Jane Lane was ... was published wi... the pen-name of ... ... nature of her books, L... ... of her grandmother, a de... ... of the Herefordshire branch of Lanes who sheltered King Charles II after his defeat at Worcester. A versatile and dynamic author, Jane Lane has written over forty works of fiction, biography, history and children's books.

BY THE SAME AUTHOR
ALL PUBLISHED BY HOUSE OF STRATUS

Bridge of Sighs
A Call of Trumpets
Cat Among the Pigeons
Command Performance
Conies in the Hay
Countess at War
The Crown for a Lie
Ember in the Ashes
Farewell to the White Cockade
Fortress in the Forth
Heirs of Squire Harry
His Fight Is Ours
The Phoenix and the Laurel
Prelude to Kingship
Queen of the Castle
The Sealed Knot
A Secret Chronicle
The Severed Crown
Sir Devil-May-Care
Sow the Tempest
A State of Mind
A Summer Storm
Thunder on St Paul's Day
A Wind Through the Heather
The Young and Lonely King

JANE LANE

Dark Conspiracy

Wilt thou conceal this dark conspiracy? A dozen of them here have ta'en the sacrament, and interchangeably set down their hands, to kill the King...

Richard II. Act V. Scene ii.

HOUSE OF STRATUS

Copyright © The Estate of Jane Lane, 1951, 2001

All rights reserved. No part of this publication may be reproduced, stored in a retrieval system, or transmitted, in any form, or by any means (electronic, mechanical, photocopying, recording, or otherwise), without the prior permission of the publisher. Any person who does any unauthorised act in relation to this publication may be liable to criminal prosecution and civil claims for damages.

The right of Jane Lane to be identified as the author of this work
has been asserted.

This edition published in 2001 by House of Stratus, an imprint of
Stratus Holdings plc, 24c Old Burlington Street, London, W1X 1RL, UK.
Also at: Suite 210, 1270 Avenue of the Americas, New York, NY 10020, USA

www.houseofstratus.com

Typeset, printed and bound by House of Stratus.

A catalogue record for this book is available from the British Library
and The Library of Congress

ISBN 0-7551-0838-8

This book is sold subject to the condition that it shall not be lent, resold, hired out, or otherwise circulated without the publisher's express prior consent in any form of binding, or cover, other than the original as herein published and without a similar condition being imposed on any subsequent purchaser, or bona fide possessor.

This is a fictional work and all characters are drawn from the author's imagination. Any resemblances or similarities to persons either living or dead are entirely coincidental.

PART ONE

Chapter One

The dark of an October evening was settling over Hampstead, when Mr Daniel Jolly, the village chandler, laid aside his account-books with a weary sigh, and, reaching for his cap, sat turning it undecidedly in his work-worn hands. It was impossible for him to concentrate while Ned, his apprentice, was making such a din with his putting up of the shutters of the shop. The lad was late, but then Ned was always either early or late for everything; a parish-child and almost a natural, he had come to Mr Jolly with a five pound indenture at the age of seven, and had been with him now for nearly twelve years. Poor Ned, thought his master, listening to him banging about outside; he could not understand how his wife had the heart to urge him to be rid of the pitiful creature.

Mrs Elizabeth Jolly was out at the moment, for this was Wednesday, and on Wednesday evenings she sallied forth soon after five o'clock, to take round the clean washing to her customers; like many tradesmen's wives of her day, she had a business of her own. It was, as Mrs Jolly was never tired of impressing upon her spouse, a great hardship that a lady of her frail physique and genteel upbringing should be forced to slave at the wash-tub, but Daniel was pleased by the knowledge that at least her Wednesday evenings gave her pleasure. At every house at which she called, she delivered not only clean linen but gossip, and in return was regaled with so many dishes of coffee or cordials or home-made wines, that her errand never finished before nine or ten o'clock.

Miss Phoebe Jolly, Daniel's daughter, was out likewise, but not in the company of her stepmother. Unless her fond old father was very much mistaken, Miss Phoebe was in some secluded nook upon the Heath, in the amorous embrace of some male companion. Mr Jolly sighed again. He ought to whip the wench; he had had a good religious upbringing, even if he had failed to give her one. But like his Sovereign, King Charles the Second, Daniel Jolly liked to be easy and to have others so. He could pay no more than a formal respect to the Deity in whom he had been brought up to believe, wit His rigid code, ruthless punitive system, and intolerance of the needs of the flesh. There was no real harm in Phoebe, wanton though she was; she had inherited a love of bed-sport from her mother; and then for the third time did Daniel Jolly heave a sigh, remembering years of connubial bliss for ever departed, when his table was ill-served, his money often wasted by a bad housewife, but his heart comforted and his bed made pleasurable by a woman who shared his easy-going nature.

Having an uncomfortably wideawake conscience, Mr Jolly frowned at himself for this third sigh and its cause, stood up with a show of resolution and put on his cap. He would go out and get a can of ale and cheer himself up. But when he was come through the shop to the street door, he hesitated again. Those cursed books. Why did they come out always on the debit side? He knew his trade, he worked hard, he was strictly honest, he sold only the best. Elizabeth told him it was because he insisted on giving credit to persons unworthy of it; he supposed she was right, but he could not alter the habits of a lifetime. It was not in his nature to demand ready money of men and women as poor as himself, his neighbours with whom he had grown up, nor could he go round dunning old customers. The result was this constant series of crises; he owed Dubs the farmer five pounds for cheeses; five pounds was a huge sum and Alfred Dubs was not the man to wait indefinitely for his money. Pox on't, Daniel chided himself, I've no right to go guzzling ale when I cannot pay my debts. There was only one thing for it, however distasteful; he must approach his old friend Josiah for another loan. A good man, Josiah Keeling, for all his strange notions, and had never forgotten that he and Daniel had shared the same bench at the parish school.

But a visit to Josiah meant a journey into the City, for Mr Keeling was an oil-merchant of the parish of St Butolph-without-Aldgate. Such a journey was not to be thought of at this time of the evening, but must be made first thing tomorrow, before Mr Jolly had time to change his uncertain mind. The best thing to do, reflected Daniel, brightening, would be for him to walk up to the Upper Bowling Green, and enquire there whether there was any wagon or other conveyance going into London in the early morning; the carrier did not go thither on Thursdays, but it was possible that some farmer might be taking in vegetables or fowls, and if such were the case the landlord of the Upper Bowling Green would know of it, for Charlie Weems knew everything about the movements of Hampstead inhabitants. Resolutely closing the street door behind him, Mr Jolly turned right up Heath Street, humming a tune to give himself courage.

The Upper Bowling Green was a large pretentious tavern, standing upon the summit of the Heath, not far from the White Stone which marked four and a half miles distance from Holborn Bars. There was a pond here, and a stray cattle pound, and just across the way was Jack Straw's Castle, where met the Court Leet and the Customary Court. Mr Jolly was not at all fond of the Upper Bowling

Green; a humble man, its size abashed him; and moreover a very odd assortment of customers frequented it. The Hampstead gentry, both the locals and that increasing urban population which was building itself houses in this healthy little village, encroaching upon the common-land with hunting and hawking, patronised it on summer evenings for the excellent bowling-green from which it took its name; apprentices and labourers thronged its shabby cock-pit; and in its vast common-room were often to be seen nameless, questionable characters, whom wise men took care not to offend, for it did not take much perspicacity to guess that they were the highwaymen, the foot-pads, and their minions, who made the Heath so dreaded by travellers after dark.

Mr Jolly entered the Upper Bowling Green diffidently, and immediately was filled with nostalgia for the homely Black Boy and Still in Heath Street, his usual tavern. The common-room was crowded, the customers being crammed so tight that the white-aproned drawers had difficulty in squeezing through with their trays of mugs and tankards. Only by the fire was there a clear space, for here, seated in a special elbow-chair reserved for him, was none other than the notorious 'Captain' George Cruckshank, the uncrowned king of all the tobymen who made the Heath their beat. He sat sprawled in an insolent attitude, his jack-boots stuck out in front of him, his horse-pistols prominently displayed on the table beside him, a bumper of brandy in his huge coarse hand, the while he discoursed with tipsy graciousness to a group of nervous locals, who stood respectfully on the other side of the fire.

Daniel, muttering at intervals, "By your leave, master," "Your pardon, sirs," edged his way through to the counter, behind which stood the hunchbacked dwarf of a landlord, Charlie Weems. He looked somewhat like a vulture, with his hunched shoulders, pigeon-chest, and his head perpetually bent forward. He had an evil, shining, polished face, a deceptively soft manner, was hand-in-glove with the highwaymen, and saw to it that the carriers and drovers compounded with these gentlemen-of-the-road by a constant rent, of which he took his pickings. Daniel waited until the landlord was for the moment free from serving, then, asking timidly for a can of ale, added an enquiry as to whether Mr Weems knew of a wagon going into the City at daybreak tomorrow.

"It is possible, it is possible, Mr – Mr Jolly is it not?" said Weems, who had a habit, oddly sinister, of repeating himself. "I have not heard positively of any such thing, but it is possible. I enquire and inform you presently, neighbour; aye, presently I will inform you."

Mr Jolly sat down humbly in a dark corner and prepared to wait. The longer he waited, the more depressed he grew. There was nothing this simple man liked better than sitting in a tavern over a can of ale, provided he had company; having no one to talk to in that crowded room, he felt his worries descend upon him in full spate, and the oftener he replenished his ale-can to drive them away, so much the more did they bombard him. He fell into that state which afflicts the sleepless in the small hours of the morning; he remembered all sorts of fresh causes of anxiety. His roof was leaking and needed repair; Phoebe, sweet child, was soon to celebrate her twenty-fourth birthday and he must give her some trinket and a treat; that lot of chamber-pots he had bought last week, and which had seemed such a bargain at the time, had turned out to be chipped, indeed two of them were downright cracked, and rather than offer his customers such shoddy wares, he must throw them out, though he could ill afford a dead loss just now. Pest take me, Mr Jolly rebuked himself, I have no right to sit here tippling; it grows late; Mr Weems hath clean forgot what I enquired of him; I must go home.

The sole result of this tippling was an urge to relieve nature; the privy stood at the back of the tavern, and to reach it Mr Jolly had to walk out of the common-room and through the yard. It was very dark out here, after the brightness of the room he had left, and being, in common with most men of his day, distrustful of the dark, Mr Jolly instinctively turned his eyes in the direction of a lighted window on one side of the yard. It was, he knew, the window of a private parlour, often rented by the landlord to customers who desired to discuss some business deal; there were red curtains at the window, but this evening they were not entirely drawn, and as he passed by, Daniel glanced within, idly at first, and then with a stare and an astonished exclamation. For in the parlour, seated by the fire, with a long pipe in his mouth and a glass of sack at his elbow, was none other than Mr Jolly's old school fried, Josiah Keeling.

At this apparition, the chandler felt an almost superstitious thrill go down his spine, for it was as though his desperate need of Josiah's help had spirited that gentleman into his neighbourhood. Never before had he seen Mr Keeling in this tavern; and never had he seen him in such odd company. For, with a second and a more unpleasant thrill, Daniel, having turned his attention to his old friend's companion in the parlour, recognised a public figure. That tall, lean body, slightly stooping, that great Roman nose, that thin jaw and sanguine complexion, and that great periwig worn almost over the eyes, were familiar from a dozen wood-cuts. Mr Keeling's companion could be none other than Robert Ferguson, Bob Ferguson the Plotter.

While Mr Jolly's slow mind wrestled with the problem as to why his friend should be in such company, he found himself looking once more at Mr Keeling, and now Mr Keeling's eyes were looking directly into his own. Filled with embarrassment at being caught thus peeping into a private apartment, Mr Jolly bobbed back and hastened upon his journey to the privy. Once more he was seized with uncertainty as to what he should do when nature was relieved; should he linger at the tavern and waylay Josiah when that gentleman left? Had Josiah recognised him through the window? Would it be best to straight home? It was characteristic of Daniel that, having decided on the latter course, he returned from the privy and immediately re-entered the common-room; but for once in his life it seemed that his indecision was favouring him, for scarcely had he pushed his way through to the counter to demand another can of ale, than he felt a pull at his sleeve, and there, greeting him with all this old friendliness, was Josiah Keeling himself.

"The Lord hath guided you thither this night, Daniel," observed the oil-merchant solemnly, as he laid a hand over his friend's to prevent him paying for his drink. "I had thought to call upon you at your house after my business here was ended, but finding the hour to be late, was about to return home when I spied you through the window yonder. We will take a tankard together, and I will stand treat, if you please."

The room was emptying now, and, when the tankard was bought, Mr Keeling had no difficulty in finding a secluded corner, where the friends sat down. The oil-merchant was a large, corpulent person, a substantial citizen, but slovenly in appearance, and of a genial disposition. Only when his fanaticism was aroused did his geniality vanish, and something almost savage and quite alien to his nature take its place. Only a few weeks ago he had "arrested" the Lord Mayor of London in the open street, for refusing to admit the Sheriffs chosen by the faction which was beginning to be called the Whigs. His friend Daniel, whose nature it was to believe the best of every man, regarded such extravagances as a mere kink in an otherwise well-balanced and admirable character, and when he and Josiah met, Daniel did his best to avoid all talk of religion and politics, which two subjects he deemed in any case unsuitable to tradesmen.

Tonight Josiah seemed to be in a particularly genial mood, and it was not long before his kindly company, combined with another quantity of ale, drove Mr Jolly to unbosom himself of his troubles. Josiah listened sympathetically, yet with a certain abstracted air which seemed to argue that his thoughts were not wholly upon his friend's financial difficulties. After a pause in Daniel's lamentations, the oil-merchant laid his large soft hand upon his shoulder, and said gravely:

"The times are evil, brother, even as they were in the days of Babylon, but the Lord in whom thou trusteth, He shall deliver thee, as He delivered that great prophet after whom thou art called, when the wicked king cast him into the den of lions."

Mr Jolly wriggled uncomfortably. The Lord, he reflected, might interest Himself sufficiently in men like the Prophet Daniel as to deliver them from their difficulties in some spectacular manner, but Daniel Jolly, the humble chandler, was not so presumptuous as to suppose that Jehovah would rescue him from the clutches of a justly incensed Mr Dubs. Moreover, the sudden turn the conversation had taken embarrassed him extremely; when Josiah began to talk in that strain, he ceased to be the familiar friend and became the fanatic. Daniel was just about to murmur that the hour was late and he ought to go home, when Mr Keeling suddenly became practical again, though his abstracted air was more noticeable than ever.

"My purse, Daniel," said he kindly, "hath been ever at your service, as indeed it ought to be for friendship's sake, but I must let you know that at present I likewise am in embarrassed circumstances, for certain ventures of mine upon the high seas have failed, and being further impoverished by a fine imposed upon me by a wicked and tyrannous Court of Justice for my late action (you wot well what I mean), I am obliged to tighten my purse-strings."

"My good friend," said Daniel, his heart touched by this speech, and his kindly nature immediately causing him to forget his own troubles, "I am much distressed to hear this ill news of you. As for any notion of a loan, I do assure you that your will to make it is as comforting to me as all the gold in the Indies."

"Stay a little, Daniel," said Mr Keeling, laying a detaining hand on Daniel's arm as the chandler made to rise, "stay a little, while I make known to you a way in which you may both strike a blow for righteousness and earn unto yourself a material reward."

Mr Jolly pricked up his ears. This talk of a "blow for righteousness" he dismissed as a mere figure of speech, or rather as something pertaining to Josiah's unfortunate kink. A while ago the phrase would have frightened him, even though he was sure that Mr Keeling was a good man, and that although he might commit such extravagances as "arresting" the Lord Mayor of London, he would never lend himself to the more treasonable actions of his fanatical friends. Mr Jolly, though living remote from the great world of politics, had read in the past such things in the news-sheets that his peaceable and law-abiding soul had fairly shuddered. There had been insurrection in Scotland, even a threat of it in England; there had been plots and riots, and the danger of the repetition of 1641. But all these things were of the past, and, poring over the week-old news-sheet in his tavern over his modest can of ale, Mr Jolly had been relieved to learn that King Charles had weathered the storms of opposition which had raged throughout the last ten years, and that save for disgruntled great lords, like the disgraced Earl of Shaftesbury, and born trouble-makers like "Dr" Titus Oates, everyone was happy and harmonious.

It was, therefore, the last sentence of Mr Keeling's speech which interested his friend, and naturally so, since his financial difficulties were so weighing upon his mind just now. He had accepted the fact that he was a failure in business, but he felt sure that if he were to have the moral backing and advice of so substantial a citizen as Josiah Keeling, any little venture into which he entered could not fail. So, turning a pathetically eager gaze upon Josiah, he begged him to explain matters to him.

"When you spied me in the privy parlour earlier this night," began the oil-merchant, not returning his friend's gaze, but playing absently with the lid of the tankard on the table before him, "you saw me in company with a gentleman who perchance may be known to you by sight and reputation."

"Why," replied Daniel nervously, infinitely disappointed by this opening, "me thought he looked somewhat like – like the gentleman they call – ahem! – Ferguson the Plotter. I would not swear to it – "

"So he is called by the sons of unrighteousness," interposed Mr Keeling sharply, "who gnash with their mouths upon all good men. But I must tell you," continued the oil-merchant, lowering his voice, "that at present Mr Ferguson goes not by his own name, but is known as 'Mr Roberts', being, you understand, somewhat under a cloud by reason of his championship of the Good Old Cause."

Mr Jolly nodded but said nothing. He was the last man to judge others, but there were certain things he had heard concerning Robert Ferguson which made him unable to avoid a mild disapproval. A dissenting minister, and then the master of a boys' school at Islington, Ferguson, he knew, had been imprisoned as early as 1663 for 'treasonable practices'. At the height of the Titus Oates plot, he had begun to write political broadsheets, and from then onwards had been one of the leading spirits of the Opposition (or the Faction, as it was often called), attacking the King, the Duke of York, the Court, the loyal Ministers, and with his lively and violent pen stirring up the rabble to discontentment with their betters. Yet on the other hand, Josiah Keeling, that worthy citizen, obviously regarded Bob Ferguson with admiration, and even, from his tone, with affection; therefore did the humble Mr Jolly strive to set aside an old prejudice and prepare himself to withhold judgement on a man of whom he had heard, up to now, only the worst.

"Mr Roberts, as we will call him," continued Josiah casting a glance at his silent friend, "is, as I have said, under a cloud, and there may be many other worthy men in like condition, for the Children of Israel are again in the Wilderness. Some of these gentlemen are, like himself, of the Scottish nation, and often it happens that they desire to visit our country upon their lawful business, yet find themselves obliged to do so under aliases, and in secret, lest some mischievous person inform against them to the authorities. It would be mighty convenient for them, therefore, if, when they are obliged to come to London, they might find some friendly and discreet persons who would give them lodging at a little distance from the City. They are all substantial gentlemen, and would pay handsomely for such a lodging, be it never so humble, so it be clean and private, and he who keeps it careful to ask them no questions concerning their business or identity, and to avoid talk of them among his neighbours."

Mr Jolly had brightened considerably during this speech, and had been obsessed with practical matters. Phoebe could move into the attic and then he would have a spare bedchamber; Phoebe was a good plain cook and never grumbled at a little extra work; Elizabeth, once she was assured that her lodger was a respectable gentleman of substance, would amuse herself by boasting of him to her neighbours; and the handsome payment promised would dispel from Daniel himself the recurring nightmare of debt. So, with a smiling face, he said impulsively to his friend:

"I am sure I could entertain one of these gentlemen, Josiah, if you would recommend me as a fitting host. You know I am not wont to tattle, but mind my own business and let others mind theirs. 'Tis true my house is small and somewhat incommodious, yet 'tis clean, and I and my family would do our best to make a gentleman easy and comfortable. Aye, I am sure it could be done."

Josiah clapped him on the shoulder and looked as pleased as though he had completed some rich business deal.

"You will hear word from me, Daniel," he promised, fastening the neck-band of his cloak preparatory to leaving the tavern, "and that very shortly, I do assure you. Meanwhile, do you set your spare bed-chamber in order; but be sure to tell your wife only that you have heard of some business gentleman who seeks lodging in Hampstead for the purer air."

But at those words, Mr Jolly was suddenly seized by doubts. A fainthearted man, and suspicious of good fortune, he was rarely able to believe that when fate seemed to smile on him there was not some trick behind the smile. He stood turning his thrum-cap in his hands, his bovine brown eyes troubled, glancing swiftly at this friend and away again.

"Josiah," he mumbled, embarrassed, "you'll pardon me if I ask you – these gentry – they are not like to bring any trouble upon me and my family? – I intend no disrespect, none in the world, but as you have said, the times are evil, and I have never concerned myself with high matters – and – and – "

He petered out, at a loss to make plain his sudden fears. But Josiah beamed upon him, patted him kindly on the shoulder, and assured him that, if he were discreet and asked no questions, he would be as safe as if he entertained a company of angels unawares. Indeed, added the oil-merchant solemnly, these gentlemen were all so godly, that almost they might be regarded as heavenly visitants.

Chapter Two

The worried frown which had worn furrows upon the brow of Daniel Jolly was not due solely to his business difficulties. Domestic troubles had taken their share in drawing those lines of anxiety on his kindly face, and indeed might be said to have been the main cause of them.

The first Mrs Jolly had died during the Great Plague of 1665, catching the infection from the fugitives who had flocked to the outlying villages of London to escape from the stricken City. She had left behind her a young and sorrowing widower, and their only child, Phoebe, then a little girl of seven. There had been more than one woman in Hampstead eager to take her place, for Daniel was well liked, and, in his thirties, personable enough; but he remained true to the memory of his wife, and, until Phoebe was old enough to do the housekeeping for him, managed as best he could. Between him and his daughter there had grown up a strong affection, the closer because they were for so long alone in the world, and it had been a real sacrifice on the father's part when, his daughter reaching her late teens, he had set himself to arrange a suitable marriage for her in the fashion of his day. He had selected a young journeyman painter, a good honest lad he had known for years, had given the pair his blessing and his daughter as good a marriage portion as his lowly circumstances could afford, and had resigned himself to a lonely future.

But fate had decreed otherwise, for, but a week after the wedding, the scaffolding around a house which Phoebe's bridegroom was engaged in painting had collapsed, and the young wife was a widow. Phoebe had accepted her loss with the stoicism which was an essential part of her character, had returned to her father's house, and very cheerfully had taken up her old duties there again. But it was not long before Mr Jolly discovered that her brief taste of marriage had changed Phoebe, or perhaps had awakened in her certain impulses which had always lain dormant in her character. She remained the affectionate child he had always known, but she now claimed the liberty of doing what she pleased in her spare time, and doing what she pleased took the form of indulging in a continuous succession of amorous affairs.

Mr Jolly was not a religious man, but he had the conventional morality of his kind, and his daughter's conduct shocked him profoundly. But when he taxed her with it, he found to his astonishment and dismay that he had to do, not with an erring and foolish little daughter, who ought to have hung her head and shed tears, but with a strong and mature personality, which had something almost masculine in its attitude to life. Phoebe not only freely admitted her sins, but expressed her deliberate intention of continuing to commit them. She had no wish, she said, to marry again, at least for a time; she was happier by far in her father's house; but she looked upon bed-sport as being as necessary to a healthy person as food and drink, and saw no more harm in it. She was sorry if her wantonness distressed her father, and she would be careful to avoid indulging it beneath his roof; she would even, if he preferred it, go into service in the country, but so long as he pleased she would stay by his side. He must remember that she was now grown up and had a right to a life of her own; he need not fear for her, she added, with an outrageous wink, she was perfectly well able to take care of herself. And with that she had put her arms round his neck and kissed him, half affectionately, half conspiratorially, as though to say, We two understand one another, and that is all that signifies.

Failing to reason her out of her waywardness, Mr Jolly had buoyed himself up with the hope that, despite her protestations, Phoebe would marry again very soon, a not unreasonable hope since she was extremely attractive to the opposite sex, and, despite the gossip which was quickly growing up about her, she had half the male population of Hampstead applying themselves to her father for her hand. But after a time it was borne in on Daniel that his daughter meant what she said, and on the subject of marriage she was adamant, ruthlessly dismissing every admirer with honourable intentions. The curious part of if was that, though she lived in that hot-bed of gossip and scandal, a small village, Phoebe continued to be liked by all and ostracised by none, even Mr Mole, the parson, making her the civility of his hat whenever they met. There was something about Miss Phoebe which disarmed criticism; she was so open and frank, so lively and spirited, so completely lacking in hypocrisy, so zestful in her love of life and all its experiences, that the sourest matron, listening to the tale of some new wantonness, found herself instinctively excusing the girl.

But Daniel had continued to worry and fret, and it was partly because he hoped that a stepmother might wield a benign feminine influence upon his headstrong and erring daughter that, two years previously, in 1680, he had taken the step he had for so long resisted, and had entered into matrimony for a second time. Fate, however, had never been very favourably disposed to Daniel Jolly, and it had not been long ere he had discovered that he had done neither himself nor his daughter any good by introducing Elizabeth into his home.

The new Mrs Jolly was no ordinary domestic tyrant. Most of her acquaintances found her charming, and deemed Daniel a lucky man; she was a good craftswoman, a hard worker, an excellent, indeed a formidable, housewife, and with her vivacity, her big blue eyes, her youthful figure, and her fresh complexion, she looked much younger than her spouse. She had a superficial charm, and the air of mystery with which she surrounded her past, before she had met Mr Jolly, made the housewives of Hampstead intrigued and admiring. She had "come down in the world," she said (with a gay, brave laugh); she talked incessantly though vaguely of a genteel upbringing, of wealthy parents who had idolised her, and of a first husband who had been a perfect paragon of all the virtues. She professed a deep affection for Daniel, but spoke of him almost as a father, conveying the impression that she had taken pity on a lonely widower and for his comfort had sacrificed her youth and natural environment.

What that natural environment was, not even Daniel rightly knew. For very early in his marriage to Elizabeth he had discovered with dismayed bewilderment that she was the most brazen romancer. When first he had met her, she had been living in one room in the City, supporting herself by laundry-work; she had told him that her mother, the daughter of a knight, had died when she was a child, and that her father, an officer in his Majesty's Navy, had been slain in the performance of his duties. Her late husband, she added, a substantial merchant, had died of a broken heart as the result of unpaid debts. Mr Jolly, a truthful man himself, had accepted these tales on their face value, and to the fascination exercised upon him by Elizabeth's charm and physical attractions, had been added admiration for the brave spirit in which she had accepted these tragedies, and a deep gratitude for her condescension in marrying him.

But soon after their marriage, he had been shocked and puzzled to hear Elizabeth telling the sad story of her life to her stepdaughter, Phoebe; for it was now an entirely different story. Her father had been a country squire, her late husband a topping physician; the father had died in prison for his loyalty to Kind Charles the First, and the husband had lost his life by remaining in London during the great Plague and attending to his stricken patients. Elizabeth had told this new tale to Phoebe in Daniel's hearing; she had told it without a blush; and when Daniel, in the first throes of his astonishment, had reminded her of the different version with which she had regaled him before their marriage, she had broken into a storm of weeping, reproached him for his cruelty in accusing her of lying, and had held it against him ever since. For two years now he had heard so many fresh versions of the story that he had lost count, and his first dismay had given place to something approaching awe at Elizabeth's brazen untruthfulness and the failure of her lies to trip her up.

Although the simple soul of Daniel Jolly could not repress a permanent shudder at the consistent disregard for truth displayed by his new wife, he was too fond of her, and too tolerant, to continue to upbraid her for it, even in his heart. But unfortunately, like all confirmed romancers, Elizabeth firmly believed in her own romancings, and consequently had come to regard herself as an injured and superior person. Possibly there was some genteel blood in her; at all events she had an undoubted air of breeding and many high-flown notions, and therefore it was all too easy for her to convince herself and her neighbours that she had conferred on Daniel a great favour when she married him. She was, as has been said, no ordinary domestic tyrant; if she nagged, it was playfully; she detested the vulgarity of quarrels, and knew by instinct that in a downright brawl she always got the worst of it; and it was part of her role to bestow upon Daniel a kittenish, patronising affection. But she could not resist the temptation of often reminding him that he was a failure in business, whereas she, brought up far above the sphere of trade, had shown herself a success as a craftswoman. She spoke frequently, with a sweet, refined nostalgia, of the days when her mother had employed a number of maids (the number varied, for Elizabeth was quite incapable of remembering the details of her lies), of the girlish petticoats and shifts starched and crimped for her by a family retainer ("and now behold! I am a laundress myself!"), and of how her dear, foolish, doting old father would have turned in his grave could he have seen her spoiling her hands at the washtub.

"I come of a dead world, neighbour," she would sigh, to some stout Hampstead housewife agog at her fortitude, "of the ruined Cavaliers who lost their all for our beloved Royal Martyr. 'Twould be foolish, as well as downright disloyal, to regret their sacrifice. Instead I bethink me how fortunate am I to have found such a dear, kind, worthy man as my good Daniel to care for me. 'Tis true he is not over genteel, but I flatter myself I am weaning him from some of his more mobbish habits; and is not a heart of gold, such as he possesses, worth more than coats-of-arms and a genteel upbringing?"

It was on the subject of these 'mobbish habits' that Daniel suffered most. Many of them were perfectly right and natural to him and the weaning process was particularly hard to bear, first because he entertained secret doubts about Elizabeth's aristocratic antecedents, and secondly because he had married her when he was middle-aged and set in his ways. He must not spit into the fireplace; he must not use certain expressions; he must not go to sleep in his chair after supper but divert his wife with a hand at the cartes; he must not fart, loudly and healthily, when he awoke in the morning. He must use a spoon and not his fingers for conveying his meat to his mouth ("My dear first husband used ever a silver fork, but so modish an instrument would not be fitting for a tradesman"), and he must wash his hands before he sat down to table. Worst of all, the second Mrs Jolly appeared to regard sexual intercourse as being 'mobbish'. Like many women of her type, she loved the first stages of love-making, the attention and the compliments, but revolted from the culmination. Adoring to be admired, she flirted openly and outrageously with every man in sight, but, by nature cold, she was affronted by the advances which her flirting provoked. Poor Daniel, essentially a warm-blooded man, found himself developing a downright apologetic attitude towards the pleasures of the bed.

If in his disillusionment Daniel could have comforted himself that in embarking upon this late marriage at least he had benefited his daughter, he would have suffered cheerfully; but it was not so. Elizabeth had the jealousy of all attractive middle-aged women towards the young, and it irked her extremely to find how popular was Phoebe with the other sex. As for her stepdaughter's wantonness, it provoked her unmitigated ire because it was so open, and therefore, according to Elizabeth, vulgar. It was well enough, she asserted, for ladies of quality to take lovers, so they were discreet; it was quite *à la mode;* but for a shopkeeper's daughter to go tumbling on the Heath with every Tom, Dick, and Harry was disgusting, low, and downright mobbish. What must the neighbours think? Had the girl no shame? Elizabeth repeated all this to her dear, sweet, pretty Phoebe until she was tired; she lectured her dear, good old Daniel nightly on the subject; she protested that the mere thought of such wantonness gave her the vapours, and that if it continued undoubtedly it would bring her to a premature decease. Phoebe listened in silence, never answered back, and went her own way, accepting Elizabeth as she accepted everything in life, good, bad or indifferent. Mrs Jolly, defeated in her attacks, fell back upon her old defence of romanticising. The poor, sweet child, she told her neighbours, had suffered a broken heart at the tragic death of her young husband; it had made her not quite normal; she was as much to be pitied as Mr Jolly's poor natural of an apprentice, Ned, said Mrs Jolly, silently inviting admiration for her own display of Christian tolerance.

There was a further cause of Elizabeth's disapproval of her stepdaughter. This girl who, except with her father, showed a certain coolness in human relationships, had an extraordinary affection for animals, and according to Elizabeth, every stray cat and dog in Hampstead found its way to the Jollys' door. It was quite true that in the back garden of the little house an assortment of cats were always to be seen waiting patiently for the milk and the scraps with which Phoebe served them; for a period there had lived in her room a badger which she had rescued from a tavern where it was being baited; and wherever she went, two or three mongrel curs trotted at her heels. Her skill, self-taught, in the treatment of animal diseases, was so widely known that her neighbours, and even those living in the next village, called for her straightaway when they had a sick horse or cow or dog; and her father, observing her with loving care, noted that in Phoebe's relationships with animals there was a gentleness and a warmth and a patience which were lacking in her attitude to human beings, always excepting himself. Elizabeth, on the other hand, though she professed a great tenderness for dear dumb creatures, was convinced that Phoebe's feeling for them was only another proof of her unnaturalness, and in moments when she was feeling particularly spiteful, would threaten to rid her sweet clean house of all those verminous strays.

On the day after his encounter with Josiah Keeling at the Upper Bowling Green, Mr Jolly was somewhat taken aback to hear his daughter enquire of him whether he would permit her to entertain her latest beau to supper at her father's board. So far she had kept to her word never to intrude her lovers under the parental roof; he had seen them hovering outside for her, and the contemporary one, Mr Derrick Calder, had called openly, on several occasions, to take her to Jack Straw's for a whet. Though Mr Calder was obviously a gentleman, Daniel had felt it only right not to show him any more open countenance than the rest, and never had invited him into the house; this morning, therefore, he was about to reproach Phoebe for making such a request when she said quickly:

"I have told Mr Calder that I thought you might give him a refusal, but he begged of me to ask it of you, since he much desires to improve your acquaintanceship."

Daniel was surprised and disarmed by this statement. For secretly he had been for some time intrigued by this Mr Calder, who was so different from the usual run of Phoebe's lovers, and had, so Daniel understood, some minor post in the household of the Duke of York, the King's brother and the Heir Presumptive. He was not altogether sure that he preferred such a beau to Phoebe's village lovers, for he had very strict notions about every man keeping to his own station; but, not being free from the snobbishness of his class, he could not but be flattered that a gentleman in so exalted a walk of life should seek his company, and from the little he had seen of Mr Calder he felt drawn to him. He scratches his head, and murmured:

"Why, I know not, child. You must ask your stepmother –"

"I have done so," interrupted Phoebe mildly, "and she is pleased to say she is willing that Mr Calder should sup with us this very night."

She looked straight at her father as she spoke, and although there was nothing at all improper in her tone or expression he knew well what she meant. Elizabeth had discovered that her disapproval of her stepdaughter was not strong enough to make her deny herself the opportunity of entertaining someone even remotely connected with the fashionable world of the Court.

As the day wore on, Mr Jolly became aware that his house was being turned upside down in a frenzy of preparation for the guest. Ordinarily Mrs Jolly left most of the domestic work to Phoebe, partly because she had her own trade to pursue, and partly that she might give herself the pleasure of criticising the girl's housekeeping. Today, however, Mrs Jolly's wash-tub was forsaken, the while she baked, scrubbed, polished, looked out the best plate and linen, borrowed from neighbours extra chairs and dishes, and chattered about what she should wear for the occasion. For some reason, quite obscure to the mere male, the whole house had to be spring-cleaned from top to bottom, despite Mrs Jolly's confession that it would wear her out. Daniel, serving out sand, cheese, firewood, and pecks of coals in his shop, listened to the upheaval with a growing uneasiness. He had looked forward to a quiet chat with Mr Calder over his usual supper of neck-beef and turnips and a tankard of small-ale; Mr Calder knew him for what he was, a humble village chandler, and would dislike, Daniel felt sure, a display of ostentation unfitting to his station in life. Devoutly did Mr Jolly hope that his spouse would not add to his embarrassment by indulging in the more outrageous of her romancings, but he feared the worst.

Like most tradesman of his day, Mr Jolly closed his shop at eight o'clock, but on this particular evening, Ned the 'prentice chose to be late in putting up the shutters, and his master was still tidying the counter when there came a knock on the door. Mr Jolly opened it, and found standing upon the threshold a young man who raised his hat politely and announced that he was Derrick Calder, at Mr Jolly's service. Daniel, guiltily aware that he ought to have been changed and washed to receive his guest, ushered him into the shop, and there, excusing himself while he locked up his cash-box and made other arrangements for the night, glanced surreptitiously at his visitor in the light of the candles.

He saw a rather slight man in his thirties, dressed modishly yet quietly; he had a modest bearing and an ease of manner; the fashionable large periwig shadowed his face, but Mr Jolly could see that his hazel eyes were at the same time thoughtful and merry, and that his mouth was good-tempered and ready with a smile. He sat down at his ease on a case of candles, and talked naturally about the weather, the state of the country, and his own love of Hampstead.

"I am country-bred, sir," said be, "being the son of parson in Sussex, and though I have been now many years at Court, I have not turned townsman in my heart. You have a sweet village here, and one with which I am very familiar. I discovered it by chance one day, when I was sent on some errand by my master, the Lord Chamberlain, and since then have come often when off-duty to ride my horse over the Heath and watch the archery in the Conduit Fields."

Nothing was more calculated to win Mr Jolly's heart than praise of his native village, and in a few moments he found himself chatting to Mr Calder with the ease of long acquaintance. By the time he was ready to take his guest into the parlour, Daniel had his hand through the young man's arm, and in an animated tone was telling him of the awesome view of the Great Fire which he had seen from the Heath in '66.

Opening the parlour door, the words died upon his lips. For the humble room was transformed so that he scarcely recognised it. Domestic articles such as the spinning-wheel, the clothes-lines usually strung before the fire, and even Phoebe's work-box, had been removed or hidden out of sight; innumerable candles, in borrowed sticks, made an almost fierce illumination; and the table was laid for supper with so many strange platters and tankards and cutlery that Mr Jolly thought with dismay that his spouse must have borrowed from half Hampstead. Phoebe was nowhere to be seen, but preening herself in front of a steel-glass was Mrs Elizabeth Jolly, decked out in her best gown which had been hastily embellished with odd bits of lace and ribbon and loaded with sham jewellery. Her plump waist was pinched in with stays, which obviously pained her, and several large patches adhered to the paint with which she had adorned her cheeks. Catching sight of the reflections of the two men in the steel-glass, the lady turned hastily, clapped a hand to her almost naked bosom, and cried "Lord!" in horrified and startled accents, as though the visitants were house-breakers.

"Why, Bess," said her husband, "here is Mr Calder come to – "

"Lord!" interrupted Elizabeth again, on a higher note, "what a man is this to welcome a guest in his shirt-sleeves! Mr Calder, indeed you must excuse my husband; he is somewhat absent-minded; he intended no discourtesy. Daniel, my love," she continued, giving her husband a false smile and a dagger glance, "be so good as to go abovestairs and shift yourself, whiles I entertain Mr Calder with a whet."

"Nay, madam," said Derrick with a smile, "you must blame me for coming before my time. I was so eager to meet with you and Mr Jolly, I vow I could scarce wait, and since I arrived have plagued him for so many stories of your charming village that he hath had no opportunity for putting on his coat."

There was so much quiet charm about this young man that Mrs Jolly forgot to repeat her order to her husband, but, fetching a piece of embroidery in a frame (to the astonishment of Daniel, who had never seen such a thing in this house before), sat down before the fire, and making a great play with needle and thread, prepared to fascinate so promising a guest. Mr Calder talked and listened politely, but his eyes kept straying from the door which led into the shop to one which obviously gave access to the upper room, and noticing this, Mr Jolly, his warm heart touched, told him kindly that his daughter would be with them anon.

"I believe she will be feeding her cats," said he. " 'Tis a nightly task she hath set herself, and she will not lay it by for anything in the world."

"Ne'er stir, but the child is devoted to dumb creatures," cut in Mrs Jolly, fluttering her eyelashes at Derrick. "The pretty dear, 'tis sweet to see her charity towards them, and I have not the heart to scold her for it, though I am in labour for the vermin they may bring into my house."

"It is one of the things for which I love her," said Derrick, quietly and surprisingly.

There was so much feeling in his tone that Daniel glanced at him in wonder. Not that he could blame any man for loving his daughter, but it surprised him that so cultured a gentleman should imply a love as deep as this for a mere village wench. Mrs Jolly on the other hand, seized upon Mr Calder's declaration as an excuse both for exercising her spite against Phoebe, and for indulging in her love of romancing.

"My sweet daughter," said she, "(for you must know, sir, I feel as though she were my own), suffered a tragedy in her girlhood which hath somewhat unhinged her and hath made her subject to whims. We must be patient and indulgent, as I am for ever telling my good Daniel here. Ah! what grief did she suffer when her young husband died. You must know, Mr Calder, that he was a painter of likenesses, and would, I verily believe, have rivalled Sir Peter Lely himself had he not been taken with a consumption and carried off in his youth. How well I understand the child's affliction, having lost both my father and my dear first husband in the prime of their lives."

"Allow me to offer you my sympathy, madam," murmured Mr Calder politely.

"Adad," cried Mrs Jolly, wiping her eyes with a wisp of handkerchief, and giving her guest a martyred smile, "I am too good a Christian, I hope, to question the Lord's decrees. He gives and He takes away, sir, and we must even continue to bless his name. My dear father – "

"I think you had best find Phoebe, Bess," interrupted Mr Jolly nervously. "Mr Calder will be hungry for his supper."

"Mr Calder will take another whet first," said Elizabeth, patting Daniel's arm. "My husband doth not quite understand, Mr Calder, the social habits with which you and I are familiar. As I was saying, my dear father was Colonel of the Militia of his country, and was slain by robbers while he was escorting treasure on the road to London. I bore my loss, I hope, as a soldier's daughter and a soldier's wife should; for I must tell you that my dear first husband (God rest him) was an officer in Prince Rupert's Horse, and fell at the Battle of Naseby, after he had recaptured from the rebels his Royal Highness' Standard and was returning it to the Prince."

There was a pause, while Mr Jolly did some agonised arithmetical calculations, and Mr Calder, nodding gravely, sipped his whet and gazed patiently at the door. Mrs Jolly, who was sublimely ignorant of simple arithmetic (a formidable handicap to so addicted a liar), on this occasion sensed that something was wrong, and remembering vaguely that the Battle of Naseby had taken place somewhere in the forties of the century, beamed her most charming smile and added, bridling a little:

"I was but a child at the time, for you must know, sir, that I was scarce out of the leading-strings when I was wed, a custom, as you will know, followed by our nobility. Aye, I was wed and widowed when tradesmen's daughters are still at their hornbook, yet continued faithful to the memory of the lord I had scarcely known, until my dear, good, honest Daniel here persuaded me to take compassion on his loneliness, and to be a second mother to his sweet Phoebe."

At this point Phoebe entered the room, causing a welcome diversion. In deference to the commands of her stepmother, she had put on her Sunday gown, but her visit to the back garden had disarranged the bright brown curls previously tortured into neatness by Elizabeth, and her holiday attire contrasted oddly with the clutter of dirty pie-dishes and saucers she was carrying with her stained fingers, and with the pair of disreputable mongrels which followed at her heels. As soon as she entered, Derrick Calder's gaze was fastened upon her, and Mr Jolly perceived in it that same depth of feeling which had marked the young man's tone when he had spoken of her.

They sat down to supper; and while Mrs Jolly, a bad hostess because she had attempted too much and had to be forever jumping up to change platters or fetch some dish, fussed and simpered and signalled to her husband and her stepdaughter with her eyes, Mr Calder strove to put the company at their ease by talking of general matters. These soon turned upon the state of the nation, and, without any ostentation, he betrayed so intimate a knowledge of political events and great personages, that Mrs Jolly soon began to pump him for details about his post at Court. He smiled at her, and answered simply:

"It could scarce be more humble a post, madam. I am a Gentleman Usher in the household of his Royal Highness, the Duke of York, and, like all the Court Officers with the exception of the Pensioners, am under the jurisdiction of the Lord Chamberlain. I seldom penetrate further than the ante-chambers of the great, opening doors, and carrying names to the Gentleman-in-Waiting on duty. You might call me but an upper servant, and would not be far wrong."

"I vow you are too modest," murmured Mrs Jolly, not quite concealing her disappointment. "But since you are in the household of the Duke, pray pardon me for asking if you are of his religion? Ne'er stir, I have no quarrel with other men's creeds, but we have had such pother with the Papists during the past few years, so many nasty plots and intrigues, that we of the dear old Church of England can scarce be blamed for looking at them askance."

"I am myself of the Church of England, madam," replied Derrick, with a somewhat dry smile, "being, as I have had the honour to tell your husband, the son of a country parson. But I must assure you that I could ask for no better master than his Royal Highness, be his creed what it may, and as for Papist plots, I believe the most of them to have been shams."

"You speak boldly, sir," said Mr Jolly, with his mouth full. "A year or two since, when Dr Oates was so high in the nation's esteem, you had been like to have found yourself in Newgate for such a word."

"Thank God, we are done with that parcel of informers," said Derrick with feeling. "Nothing was more like to have brought the Church of England, and the kingdom, into discredit abroad than the countenance given to rogues like Oates. I cannot but think the Government had been wiser to have probed the counsels of the fanatics, than to have persecuted men and women of a faith which hath showed so much loyalty to the Crown, both in the time of the late King and his son."

Mr Jolly put down his knife and stared at the young man keenly. That word "fanatics" had caught his attention and made him faintly uneasy; for was it not but yesterday that he had seen his friend Josiah Keeling in company with an avowed fanatic, Bob Ferguson the Plotter, and was he not pledged to entertain beneath his roof some of Bob Ferguson's friends?

"Come, sir," said he nervously, "the fanatics are become harmless enough. I wot well they have made a stirring in Scotland, but that is quelled, and in England we have his Blessed Majesty more securely established than ever before, and all opposition to him clean withdrawn."

"It would seem so, sir," replied Derrick slowly, "and I trust in God it is so. Yet I cannot but remember that many of these fanatics were Cromwell's men, in rebellion against the King's father, that they never in their hearts accepted the Restoration, and are fit tools for certain lords and gentlemen who, throughout the present reign, have opposed his Majesty on principle, and are still pledged to prevent the Heir Presumptive, the Duke of York, from acceding to the Crown when King Charles comes to die."

"Pox on't," exclaimed Mr Jolly disapprovingly, "that's foolish talk. 'Tis true these great lords of whom you speak, sir, and notably the Earl of Shaftesbury, disliked his Royal Highness' religion, and feared for the safety of the Protestant faith should he succeed his brother. (So I have heard tell; I am a simple man, sir, and know little of great matters.) But they failed to exclude him by lawful means, I mean a Bill in Parliament, and those who sought their ends by plots and intrigues are disgraced, while the rest, I vow, are resigned to accepting a Papist King so he meddles not with the Established Religion, as the Duke hath promised he will not."

"Fie, Daniel," broke in Mrs Jolly, bored, "you chatter as much as ale-wives at a christening. What talk is this from a laborious man? Mr Calder, I vow, will deem you altogether too knowing if you tattle of subjects you should leave to your betters."

"Nay, madam," said Derrick, before his host could reply, "the opinions of laborious men are mighty valuable, for they are the bulk of the nation, and keep her balanced between the ambitions of nobles and the unruly passions of the mobile. You must blame me for having strayed upon a subject which can have little of entertainment for fair dames, and is in truth mighty dull. Come, what shall I tell you of the Court? 'Twill be little better than coffee-house talk, for I am, as I have said, but on the fringe of it, but perchance will serve to make you laugh."

So he entered into a description of a recent visit of the Moroccan Ambassador, fascinating his rural audience with his tales of rich scimitars, silk turbans, and gifts of ostriches and lions. When the cloth was removed, they played angel-beast, a round game with cards, sipping meanwhile some blackberry cordial distilled by Mrs Jolly with her own fair hands. Mr Jolly, observing how on the one hand Derrick kept glancing at the silent Phoebe, obviously yearning to be alone with her, and how on the other his spouse was becoming more and more foolish as the wine got into her, laughing at nothing, and occasionally lapsing into tears as she recalled "our beloved Royal Martyr," whose hand she now claimed to have kissed, "when I was a babe in arms," was not ill-pleased when Mr Calder, openly drawing his watch from his pocket at last, said that he must be gone.

"I left my horse at Jack Straw's," said he. "He seems to have a trifle of lameness in the shoulder, and were the hour not so late, I had hoped that Mistress Phoebe would examine him, she being so knowledgeable in the treatment of beasts."

It was said so awkwardly that Mr Jolly felt his heart warm further towards this young man with the mature mind and the boyish devotion. Phoebe, always the realist, rose at once and said she yearned for a can of the Jack Straw's ale and would go thither with Derrick there and then; her stepmother, who would have voiced her disapproval in no uncertain terms had Mr Calder been other than a gentleman of the Court, rose with her and, announcing her intention of making sure that the dear pretty child wrapped up warmly against the cold of the night, followed Phoebe upstairs to give feminine advice in the management of so aristocratic a lover.

There was silence for a while when the two men were left alone. Mr Calder was somewhat sleepy, being accustomed, like all working men of his day, to early hours, and quite unaccustomed to blackberry cordial. Derrick strolled to the window which looked out upon the garden, stooped suddenly, picked something up from the floor, and returned with slow steps to the fire.

" 'Tis exactly the colour of her hair," he murmured; and, meeting Mr Jolly's puzzled glance, opened his hand and showed him a pale brown oak-leaf, blown in from out-of-doors.

"You are a poet, sir," said his host shyly.

"Nay, I am no poet, but a man in love." His smile died, and looking down at the chandler, he said with great earnestness and sincerity: "I love your daughter, sir, deeply, desperately; I love her as I love myself, for in truth she is part of me, the better part. Mr Jolly, I am a married man. I will not enlarge upon the failure of my marriage; 'twould not be fitting, or fair to my wife. But you have, I am sure, both wisdom and charity, and will know that the heart cannot be ruled."

"My Phoebe is a simple wench, sir," said Mr Jolly, stirring uneasily in his chair, and embarrassed by the turn the conversation had taken. "A good girl, I assure you, though some would deem her otherwise, but affectionate at bottom, and honest as the day. Yet, Mr Calder," went on the chandler, rousing himself to be fair to this quiet gentleman for whom he had conceived already so great a liking, "I must let you know that I presume to think you somewhat of a romantic, and it sticks in my mind that you see my Phoebe through the rosy spectacles of love, and perchance deem her other than she really is. I am a simple man and am in labour to express what I intend; but I am growing old, and have, as you say, a certain homely wisdom. Come, sir, be plain with me; what is it in Phoebe that makes you so deep in love?"

Mr Calder gave a rueful little laugh.

"A question which cannot be answered, sir. We may say we are fond of such a one because she is kind, because she is generous, because she hath wit or beauty; we can give a reason for fondness; never for love. It is indeed a spirit which bloweth where it listeth; it is a flame which is lit no man knows how. I do not deem Phoebe other than she is; I have learned enough about myself and life to be sure that I can but accept her as I see her through human eyes. The reality of her, the essential Phoebe who draws forth this mysterious love of mine, that I shall know hereafter; I am convinced of it."

This was too deep for Mr Jolly, and he could make no comment on it. It seemed, however, that the young man was thinking aloud rather than addressing his host; with a preoccupied air, in which there was something both of exaltation and of sadness, he wandered about the little room, talking quietly yet with deep feeling.

"Have there not been times when you have had the conviction that this human life of ours is but the shadow of a substance which is very near? Have you not often, out in the country on an autumn morning, when the green and yellow trees stand as it were painted against a sky of tender blue, the grass shimmers with moisture, and a faint mist enshrouds the further view, have you not felt then that if you could but push aside the trees and the houses you would find that of which they are but the reflections in a mirror? They are unreal; but just beyond them, but just out of reach, are the real trees and houses and people, whom instantly we should recognise could we but see them. Is this not, perchance, what was meant by the saying that now we see in a glass darkly, but then face to face?"

He paused; and again he turned in his hand that light tan oak-leaf.

"When I was a child in Sussex," he went on, smiling down on Mr Jolly in the light of the now guttering candles, "we had for neighbour the lord of the manor, his estate separated from my father's vicarage by a great high wall. It was in the time between the execution of King Charles the First and the Restoration of his son, an evil time for men who loved the Monarchy. My father was a staunch Royalist; God knows how he kept his living, save that the squire, who was his friend, was something of a trimmer, and having influence with the Parliament, persuaded them to leave us in peace. My father could not forgive him for this toadying to rebels, and when I was a child still in the 'coats, forbade me ever to visit his friend's family, with whom I was used to play. I understood not the command, and grieved at it, for though I was not yet seven, my chief happiness had lain in the visits I had paid to that great house which lay so close to us, and in my playfellows who were the squire's sons."

He sighed a little, looked again at the oak-leaf, then slipped it into his pocket.

"I used to wander beside that high wall, and staring up at it, I thought that all my happiness lay upon the other side, all the things and the persons I knew and loved most vividly. And sometimes now, Mr Jolly, I have the fancy that our mortality is somewhat akin to that high wall; we are in exile on the one side of it, and on the other lies our home. So close, yet so hidden; so near and yet so far. But for all of us there is a private door, and when we have wandered long enough, we shall come upon it; it will have our name writ over it, and its own name is death. When my time comes, and only then, shall I find the real world, and the real Phoebe."

"These are deep matters," murmured Mr Jolly gruffly, greatly moved, he scarce knew why, by the tone rather than the words.

"Plague on't," replied Mr Calder, on a lighter note, "I have come near to delivering a sermon to one far older and wiser than I. My apologies, Mr Jolly; 'twas an ill return for all your kindness and hospitality."

When Mr Calder had taken his leave and had gone off with his mistress to Jack Straw's, the chandler, worn out, fell asleep in his chair, and so was spared Elizabeth's tipsy dissertations on the evening. But he was not spared a very evil dream. He dreamed that he roamed beside a high wall, and that coming to a door therein, it opened, and standing there was the sinister figure of Bob Ferguson the Plotter, who uttered the one word "Death".

Chapter Three

At the hour of noon, two days later, Mr Jolly was taking his usual dinner of bread and cheese and onions in a little recess he had partitioned off for this purpose in his shop (for this was often a busy hour and he could not trust Ned to serve single-handed), when his apprentice came shambling round the pile of saucepans and other domestic articles which shielded Mr Jolly from the public gaze, and in his usual slobbering speech informed his master that there was a gentleman demanding to see him upon urgent business.

Mr Jolly's heart sank at these words, for he lived now in a perpetual fear of being dunned by his principal creditor, the stony-hearted Mr Dubs. Peering cautiously through an aperture in the tower of saucepans, he saw to his relief that the visitor was a stranger to him; and hastily wiping his mouth on his apron, he trotted round the counter to enquire how he might serve the gentleman.

The stranger was a very feeble, ancient person, so tiny as to be almost a dwarf. He wore his own sparse grey hair, and his wrinkled face was ornamented here and there with a thin crop of whisker; he leaned upon a cane, and Mr Jolly observed that this was of fine ebony, with a silver knob, and that the dress of the old gentleman, though sombre, had an air of richness about it. When he saw Daniel, the stranger bowed in a gracious fashion, and in a high squeaky voice and strong Scots accent, thus addressed him:

"Ma name, sir, is Baillie, Robert Baillie o' Jerviswood in the kingdom o' Scotland. I cam' doon last night on the stage, and meeting as arranged wi' a guid friend o' mine this morning, was informed by him o' an honest man, yoursel', sir, wha wad gi'e me the hospitality o' his hoose. He's a friend o' your ain forbye, Master Jolly; his name is Josiah Keeling; ye ken wha I mean."

Here, it seemed, was one of those angels in disguise promised by Josiah as a lodger, and Mr Jolly was thankful that, on the morning after his encounter with the oil-merchant, he had prepared his wife for the possible advent of a lodger, and had bidden Phoebe move her goods into the attic.

"At your service, sir," said he to Mr Baillie. "Josiah was very kind, and told me he would recommended my house to such good friends of his who had occasion for board and lodging where privacy might be had."

"Ay, yon's the word, privacy," rejoined the stranger, casting a significant glance in the direction of Ned, who was standing goggling at him with his foolish mouth wide open. "Privacy and the caller air o' Hampstead, for I must tell you, sir, I suffer somewhat wi' ma lungs." Here he coughed a little, to give point to this remark. "I made sae bold as to carry ma baggage wi' me; it is oot i' the hackney yonder, and if convenient to you, Master Jolly, will tak' up ma residence straightaway."

Sending Ned to help carry in the gentleman's baggage, Daniel escorted Mr Baillie into the parlour, where he called loudly for Phoebe.

"The room I can offer you, sir," said he, "is not large, I fear, but it looks upon the garden, and you will not be teased with the street cries. I assure you, you will find the bed aired and all things convenient – "

"Say nae mair, Master Jolly, say nae mair," interrupted the other with a gracious gesture. "Ye'll no' find me a difficult man to please. Ma wants are small, Master Jolly; I eat like a birdie" – he gave a little cackling laugh – "and willna put ye aboot wi' fetching and carrying."

Phoebe now arrived from the kitchen, accompanied as usual by her two mongrel dogs. No sooner did these curs perceive the stranger, than they set up the most ferocious barking, and but for Phoebe's management of them, would have flown at his throat. Mr Jolly was astonished and dismayed; never before had he seen the curs act so, and he cursed them in his heart lest they lose him a lodger. But Mr Baillie took it all in good part, and when Phoebe had locked her dogs into a closet, followed her and her father upstairs to the bedchamber set aside for him. It was, indeed, very small, for it was a humble dwelling, but Phoebe has seen to it that it was clean, the bed made up, and a fire laid ready on the tiny hearth. She lit this in silence, while Ned and the coachman staggered in with Mr Baillie's valises; there were two of these, and with them was a small iron box, which latter its owner, having discovered in the room a cupboard with a key, straightway locked up with some care. The coachman being paid off, and Phoebe and Ned having taken their departure, Mr Baillie lowered his feeble little frame into a chair by the window, and, learning on his cane, addressed his new landlord.

"Master Jolly, there are certain particulars wi' which I tak' leave to acquaint ye right away. I hae privy business i' London, and being unco' obnoxious to certain gentlemen there because of ma religion and ma politics, desire to live very private and retired – ye understand me?"

"Josiah so advised me, sir," answered the chandler, feeling somewhat uneasy all the same.

"That's guid, that's guid," approved the other. "Noo, I'll be haeing maybe some visitors, wha will wish to come here and transact business wi' me, for being, as you can see, somewhat feeble in ma body, I'm no' verra guid at travelling aboot. Forbye, as I hae said, I desire to keep masel' verra retired. They'll no' interfere wi' you or your family, sir, but come and gang. I'll answer for them as for masel', they being peaceable honest gentlemen, and wishing ill to no man. Aiblins there might be, whiles, some letter connected with ma business which must be taken to the letter-office or to the inn hereabouts where a post-boy may be hired to carry them instanter to their destination. I'd be much obliged if when this happens, you'd tak' these letters yoursel', for I wadna hae them miscarry by any means."

Daniel looked somewhat blank at this. He had his shop to attend to, and he felt it a little hard that his duties as a landlord should be expected to include those of a messenger. Sensing something of his resentment, Mr Baillie said blandly:

" 'Tis asking a lot o' ye, friend, but I'm no expecting ye to dae it for naething. I propose to pay ye five and twenty shillings for ma rent, and any wee extra services will no' gang wi'oot their just reward. I'm a strict man i' business, Master Jolly, taking care to mak'nae man the poorer for serving me; and if five and twenty shillings doesna seem to you a fair rent, prithee name your ain terms; I'll meet ye, so they be reasonable."

"Sir," said the jubilant Daniel, "five and twenty shillings weekly is a handsome rent indeed; bless me, 'tis more than Charlie Weems demands for the best bedchamber and privy parlour at the Bowling Green."

"Yon's settled, then," said Mr Baillie, with another of his gracious gestures. "And noo, sir, I'll even tak' a wee rest, if you please, being somewhat fatigued by ma lang journey."

Mr Jolly took the hint and left him. Going into the kitchen to bid Phoebe notify her stepmother of the new lodger's advent, so soon as Mrs Jolly returned from shopping, he found the girl kneading dough and looking somewhat preoccupied. She merely nodded as he gave his orders, but just as he was returning to his counter, she said suddenly:

"I have never known Tangle bark so at any man save the fellow who came hither begging last summer, and the very next night robbed two men on the Heath."

Mr Jolly's ire rose at these words.

"Those curs of yours had been like to have lost us a lodger, my wench," he snapped. "Pox take 'em, if they make any more touse, out they go and there is an end of 'em."

"I protest, you need not be so sharp with me," said Phoebe mildly. "My dogs will behave themselves, for I have told them that they must. Yet I cannot but fear this stranger is an ill person, for these dogs of mine are quick to scent evil, and cannot stomach it."

"Pish!" exclaimed her father irritably, "you're full of fancies, girl. Mr Baillie is a gentleman, as you can see if you have eyes, and I'll ask you to keep your silly notions to yourself."

Indeed, in the days that followed, Mr Baillie showed himself a model lodger, appreciative and considerate. Mrs Jolly was quite charmed with him and his gracious airs, though she regretted that he did not seem inclined for conversation and excused himself from her repeated invitations to take a whet in the parlour or a hand at the cartes. It having been impressed upon her by her husband that if she gossiped about their lodger he instantly would take his departure, she managed to deny herself this pleasure, and found some compensation for the hardship in weaving romances about him in the bosom of her own family. Mr Baillie kept strictly to his room, only very occasionally ordering a hackney when he was obliged to make an excursion into London.

He appeared to have a great deal of writing to do, for every time Mrs Jolly or her stepdaughter entered his chamber to bring him his meals or other necessities, they would find him busily engaged with quill and ink-horn, and usually with the little iron box open on the table before him, quite overflowing with papers. On the rare occasions when he went abroad, however, Mrs Jolly, seizing the excuse to give his room a good cleaning, was disappointed to find that the iron box was locked away in the cupboard, and that nothing of the lodger's personal effects was left lying about. Two or three times a week, Mr Jolly would be commissioned to carry letters to the Upper Bowling green, where, it seemed, Charlie Weems saw to their further dispatch. Mr Jolly was not by nature a curious man, yet he could not resist a glance at the inscriptions on these letters as he walked to the inn with them in his hand. It seemed that Mr Baillie had a great many correspondents; some of the letters were addressed to "Mr Roberts, in the care of Mr Bourn, at the sign of the Cock-in-the-Hoop, in the Poultry," others to "Mr Smith, to be called for at the dry-salter's in Minns Wynd, Edinburgh," others again to "Colonel Rumsey, at the cutler's over against Hill's Coffee House, Soho." Daniel remembered that Roberts was the alias of Ferguson the Plotter, but the other names meant nothing to him. Whenever he delivered these letters, there were always some to collect in return, in many different handwritings, and nearly all of them were thick packages for which Mr Baillie had to pay dear.

The lodger had not been established in Hampstead many days before his first visitors came to call on him. They arrived one evening when Mr Jolly had just closed his shop and was counting over the day's takings before going into the parlour for supper. There was a peremptory rap upon the street door, and when he opened it he found two men standing there. Both were muffled up in cloaks, which they wore with one end flung over their shoulders, and slouch hats pulled well down over their eyes; the light from the shop falling upon them, Mr Jolly observed that one was a big burly fellow, red-faced and heavy jowled, the other tall and thin with a wooden leg.

"How now, friend," said the big man gruffly. "Is all in harmony?"

Mr Jolly gaped at him. It was an ill time of night for visitors, pitch dark, and the village street deserted. Secretly wishing that he had his old blunderbuss handy, he muttered:

"Whom is it ye seek?"

The burly man exchanged a meaning glance with his friend, then, pushing past Mr Jolly without ceremony, he turned and faced him, and very deliberately began to undo the two top buttons of his coat. Fearful that he was reaching for a pistol, Mr Jolly looked hastily round for something he could use as a weapon, but even as he did so, the thin man clapped him on the shoulder, told him to be of good cheer, that they were friends of Master Baillie and would have speech with him. He spoke in an educated voice, yet Mr Jolly liked the looks of him no better than those of his red-faced friend; he with the wooden leg had eyes which roved continuously, never gave a direct glance, and seemed full of dark secrets.

Taking up a candle, and requesting the visitors to follow him, the chandler led the way through the parlour, signing sharply to his wife in passing to take no notice of his companions. Preceding them up the stairs, he heard the tap-tap of the wooden leg and crutch coming up after him with an agility which was somehow unnerving.

"Wait," commanded the burly man, as Mr Jolly was about to knock upon his lodger's door. "I'll announce myself, if you please."

With that, he raised his hand and rapped with his knuckles in a peculiar manner: two soft strokes, three loud, and then two soft again. There was a faint exclamation from within, and then Mr Baillie's squeaky voice cried to enter. The two men went in, and with scant ceremony shut the door in Mr Jolly's face just as he was about to follow them and enquire of his lodger whether he desired any refreshment brought up. Somewhat affronted by this rude treatment, the chandler stood a moment on the landing, muttering to himself about some men's ill manners; as he did so, he heard the thin man say:

"He knew neither the sign nor the password. Is he not, then, one of us?"

"Nay, but a guid honest man, Frank," replied Mr Baillie, "recommended by Josiah, and nae blabber wi' his tongue."

The man who had been addressed as Frank made some reply which Mr Jolly could not catch, and not wishing to eavesdrop, the chandler made his way downstairs again.

But he was very uneasy in his mind. He realised now that he had felt a vague disquiet ever since that night at the Upper Bowling Green when he had seen his friend the oil-merchant in close converse with that sinister character known as the Plotter; he had persuaded himself that such disquiet was foolish, and the gentlemanly appearance and behaviour of this lodger had gone far to remove it. Yet it had remained at the back of his mind, and with the advent of Mr Baillie's first visitors it returned in strength. There was an air about them he did not like; they had looked so like ruffians, standing there at the street door, and what could they have meant by saying that he knew not the password or the sign? It was plain that they were well acquainted with Josiah, since Mr Baillie had mentioned that gentleman to them by his Christian name, but although he still could not suspect his friend of being mixed up with anything improper, Mr Jolly could find no comfort in the fact of their acquaintanceship with him.

He ate his supper with a preoccupied air, and during the process came to a resolution. Immediately afterwards, muttering to his wife that he would go upstairs to see if the gentlemen lacked for aught, he tiptoed up in the dark to Mr Baillie's door. His honest soul shrank from listening at keyholes; his practical mind revolted from the risk of losing a rent which was a fortune to him, and which, if he continued to receive it, would enable him very shortly to pay off Mr Dubs; yet he could not rest until he had attempted to satisfy himself that the gentlemen closeted behind that closed door were indeed engaged upon some harmless business transaction.

He felt very guilty as he stood on the dark little landing, holding his breadth and straining his ears to catch the voices within. At first these voices were drowned in a crackle as of some stiff parchment being unfolded, accompanied by Mr Baillie's dry little cough. Then the man with the wooden leg, who had been addressed as Frank, began to speak, and as he did not trouble to lower his voice, Mr Jolly could hear quite clearly all that he said.

"This is an exact copy of the map which hangs in West's chamber; you will observe, sir, that it contains the City and the liberties, and is divided into twenty parts. These divisions have been made by Goodenough, who, from being so often Under Sheriff, knows the City and its temper best than the rest of us. Over each division is to be placed a leader of trust and zeal, who is to choose him nine or ten more in whom he can confide and can make his lieutenants. From time to time these lieutenants are to make returns to their leader of the number and nature of the recruits they have enrolled, and their leader will communicate the information to my lord."

"Ay, yon's guid and neat," Mr Baillie's squeaky voice approved. "You will be Ferguson's arrangements, dootless. A canny man, oor Rabbie; nae mixtie-maxtie methods whaur he's concerned."

"Nay, for my part I like it not," interposed the gruff voice of the third man. "There are too many in it already for safety."

"And that's the reason why my lord presses for the thing to be done without loss of time," replied Frank. "Delay is exceeding dangerous, saith he, and methinks he is in the right of it."

"And wha's for delay then?" enquired Mr Baillie sharply.

"Why, our Prince Perkin, of course," answered Frank contemptuously. "You know his nature; he blows hot, and he blows cold, and no resolution is to be found in him. If he continues in this strain, my lord will tire of him ere long, and the thing will be done without him."

"Nay, that were madness," exclaimed the third man. "He alone can protect us when the thing is done."

"Weel, let's hear about these recruits i' the City," said Mr Baillie soothingly. "I've muckle faith i' oor Rabbie, and ken fine he'll be taking nae unnecessary risk."

"He has indeed laid down most careful rules for recruitment," agreed Frank. "The true nature of the design is to be concealed at first; there is to be but a discreet probing of the sentiments of possible recruits, by tactful question and insinuation. As, What would you do in the case of foreign invasion? Would you contribute the assistance of your purses or persons or both? If the answers to these questions prove satisfactory, the man is then told that there is an actual invasion of English liberties; that the only obligation the subject has to the King is the mutual covenant; that this covenant is manifestly broken on the

King's part, and that therefore the people have the duty to assert their rights as justly against a domestic as against a foreign invader. These arguments – "

The voice broke off abruptly, as Mr Jolly in the passage, absorbed in the strange talk, shifted his position and trod upon a loose board. His first thought was flight, but so unfamiliar was he with the role of eavesdropper, so bewildered by the whole situation, that he found himself incapable of moving a foot. Then, as he heard a footstep in the room as though someone were about to open the door, some instinct told him what to do. Going quickly up to the door he rapped upon the panels. The door opened immediately, and the burly man stood there, with a candle in his hand and a very suspicious look upon his face.

"Your pardon, sirs," babbled Mr Jolly, trying to keep his voice steady. "My wife sent me to say she would take it as a favour if you would taste her blackberry cordial. I will fetch it, sirs, if you would condescend; I – I hesitated to intrude, but – "

"Please to say to that charming wife o' yours," interrupted Mr Baillie graciously, "that I and ma friends here tak' it verra kindly o' her, and will drink a glass wi' pleasure if ye'll bring it up."

As Mr Jolly stumbled down the stairs, he found that he was sweating with relief. It was absurd, of course, he assured himself, to imagine that he would have been in any danger from these gentlemen if they had suspected him of eavesdropping; ridiculous to imagine the courteous and well-bred Mr Baillie permitting harm to come to an innocent man. Yet he continued to bless the kindly guardian angel who had put the excuse of the blackberry cordial into his head, and when he carried it above stairs he found that his hands were trembling so violently that the glasses shook and tinkled on the tray. He would have set down his burden and withdrawn at once, but that the burly man, as he made to do so, clapped him on the shoulder, and with a jollity which somehow rang false, cried to him:

"You'll take a whet with us, my good friend. Come, we'll have no denial, and you being so honest a man shall join us in a toast: Here's to liberty and the Protestant faith."

Mr Jolly drank the toast; in other circumstances he would have done so with enthusiasm, for both his liberty as an Englishman and the vague something, secure and respectable, which he understood by the words Protestant faith, were very dear to him. But it was as much as he could do to drink with these men at all, and the honest toast they had proposed sounded on their lips ominous and almost sinister.

Mr Baillie's visitors remained with him for many hours, and until they left Mr Jolly could not lock up and go to bed. His wife retired at her usual time, despairing of satisfying her curiosity with a glimpse of the strange gentlemen, but Phoebe, for some reason she did not mention, chose to sit up with her father, mending a sheet beside the fire. Her dogs, curled at her feet, were restless, often raising their heads to give a gruff bark as the voices above stairs rose and fell, and sometimes running to the door which gave on to the staircase, and sniffing beneath it with hackles raised. Daniel, a cold pipe stuck in his mouth, stared at the glowing logs, his mind a-whirl with confused doubts and fears, which articulated themselves only in an occasional heavy sigh. At last Phoebe said abruptly:

"Who are those men above, father?"

It was the first word she had spoken since her stepmother had retired, and Daniel started at her voice.

"I know not, child," said he, stirring uneasily. "Save that they are friends of Master Baillie. I would they would take their leave, for I am woundy tired."

"Methinks you like them no more than do my dogs," said Phoebe, in that direct way of hers. "I have observed you have been troubled in your mind ever since this Mr Baillie came to our house. Why do you not confide your uneasiness to Derrick and seek his advice?"

"To Derrick – to Mr Calder?" exclaimed Daniel, astonished. "Why, child, what would make me do that?"

"He is a man who knows the world," replied Phoebe, "and one who hath conceived a great affection for you. He tells me so often, since he came to supper that night."

"I am much obliged for his good opinion, wench," said Daniel, touched and surprised, "which indeed I do return. Yet I cannot see how I am to confide my troubles to him, since they are not at all clear to me, and are, I am sure, quite without foundation."

But he did not think they were without foundation. It was from this evening that he began to be filled with a pervading anxiety, still vague and formless, but so persistent that he tossed and turned in his bed at night and grew absent-minded even in his shop. Much of the conversation he had overheard between Mr Baillie and his visitors had been unintelligible to him; but certain phrases had stuck in his mind, and he did not like them. "The people have the duty to assert their rights as justly against a domestic as against a foreign invader." "He alone can protect us when the thing is done." "There are too many in it already for safety." "I've muckle faith i' oor Rabbie, and ken fine he'll be taking nae unnecessary risk." Ominous phrases, whatever their true meaning; almost the phrases of men hatching some plot. But that was fantastically absurd. What chance had a few fanatics in this year of grace, 1682, when the nation had never been more tranquil and more wholly devoted to the King, to play the game of '41 again? But then there was that mention of "my lord." "My lord presses for the thing to be done without loss of time. Delay is exceeding dangerous, saith he." What my lord could this be? And "Prince Perkin"; was that one of the nicknames of the King's favourite bastard, the troublesome Duke of Monmouth? If so, what could such great personages be up to, consorting with men like Ferguson the Plotter, Frank of the wooden leg and shifty eyes, a frail old Scottish gentleman, and Josiah Keeling, the respectable oil-merchant?

Thus did poor Daniel Jolly's simple mind wrestle with a cloud of doubts, the more horrid because they were intangible; now it presented to him an awesome picture of conspiracy and rebellion being hatched under his roof, now desperately assured him of his presumption in questioning the good faith of gentlemen. But his doubts triumphed more and more over his optimistic reasoning, and he grew so drawn in countenance, and so preoccupied and even irritable in behaviour, that his neighbours began to ask of him if he ailed.

One fine Sunday afternoon towards the end of October, Mr Jolly and his family were taking their usual Sabbath promenade about the Heath. It was a custom Daniel relished greatly; from Monday morning till Saturday night he worked hard and long and Sunday was for him his only day of rest and simple recreation. Dressed in a suit which all the week was laid up in lavender, with his wife and daughter gaily attired on his either arm, he strolled gently about the Heath he so loved, stopping often to chat with his promenading neighbours, exchanging village gossip, and pausing at various vantage-points to admire the view from this high village. On Sundays the Heath was transformed; the many laundresses who plied their trade here had taken in the sheets and shifts which on week-days lay bleaching on the grass, and even those nuisances, the pig-keepers, observed to keep their swine from straying about as they did on week-days to the indignation of the rest of the community.

On this particular Sunday, the Jolly family had walked as far as the windmill on the old highway between London and Hendon, had admired the fine new houses which wealthy citizens were building themselves along this road, had enjoyed anew the grisly Gibbet Trees, two huge elms, which held between them a chain from which dangled the bodies of highwaymen suspended there until they became mere skeletons, and had examined from a respectful distance the bleaching bones of Francis Jackson, alias Dixie, which had hung there now for eight years. So they climbed the hill by Jack Straw's Castle, skirted the White Stone and its pond, and reached the highest point of the Heath, where stood the famous Hampstead Elm, a favourite place of pilgrimage for Londoners, with a winding staircase inside its hollow trunk and an octagonal turret at the top which afforded sitting accommodation for six persons and standing-room for fourteen more. And here, as always, Mr Jolly made his longest pause, for from this altitude could be seen the whole of London-town, lying in its hole far, far below. The afternoon was so clear that one could identify famous City churches and make out clearly the scaffolding round the new cathedral of St Paul's.

It was while he was gazing upon this view so dear to him, that Mr Jolly was struck with an idea. And now he wondered why he had never thought of it before, since it promised the solution to all his problems. Somewhere down there, amid the confusion of house roofs and chimneys and steeples and the smoke of the sea-coal lived his dear old school friend, Josiah Keeling. He would go and see Josiah; he would venture into that horrid place, the City of London; the very next morning he would catch the carrier, leaving Ned to run the shop as best he could for a few hours. He would seek out Josiah at his place of business, which was also his residence, and into that kindly and understanding bosom he would pour out all the doubts which were tormenting him.

Josiah had been the indirect means of causing them; only Josiah could drive them away.

Chapter Four

Awakening on Monday morning, Daniel was half-inclined to lay aside yesterday's resolution to go into the City. He feared and hated London, with its lurking pestilences, its crowded streets, and its confusion of noise so daunting to a countryman. But as he lay irresolute in bed, he heard through the wall the dry little cough of his lodger, and somehow the sound brought back most vividly the evening when he had lurked outside Mr Baillie's door and had heard such strange and frightening conversation from behind it. He rose determinedly, put on his Sunday suit again, stole out of the room without awaking his wife, and going downstairs scrubbed himself at the pump in the back garden; by the time Ned arrived, soon after seven o'clock, his master was waiting to give him prolonged and minute instructions as to how to conduct business in his absence.

Hampstead was already astir as Mr Jolly hurried down Heath Street towards the King of Bohemia in High Street, from which hostelry started the carrier for London. He could hear the clatter of wooden pails from the spring in Conduit Fields as the water-cobs drew the fresh water which they would sell to Hampstead housewives. Cocks crew in back gardens, and from his parsonage hurried Mr Mole, the clergyman, going to church to read Morning Prayer to a few old women and a sleepy clerk. The carrier's cart was already half full as Mr Jolly turned into the inn yard; crates of squawking hens, bulky packages, and sacks of vegetables incommoded an unusual number of passengers, who consisted mostly of women. Mr Jolly was surprised to see several plump housewives, his neighbours, decked out in their best as though sallying forth to some treat; saluting them, as he squeezed into the cart beside them, he enquired their errand.

"Lord, Master Jolly," replied one excitedly, "do you not know this is a hanging-Monday? We are bound for the Green Dragon on Snow Hill, where we may get a good view of the start of the March to Tyburn. Captain Baker is Ketch's chief subject today, he who was called the Terror of Houndslow, and you know what sport the highwaymen always give in the cart. They say Ketch is bribed to cut him down immediately he swings, for his friends have hired a surgeon to nurse him back to life again, and so cheat the law and the Barber Surgeons of a corpse."

Mr Jolly was not at all pleased to hear all this. Not that he was averse to a view of the March to Tyburn, which was, indeed, the favourite spectacle of his kind, but it would mean that the City would be more crowded than ever, and as the carrier went no further than this same Green Dragon on Snow Hill, his long walk to Aldgate would be delayed at the very start by the huge crowds milling round Newgate and St Sepulchre's. He has an idea that at a set hour every morning, Mr Keeling went upon 'Change, and if the delay in getting to Aldgate was very great, Daniel might miss him.

As soon as the cart, jolting slowly along, and often stopping to pick up goods and passengers, has passed through the village of Camden and was come in sight of the Tyburn Road, the holiday crowds became observable, some hastening towards the gallows, others concentrated upon getting a good vantage-point on the road to it. There were hundreds of apprentices in their blue frocks, for though many of their masters refused to close their shops on hanging-Mondays, these lads took french-leave. Mingling with them were housewives with their children, vendors of oranges, gingerbread and sweetmeats, street musicians and tumblers, with a sprinkling of craftsmen and shopkeepers who loved the sight of the hangman's cart better than a morning's business. The carrier's progress became slower and slower as it neared Holborn, the driver's warning shouts and the flourishing of his whip having little effect upon the seething mob; and by the time they reached the Green Dragon, Mr Jolly's female friends were quite beside themselves with anxiety lest they by too late to see the condemned put into the cart.

Mr Jolly himself had caught now some of their excitement, and was craning and chattering as animatedly as his neighbours. Throughout the last stages of their journey, they had heard, high above the noise of the mob, the booming bell of St Sepulchre's tolling, and now, approaching the church, they heard also the hand-bell of the sexton who, according to custom, was perched upon the graveyard wall, snuffling out an exhortation to pray for the victim's repentance, an exhortation quite drowned in the laughter and voices of the excited crowds, the shrilling of penny whistles, and the confusion of footsteps. As the carrier turned into the inn yard, a great roar broke out, and one of the women passengers, standing up in her seat beside Mr Jolly, cried out that there was Captain Baker himself, with his fetters and darbies knocked off, just stepping into Jack Ketch's cart and exchanging the traditional jests with the hangman and the constables.

"Rein in your horse, Will Fleming!" she screamed at the carrier. "Venture you not another yard lest we lose the view. Lord! There is the City Marshal with his peace-officers, and there comes the Sheriff's coach. See, there's a wench among the condemned; that will be Nan Banker, she who was caught for thieving and pled her belly at the trial, but a jury of matrons found it a sham. They say she's weighted her gown with stones that she may die the quicker, being such a lightweight, but I'll warrant she'll dance awhile on the Three Legged Mare for all that."

The carrier, nothing loth, had halted his cart in the entrance to the yard, and it being impossible for Mr Jolly to jump down because of the press of people, he was obliged to stay where he was, whether he would or no, until the procession had passed. For the moment he had forgotten the errand which had brought him into the City, as he watched the hangman's cart making its first halt not a stone's throw from him, where by ancient custom a party of damsels, armed with nosegays, waited in the porch of St Sepulchre's to claim a kiss from such of the condemned of the opposite sex who were young and personable; he had an excellent view of the shoddily picturesque procession, with its javelin-men, its mounted constables, the City Marshal on his richly caparisoned horse, the Sheriff's fine coach with its outriders, and Captain Baker, the highwayman, gaudily attired, standing up in the hangman's cart to salute his friends and jest with the mob according to the tradition of his kind.

But when at last the horses' hooves and the rumble of wheels had died away down Snow Hill, and the greater part of the mob had gone jostling and hurrying after them, Mr Jolly recollected himself with a start, and found to his dismay that it was already half past ten. He had yet to walk to Aldgate, and his progress looked like being impeded by the many street entertainers who, now that the chief attraction of the day was passed, were busily catching the interest of the crowds that remained. There was one in particular who seemed to be doing good business, the folk collected round him quite blocking the narrow street, and as Mr Jolly strove to push his way through them, he was carried to within a few yards of the centre of attraction. The man was selling what purported to be the Last Dying Speech and Confession of Captain Baker, and likewise a ballad which, he swore, had been written by the highwayman's sweetheart, in which she bewailed his untimely fate and described the pleasures she had shared with her lover. Well, thought Daniel, I might as well buy one of these now I am so close, for Elizabeth will relish it; he was struggling to get a penny from his pocket when something happened which made his mouth fall agape and a cold shiver to run down his spine.

Anticipating him in buying from the ballad-monger was a gentleman of seedy appearance, and with a curious resemblance to a fox. He wore a red periwig, and the wind blowing the folds of this aside, his face was seen to be sharp and pointed, with yellow teeth exposed in a grin. Mr Jolly, standing pressed against him, heard him say, in low yet distinct accents to the ballad-monger:

"Is all in harmony?"

And as he did so, he unfastened the two top buttons of his coat. The ballad-monger, handing him a paper from the bottom of his pile of ballads, answered in the same tone:

"In harmony and liberty."

The fox-coloured gentleman took the paper, did up the buttons of his coat again, flung a penny into the man's tin can, and without another word began to push his way through the crowd in the direction in which Mr Jolly himself had been making.

Mr Jolly stood staring after him for a moment, forgetting his intention to buy a ballad for his wife. "Is all in harmony?", and the unfastening of the two top buttons of a coat; these, he was convinced, were the very same password and sign he had failed to understand when they had been given him by one of Mr Baillie's visitors. What could they mean? They hid, it seemed, a secret shared by the most strangely assorted characters. Suddenly Mr Jolly was not only frightened; he was excited; the boy in him scented a game, caught an old thrill from his school days, of gangs and secret societies and cryptic signs. He never knew afterwards what cursed instinct had made him act so, but before he knew what he was about he had pushed and jostled his way till he was alongside the fox-coloured gentleman, laid a hand upon his sleeve, and having caught his attention, in silence began to undo the two top buttons of his Sunday coat.

The fox-coloured gentleman stopped dead in his walk; his eyes, pale, hooded, with a hint of savagery, scanned Daniel up and down. He leaned against one of the white posts which separated the footwalk from the street, thus saving himself from being swept away from Mr Jolly in the mob, and shot out at him:

"I do not know you, sir."

Mr Jolly blinked, and swallowed hard. The instinct which had made him accost the stranger deserted him on this hostile response, and he felt only very foolish and rather afraid. But then again something seemed to impel him to act out of character, and he heard his own voice say tremulously:

"Your pardon, neighbour, but I heard the password, and wondered if there was news."

"Did you get a paper?" asked the gentleman sharply, jerking his head backwards in the direction of the ballad-monger.

Daniel shook his head in silence.

"H'm," grunted the other, still scanning him closely, "the fellow is new to us, but safe. If you wish to hear the news, return to him, give him the password and sign, and he will hand you one of these," he tapped his pocket into which he had slipped whatever it was he had got from the ballad-monger, nodded curtly, and mingled with the crowds before Mr Jolly could detain him.

It was now that Daniel Jolly's only serious weakness of character asserted itself. He was, as has been seen, one of those person who, having made a decision, are apt to act clean contrary to it. As he stood there staring after the fox-coloured gentleman, an old adage piped up in his mind, "Curiosity killed the cat," and his reason applauded the truth of it. Had he not assured Josiah, at that meeting at the Bowling Green, that he was not one for prying into other men's business? And it was true. Whatever the significance of all these passwords and signs and strange doings, they were no concern of his, and the only right and sensible course was to ignore them. Besides this he was already late in getting to Josiah; what he must do was to hurry to Aldgate as fast as his legs could carry him, and forget what he had seen and heard just now. And even as he told himself all this, he found that he was retracing his steps and was pushing his way through the crowd in the direction of the ballad-monger; perversely he fought with elbows and shoulders until he was within a yard of the man, then, catching his eye, he went through the mummery of unfastening buttons, murmured the strange password, and found thrust into his hand a paper. Suddenly terrified at his folly, he pushed the thing deep into his pocket, and having fought his way to the ballad-monger, wrestled like a mad creature to get out of this vicinity.

He was distraught in mind and out of breath in body when at last he arrived at Mr Keeling's place of business; the unfamiliar atmosphere of the place, hinting of weighty business transactions and high finance, completed his discomfiture, and when a clerk informed him that the oil-merchant was out, he could have wept. But he had not come all this way to give up at the first obstacle, and what had transpired on the start of his walk had made him more desperate than ever to seek the sanity and comfort of his friend's advice. So he pleaded with the haughty young clerk to let him know where he might find his master, and received the grudging information that in all probability Mr Keeling was to be found at the Amsterdam Coffee House near the Royal Exchange. Thither did Daniel direct his steps, but after a few minutes seized upon the excuse of a heavy shower of rain to hail a hackney. He was in such a state of nerves that he could not face another walk just yet.

Like most men of his kind he was inclined to distrust these new coffee-houses which were springing up all over the town. Not only was honest English ale being superseded by a heathen beverage, but from their first advent under the Commonwealth, the coffee-houses had come to be identified in the public mind with disaffection and rebellion. "Coffee and Commonwealth came in together," had written a Whig pamphleteer, "to make us a free and sober nation," and the nation generally, which remembered the tyranny of the Commonwealth and had no very great love of sobriety, disliked the new institutions on that very score.

The Amsterdam was one of innumerable coffee-houses which were situated around the Royal Exchange and was definitely Puritan and Whig in tone. Mr Jolly, diffidently entering its pretentious portals glanced with distaste at a notice, prominently displayed, which asserted that a fine of twelvepence would be exacted for an oath, and noted with contempt that a perusal of the news-books cost the customers a penny, whereas any self-respecting tavern let its habitués read them for nothing. The place was crowded, mostly with merchants discussing their business, but there were other groups which argued about politics, and, unmellowed by ale, grew heated and quarrelsome; a white-aproned serving-man bustled to and for with trays of shallow wooden dishes, and upon a stand in one corner of the room there stood a white iron machine, turned by a spit, wherein the coffee was being roasted. Some coffee-houses permitted their customers to drink ale or wine, but not so the Amsterdam. There was either coffee, drunk without milk or sugar, or, for those who could not acquire a taste for this bitter beverage, there were saloop, tay, chocolate, sherbet, and this new China drink called tena.

Slowly threading his way between the tables, Mr Jolly searched anxiously for his friend, and at last spied him in the centre of a group around the fire at the far end of the room. The oil-merchant was deep in talk, emphasising his words with what looked like a pamphlet which he held in his hand. Not liking to intrude, but absolutely resolved for a talk with Josiah, Daniel hovered upon the edge of the circle, and presently found himself listening to the conversation. The more he listened, the more bewildered he became; it was true that he knew little of the jargon of the merchants, but this group was sprinkling among its unintelligible terms certain names which were ominously familiar to Daniel, yet seemed altogether out of place in such a company.

"The General Point," said one, "is settled then for the 19th, but what of the Lopping Point?"

"Hannibal is the trouble there," replied another, "for he will not undertake for less than six hundred pounds and forty men."

"Nay, 'tis not only Hannibal," interposed a third. "We are yet uncertain of Prince Perkin. If the Blackbird and the Goldfinch are shot down, he may turn round upon us and disown his part in the sport, unless we can bind him to us before 'tis done. My lord insists that Prince Perkin have some of his servants among the men at the Rye, but Perkin is too brisk for him there, and absolutely refuses."

"Mr Roberts is strong for the Lopping Point," retorted the man who had spoken first, "for it is, saith he, the more pious design of the two, and the only way of preventing the shedding of Christian blood, which would happen if the General Point only were followed. We have seen how hot they were for the Blackbird at Oxford, and the General Point entered upon without the Lopping Point accomplished first, would be a thing of huge risk for us all."

"If it must be done," sighed Mr Keeling, "I would not have it on the 19th for anything in the world, that being the Sabbath. I know what Mr Roberts saith, that they have a proverb in Scotland which runs, The better the day, the better the deed, but his appears to me plain blasphemous, and – "

He stopped short, for, half turning, he had caught sight of Mr Jolly's figure standing on the fringe of the group.

Josiah Keeling's first reaction to this vision was one of obvious annoyance. His genial face clouded and went red, a frown creased his forehead, and with the paper in his hand he signalled sharply to his companions to cease their talk. Then, observing his old friend's look of dismay and embarrassment, he forced a smile, and laying a hand on Daniel's sleeve, said with his old kindness:

"Why, friend, what brings you here so far from your counter?"

"Your pardon, Josiah," mumbled Mr Jolly, nervously twisting his cap in his hands. "I did not intend to intrude, but I greatly desired some speech with you, and they told me in Aldgate that I should find you here."

Mr Keeling glanced hastily at the clock above the fireplace; then, murmuring an excuse to his friends, took Daniel's arm and guided him through the throng to a vacant table.

"I must be on 'Change at noon," said he, as they sat down, "and have some business to transact ere then, but can always find time, I hope, for a talk with mine old school friend. Will you take coffee, or this counterfeit stuff called saloop? 'Tis a pleasant drink enough, and warming on a cold day."

"I thank you, nothing, nothing," replied Daniel. His desperate anxiety had been a little allayed by Josiah's kind manner, and now he was yearning to unburden himself without loss of time. "I came to seek comfort from you, Josiah, being in much perplexity and trouble of mind."

And with that he poured forth some of the doubts and fears which had plagued him so greatly during the past few weeks; he was, he said, a plain man and did not presume to meddle with high matters; he was sure that Mr Ballie, his lodger, was an honest gentleman, but he had visitors who spoke and looked strangely, and some talk which Daniel had chanced to overhear when certain of these had called on Mr Baillie had made him fear lest some conspiracy were being hatched under his roof. Daniel contradicted himself several times during this recital, being very much put about how to make plain his fears on the one hand, and say nothing derogatory about Mr Baillie on the other; he was not very coherent, but he was encouraged to continue by the kind way in which Josiah listened, occasionally nodding his head as if agreeing with the reasonableness of his poor friend's doubts. When Daniel had rambled to an end, the oil-merchant sat silent for some moments, evidently deep in thought. Then, laying a hand upon the chandler's knee, and pressing it affectionately, he began in a low and confidential voice to talk.

"Neighbour," said he, "you are a very honest man, and a discreet one, and because I know you to be both I will be frank with you. You heard, no doubt, somewhat of the talk in which I was engaged with my friends yonder by the fire; mighty strange talk you must have deemed it, as strange as that you overheard betwixt Mr Ballie and his two visitors.

The truth of it is, Daniel, that we and they spoke in ciphers, not because there is aught being discussed which is at all improper, but because, as I said to you upon a former occasion, the times are evil, and there be good men among us who are in peril for their zeal to their religion and their country."

He then embarked upon a résumé of the history of the present reign, that of King Charles the Second. Daniel did not need to be reminded, said he, of how the Papists had plotted for years to slay the King, because he would not own himself a Papist, and bring in the Duke of York, who was openly of their persuasion; had it not been for good Dr Oates, King Charles would have met his death at an assassin's hand in '78. He would say nothing against the Duke of York; he seemed an honest gentleman and he was the King's brother; but there was no doubt that he was surrounded by priests and Jesuits, and did what they bid him. There were some, went on Josiah, casting a sidelong glance at his silent friend, who declared that the rightful Heir to the throne was the Duke of Monmouth; Daniel would remember how Mr Ferguson had published the story of a mysterious Black Box, in which he declared had been found the marriage certificate of the King and Monmouth's mother. For himself, he did not presume to judge how far this was true; only he could not help but think that it would be a mercy if it were, for then they might have a Protestant instead of a Papist King when the present one died. Noting Daniel's uneasiness at such delicately phrased treason, he quickly left it aside, and went on to say that after the recent rebellion in Scotland of those men called the Covenanters, many gentlemen up there who were good and peaceable men had found themselves deprived of their estates and persecuted; perceiving, therefore, no likelihood of maintaining themselves and their families upon their native soil, certain among them had banded themselves together and had formed a project for founding a colony in Carolina for such as were of their way of thinking.

"Yet the malice of their enemies is so strong, Daniel," concluded the oil-merchant, "that were this project to become public, 'twould be stopped. Therefore is all talk of it kept secret, and it is discussed under such cant terms as those you have overheard today."

Daniel Jolly's relief at hearing this plausible and innocuous explanation of the mysteries which had troubled him, was so great that he was almost abject in his apologies to Mr Keeling for having even remotely suspected friends of his of being concerned in anything improper. Mr Keeling listened sympathetically, patting the chandler's knee at intervals as if to give him reassurance; but when Daniel had stammered himself silent again, he leant towards him, and said very earnestly and gravely:

"One word of warning I must give you, neighbour, or I were no true friend of yours. Do not, I pray you, seek to concern yourself any more in this business; do not mention to any living soul what I have told you, or what you feared before; and above all, let not Mr Baillie or any of this visitors who come to call on him, suspect that you seek to overhear their talk."

"Nay, Josiah," cried Mr Jolly, reddening at this last blunt intimation that his friend guessed he had been eavesdropping outside his lodger's door, "I vow I – "

"Harkee, Daniel," interrupted Mr Keeling, more earnestly than before and in a tone of even greater gravity, "I warn you for your own good. I must tell you that certain of the gentlemen concerned in this project are apt to be hasty and blunt in their displeasure against any man whom they may cause to suspect to be meddling in what doth not concern him. They are hot in their zeal for their cause, and they hold that the Lord approves the destruction of the ungodly; I will not go all the way with them in this, yet I assure you I should be powerless to protect you from their wrath if you were unwise enough to offend them."

A thrill of fear had been working its way up and down Mr Jolly's spine throughout this speech; now he sat staring open-mouthed at his friend, his brown eyes hurt and bewildered. Mr Keeling, giving the chandler's knee a final pat, rose, and saying he must now return to the discussion of business with his friends, nodded genially to Daniel, and walked towards the fire. There was nothing for Mr Jolly to do but go home, and as fast as his shaky legs could carry him he hurried towards and door. Just as he was about to leave the coffee-house, a man entered it; they met in the doorway; and with a further shock Daniel recognised the fox-coloured gentleman who had bought a paper from the ballad-monger in the vicinity of Newgate. It was plain that the fox-coloured gentleman in his turn recognised Daniel; he stopped, stared hard at him, seemed about to speak, then, without a word or sign of greeting, proceeded into the room. The chandler, glancing nervously over his shoulder, saw him stalk straight towards the group by the fire.

It was then, as he hurried down Change Alley, that Daniel remembered the paper in his pocket.

He had intended to show it to Josiah, but during their talk had clean forgot it. He stood still on the foot-path, jostled and pushed by hurrying merchants and clerks, trying to decide what to do. Almost certainly the fox-coloured gentleman would mention his encounter with Daniel to the group by the fire; he would tell them that Daniel knew the password and sign, and he would enquire who he was. Josiah, worthy man, would speak for his honesty and harmlessness; but might not even Josiah wonder why he, Daniel, had not mentioned the paper in their private talk? And then again there came down on Mr Jolly that shivering fear which had possessed him when Josiah had warned him of the vengeance which might overtake any man who meddled in this business; and with this fear spurring him on, he began to run as fast as he could through the crowded streets of the City towards the refuge of his own village. Panting and breathless, with a stitch in his side, now pausing for a little rest, now pelting on again harder than before, with the rain mingling with the sweat which poured down his face, he kept on until this frightening City of London was left behind him, till the houses and the shops began to thin, and the smoke-laden air gave place to a breath laden with wet earth and sodden leaves. And all the while as he ran, the paper in his pocket seemed to burn him.

When he was come to the edge of the Conduit Fields, he turned into a little wayside inn, and sinking down on a bench, ordered a can of ale. There was no one else in the tavern, and as he drank his hand kept stealing to the paper in his pocket, the accursed paper, obtained in a moment of childish folly, capable, perhaps, of bringing upon him and his family some nameless destruction. At last, unable to bear the suspense any longer, he took it out, gingerly unfolded it, and laid it on the table before him. Clasping his head with his hand, he laboriously spelled out the writing.

What he had expected to read there he scarcely knew. What he did in fact read there made his mind a chaos of mingled relief, bewilderment, and incredulity. It was a letter, written without date, beginning "Sir" and ending "Your Friend in Harmony." It was, apparently, a letter of condolence for some bereavement unspecified, very peculiar in phraseology and more so in punctuation, as even the unlettered Mr Jolly could perceive. Certain sentences seemed quite irrelevant, as "The Young Devil will try his Fortune at getting a Horse Shoe," and such cryptic statements, combined with the old punctuation, the circumstances in which Mr Jolly had obtained the letter, and all that he had heard from Josiah, convinced even his simple mind that this "letter" was really a paper written in cipher.

When he had finished his ale, Mr Jolly still sat for a long time, debating with himself whether to destroy the letter and have done with it, or keep it and lock it away in some secure place at home. Reason was all for the former course; Josiah's warning still rang in his ears and filled him with a dreadful apprehension. But besides that weakness of his, which made him decide on one course and then embark on the opposite, Daniel Jolly possessed an obstinacy which is sometimes to be found in timid, easy-going characters. Moreover, though he did not realise it, all these mysterious doings with which he had become entangled tempted him with their spice of novelty and adventure. His life was dull and hard; the boy in him, which originally had prompted him to obtain the paper, now urged him to keep it, so that at odd moments he might amuse himself with trying to puzzle out the meaning.

When he left the tavern, the paper was back in his pocket; several times, as he ploughed through the long wet grass of the Fields, he stopped, took it out, and made to tear it up. But when at last, weary in mind and body, he entered his little shop, and saw Phoebe running anxiously from the back to greet him and enquire where he had been all morning and whether he would like a mug of mulled ale, he still had the paper with him; and when he had drunk his ale and gone to his bedchamber to change his wet clothes, he locked the thing carefully into his moneybox, and with more than ordinary care, pushed this receptacle of all his wealth into a recess within the chimney.

Chapter Five

The date on which Mr Jolly had gone into the City to see his friend Josiah was Monday, November 13th. The following two days were uneventful; Mr Jolly absorbed himself in his business, striving to put from him all thought of the mystery which had intruded itself into his life, and to reassure himself with the knowledge of Josiah's friendship and willingness to protect him so long as he did not meddle in what did not concern him. On each of these two evenings Mr Baillie had visitors; they stayed late, which meant that the chandler had to sit up far beyond his usual bed-time, but being an extremely kind-hearted man, he was less concerned with this than for the fatigue which such prolonged visits must cause his lodger, for the bad weather had made Mr Baillie's cough much worse, and he looked very frail indeed.

The third day, that of Thursday, November 16th, dawned in thick fog. Even up here upon the heights of Hampstead, Mr Jolly could feel and smell the stifling blanket of it when, grunting out of bed as usual at six o'clock, he opened his window to look at the day. Dressing in the dark so as not to wake his wife who, though a hard worker, was never able to rise early in the morning (a weakness, she loved to point out, which must be excused by her genteel upbringing), he went downstairs and into his shop to examine his supply of links. Every man who had business abroad today would be sure to seek one to light him through the fog, and what otherwise would have been a bad day for trade could be turned into a good one if he had sufficiency of links. He was routing among his stores for these articles, when he was surprised to hear from the stair-foot the dry little cough which announced the presence of his lodger; supposing that Mr Baillie was making an early excursion to the privy, he took no notice, until he heard the lodger's voice calling urgently to him:

"Master Jolly! Master Jolly! Are ye there?"

"At your service, sir," replied the chandler, running through into the parlour, where he found Mr Baillie, clad only in shift and nightcap, leaning weakly against the wall at the foot of the stairs. "Do you lack for aught?"

"Nay, I do fine," answered the lodger, his wheezing breath contradicting this statement. "This is a waefu' haar – a fog ye'll ca' it downby – but however ye ca' it, it vexes me sair, for I hae urgent privy business in the City the day and must hae conveyance thither."

"There's not a hackney will be stirring from his stable today, sir," Mr Jolly told him, wondering at the gentleman's urgency and agitation. "If it is thick up here 'twill be smothering in London, and the only passengers you're like to find upon the road will be the tobymen."

"I maun gang into the City the day," reiterated Mr Baillie obstinately; and with that, before Mr Jolly could argue further, he retreated up the stairs again.

The fog grew a little thinner with daylight, and about noon seemed inclined to clear. Busy at his counter, Mr Jolly was called several times into the parlour by Phoebe, who told him that his lodger desired speech with him, and each time this happened it was only for news of the weather. Mr Baillie, Daniel observed, was doing no writing today; whenever the chandler entered his room in response to one of these summonses, he found the old gentleman pacing about, his stick tap-tapping in peevish impatience, his thin whiskers awry as though he had been fidgeting with them. It was plain that something was very much agitating him, and this agitation increased his cough, so that by dinner-time, when Mr Jolly was summoned yet once more, the little man could hardly speak.

"It looks like clearing for a while, sir," Mr Jolly told him, to hearten him, "but I doubt will do so in the City. Would you have me enquire at the Bowling Green if there be any man going into London who would carry a message for you?"

"Nay, nay, I maun gang mysel'," asserted Mr Baillie, between two fits of coughing, "and I canna gang till it be evening."

"Evening!" exclaimed his landlord in dismay. "Your pardon, sir, but you are clean out of your senses if you look to make a journey in your condition and in such weather, in the evening."

"Och away!" snapped Mr Baillie with unaccustomed rudeness. "Ye're havering, sir, and may spare yoursel' breath. I ken fine what I maun do."

Easily hurt, Mr Jolly retired in some dudgeon, and when, at five o'clock that same evening, when Hampstead was once more shrouded in a blanket of thick mist, he was summoned yet again to his lodger's chamber, he was half inclined to send Phoebe to say he was engaged. However, his kindness of heart was too great for this, so patiently he climbed the stairs once more, and this time, on being admitted, was told to shut the door and attend carefully to what was said to him.

"I canna gang, Master Jolly," said the lodger, seated in his elbow-chair by the fire and looking really ill. "The guid Lord hath sent this sickness upon me for His ain wise purposes, nae doot, and I'll no' complain. But there is news I maun hae ere the nicht be spent, and you news canna be got save in London-toon. Ye maun e'en gang yoursel', Master Jolly, and fetch it for me."

"I, sir!" exclaimed the chandler, aghast. "I make a journey into London in this fog and at this hour? You must excuse me, sir, it cannot be done indeed."

"Ye'll gang and ye'll gang instanter, sir!" cried the other, suddenly belligerent, and banging his feeble fist upon the chair-arm. "I'm no' a man to be trifled wi' when I gie a command."

An indignant flush spread over the chandler's face.

"Sir," said he stiffly, "under your favour, I am not your hired lackey, but a freeborn Englishman, the master in my own house, and am not to take orders from those who enjoy its hospitality."

Mr Baillie looked at him, and his manner changed.

"Oblige me, Master Jolly," said he, reverting to his gentle tone, "by bringing me a wee baggie ye'll find in the cupboard. Here is the key. Ye see I'm no' just verra fit to fetch it mysel'."

Somewhat ashamed of his late indignation, Mr Jolly complied with this request, and unlocking the cupboard lifted from it a small canvas bag which gave forth a suggestive jingle. Taking it from him with one of his courteous inclinations of the head, Mr Baillie undid the tape which bound its neck, opened it, and shook into the lap of his bedgown a shower of golden guineas.

"Ye'll mind me saying, sir," said he, his aged fingers playing with the coins, "that I asked naebody to serve me for nought. If ye'll e'en do as I ask, five o' these guineas are yours ere ye set oot, and anither five when ye return, if ye bring me the news I seek."

Mr Jolly stared at the heap of gold in his lodger's lap, and his eyes fairly goggled. Ten guineas! a small fortune for a poor chandler; at one fell swoop he could pay off all his debts. But then the price of this fortune cut short his mounting exultation; the risk, the appalling risk of a journey on foot (for he would never be able to get a conveyance) into London at this hour of the evening, the deserted lanes, the lurking highwaymen and foot-pads, and then the return, perhaps at some late hour – no, not even for ten golden guineas could he brave such perils.

"You are mighty good, Master Baillie," he muttered, "mighty generous indeed, but you must excuse me; you know not the danger; I could not find my way in this fog; besides there is my shop to attend to – "

"Master Jolly," interrupted the other quietly, looking up at his landlord from beneath lowered lids, "ye do ill to thwart me. This is a matter o' life and death; nae less, ma mannie, nae less."

Daniels lips were dry as he echoed fearfully:

"Of – of life and death?"

"Ay, yon's the tune o' it. Noo, will ye gang?"

Half-formed questions struggled on Daniel Jolly's tongue, but he could not give them utterance. A matter of life and death – most ominous phrase! Was Mr Baillie referring to his own concerns, or was he uttering a veiled threat? The strange paper hidden in his chimney, the look the fox-coloured gentleman had given him at the Amsterdam, Josiah's urgent warning about the ruthlessness and zeal of certain friends of Mr Baillie and his own inability to protect Daniel from them if they suspected him of meddling in their affairs, all these recurred to Mr Jolly's mind. Perhaps it was not enough that he had kept to his resolve not to concern himself further with the mystery upon which he had stumbled; perhaps he had meddled too much already, and Mr Baillie and his odd friends were resolved to blackmail him. These hideous apprehensions overcame the terrors of the lonely road and lurking tobymen, and, involuntarily stretching out a shaking hand towards the pile of gold in Mr Baillie's lap, Daniel murmured miserably:

"I'm at your service, sir."

"That's fine," approved Mr Baillie, becoming again the courteous, gentle personage which was his ordinary guise. "Here's your five guineas for a start, and ye'll find their companions waitin' for ye whey ye return. Noo harkee, and gie me your close attention. Ye maun gang to Southampton Hoose in Bloomsbury, which is the residence o'my Lord Russell; ye ken whaur I mean?"

"I think so, sir, I think so," replied Mr Jolly, experiencing a wave of relief. He had feared that he would be sent to some obsure tavern or coffee-house in the City, for he was convinced that this urgent business of Mr Baillie's must be connected with the Carolina project of which Josiah had spoken. Instead, it seemed that he was to go to the house of a nobleman, of a nobleman moreover whom he knew by name and reputation. Since the year 1678, Lord Russell had been heir to the earldom of Somerset; a bitter Exclusionist, and kin by marriage to the digraced Earl of Shaftesbury, the Opposition leader, Russell yet enjoyed a reputation for strict honesty and even piety. He was known to be deeply in sympathy with the religious views of the dissenters, and probably, thought Daniel, it was this which was causing him to lend his support to the Carolina project.

"Ye maun present yoursel' at the main door o' Southampton Hoose," continued Mr Baillie, "and enquire for Mr Essex. Mr Essex; ye mark yon?"

"Ay, sir, I follow you."

"Mr Essex is supping wi' my Lord Russell the nicht. Noo, when Mr Essex comes doon to ye, ye maun say this to him: 'I am sent frae Master Baillie to enquire if a' is in harmony.' Nae mair than that. He'll conduct ye into the hoose, and nae doot ask ye to wait in a chamber by yoursel'. Aiblins ye'll be obliged to wait a lang time, whiles the gentlemen discuss their business. When they hae done, Mr Essex, or one o' his friends, will come to ye and gie ye a message to carry back to me. Ye'll ask nae questions, but thank the gentleman and return here instanter. And, Master Jolly, if ye should chance to recognise this Mr Essex, ye'll keep it to yoursel', for he'll no' thank ye for seeming to ken him."

"Is he, then, some public figure, sir?" enquired the mystified chandler. "For indeed I know no Mr Essex that I can recall."

"That's as maybe," replied the lodger shortly. "Noo, repeat a' I hae told ye, if ye please, and let me see ye hae your lesson perfect."

Mr Jolly repeated his instructions, which were, indeed, very simple, and, receiving the five guineas, was bidden make haste and start upon his errand. He left Mr Baillie coughing feebly in his chair, and still bidding him, by means of gestures, to make no more delay. Summoning up all his courage for the ordeal before him, and laboriously comforting himself with the harmlessness of his mission, Daniel went first to his bedchamber where he locked the five guineas into his strong-box; then, passing through the parlour where his wife was busy ironing, he said nothing to her of what he was about to do, but went straight into his shop where he heard Phoebe attending to some customers. Drawing the girl aside, he informed her that he had to go abroad on business which might occupy him for several hours, adding that she must take pains to calm her stepmother's fears if he were delayed. She gave him an anxious glance and seemed inclined to question him, but he patted her head reassuringly, bade her wait up for him like a good wench, and, muffling himself in an old hooded cloak which hung upon the door, and taking a thick cudgel from the same place, he stepped forth manfully into the fog.

It was fortunate that Mr Jolly knew every step of the way for the greater part of his journey, because the weather was so thick that otherwise he must have lost himself. It was, nevertheless, an uncomfortable and anxious walk; the fog got into his lungs and made him cough, his eyes smarted, and every now and then, as he crossed the lonely Conduit Fields, a looming tree put his heart into his mouth with the thought of foot-pads. He met no one; already, though the shops were not yet closed, London and her surrounding villages had gone indoors, and no man with lawful business would venture forth again on such a night.

The journey was accomplished in safety, and presently, looming through the thick grey blanket, Mr Jolly saw a dim radiance which informed him that he was come to the verge of the town. He was thankful that he would not have to penetrate far into it, for its streets after darkness fell held worse terrors for him even than the lonely fields. Soon he was aware of houses on either side of him, some with the regulation lanterns hung over their doors, others with flaring links in holders; a watchman's dog barked at him, and guided by this and the tinkle of a hand-bell, Daniel approached the man and enquired the way to Southampton House. The watchman was suspicious; he enquired Daniel's name and business, moving his lantern up and down to take a view of him; then, having satisfied himself that here was an honest citizen, though certainly a mad one to be out on such a night, he directed Daniel to Bloomsbury Square.

The fog was a little thinner here, and what with this and the blaze of links, Daniel could see something of the part of London into which he was come. It was of the new London, risen on the ashes of the great Fire, a square of neat, flat-faced brick houses, somewhat Dutch in style, many with small iron balconies, all with well-lit windows, and here and there could be seen link-boys and footmen lounging under the porticoes. All these houses looked alike in their neatness and suggestion of unpretentious wealth, but Southampton House was, as the watchman had told Daniel, impossible to miss. It occupied one whole side of the square, set well back from it, and protected from the common street by high railings of beautiful iron-work, and a courtyard in which were drawn up a hackney and two private coaches, besides a number of sedans. The great house blazed with light as though some feast were being held therein; figures passed and repassed behind the illuminated windows, and as Daniel came slowly through the outer gateway, he heard the sound of fiddles and guitars.

Mr Jolly's fears of lurking tobymen and foot-pads were replaced, as he approached this great mansion, by others, more vague, indeed, but daunting enough. He was entering a world unknown to him, the world of fashion, of vast wealth, of the beaux with their nightly pranks, of haughty footmen; brought up in an era in which each man knew his place and took a pride in keeping to it, Daniel shrank from intruding himself into such a world, especially by way of the front door. He became suddenly aware of his appearance; his cloak was old, patched, countrified; he had forgotten to take off his apron; he had not shaved today; and altogether he was convinced that at the very first sight of him some indignant lackey would throw him into the street. However having come so far he durst not turn back; so he walked timidly over the vast expanse of courtyard towards the double flight of steps which curved up to the main doors of the house. In order to climb them, he was obliged to pass close by one of the private coaches; glancing curiously at it as he did so, he saw, in the light of lanterns and links, a coat-of-arms painted on the doors. His breath caught in his throat, for ignorant countryman though he was, there was no mistaking them; they were the Royal Arms, but they were crossed by two horizontal parallel lines upon the shield, the bend sinister of illegitimacy.

The main doors of the house were wide open, and on the threshold hovered a group of flunkeys in various liveries, all very splendid, talking together in low voices while retaining the watchful air of well-trained servants. As Daniel approached, these fellows broke off their conversation to stare at the uncouth figure looming up out of the fog, its cropped head shining with moisture, as, with an instinctive gesture, Daniel pulled back his old-fashioned hood. Fearful that he would be driven off before he had time to state his business, Daniel approached the nearest lackey and, in a voice made hoarse by fog and nervousness, desired speech with Mr Essex, adding that he had urgent business with him. The man gave him a hard look, then, without a word, jerked his head in the direction of an especially splendid personage who, with a gold chain about his neck and a white wand in his hand, stood a little apart from the group. Supposing this to be Mr Essex himself, Daniel approached him and began to falter out his message for the second time, but the only result was that he was told sharply to wait and the personage would fetch Mr Essex down to him. When he had gone, the lackeys, released from his overawing presence, began to jest among themselves at Daniel's expense.

"Death and hell!" cried one to the rest, "here's a country booby mistook my lord's steward for my lord."

"Nay, let him be," said another contemptuously. "There's no making a whistle out of a pig's tail. Phew! His breath's like the fume from an alm's-tub. I warrant you he's the keeper of a lay-stall or some carter of night-soil."

"He's like to lose his ears for enquiring for my lord as 'Mr' Essex," chimed in a third. "Is he so ignorant that – "

"Hold your tongue, or you will lose that," snapped the one who had spoken first. "Here comes my Lord Essex himself."

And there, walking briskly across the great hall within, with its tessellated wood-work in the new Paris mode, came a tall, thin, middle-aged gentleman, dressed in a coat which had the fashionably emphasised waist and full skirts, with shortened waistcoat, tight breeches, and fine silk stockings rolled up over the knee. He stepped up to Daniel, and, without a word, put a hand upon his sleeve and guided him through the hall. Mr Jolly, stepping on tiptoe as though he were in church, glanced from the Venetian mirrors on the wall, the crystal candle-scounces, and the inlaid furniture, to the silent gentleman by his side, this gentleman who, it seemed, was not Mr Essex at all, but my Lord Essex. Daniel knew him, as he knew Lord Russell, by name and reputation. Son of a Royalist martyr who had lost his head for Charles the First, made an earl at the Restoration, but gradually becoming infected with Opposition principles, Essex was by this time a strong opponent of the Court. He seemed a ponderous person, and looked ill; his face within the heavy folds of his peruke was lined and sad, and he had the largest and most melancholy eyes Daniel had ever seen. It was whispered in the taverns, Mr Jolly remembered, that my Lord Essex was not entirely normal in his mind, and now that he was having this personal view of him, Daniel reflected that for once such gossip might have truth in it.

Halting abruptly when they were out of ear-shot of the servants, Essex said in a low voice to his companion:

"You bring some message, sirrah?"

"From Mr Baillie, my lord – sir," stammered the chandler, so flustered he scarce knew what he said. "He is mighty sick and could not come himself. He pleases to lodge at my house in Hampstead, and bade me seek you out."

"And is that all?" enquired the other sharply.

Daniel stared at him, discomfited by his tone; then, hastily recollecting himself, he faltered:

"All except to – to – that is, I was bidden enquire if all is in harmony."

As soon as he said that, Essex gave a quick little nod as though satisfied, and going forward without another word, beckoned Daniel into a little room which opened off the hall.

"You must wait here," said he, not unkindly. "Your vigil may be long, but rest assured you will not be forgotten. I will direct a servant to bring you some refreshment, for you have had a tedious journey, friend."

With that, he hurried out again and closed the door; Daniel was a little dismayed to hear him lock it on the outside. He was timidly examining the apartment, when the key turned in the lock again, and as he started guiltily a lackey in splendid livery entered, bearing a tray on which stood a tankard of ale, a pewter mug, and some bread and cold meat. These he set down on a little table, and bade Daniel fall-to. The lackey had a genial if condescending manner; he was inclined to linger and gossip, being a young man and probably new to service. While Daniel ate and drank, the lackey boasted largely of the wealth and grandeur of his employers; this, he said, was really Lady Russell's house, she being the daughter of the Earl of Southampton and a great heiress; she entertained in style every night, the least of her guests being some rich merchant, and never sat down to less than fifty covers.

"Her worst servants eat in plate," said he, "and her maids all have silver chamber-pots."

Such fabulous tales were pleasing to the simple Daniel; but when he began to ask about Lord Russell, his informant became less enthusiastic, muttered that he was a good master but so gloomy a Puritan that he could not enjoy himself as a gentleman should, and then, before Daniel could question him further, took himself off and locked the door again.

Two hours passed by, as Daniel could tell from the chiming of innumerable clocks in different parts of the great house.

He felt lonely and anxious and ill-at-ease; unfamiliar sounds drifted in to him in his elegant imprisonment, women's high laughter, men's affected voices, music and singing, the clinking of silver dishes, and the rich rustle of satin petticoats. He sat on the very edge of the most uncomfortable chair he could find, swallowing hard at intervals, and trying not to think of his homeward journey, his neglected shop, and what he should say to Elizabeth to explain his long absence. And then, suddenly, his nerves jumped and jangled, as from somewhere in the house came the sounds of a noisily opened door, a man's tipsy laugh, a confusion of voices, and footsteps, which seemed unsteady, approaching nearer and nearer the very room in which he sat. What should he say, how explain his presence here, if guests from my lady's party came in and discovered him? My Lord Essex had disappeared and left him friendless; he dared not mention Mr Baillie to anyone else. Suppose they threw him out before he had received the promised message; worse still, suppose they suspected him of being a house-breaker and sent for the constables and had him flung into jail?

Even as these terrors chased each other across Daniel's simple mind, there was a quick footstep outside, the sound as though someone had set his back hard against the door, and a voice he recognised as belonging to my Lord Essex said sharply:

"Your Grace, I implore you, lay by this folly. The fellow is unknown to us, and your tongue is loosened with wine – "

"D'you dare say I'm drunk, you old Puritan?" interrupted another voice, the same which had given that tipsy laugh just now. "Nay, your martyred father was a better man with a bottle than you, whatever his politics. Ha! You shrink from talk of him, d'you not, Arthur? 'Whatever becomes of me,' " went on the drunken voice, imitating some grave and solemn old gentleman, " 'never let my son be a traitor to his King.' Alack, poor old lord; I'll warrant the axe seemed sweet to him with your false promises ringing in his ears – "

"Russell, you have more influence with him than I," interrupted Essex in great agitation. "Pray get him home ere he hangs us all. Here, Jepson! the Duke of Monmouth's coach instanter. Nay, your Grace, you must – "

"Don't you be giving me orders, Arthur Capel, son of loyal Lord Capel, Royalist martyr," broke in the other voice in drunken fury. "A fine subject of mine you'll prove when what is to be done is done. I know my true friends and will reward 'em when the time comes, ay, and will know how to deal with those who took up my cause but out of spite at not being made Lord Lieutenant of Ireland again in '77 – "

The harsh grating of the key in the lock interrupted this furious outburst, and Daniel, who had been standing petrified on the other side of the door, leapt back with a kind of squeal as it was flung open and a young gentleman, with his fine clothes and wig in disorder, his face flushed with wine, and his handsome mouth still twisted in a sneer, was half pushed, half pulled into the room.

"Mr Howard," panted Essex in great agitation, to one of the gentlemen who had entered with him, "see that the servants come not hither. Russell, prithee shut the door behind Howard. Such talk in the open hall! – "

He seemed to have forgotten the presence of Daniel as, in extremity of agitation, he issued these orders, the while he endeavoured to coax the drunken young man to a chair before the hearth. Daniel, for his part, had no eyes for any of the newcomers except this same drunken young man. Here, his awe-stricken mind informed him, was the owner of the coach with the Royal Arms and the bend sinister painted upon it, the "your Grace" of Essex's protestations, the outstanding figure in many a public spectacle, dining in state with the Lord Mayor, riding beside the Opposition leader through hysterical mobs, setting forth on semi-royal progresses, James, Duke of Monmouth, the King's eldest and most beloved bastard, the storm-centre of a stormy reign, set up as a rival for the throne of England by the faction which hated the Duke of York.

Whatever Mr Jolly's private opinions of Monmouth had been when he had read of him in the news-sheets or seen him from afar in public, now that he was at close-quarters with him, he experienced only a shocked disgust. The extravagance of dress proclaimed the beau – the pure white damask coat and waistcoat, embroidered all over with true-lovers-knots, the foolish little muff slung on one arm, the scented peruke, the paint and the patches on the handsome face; and that handsomeness, seen thus, was clearly only a veneer; drink had rubbed off the charm and showed all too clearly the weakness behind it, the weakness and the spite and the fathomless vanity. Rabidly conservative, Mr Jolly held that a man in whatever walk of life should conduct himself according to his station; here was only a bully of the town, the son of a guttersnipe mother, screaming abuse like any fishwife of Billingsgate.

Forgetting the necessity of receiving a message for Mr Baillie, Daniel was endeavouring to make an unobtrusive exit from the apartment, when Monmouth, sprawled in his chair, caught sight of him, and waving a heavily beringed hand in his direction, cried to his companions:

"Lord, we had almost forgot our good country bumpkin yonder, him I came hither on purpose to view. Where is my spice-ball, Russell? I protest, he stinks like a Tom-turd man, yet I'll warrant is a true Protestant at bottom, and so shall join us in a toast. My good Essex, where's the wine? Let's whet; here's to the man who first draws his sword against Popery and Slavery! Come, my fine countryman, stand not there as stiff as a figure in a raree-show, but drink with your future King."

Before Daniel, aghast and bewildered, could make any reply, Essex had him by the shoulder and was propelling him out of the room so fast that Daniel was near falling on his nose. As my lord slammed shut the door behind them, Daniel could hear the Duke's drunken laugh, Russell's voice raised in protest and exhortation, and the others joining in a confused babel of talk. Essex, his face white and working, drove the chandler before him across the great hall, where groups of servants broke off their whispered conversations to stand stiffly to attention at the sight of one of their master's guests. Without a word, Essex guided the chandler into a chamber where there was a writing table, and, curtly bidding him wait, sat down thereat and agitatedly and rapidly began to write. After a few minutes he rose again, sanded the paper, sealed it with a wafer, and handing it to Daniel bade him put it safely in his breasts.

"Get you back poste-haste to Hampstead," he ordered, "and deliver this paper to Mr Baillie with all speed. As you value your life, guard it well upon your journey, and at whatever hour you reach your home, you must be sure to give it instanter into the hands of your lodger. Do you understand me? Instanter."

Daniel, past speech, merely nodded, tucked the paper away in his breast with trembling fingers, and obeyed Essex's curt gesture of dismissal by fairly running from the room. Across the hall he scurried, out through the main doorway and over the courtyard; only when he had left Bloomsbury Square behind him, and the fog, thicker than ever with the coming of night, had engulfed him, did he lessen his pace and permit himself to wipe the sweat from his brow and rest a moment ere starting on his long walk back to Hampstead.

Chapter Six

It was not until Daniel Jolly had come as far as the Conduit Fields that he had leisure once again to attend to those fears which had beset his outward journey, those terrors connected with being out at night on a lonely road. For until then his simple mind had been striving to digest the astonishing things he had heard and seen at Southampton House.

He had been indeed in the company of the great and mighty; he had seen at close quarters the personages of whom he had read in the news-sheets or had viewed from afar in public processions. In any other circumstances, how happy and proud would this have made him, how he would have chattered of it to his neighbours, how have diverted his family with a minute description of the dress and manner and speech of public men. But he was neither happy nor proud; he was disgusted by the Duke of Monmouth's behaviour, vaguely terrified by what that painted mouth had said. And, above all, he was hurt as he had never been hurt in his life before, because Josiah Keeling had betrayed his friendship.

For Monmouth's blabbings, though still half unintelligible to Daniel, had convinced him that there was more in this business than the founding of a Scots colony in Carolina. Essex and Russell might put themselves about to succour a part of rebel Scotsmen and establish them overseas; Monmouth certainly would not put himself about for any man, and apart from this, he had talked openly and confidently of getting the throne "when what is to be done is done"; he had given Daniel a toast to drink "to the man who first draws his sword against Popery and Slavery"; he had invited the chandler to drink with "his future King." Oh, it was no secret that Monmouth nourished an ambition of succeeding his father, an ambition fostered by every malcontent throughout the reign; this very autumn, on a semi-royal progress through the north of England, he had been brought back under arrest for going about the country in a riotous and unlawful manner, and the previous year, having taken the bend sinister out of this coat-of-arms, he had become such a storm-centre that an Order in Council had forbidden persons of quality to correspond with him. All this, and more besides, Daniel had read in his news-sheets or heard over his can of ale at the Black Boy and Still; but he had believed that, released on bail, Monmouth was living quietly at his house in Hertfordshire and had laid-by a folly which had no chance of success.

Yet it seemed that it was not so; and again and again did Daniel's memory wince at those words "To the man who first draws his sword." All the fears which had been so greatly allayed by his talk with Josiah Keeling at the coffee-house returned upon him, a thousand times augmented, and sharpened by Josiah's deceiving of himself. There might be a project for establishing a colony in Carolina; but there was another project also, of which this might well be the cover; there was a plot hatching, insurrection, and bloody revolution; and he, loyal and simple Daniel Jolly, risked being implicated in it against his will. Yes, there was a link, however fantastic it appeared, beween these great lords, the rakish, whoring, insolent Monmouth, the grave and honest Russell, the wise and sober Essex, and such disreputable personages as Bob Ferguson the Plotter and even an illiterate ballad-monger in the street. All used that same password: "Is all in harmony?"

The sinister conversation Daniel had overheard in his lodger's chamber, the cant talk at the Amsterdam, and the curious "letter of condolence" obtain from the ballad-monger, all these Daniel now saw in a new light, the ominous light of treason and plot. It was no longer any use trying to comfort himself with the conviction that men like Josiah Keeling would not lend their support to anything improper; Josiah Keeling, his friend remembered too late, was two persons, the sober, substantial merchant, and the fanatic who 'arrested' the Lord Mayor of London; was it not possible, then, that lords like Essex and Russell were dual personalities, and through discontentment, ambition, or fanaticism could be induced to play the game of '41 again? And if in truth there was treason hatching, he, Daniel Jolly, had got himself entangled in it. He sheltered in his house this mysterious old Scotsman who was hand-in-glove with Ferguson and his group, and who was deep in the confidence of Essex and his friends. He had carried a message asking for news, almost certainly treasonable news, from Mr Baillie to my Lord Essex; in his breast at this very moment there reposed an answer which, if found upon his person, might put his innocent neck in the noose and his family upon the parish.

And it was when he reflected upon this (his face fear-white, his legs trembling so much he could scarcely walk), they more normal fears began to mingle with these horrors, and he became aware that he was walking solitary through the foggy night in one of the most lonely spots round London. My Lord Essex had been mad, criminally mad, to have sent him unprotected into the perils of this journey and at the same time to bid him guard the letter with his life. My Lord Essex, of course, in his exalted station, could not have known what it meant to go solitary on foot over the Conduit Fields after darkness had fallen. And such darkness! Never in all his life had Daniel seen a night more favourable to robbers.

And so he became aware, horridly aware, of his surroundings. As he climbed the steep fields, the fog became patchy, drifting, here thick as a shroud, there parting slightly to show him an object looming up, a solitary tree, a recumbent cow, unrecognisable now, taking on sinister and unfamiliar shapes; and in this blanketed world, in which even his own footsteps sounded muffled, his straining ears caught now and again some unidentifiable noise, which might have been the fall of leaves or a stealthy footstep behind him, the grunt of a beast or the signal of a robber to his companion that a solitary traveller approached. A little eerie wind was risen, moaning to itself; and to the terror of tobymen and foot-pads was added the fear of ghosts. Halfway across the fields was a spinney of great old oaks; distrusting them because of the shelter they would afford to any lurking robbers, Daniel had intended to avoid them, but not being able to plot a proper course because of the fog, he found himself, all unawares, in their midst. They loomed up suddenly, giant ghosts, their damp leaves feeling like clammy fingers as they touched him. Amid the patter made by the drops of moisture which fell from their branches, he heard his own teeth chattering like castanets, horribly loud in this silent world. Muttering a prayer, which was choked by sobs of terror, he began to run, stumblingly, his long cloak tripping him, the breath rasping in his throat.

And then his bowels moved as, clumsily seeking to avoid a tree which had loomed up directly in his path, he heard from behind it a rough voice utter the dreaded challenge:

"Stand and deliver!"

He stood; indeed, he was incapable of moving another step, however great his desire to run for it. The blood froze in his veins, and a great trembling shook his limbs. Like a man in nightmare he stared as from round the tree came a figure on horseback, and, as the fog dispersed itself a little, he saw a face masked by a vizard beneath a big slouched hat, and a gauntleted hand which was levelling at him a long horse-pistol.

"Put up your pickers and stealers and stow you!"[*] continued the voice, which Daniel now recognised as that of Captain Cruckshank, the most notorious tobyman of these parts. "You are come into the company of a high-lawier, and if you are so clay-brained as to squeal, my buzzard, I'll let off my popp at your nab. Stand, and prepare to be boarded! I know there's but one of you, and if you're geck enough to scamper, I'll call up my oakes."

Mr Jolly, good man, would have deemed it beneath him to have acknowledged an acquaintanceship with this thieves' language called cant, yet he had no difficulty in translating Captain Cruckshank's orders, since they were accompanied by a flourishing of his horse-pistol, which he called a popp, in the direction of Daniel's "nab" or head. Scarce able to speak for terror, Mr Jolly managed to stutter wretchedly:

"Sir, I protest, I am a p-poor man, and have no b-booty on me worth your taking."

"Stow you!" commanded the highwayman unkindly. "I'll frisk you and discover for myself, if you please. Many a geck has thought to coney-catch me with that tale, yet has proved rhinocerical enough." He dismounted, and, with his rein over his arm, roughly seized upon Daniel, and, with his rein over his arm, roughly seized upon

---

[1]An explanation of this thieves' slang is to be found at the end of the book.

Daniel, and with expert fingers began to go through his clothes in search of valuables. "What's here?" he muttered as he worked, "the duds of a swad upon whom the generous way of padding is quite wasted. This mads me; what, not a meg, not a smelt, no scout or famble, not so much as a sice! I've a mind to pluck out porker and lay you on thick to have me so caravaned. Here is no martin, but a cully for hookers and anglers, rot him! Stay! What's here? A money-bill, by God! Now I say by the Solomon, if you thought to caravan me thus, you'll make me have hay in my horn, and may fall to your prayers."

"You mistake, sir, you mistake," cried the anguished Daniel, as the highwayman's exploratory fingers, having come upon the letter in his victim's breast, plucked it forth. "This is no money-bill but a letter, a most important letter, which I was bidden carry from one – one honest gentleman to another. 'Twill cost me my life if I miscarry with it; have pity, sir, have mercy, I am a married man, my wife – "

"The devil take this dark!" interrupted the highwayman, as he sought unsuccessfully to examine the paper in his hands. "Pearly!" he cried, to some unseen accomplice, "bring a glim here and let's see if this swad thinks to play crimp."

From out of the fog loomed a second figure, masked like the first, and carrying in its hand a darkened lantern, the rays from which struggled feebly with the surrounding gloom. Cruckshank seized it, impatiently snatched off the black rag which had shrouded it, and holding it close over the paper, earnestly examined his booty. He had not done so for more than a minute or two before he gave vent to a muttered oath, and ordering his accomplice to stand back, God damn him, became quite absorbed in what he read. At last, raising his head, the highwayman astounded Daniel by addressing him with a complete change of tone and manner.

"Friend," said he, in a low voice, "your pardon, but you should have given me the password. I know you not, but from your being the bearer of this letter, I perceive you to be of the Friends in Harmony. Come, tell me your name, fair and honest, and likewise that of the gentleman to whom you carry this."

"My name, so please you, is Daniel Jolly," replied the trembling chandler, frenzied relief struggling with a new bewilderment. "And I am bid carry this letter to a Scottish gentleman who lodges at my house, by name Mr Baillie. But I protest, sir, I know nothing of – "

"Baillie," interrupted the other gruffly. "Ay, I know him well". He seized Daniel's arm, and thrusting his masked face close to that of the chandler, gabbled excitedly: "But tell me, friend, what of the Lopping Point? Here in this letter is brave news enough of the General Point, but not one word of the other. God damn them, they are mad if they think to rise without it. Buy yesterday I was with Hannibal and his boys at the Rye, and they looked for news."

"Sir," pleaded poor Daniel, "I do protest I know nothing of what you say. I was bidden carry the letter and deliver it instanter, but I know not what it contains, nothing of these Lopping Points and General Points of which you speak, upon my salvation I do not."

There was silence awhile, as the highwayman, swinging the lantern backwards and forwards across Mr Jolly's face, seemed striving to make out his expression. Then a huge hand fell upon the chandler's shoulder, making him yelp with fear, and with a rough laugh the tobyman observed:

"Snck up, you, you're close! But it is a good fault in one of our company, and rare, for there's more clack-dishing among us than can be heard from behind a red-lattice on a

Saturday night. Go your ways, friend, and deliver your letter; but may I come to the Three Legged Mare before my time if I understand what they would be at. Harkee now, perchance I should conduct you to your house, lest some whoreson cur of a nip draws you, and you lose the letter in a silly cheat."

"I shall do well, sir, I assure you," cried Mr Jolly hastily, thinking with horror of entering his native village under the protection of a notorious highwayman. "Pray excuse me now, I must hasten – but stay," he added, as an uneasy thought struck him, "you have broke open this letter, and how am I to explain that to Master Baillie?"

"Why, you must tell him the truth, brother," answered the highwayman lightly, "and make my humble apologies for the mistake. I know him and he knows me, and I assure you he is no bum-bailly to send me to the Whitt for a trifle of high-law, when else I must clem. Away with you now; and if any nip and his stale have the impertinence to board you, tell 'em you have Captain Cruckshank's protection, and they'll scour as quick as a bolter of the Friars when he spies the bluebottle and his nut-hooks."

Daniel needed no second bidding. As fast as his shaking legs could carry him, he was soon racing on over the fields again, once or twice looking fearfully over his shoulder to make sure that the highwayman had not determined to force upon him his sinister protection after all. Thus, without further mishap, did Daniel come to the High Street of his village, as he felt rather than saw, for the street was as solitary as the grave, and as dark. As the hurried up it, he heard the clock on the parish church boom out the hour of midnight, muffled and solemn as a passing-bell; and with this reminder of the lateness of the hour, the whole bevy of his fears attacked him in such force that he felt he must swoon. Feeling his way along the shop-fronts of Heath Street, he paused under a sign which creaked faintly in the wind; a sudden resolution came upon him, and raising his fist he hammered on the door beneath the sign, careless of this affront to his sleeping village, frenzied for human companionship, for a cordial, and for the face of a friend. Presently a window was opened above, and a man's voice asked crossly what was to do.

"Noll," gasped out the stricken chandler, "for the love of God come down and let me in. I must have a quarton of brandy or I perish."

The voice above exclaimed in surprise; then the window was shut again, and presently footsteps sounded in the downstairs passage, the door was unbolted, and a big man stood there in his shift, with a rushlight in his hand. He said nothing, but putting out a strong hand drew Daniel within. Then he refastened the door, led the way into the kitchen, set the rushlight down upon the table, and surveyed his friend with the utmost curiosity. Daniel for his part, comforted by the presence of this good friend of his, Noll Smart, the landlord of the Black Boy and Still, staggered to a chair by the dying fire, flopped into it, and hid his face in his hands.

"Pox on't," cried Noll, surveying him, "what do you abroad at such an hour and on such a pesty night? By your looks, you have seen a ghost, and small wonder, if you will stray at an unchristian hour when you should be in your bed. Come, drink this, and let it cheer you."

His teeth chattering upon it, Daniel gulped from the glass of brandy which his friend extended to him, and as the spirit burnt his throat and flowed warmly down his gullet, he began a little to recover himself. But as the height of his panic subsided, a desperate resolve took its place; he knew too much, and yet it was not enough; he must convince himself that all the horrible doings of this night were not part of some evil dream; only so could he know how to act in future. As he related to the sympathetic Noll how he had been sent into London by his lodger with an urgent message, had strayed in the fog, and had been waylaid by highwaymen in the Conduit Fields, the urge to read this mysterious letter grew and grew. It might be, it probably was, in cipher and he would be able to make no sense of it; but just in case it was writ plain, he must examine it and know the worst. So presently, persuading the kind Mr Smart to go and draw him another measure of brandy and warm it a little that it might prevent him from catching an ague, he immediately, as soon as the other had left the kitchen, drew out the crumpled letter from his breast, smoothed it out, and began to spell his way through it as fast as he could. It ran thus:

"Sir,
  Prithee burn this as soon as read, for I have no time to write in ciphers.
  'Tis agreed that the General Point be set in action upon the 19th instant, a Sunday being chosen because, the streets being then more full of folk than ordinary, our men may muster unperceived. The rendezvous are various, that which concerns your party being at Bedford House. These have the ordering of the Tower, one body coming thither in coaches on pretence of visiting prisoners, another as sightseers going to view the Armoury and the lions. A quarrel being feigned at the gate is to be the signal for all parties to join and fall on the guards. I would have you note that Dartmouth must be dispatched immediately, for otherwise, if he cannot find another way of resisting, doubtless he will blow up the powder magazine.
  The chief posts in London being captured, other of our forces will take the Guards in the rear, and yet others, crossing in lighters to Westminster, will assault

Whitehall. Immediately upon our first successes, a proclamation is to be read, proclaiming M as King, and Mr Robert's declaration of grievances to be read likewise. Meantime the mobile will be diverted with tales of another Popish Plot. My lord asserts that if we can hold London, the country is ours. I have no time to write more, only to urge you to notify your party with all dispatch, the time being exceeding short.
    Your friend in harmony,
      E"

 Scarce had Mr Jolly come to the end of this letter, than his friend returned with the brandy; seeing the pallor and renewed anguish on the chandler's face, Noll Smart urged him to drink quickly, while he roused the Watch and had search made for his friend's assailants. But Daniel, gulping down the second measure of spirit, waved this away; he must get home, he said, and that without further loss of time, or his wife would be fit for Bedlam with anxiety. Rising, and squaring his shoulders, he bade Noll a somewhat curt good night and strode out of the tavern looking very fierce.

 For since the reading of the letter, his terrors had given place to an honest anger. He was the small man roused. He breathed hard and harsh as he climbed the hill towards his house, but it was less from exhaustion than from a seething indignation. That he, Daniel Jolly, a respectable, law-abiding shopkeeper, a loyal subject of King Charles, should be so tricked! That he should be forced to run errands for a parcel of low conspirators, however nobly born some of them might be – it was not to be endured for an instant. Rage combined with the effects of two large measures of brandy on an empty stomach, eclipsed for the time all thought of his personal danger; dishevelled as he was, there was a simple dignity about his stout little figure as, careless now of rousing his family and neighbours, he thundered with his fists upon his own door. Only a second or two elapsed before his wife's voice, shrill with apprehension, demanded to know who it was.

"It is I," roared Daniel. "Open the door this instant, wife and let me in."

The sound of bolts being withdrawn was followed by the door being opened a few inches; Daniel pushed it wide, and strode into his shop. There he paused, for Elizabeth's figure, fully dressed, confronted him, one hand holding a vial of hartshorn, prominently displayed, known of old by Daniel as a danger-signal. In the background, also fully clothed, hovered his daughter, bearing a candle.

" 'Ounds!" screamed Mrs Jolly, clutching at the counter for support, "you have come home, you rogue you, when I made sure I was a hempen widow. What a monster is this to put his poor wife into such extremity of anguish. Have you no heart, no bowels, sir, that you would go gadding all night and leave a frail woman, who was brought up genteel, to torment herself near into her grave with fears for your safety. Phoebe will tell you that had I not prevented her she would have fetched in the surgeon to bleed me, I have swooned so oft these last few hours."

"You would do better," said Daniel shortly, "to be thanking God upon your knees that by His special mercy I have come home safe, than be making such a touse. Go to bed, wife, and I will come presently. I have business with my lodger first."

"Now God forgive you, I believe you have been baiting the bombard," panted Mrs Jolly, sniffing hard as her husband passed by her. "Your breath stinks like a tavern. Lord! that my father's daughter should be wed to such a monster that comes home boozed at midnight – ay, and would speak with gentlemen in such a state. I vow I think you have beshit yourself, husband, there is such a close-stool stink hangs about you. Phoebe, sweet wench, assist me to a chair; I much fear I shall swoon again. As for you, sir, positively I must tell you that I will not have this affront put upon Master Baillie, nor have him see you – "

She spoke to empty air, for Daniel, without another word, had stalked through the parlour and up the stair. Awaiting him in the doorway of his chamber, dressed in bedgown and night-cap, he found his ancient lodger.

"Come awa' in," commanded Mr Baillie, on sight of the chandler. "Whaur the deil hae ye been, man? I sent ye into the toon when it lacked seven o' the clock, and noo 'tis after midnicht. Whaur's yon letter?"

This insult added to injury merely fanned the flame of Daniel's rage. He strode to the table, and swinging round upon his lodger, wagged at him a shaking finger.

"You may well ask where I've been, sir," cried he, "you may well ask that, and I will tell you. I have been this night upon the nastiest business ever an honest man was bubbled into undertaking, and I trust the Lord will forgive you for it, for I shall not. I am poor and humble, sir, yet I would have you know that I value my reputation as an honest, peaceable subject of my Sovereign Lord, the King, and am not, sir, to be made the tool of plotters, be they great lords or Scottish gentlemen or ruffianly highwaymen, and so I tell you fair and square."

Mr Baillie regarded him with his head on one side.

"Losh, I'm thinking ye're a wee bitie foxed, Master Jolly," said he mildly. "Ay, aiblins they gave ye a glass o' strong liquor at Southampton Hoose, and it's undone ye; ye hae the smell o' it on your breath yet. I'm taking the charitable view, ye mind; I'll no' believe that in our sober senses ye'd be so dolted as to rave at me in sic a fashion, and haver aboot plotters. Yon's an ill word to use, Master Jolly, an ill word indeed."

The Scotsman's manner, much more than his words, damped the first heat of Daniel's indignation. That manner was calm and gentle, mild and courteous, yet Mr Jolly was sure he did not only imagine that it veiled a threat. Some of his former fears returned to him, and he felt his sustaining anger drain away. He said nothing as, with trembling fingers, he unbuttoned his coat and drew from beneath it the crumpled letter. Then, as he handed it to Mr Baillie, he mumbled sulkily:

"The seal is broke, but not by me. I was stopped by Cruckshank the highwayman in the Fields, who would have taken it from me, but having made so bold as to read it, he returned it to me. He bade me offer you his apologies, and seems to think you would not take it amiss," added Daniel significantly.

"Is that a fact?" remarked the lodger, not at all put out. "The guid Lord, Master Jolly, makes use o'unlikely instruments for His ain wise purposes, and is still the friend o'publicans and sinners. Did Captain Cruckshank tell ye what was in this letter?"

Daniel hesitated. Exhaustion was coming down on him again, and this, combined with that hint of a threat beneath his lodger's mildness, and the desertion of him by his own honest rage, made him confused and uncertain how to act. It was on the tip of his tongue to tell his lodger that he knew nothing about the contents of the letter, when that old perversity of his caused him to answer gruffly instead:

"He told me enough to assure me that the letter contains somewhat that I like not at all. You may choose to consort with tobymen, sir, and name them the Lord's instruments. I for my part am a plain man and name them rogues, howsoever they may enjoy the confidence of gentlemen. And I must tell you, sir," continued Daniel, suddenly heartened by his own boldness, "that things having come to this pass, I can no long longer afford you the hospitality of my house, and would be obliged if you would quit it in the morning."

"We'll speak o' it the morn," answered Mr Bailllie abstractedly; he was now altogether engrossed in reading Essex's letter. "Awa' wi' ye noo, ma guid mannie, and leave argy-bargying. Stay, here's the rest o' your fee for the errand; tak' it and gang awa' to your bed."

Again did Daniel Jolly hesitate. On the one hand, he had earned that other five guineas; indeed, it was the hardest money ever he had earned in his life. But on the other hand, if he accepted it, he would be receiving payment from traitors and conspirators and so in some measure would be partaking in their iniquity. He scratched his head, shuffled his feet, and wrestled with his conscience. In the end, the amount of the money overcame his scruples; he was a poor man, he was still in debt, the money was rightfully his, he was determined that whatever else he did about this business he would get rid of Mr Baillie in the morning, and it was only just that this wolf in sheep's clothing should pay the price of having bubbled a poor and honest man. So he took the gold, and without another word stalked out of the room towards his own chamber, where he found to his infinite relief that his wife, already in bed, had decided to postpone the remainder of her lecture until sleep had given her strength.

Daniel himself slept fitfully, and when he did was troubled by nightmares. Self-pity, indignation, fear, and uncertainty as to what he ought to do with the information he had obtained from the letter, these robbed him of his rest. He longed to unburden himself to some wise and sympathetic friend, but could not think of any man fit to be consulted. Josiah Keeling was no longer a friend of his; this mysterious "General Point" which he and his friends had been discussing at the Amsterdam had nothing to do with the founding of a colony in Carolina, but was the cant name for some sort of armed rising; so much was clear from the letter. Noll Smart, Daniel's particular crony, though honest as the day, was not altogether free from the weakness of gossiping, and in any case was incapable of offering advice on so delicate and extraordinary a problem. As for going to the authorities with his tale, Daniel shied away from the thought. The history of the last few years pointed the moral that when there was talk of plots abroad, wise men took care to remain ignorant of them, lest, however innocent, they found themselves regarded with suspicion.

Thus did poor Mr Jolly argue away the night, and when morning dawned had come to no decision on his main problem. His resolution to get rid of his lodger was, however, more fixed than ever, and as soon as he had risen and dressed, he went straight to Mr Baillie's room and rapped upon the door. A courteous voice bade him enter, and going in he found his lodger sitting up in bed, looking so feeble and ancient in the dim light that almost the chandler's heart smote him for what he had to say.

"Sir," said he abruptly, "the fog is cleared, and you may travel abroad without inconvenience. Therefore, under your favour, I will order a hackney for you and your goods, if you will please to let me know at what hour you will be ready to leave my house."

"You're unco' anxious to be rid o' me," replied Mr Baillie, with a rueful smile, "but nae doot ye ken your ain business best. If ye'll bring me ma morning draught and a manchet o' bread to break ma fast, I'll pack and gang wi'oot loss o' time, for Robert Baillie o' Jerviswood ne'er was a body to stay whaur he wasna wanted."

This unexpectedly compliant attitude made the gentle Daniel, in the first flush of relief, feel unreasonably ashamed of himself, and he was beginning to mumble out some excuses for his harsh conduct, when Mr Baillie cut him short.

"Say nae mair, Master Jolly, say nae mair. You and I will part friends and nae ill feelings. Ye'll oblige me, I'm sure, wi' one last favour. Will ye carry this letter to Chairlie Weems at the Bowling Green? He's a guid wee mannie, and will let ma friends ken whaur I've gaed wi'oot putting ye to the trouble o' it. Ye may order a hackney at the same time."

Mr Jolly readily complied with so reasonable a request, and having told Phoebe to take Mr Baillie his morning draught of small-beer, he hastened up to the Bowling Green without staying for his own breakfast. A yawning serving-man at the inn informed him that the landlord was in his cellar, checking his stock, and thither did Mr Jolly betake himself without loss of time. The little hunchback seemed surprised to see him at this early hour, but look Mr Baillie's letter without comment, read it through carefully, nodded to himself, and said:

"I shall not trouble the gentleman with a written reply, Master Jolly, not with a written reply. Be so good as to tell him that I will carry out his wishes; be so good as to tell him that. And for the matter of the hackney, I will attend to it; I promise you I will attend to it myself."

Much relieved in his mind, Daniel returned to his shop, where he found Ned just starting to take down the shutters. Realising suddenly that he was very hungry, having eaten nothing since the cold meat and bread he had been given at Southampton House last evening, Daniel was about to go into the parlour in search of breakfast, when a sudden shrill outbreak of female voices from the stairs took away his appetite. Muttering to himself that a man had no peace nowadays, he waited at the parlour door to discover what this new uproar portended, nor had he long to wait. In another moment, Mrs Jolly, half dressed, with a shawl clutched round her bosom and her hair done up in rags, debouched upon him from the stair-foot.

"Take shame to yourself, Daniel Jolly," she screamed, "for I swear I think you have slain him with your cruelty. 'Tis true you know not how to conduct yourself towards gentlemen, which is no fault of yours, being a laborious man, but it seems you have no heart in your bosom, that you would order a fellow Christian, be he gentleman or mechanic, out of your house so rudely when he is at death's door."

"What touse is this?" asked the chandler wearily. "Master Baillie leaves us willingly, wife, and I beg you will not concern yourself in matters which are not a woman's business. I had my reasons for what I have done, and I – "

He was interrupted by the entrance of Phoebe, who looked unusually grave.

"Methinks he has suffered some fit," she told her father, jerking her head in the direction of the lodger's room, "and is in no state to travel, yet swears he will."

"If he goes, it will be over my corpse," announced Mrs Jolly dramatically. "Ne'er stir, I will not have it said that I have neither bowels nor manners, howsoever they appear to be lacking in the wretch on whom I bestowed my hand."

Mr Jolly, now in so irritable a frame of mind that he longed to bestow his hand hard on Elizabeth's bottom, pushed past that lady, who seemed about to indulge in another swoon, and once more mounted the stair to his lodger's chamber. Mr Baillie was sitting slumped in his elbow-chair, with his valises ready strapped up beside him, and his little strong-box clutched in his lap. He was fully dressed, and had his hat upon his head; beneath it his wizened face looked ghastly in the morning light, and his frail old hands, blue-veined and delicate, trembled violently as they lay clasped upon the box. He turned his head feebly at his landlord's entrance and attempted a smile.

"What's this, sir? You are mighty sick," said Daniel anxiously, his kind heart upbraiding him for his decision to get rid of so infirm a lodger.

"A wee bitie, a wee bitie," gasped out the Scotsman. "Yet I'll no' be pitting ye to ony trouble on ma account. Did ye deliver ma message to Weems and order the hackney, sir?"

"I did both, Master Baillie," replied Daniel. "But it sticks in my mind that you are not in any state to make a journey this morning, and if you will rest here, I will call an apothecary – "

"Na, na," interrupted the lodger, with a feeble gesture. "I've made ma arrangements and will e'en bide by them. The Lord will tak' care o' me, hae no fear. Harkee, you will be the hackney arriving; oblige me, Master Jolly, by lending me your arm doon the stair – so – I'll manage fine, even if 'tis a wee bit slowly."

Leaning heavily upon the chandler, who muttered confused expostulations and protests against his rashness in venturing forth, the old gentleman staggered out of the room and descended the stairs. In the parlour, while Ned and the hackney-coachman were fetching his luggage, Mr Baillie took a most kindly and gentlemanly farewell of Mrs Jolly, sweeping aside her denunciations of her husband's cruelty in thus turning him out, and thanking her effusively for all her kindness on his behalf. Phoebe, meanwhile, holding by the scruff of their necks her violently excited dogs, which seemed as desirous of flying at Mr Baillie's throat now that he was leaving the house as they had when first he had entered it, watched the scene with an enigmatic expression, and when her turn came to say farewell, bobbed a small curtsey and said nothing.

Having settled his account for the remainder of his rent, Mr Baillie, still assisted by his landlord, limped feebly through the shop; but just as he was about to go past the outer door, he seemed taken by another faintness, and but for Mr Jolly's supporting arm would have fallen. The coachman, who by now had got his passenger's valises into the boot, took the sick man's other arm, and said over his head to Mr Jolly:

"You had best come with us, neighbour, and see him safe delivered. He goes at his own risk, mind you, and if he's a dead 'un by the time we reach the City, I am minded to have a witness that it's no fault of mine."

"Bless me!" cried the exasperated chandler, "here is a fine to-do. Pest take it, the gentleman needs not to travel at all until he is recovered, as I have been telling him till I am tired. As for accompanying him, I have my shop to attend to, and," added Mr Jolly, his spleen rising as he remembered the events of last night, "have suffered sufficient already upon Master Baillie's account."

His last words were quite drowned in a clamour of voices. Mrs Jolly, who had come through from the parlour, began for some obscure reason to talk rapidly and incoherently about her grandfather (a relation not hitherto mentioned in her romancings) who, it appeared, had been a Gentleman of the Bedchamber to King James the First and had come to an untimely end in some way resembling the present situation; a housewife who had found herself out of besoms was trying to enter the shop and buy one before she could start her work; the hackney-coachman, who, in the manner of his kind, was always liable to suspect himself of being put upon, kept demanding a witness to his fare's insistence on travelling in this state; Phoebe's two dogs were barking harder than ever, and Phoebe herself was exhausting her rustic vocabulary of oaths in trying to quieten them; and Mr Baillie, now partially recovered, feebly entreated the chandler to do him the charity of seeing him safe to his destination, promising that he should return instantly in the hackney at the Scotsman's expense.

Mr Jolly, red in the face with annoyance, his brain a-whirl from the general clamour, gave in at last to these entreaties, it promising to be the line of least resistance. Between them, he and the coachman half carried the sick old gentleman to the vehicle drawn up in the street, and deposited him upon the tattered leather cushions within; Mr Jolly followed, just as he was in his apron and shirt-sleeves without cap or coat; the steps were clapped up, and, speeded on their way by the shrill voices of Mrs Jolly and the female customer, protesting, advising, commiserating, and exclaiming, the hackney and its occupants jolted down Heath Street and started on the journey to London-town.

Chapter Seven

During the greater part of the journey, Mr Jolly was so intent on observing his fellow passenger, dreading lest at any moment he should expire before his eyes, that he had no leisure to look out of the hackney to see whither they were going. It was not until the iron wheels of the vehicle began to rumble over cobble-stones, and the uproar of street cries, apprentices bawling at their masters' doors, and a confusion of footsteps and horses' hooves informed him that they were come into London, that, letting down one of the tin sashes at the window, he saw that they were already past Temple Bar and were progressing slowly towards Ludgate. A glance at his former lodger showing him that Mr Baillie seemed a little recovered, he enquired whither they were bound.

"To a guid friend o' mine who lodges in Queen Street off Cheapside," replied his fellow passenger. "We'll no' be lang noo in arriving, and then ye may be quit o' me and hasten back to your shop."

Much relieved by this information, Mr Jolly sank back upon the leather cushions and prepared to endure with resignation the remainder of the journey and the torturing of his bones by the bumping and jolting of the unsprung vehicle over the innumerable pot-holes of the streets. Fishing for his handkerchief, he wiped his sweaty face. Not until this moment, when the end of the strange and frightening period of his adventures was in sight, did he realise how they had unnerved him. As for the treasonable letter, he found that he had made up his mind. He was not an unpatriotic man, but he possessed in good measure that instinct to avoid trouble of a public nature which was a characteristic of the class. Plots were the business of the King and his Ministers, who could be trusted to deal with them without his assistance. Moreover, simple though he was, he was astute enough to be aware that he had no proof to offer that there really was such a conspiracy on foot as seemed evident from Lord Essex's letter; the letter was no longer in his possession; and the bare word of a village shopkeeper would have little chance against the inevitable denials of lords and gentlemen and experienced plotters like Bob Ferguson. In any case, his first duty was to his own family; by removing from their midst this Mr Baillie, he was, he felt, doing all that a man could do, who against his will had become entangled in the fringes of treason, to safeguard his wife and daughter and his livelihood. He was innocent, and in ridding himself of Mr Baillie he was proving himself so. If Mr Baillie and his friends continued with their vile schemes, it was no affair of his, and doubtless, sooner or later, they would pay the penalty of their treason; for Daniel had great faith in the triumph of good over evil.

These meditations were interrupted by the sudden halting of the hackney, and letting down the sash once more, Daniel observed that it has stopped in a narrow street before a tavern, which bore the sign of the Horse Shoe. The name stirred a memory within him, an uneasy memory, but even as he strove to discover what it was, his fellow passenger plucked his arm and entreated Daniel's assistance in alighting. Mr Baillie seemed very feeble again, and it required the combined aid of Daniel and the hackney-coachman to lever him out of the vehicle and into the tavern. When they were come into the entrance, Mr Baillie, racked by another fit of coughing, made a weak gesture towards the staircase, and when they had got him up to the first landing, guided them towards a closed door. Releasing his arm from the coachman's, but keeping a firm hold of Daniel's, he lifted his silver-knobbed cane, and rapped with it upon the panels; with a sudden shiver, Mr Jolly recognised the manner of the knocking; there were two soft raps, then three loud ones, then two soft again. It was the same signal as that given upon Mr Baillie's door at Hampstead when the burly man and the one with the wooden leg had come to call upon him last month. The door was opened by someone unseen, and, still supported by his two companions, the ancient gentleman went feebly yet hurriedly into the room.

A man, the sole occupant of the apartment, had returned to a table by the window after opening the door, and now sat there, saying nothing, but staring straight at Daniel. And now the vague alarm, which had been aroused in the chandler by Mr Baillie's manner of rapping on the door, rose higher and became less vague; for the man at the table was that same fox-coloured gentleman with the hooded eyes and sharp yellow teeth whom he had encountered near Newgate when he had gone to visit Josiah.

Daniel drew a shuddering breath which sounded loud in the silence.

"My – my compliments, gentlemen," he stuttered. "I will t-take my leave now, if you p-please; I am glad to have been of service, Master B-Baillie; your servant, sirs, your servant."

Snatching his arm from the Scotsman's as he spoke, he made for the door; but there, straddling before it, biting the end of his long whip, he found the hackney-coachman, who, grinning unpleasantly, made no move to stand aside.

As Daniel was about to order him to do so, a voice spoke from the other side of the room.

"Nae sae fast, Master Jolly, nae sae fast," said the voice of Mr Baillie, and it was no longer feeble, nor yet kindly. "Allow me to present to ye ma friend, Mr Aaron Smith, a canny lawyer of whom ye may hae heard, since he had the honour to be counsel to Dr Titus Oates and assisted him in a' his evidence. Noo, Mr Smith, it grieves me sair to hae to tell you that I've a charge to mak' against oor friend here. He has ten guineas o' mine, which he stole frae ma strongbox whiles I was unco' sick, and sae was I fain to bring him hither by a wee deception, being altogether in his power at Hampstead and withoot the protection o' ma friends."

For a moment Daniel was quite bereft of speech. Up to a few weeks ago, his life had been uneventful, and he had encountered only the ordinary misfortunes and injuries which beset the run of lowly men. Faced with this monstrous wickedness, this bare-faced persecution, he had for the moment all he could do to persuade himself that he had heard aright. Mr Aaron Smith, however, quickly convinced him that it was so.

"This is a very serious charge," said he, his voice grave but his pale eyes horridly twinkling. "You had best answer to it, Master Jolly, and endeavour to clear yourself before I summon a constable."

"It is a lie!" shouted Daniel violently. "A damnable, hellish lie, and I marvel that you, sir, are not struck dead this instant for daring to utter it."

"D'ye deny that ye hae ten guineas o' mine, Master Jolly?" enquired the ex-lodger softly.

"I do not deny it," stoutly replied the chandler. "But as you very well know, sir, you gave it to me, freely and unasked."

"He *gave* it to you?" echoed Aaron Smith, with an unpleasant laugh. "Nay, come, sir, you must do better than that, you know. For what possible reason could a gentleman like Mr Baillie give you this huge sum?"

Daniel licked dry lips. He suspected a trap in the question, and knew that he was not quick-thinking enough to evade it in his answer. But, sustaining himself with the knowledge of his own innocence, he replied bravely:

"For carrying a message into London for him, when he was too sick to go himself. Whey he should think the errand worth ten guineas you had best ask him, and let him answer frankly if he can."

"Master Jolly," said the Scotsman, who was now ensconced in an elbow-chair beside the fire, and who, leaning upon his cane, was regarding his former landlord with a gentle pity which was most exasperating to the chandler, "I ken fine ye're a puir man and puir men hae muckle temptations. I blame mysel' that I was sae careless as to leave ma strong-box open when ye visited ma chamber and let ye hae a sight o' yon gold, for it was no' verra fair o' me, I ken that noo."

With a bellow of rage, Daniel strode over to him, and, clenching and unclenching his fits, roared out:

"Did you not send me to Southampton House, sir, but last night, with a message to a Mr Essex? And did you not give me ten guineas for my pains, five ere I set out, and five when I returned? Have you the face to deny this, sir? Have you, I say?"

"Ye were guid enough," replied Mr Baillie gently, "to offer to carry a message for me to my Lord Essex, whose friend I hae the honour to be, and for yon service I gave ye a shilling. Guid grief, man, if I'd needed to send ye to the Americas and back, it wadna hae cost me ten guineas."

"But I will tell you why it cost you that sum to send me to Southampton House," raged Mr Jolly, now thoroughly desperate and reckless; " 'twas because you and your fine

Lord Essex were hatching beastly treason, as I know, sir, because, let me inform you now, I read the letter he sent you, after I had been waylaid by a tobyman, your friend, and he had broke the seal."

"What's this?" interposed the lawyer sharply, "what is this I hear you say, fellow? You own you carried a letter containing matter of treason? Have you notified a magistrate of this? Pray don't let me hear that you have suppressed knowledge of this kind, else I fear me you are altogether undone. Misprision of treason is a far greater charge, my man, even than that of the theft of ten guineas."

Then once again was poor Daniel bereft of speech. It penetrated into his distracted mind that this was indeed a trap, that he had walked straight into it, and could see no way of getting out again.

"If you are wise, sir," continued the lawyer, those pale eyes of his glinting with laughter, "you will say nought of this matter outside these walls, else are you like to find yourself in Newgate. Master Baillie here, myself, and the worthy coachman yonder, will pledge ourselves to keep mum concerning what you have confessed, seeing that you are already lying under an accusation which is heavy enough. Take comfort, my friend, that though the theft of ten guineas may transport you to the Plantations, at least it will not bring you to the quartering-block, as might misprision of treason. You, fellow," he added, addressing the hackney-coachman who all this time had stood silently on guard before the door, greedily drinking in every word of the conversation, "summon a constable, and say to him that there is a hackney waiting here in readiness for the conveyance of a prisoner to the Poultry Compter, and that if he will be good enough to step up to this apartment, I will acquaint him with the charge."

When the coachman, nothing loth, had gone upon his errand, Daniel found his tongue with a vengeance. He raved, expostulated, threatened, pleaded, and denounced; in the extremity of his terror he even went down on his knees to Mr Baillie, reminding him of how often he had larded his talk with the name of God, of how, if he were indeed a religious man, he must expect to find the wrath of the Lord unloosed upon him for his wickedness towards a poor and defenceless shopkeeper. Despair making him eloquent, Daniel drew a painful picture of the plight of his wife and daughter, if the threat to carry him to the Compter were carried out, and in the next breath threatened to have his revenge upon the maker of so monstrously false an accusation, if he could find justice anywhere in England. Meeting only gentle smiles and grave rebukes, Daniel, suddenly panic-stricken, made for the door again, and finding it locked upon the outside, hammered on the panels with his fists, shouting for help to the inmates of the tavern; so that presently, when the coachman returned with a constable and his halberdiers, a crowd had collected not only in the passage but in the street outside.

"You will note that the fellow is violent, Mr Constable," said the lawyer, as that worthy, grasping his painted staff of authority, demanded to know what was all this to-do. "I am here to witness that he threatened my client, which I much fear will prejudice his case when it comes to be heard, especially as my client is, as you can see, an exceeding frail and ancient gentleman. Prithee guard the fellow close, for he is a desperate character."

"Desperate quotha!" bellowed Mr Jolly, suiting the action to the word by wrestling with the halberdiers. "Ay, do but take me before a magistrate and you shall see how desperate injured innocence hath made me. My word upon it, I have that to say which shall make more than one head to fall."

"Hold your peace, rogue," commanded the constable. "You shall be taken before a magistrate at the proper time. Now, sir, let me hear the charge against him."

Mr Baillie, addressing the constable with a nice mixture of patronage and deference, as became a gentleman to a minion of the Law, told him that, being a lodger in Daniel Jolly's house, he had the folly to leave his strong-box open on the table yesterday when he went to relieve nature, and returning, had found to his dismay that ten guineas had been taken from it. There could be no doubt, he added, that his landlord had been the thief, because they two were alone in the house at the time, and besides, as he had climbed the stairs towards his chamber, he had seen the chandler coming out of it: if search were made, said he, he suspected that the money would be found secreted in the house. In the meantime, perceiving that his landlord was a desperate man, he had by a trick conveyed him to the lodgings of his friend here, Mr Aaron Smith, a lawyer of the Temple, had laid the information before him, and now begged that Master Jolly be conveyed to a place of security until the matter could be investigated.

"Don't concern yourself, sir, but it shall be done," replied the constable officiously. "We'll clap the rogue in the Compter and he shall appear before his worship in due course. Come, fellow, conduct yourself peaceable, or I shall be constrained to bid my men use force with you. I thank you, sir, I thank you," he added, as Mr Baillie slipped a shilling into his ready palm. "My best respects to you, gentlemen, and pray don't be uneasy; his Majesty's representative shall see the rogue secured."

So they marshalled the now exhausted and despairing Daniel through the mob in the passage, and down the stairs. In the street a second crowd was collected about the waiting hackney, and in the manner of their kind had armed themselves with horse-dung and other filth so that they might indulge in the pleasure of pelting the unhappy captive, knowing little and caring less for what reason he was under arrest. Bundled into the hackney, his face and clothes besmeared with the artillery of his mobbish tormenters, Daniel, almost crushed to death by his guard, had some leisure to reflect most bitterly upon the injustice and ingratitude of mankind as he was jolted towards the jail in the very hackney in which, out of the kindness of his heart, he had accompanied his sick lodger to Queen Street.

The Poultry Compter, newly rebuilt after the Fire, but its brick already blackened with the London smoke, stood at the top of Scalding Alley on the north side of the Polutry, which thoroughfare, at this busy hour of the morning, was crowded with the stalls of those who sold fruit, fowls, and oysters. The hackney, having with difficulty negotiated a passage between these stalls, stopped before a frowning wall in which was set a huge grate guarded by a porch. The constable, descending first, knocked loudly upon the grate with his staff of office, a summons answered after a short delay by the sound of a chain being unfastened and that of bolts withdrawn; a wicket within the grate creaked open, and an evil-looking fellow in a mangy fur cap, and with a key of enormous proportions in his hand, appeared and exchanged a few words with the constable. Then the latter, beckoning imperiously with his staff to the halberdiers, bade them bring forward the prisoner, and Daniel was bundled out of the hackney and through the wicket. His former guardians, apprehensive of jail-fever, retired with haste, leaving him in charge of the porter. The wicket was shut and bolted behind him, the huge hey turned in the lock, and Daniel, looking wildly about him, saw that he was in the porter's lodge, on the walls of which leg- and hand-fetters of all shapes and sizes ominously dangled.

A turnkey, rising reluctantly from a bench on which he had been lounging, took one look at the newcomer and summed him up with an experienced eye. A first offender, undoubtedly, and by his looks a respectable small tradesman; such were usually fair game.

"For a trifle, sir," said the turnkey, "you may lie in the King's Ward, where you may have a bedstead and all things convenient. And for a trifle more you may buy yourself free of the irons, which I may tell you is a great privilege."

But despair had for the moment restored Daniel's self-respect and reawakened his righteous wrath. Therefore, without troubling to mince his words, he told the turnkey exactly what he could do with his King's Ward and his fetters.

"I scorn," added the chandler, with pathetic dignity, "to buy privileges from such as you. I am an innocent, respectable subject of his Majesty, and until such time as I may have justice done me and my fair name cleared, you and your like may do your worst."

It was a rash challenge, but then Mr Jolly was quite unacquainted with the inside of a jail and the ways of turnkeys. Denied his garnish, the warder promptly fitted Daniel with the heaviest pair of fetters he could find, and, keeping up a stream of blasphemous abuse all the while, hustled his clinking captive to the Common Side, where the lowest scum in London, unable to pay for any privileges, were housed. Thus did Daniel find himself locked into a large apartment, the floor, walls, and roof of which were of foul and slimy stone. In the centre stood a large iron stove; round the walls were ranged bunks, tier upon tier of them, of bare and exceedingly filthy boards; and prominently placed in one corner stood the common excreting-tub.

Immediately upon his entrance, the inmates of this apartment crowded round him, screaming "Garnish!

Garnish!" pushing and jostling him as they went through his pockets in search of any coins the turnkey might have missed, and chattering to one another in the secret language called cant. It was a nightmare crew, unshaven, ragged beyond belief, crawling with vermin, some with their heads thrust into the tops of old stockings, some covering their nakedness with sacks, some old, some young, a few with an air of decayed respectability still clinging about them, others looking as though they had been nurtured in vice from the cradle, but all banded together in a common misfortune, and determined, one and all, to milk a newcomer of all he had before admitting him to their miserable society. Within a few minutes of this entrance, they had snatched from Daniel's pocket the few small coins which reposed there, and a free fight ensued for the possession of them, old and young fighting each other like dogs. When this fracas subsided, a villainous-looking fellow, his face deeply pitted from the smallpox, informed Daniel in an educated voice that he was now made free of the Common Side, and "to all the privileges and immunities thereof". His fellow prisoners then lost interest in the newcomer, and returned to their several occupations, which consisted in playing with a pack of greasy cards, exchanging bawdy jests and stories, sleeping, and scratching themselves.

 It is fortunate, perhaps, for Daniel, that he had so much physical discomfort to contend with, for thus he was spared for the time the full force of the mental anguish which otherwise might have unhinged him. His nose was assaulted with the abominable stink of the place, his eyes with sights of filth, vice and poverty never before imagined, his ears with obscene noises and with that thieves' talk he had heard on the lips of the tobyman in the Conduit Fields. Much of this was quite unintelligible to him, but here and there he caught words and phrases at the meaning of which he could guess from their context. To his astonishment he found that the majority of these wretches were quite undismayed by their condition, seemed in high spirits, and talked with animation of the crimes which had placed them here, and of the offences they would commit as soon as they were released. Besides this cheering topic, they chattered endlessly of women, referring to some as 'dells', to others as 'kirchen morts', and to others again as 'commodities', 'bawdy baskets', 'pures', and 'naturals'. Presently, a wretch who had been loud in boasting of how he had "sucked the rhino from a shot-shark but had got so clear upon it that I was putt enough to lose it to a tat-monger," obliged the company with a song, which, though many of the terms used in it were meaningless to Daniel, shocked him by its obvious exaltation of crime:

>"The budge it is a delicate trade,
>   And a delicate trade of fame;
>For when that we have but the bloe,
>   We carry away the game;
>But if the cully nap us,
>   And the lurries from us take,
>Oh then they rub us to the Whitt
>   And 'tis hardly worth a make.

>"But when that we come to the Whitt
>   Our darbies to behold,
>And for to take our penitency
>   And boose the water cold;
>But when that we come out agen
>   And the merry nick we meet,
>We bite the cully of his coal
>   As we walk along the street."

When darkness fell at last, the company made for the sleeping-huts, fighting like dogs over the bunks which were not sufficient to accommodate all of them. Mr Jolly being a newcomer had no chance at all of securing one, and so lay down upon a bench, under which another prisoner curled himself up like a hound; others lay down on the ashes round the stove, heaped one upon another for warmth. Night might have brought poor Daniel's worries down upon him in a swarm, but he was so obsessed with disgust at the sounds around him, the scratching and growling as of dogs, the cracking of lice, the chorus of snores, and other more obscene human noises, that while sleep was impossible, so also was any meditation upon his predicament.

Morning brought a general rush for the excreting-tub, and so dreadful became the atmosphere that the chandler was forced to go into a corner and vomit. At last he heard from outside the rattle of keys, and the turnkey, opening the door, admitted the prisoners into the yard for exercise, where they found those who lodged in the "King's Ward" already engaged in their favourite game of rackets, which consisted in hitting a ball against the high outer wall of the jail. Such among the wretches from the Common Side who had money in their pockets trooped down to the cellar, from which the clink of tankards and the sound of female voices proclaimed that refreshment of two sorts was to be had there. Mr Jolly, from whom every penny had been taken last night, and who in any case was not in a mood to drink or wench, turned his back upon the cellar and sought out a turnkey, demanding to know when he might be brought before a magistrate.

"Why, on Monday," replied the man. "You don't suppose his worship wastes his Saturdays with committing such scum as you to the Sessions."

This was the bitterest blow of all to poor Daniel; and now to all his other troubles was added the pain of knowing that he had no means of communicating with his family, and that Elizabeth and Phoebe must go a whole weekend in ignorance of what was become of him. His stricken looks touched the heart of one of the less hardened of his fellow prisoners, who, taking his arm, drew him down into the cellar, where he treated Mr Jolly to some very raw spirit. Discovering by tactful questioning that the newcomer was a shopkeeper with a small but solvent business, the company in the cellar soon made him aware that the turnkeys would let him drink upon credit, and pressed him to treat himself (and them) and so cast away his cares. It was not long before Daniel, at the end of his tether, fell to this temptation, and thus, imbibing a great quantity of spirits, to which he was quite unaccustomed, passed most of the weekend in a merciful stupor.

On Monday morning he awoke with a dry mouth, an aching head, and a fathomless depression. By this time he had convinced himself that his innocency would afford him no protection against the malice of his enemies, so that even the thought of being taken before a magistrate failed to hearten him. Therefore, when the turnkey, after unlocking the door, roughly bade him stand aside while the rest trooped out into the yard, Daniel obeyed in a dreary and hopeless manner, feeling only regret that he could not deaden his despair with another bout of drinking.

The turnkey led him across the yard and into the porter's lodge, where a smith was waiting to knock off his fetters. When this was done, the turnkey, to Daniel's surprise, turned his back upon him, and stalked away on his own business; but this surprise was nothing to the blank bewilderment with which Mr Jolly now heard the porter tell him to get him gone out of the jail, for he was free.

"Free?" gasped the chandler stupidly.

"That's what I said," replied the porter impatiently, "therefore do you scour away, my cully, and presume not any longer to enjoy his Majesty's hospitality. Yet remember that you have drunk much upon tick, so that one will call upon you at your house anon to collect the debt."

"I cannot understand – " faltered poor Mr Jolly, supporting his weak limbs against the wall. "The charge against me – "

"Is withdrawn," interrupted the porter, more impatiently than ever. "The gentleman who accused you has withdrawn it, why I know not, so waste not my time in asking questions, but rub away fast and make room for your betters," and with that he fairly pushed Mr Jolly through the wicket in the grate and slammed it after him.

Convinced that there must be some mistake, Daniel, once the wicket was shut behind him, was seized by an urge to get away from the vicinity of the jail as fast as ever he could, so he took to his heels and ran down Scalding Alley at so hot a pace and with such desperate looks that passers-by, fearing that he was mad, gave him a wide berth. Panting and sweating, he ran through the busy street, sustained by the burning desire to get home, to scrub the filth of the jail from his body, and to fortify his exhausted spirit with the sight of familiar things. Having no money left, he could not treat himself to a hackney, and never had the miles to his native village seemed longer.

It was when he had reached the Conduit Fields, and, taking in great breaths of the clean country air and feasting his eyes upon the sight of trees and grass, had slowed down his pace, that a sudden thought hit him. He remembered the date; it was Monday, the 20th of November. He remembered it because his surroundings had recalled to him his encounter with the highwayman in these same fields, and this in its turn had brought recollection of something he had read in that sinister letter from Lord Essex. " 'Tis agreed that the General Point be set in action on the 19th instant... " So that was it. The conspiracy, insurrection, or whatever was meant by the "General Point", had been planned for the 19th, which was yesterday. For some reason it had proved abortive. Obviously this was so, for otherwise he would have seen or heard some signs of it in the London through which he had just come. And because it had failed, Mr Baillie had withdrawn the odious charge against his former landlord and had allowed him to go free.

So the mystery of the charge itself, hitherto quite inexplicable to Daniel, was plain to him at last. The conspirators, aware that he suspected their designs, and afraid lest he should blab of them, had taken the precaution of clapping him into jail until such time as their plans had been put into action. These plans having gone awry, he was no longer a danger to them, and therefore might have his liberty.

There was food for all sorts of emotions in this discovery, but in his present state Daniel Jolly was capable only of enormous relief. The problems, the doubts, and the vague threats which had been overshadowing him for more than a month, were plucked away. Without his having to risk laying an information, which would, he was convinced, have obtained no credence and might have brought all sorts of inconveniences to himself, a vile plot had proved abortive. His troublesome lodger was gone; his house no longer would be invaded by sinister visitors; passwords and signs and unintelligible jargon were vanished from his homely world; and he was back where he had been before he had encountered Josiah Keeling at the Upper Bowling Green on that fateful evening in October: a failure in business, it is true, still somewhat in debt (yet he had that ten guineas, he thought exultantly, though whether he would venture to make use of such money or not, he did not yet know), but rescued from dangers intolerable to an honest and peace-loving man.

So great was Daniel's sense of a burden being lifted, that as he strode across the lonely, sunlit fields, he heard himself breaking into song. It was the very song which had so shocked him when he had heard the wretch sing it at the Poultry Compter, yet so suddenly carefree and intoxicated with happiness did he feel now, that it was without any sense of shame that he roared out the last verse; which was all he remembered:

> "But when that we come to Tyburn
>   For going upon the budge,
> There stands Jack Ketch, that son of a whore,
>   That owes us all a grudge.
> And when that he hath noosed us,
>   And our friends tip him no coal,
> Oh then he throws us in the cart
>   And tumbles us into the hole."

Part Two

Chapter One

On an evening in December of that same year, Derrick Calder rode up to Hampstead to keep a supper engagement with the Jollys.

These invitations, conveyed to him by Phoebe when the lovers met at Jack Straw's, had become very frequent of late, but it was not very often that Derrick accepted. His duties at Court, and the social engagements of his wife, occupied most of his evenings; but apart from this, though he had conceived a great affection for Phoebe's father, her stepmother acutely embarrassed him. Elizabeth made no secret whatever of the fact that, having discovered to her disappointment that Derrick was married and therefore could not take her stepdaughter off her hands, she was determined to persuade him to acknowledge the girl as his mistress and set her up in style. Mrs Jolly did not actually say this, but she made it plain that, it being quite the fashion for gentlemen to 'keep', she expected Derrick to rent some expensive lodging for Phoebe, preferably in the vicinity of the Court, so that her stepmother could boast of it to her neighbours. It was in vain for Derrick to try to convince Mrs Jolly either of his own poverty or of Phoebe's utter distaste for such an arrangement; Elizabeth had a habit of simply disregarding facts which did not fit in with her own romantic notions. Derrick was a gentleman attached to the Court, and therefore, obviously, a man of means; he was in love with Phoebe, and the girl's brazen unfaithfulness to him must be distressing; therefore the only sensible solution was to take her away from her vulgar intrigues with villagers, make her a handsome settlement, and give her the standing accorded to the kept courtezan.

So the atmosphere of the Jolly household was apt to be strained when Derrick accepted an invitation to supper. Nevertheless, there were times when he did so accept, and not only because of his genuine pleasure in Daniel Jolly's company, but because it had seemed to him of late that the chandler had something on his mind of which, given the opportunity, he might wish to unburden himself to Derrick. Mr Calder was one of those persons acutely sensitive to atmospheres; having acquired through much mental suffering sympathy with that of others, he had a keen desire to use what wisdom he had for the benefit of those who aroused his affections. In this particular instance, he had the added incentive of the fact that Daniel was the father of his beloved, and probably, he suspected, was the only human being for whom she felt any real warmth.

So far, however, there had never been an opportunity for Derrick and his host to have a private talk, for Mrs Jolly, whenever the young man came to supper, monopolised his company. But on this particular evening in December, Phoebe vanished immediately after the meal, ignoring her stepmother's furious glances and playful chiding, and saying that she had to visit a sick sheepdog and that it would only embarrass the farmer if Derrick accompanied her. She would be back presently, and then Mr Calder could take her to Jack Straw's for a whet. Scarcely had she gone than one of Mrs Jolly's favourite gossips called to seek the good lady's advice on a new gown, and, her love of advising on such matters overcoming Elizabeth's relish of

Derrick's company, she retired upstairs with her neighbour, and left Mr Jolly and his guest to their tobacco.

Derrick Calder was a shy man, introspective and deep-thinking, and though the young sparks at Court deemed him dull, a certain quiet charm made him generally liked. From his childhood days he had been much alone; he was an only child, and his mother had died in giving him birth; his father, a fiery, opinionated old country parson, had attended to the boy's education himself, fearing the revolutionary influences of school and university. Sent at the age of twenty into the gay world of the Court, Derrick had found his poverty, inbred seriousness, and lack of any desire to push himself a barrier to complete acceptance by that world, and in his loneliness had fallen an easy prey to the first designing woman who found his good looks, ancient name, and excellent manners attractive. Thus had he become the poor husband of a rich wife, for Ella was the daughter of a wealthy merchant, and very quickly had been made aware that his bride, having attained by her marriage the thing she coveted most, an *entrée* into polite society, had no further use for him. This he had accepted with the philosophy he had built up for himself and had fallen back upon those consolations which never yet had failed him, the consolations of the mind; until that fateful day when, being in Hampstead on some errand, he had encountered Phoebe Jolly.

But he could not talk to Phoebe, and like many lonely men there was nothing he relished more than a discussion of abstract matters with someone sympathetic. Strangely enough, such a one he had found in the simple old chandler, Phoebe's father. It was true that Daniel listened more than he talked, but he listened with plain interest, and often stimulated Derrick by some shrewd remark which was born of a genuine simplicity and humility, and a long experience of the microscopic world of a village.

Thus on this December evening, sitting in the candlelight on one side of the fire, with only the whisper of the flames and an occasional barking of a dog without to break the country silence, Derrick began to talk of himself with that detachment and freedom from embarrassment which often distinguishes the genuine seeker after truth.

"You must know, sir," said he, watching the smoke from his pipe curl up into the air, "that ever since I can remember I have been plagued by a desire to probe into the hidden meanings of life. Never was I able to accept second-hand opinions, nor could I ever rest content with beliefs and theories which I could not understand. Perchance it is a form of pride; my father would say so, I don't doubt; but if it is, 'tis one I would willingly forbear, for though I cannot accept the orthodox, I envy those who can and are not plagued with the urge to think out such weighty matters for themselves."

"I trust, Mr Calder," said Daniel uneasily, "that you are not one of these modern men who question even the existence of God."

Derrick smiled at him.

"I am sure of the existence of God," said he, "only I do not know His nature, nor can I see any justice and meaning in much of His creation. I am convinced that both exist, but equally convinced that I must discover them for myself, since nothing else will satisfy me. You may say that such things are mysteries, rightly kept hidden; yet we are given minds, as well as hearts and wills, and methinks we were intended to use all three. I protest, I do indeed envy that man who can accept without question any religious creed, be it only that of the fanatics, for I know nothing more intolerable than for the spirit to drift anchorless, unsure of the port from whence she came, the harbour for which she is bound, and the reason for her voyage."

"For my part," said Mr Jolly, with unusual vigour, "I would prefer to believe in nothing whatsoever than to give house-room in my breast to the abominable falsehoods of the fanatics."

Derrick, sensitive to the feeling which underlies words, glanced curiously at him, for his experience of the chandler had led him to believe the old man to be peculiarly tolerant for one of his class and age; he spoke even of the Papists with no more than conventional disapproval. After a pause, in which he waited in vain for his host to enlarge upon what he had just said, Derrick continued, half to himself:

"There are times when I am seized by the fancy that this world, and human life, are but pictures, such as we are shown in the chap-books when we are children, poor, ill-drawn pictures of a home we have lost but may one day find again. I cannot believe in the Heaven of which I was taught, with its glassy sea, its golden streets, its harps and its endless alleluias; the only Heaven in which I could believe would be the model for this lovely world of ours, a world defaced by we poor humans. If there are streets in my Heaven, they will be country lanes, if seas, the foam-flecked restless waters which lick the shores of my native Sussex, if voices, those of the friends I have loved upon earth. At other times, I am tormented by the notion of some secret which, if I could but light upon it, would explain all the problems of life, even as the key-word to a cipher makes plain that which was quite unintelligible before."

"A cipher?" repeated Mr Jolly; and once again Derrick caught an unusual sharpness in his tone.

"Why yes," said the young man, smiling. "The study of cryptograms has been a pastime with me since my boyhood, and I find it most diverting. It is a part, I suppose, of my obstinate desire to find out the hidden realities in all things."

Mr Jolly made so restless a movement, that his guest became silent, watching him covertly as he made something of a business about knocking out his pipe.

"H'm," said the chandler, speaking rather too casually, "it is a subject of which I know nought, but one diverting doubtless. Tell me, sir, something of it, if you please."

It was now plain to Derrick that, all unawares, he had made some remark which had a bearing on the mysterious preoccupation of mind which he had noted in the chandler of late. Too tactful to question him, he began instead to discourse upon his favourite hobby.

"Why, sir, to begin at the beginning, you must know that a cryptogram is a hidden message, a cipher the method of writing that message so that it cannot be understood by any man ignorant of the key, and the clear is the communication which it is desired to make. It is an art exceeding ancient, used in all ages by rulers, military commanders, and conspirators, and the methods are so numerous that I believe there never has been a complete list made of them. Some are simple, some very intricate; the crudest of all, I suppose, is the diagram-cipher, which is composed of pictures roughly chalked on house-walls, play-bills, and door-posts by thieves and other illiterate persons. And I must tell you that, with some of the more cunning methods, while a man may succeed in deciphering a message, 'tis quite another thing for him to discover the system by which it was composed. What are called frequency tables are the most important tools of the cryptographer, for these show the relative frequency of letters, pairs of letters, triplets, syllables, and words in ordinary text."

"I understand you, sir, I understand you," observed Mr Jolly, who quite obviously did not. He appeared deeply interested, but, Derrick suspected, more in some secret of his own upon which the subject had a bearing, than in what his guest was telling him. After a pause, during which he shifted uneasily, he blurted out: "I must let you know, sir, that not long since I – I chanced upon a paper, which I strongly suspect to be writ in cipher; knowing nought of these things, as I have said, I yet kept the paper by me and have it yet – only as a novelty, sir, you understand me, only as a novelty, nothing more."

"Why, 'tis quite natural you should keep such a thing," said Derrick soothingly. He paused for a second, then added: "It would much divert me if I could glance at it, yet I would not have you think, Mr Jolly, that I seek to pry into what may be your personal affair."

"I assure you, 'tis no affair of mine, none in the world," replied Mr Jolly hastily. "In truth, I believe I ought to have destroyed this paper, or let it lie where I found it."

"Do you think, then, it may be dangerous?" asked Derrick.

"Dangerous, quotha!" cried the chandler, and in the firelight his face seemed flushed. "I know not, I cannot tell, but you mentioned, sir, that such secret writings are used sometimes by – by conspirators, as well as by those whose duty 'tis to conceal matters for the public weal."

"Why, sir," replied Derrick with a smile, "conspirators have the best reason of any to resort to ciphers, and have done so since the days of ancient Rome. But if it makes you uneasy to speak of this paper, pray let's forbear further talk of it."

"Nay, I shall show it you," asserted Mr Jolly, suddenly firm. "I shall fetch it this instant, and you may make of it what you will. Only I beg, Mr Calder, that all this be under the rose, for I am a plain and honest man, sir, and like not to meddle in what doth not concern me."

"Sir," said Derrick gravely, in replay to this somewhat cryptic statement, "rest assured that anything you say to me in this matter, or anything you may show me, shall go no further than this room. You have my word on that."

Mr Jolly, nodding as if satisfied, left the parlour and retired upstairs, returning after a minute or two with a folded paper which, handling it gingerly as though it were something which might explode, he placed upon the table by his visitor's elbow. Then, reseating himself, he lit his pipe again, glancing over the spill in a fashion which seemed half excited, half disturbed.

Derrick, having unfolded the paper and begun to read, forgot for the moment his host's strange manner, as he became engrossed in his favourite hobby. He read and re-read for some moments in silence, then, desiring pen and ink, drew out his tablets and began to make some notes. His own voice held a note of excitement as at last he looked up and said:

"This is enciphered by one of the methods used often during the rebellion against King Charles the First. I have seen many specimens of it from those times, but believed it had been laid-by because, the system being very well known, and a simple one besides, few men would risk employing it if secrecy were vital to them. The method, Master Jolly, is this: He who sends the message, writes as it were an ordinary letter, of business, condolence, or friendship, according to his fancy. To those who know not the key, the wording, and in particular the punctuation, may seem somewhat strange, yet such messages were frequently conveyed to Royalist prisoners during the late troubles and were passed after the most strict examination by their warders. The solution is to be found by reading every third letter after a punctuation mark until a sentence be made; unless the cipher letter be very long, only brief messages may be conveyed by this method, yet, as I suspect to be the case here, a word or even a phrase may be inserted in plain hand, these seeming innocent enough if read by those for whom the letter is not intended, but conveying additional information to the recipient who has the key."

"Proceed, sir, proceed, I beg," cried Mr Jolly, no longer troubling to hide his excitement. "Let me know what this paper saith, when the key to the cipher is known."

Derrick looked again at the notes he had made on his tablets, and his face grew grave.

"The message contained is this-wise," said he quietly.

" 'Meetings will be held tonight at the Young Devil, Fortune, and Horse Shoe. Those with arms to convey to go to the Horse Shoe. All at eight of the clock.' And that is all."

"The Horse Shoe," muttered Mr Jolly; and Derrick, watching him closely, observed that the hand with which he conveyed his pipe from his mouth trembled a little. "Now it hits me why that name – " He stopped abruptly, gave Derrick a fleeting glance, and closed his lips tight.

There was a short pause. Then, leaning a little forward, and speaking with great earnestness, Derrick said to him:

"Master Jolly, I would not press you to disclose to me what may very well be no concern of mine. Yet I must tell you that I like not this message, and in particular that word 'arms'. You cannot, I believe, doubt my discretion; you have my word that this matter shall go no further than this room, unless you would have it so; and if you think I might assist you with the benefit of my experience, humble though it is, of living upon the verge of the Government and the Court, I believe you would be well advised to tell me where you obtained this paper, and in what manner, for I suspect the matter to be troubling you, and you may gain some comfort in unburdening yourself to me."

"I got it by chance from a ballad-monger," replied Mr Jolly, speaking hastily, abstractedly, and with obvious reluctance. "He mistook me for another, I suppose. I was a fool to keep it by me; but thank God no harm hath come from it. The matter is stale, sir; 'tis finished, I am sure of it; and by your leave I will now put this paper where I ought to have put it in the first place," and with that he fairly snatched the cipher letter from Derrick, and thrust it well into the red heart of the fire.

Before Derrick could make any comments on this action, or question his host further, the sound of the street door being opened and closed again, and the scrabbling of dog's feet on a stone floor, made the younger man forget, at least for the moment, all such things as secret writings, as, with that rapt look which came upon his face whenever he was in the presence of his mistress, he rose to welcome Phoebe.

It was the habit of this cheerfully wanton young woman to entertain her lover in a small private room at Jack Straw's Castle, a room placed at her service, wherever she had need of it, by the landlord of the tavern, a husky, cheery toper, with a shock of frizzy grey hair and an Elizabeth beard, who was known to his friends by the nickname of the Pirate. What price, in money or favours, Phoebe paid for this privilege, was known only to her and the landlord. It was an arrangement which Derrick, in the first stages of his infatuation with the girl, had regarded with the utmost distaste, especially as Phoebe made no secret of the fact that it had been her rendezvous with other lovers. He protested no longer, because his wisdom, learned in a hard school, had taught him that the only recipe for peace of mind was to accept his fellow men and women as they were, instead of endeavouring to make them what he wished them to be. Phoebe was Phoebe, with vices and virtues, strengths and weaknesses, all her own, and as such he loved her; why he loved her was a mystery into which even he, with his passion for solving the problems of human life, did not attempt to pry. Though he could not kill the hurt which Phoebe's unfaithfulness and crude vulgarity often wrought in him, he had succeeded in killing all resentment, a success which made the relationship between these oddly assorted lovers genuinely and consistently harmonious.

As they walked towards their rendezvous on this December evening, Phoebe kept up an animated monologue on the subject of her canine patient, the sheep-dog she had just been to visit, describing how she had plugged its deaf ear with the juice of leeks and the drippings of eels, overlaid with wool from a black sheep's belly, and as she talked he noted again that unsentimental but very real affection which crept into her voice whenever she spoke of animals. He listened, encouraged, and tried to make intelligent comments; and all the while the old wonder deepened in him, the wonder of their mutual love. Though he was too wise to ask, Why do I love Phoebe? he was too humble not to ask himself, Why does Phoebe love me? For, physically faithless though she was, he was convinced that she did. There were times when he feared that he bored her, yet she continued to relish his company; she was a robust young animal, with a dozen rustic lovers at her beck and call, and yet, although she made no secret of despising Court gallants and townsmen, she would cancel, without hesitation, an engagement with some Hampstead admirer if she knew that Derrick was free to visit her; and though she never, in their intimacy, displayed that warmth of affection which she reserved for her father, Derrick was aware that her heart and not only her passions responded to his love. There was some bond, some link, between them which had its roots in eternity; it could be seen now only with the gift of faith; hereafter, he was sure, it would become as plain to him as an enciphered message to one who has the key. He knew that Phoebe herself was almost entirely unaware of it; she was young and plain and fortnight, and did not trouble to analyse her emotions; yet one day, whether in this life or in the next he did not presume to guess, she too would find the key to the secret message of her heart.

When they came to Jack Straw's this evening, they followed an habitual routine. Phoebe liked things to be ever the same, and no matter how late the hour when she arrived at the tavern with her lover, and the shortness of the time they could spend together, she would insist that before going upstairs, they go into the common room and treat the Pirate to a can of ale. Derrick had undergone much inner conflict before he had come to accept without distaste this part of the evening's routine; the rustic crudeness of the jests his mistress exchanged with the landlord made him incapable of entering into them, and also had he found it hard to endure the way in which Phoebe, scorning subterfuge, talked openly and ribaldly with the Pirate concerning the reason why she desired his private room.

Having thus regaled herself as usual this evening, Phoebe hastened above stairs in front of her lover, and as soon as the door of the little chamber closed behind them, flung herself into his arms with that warm abandonment which was one of her chief attractions for him. There was no coquetry about Phoebe; and on the other hand a certain affection which betrayed itself in her most amorous embraces robbed them of plain lust. She gave generously and heartily and with frank enjoyment. After this prolonged ecstatic ritual was over, she loved to linger in the room and drink with her lover, chattering to him about her activities since last they had met, sometimes asking him for news of his own world, but this in a polite and perfunctory fashion, for she had no talent for dissembling, and it was plain that his life apart from her could not arouse her interest.

This hour of sitting quietly together, she on the bed, he at her feet or leaning over to caress her, was very sweet to Derrick. Starved of affection through his boyhood and young manhood, he valued intensely the little things which go with it, and this sordid little chamber at Jack Straw's had become for him a shrine which held the memory of a hundred endearments and fond caresses. Every detail of its furnishings was imprinted on his memory, so that when he was absent from it he had only to close his eyes to see most vividly the truckle bed, the poor scratched table with one leg shorter than the rest, the dingy hangings at the slit of window, even the very cobwebs on the wall and the stale rushes on the boarded floor. There fell tonight, during this hour before Derrick must escort his mistress home, one of those silences which, thinking of them afterwards, disturbed the lover because he feared that Phoebe, having exhausted her tale of her own doings, and having no interest in his, was become bored. He was acutely aware that he was ten years older than she, and suspected himself of being dull to boot. He was trying desperately to think of something to divert her when he remembered of a sudden his recent conversation with her father, and asked her guardedly whether it had seemed to her that Mr Jolly was troubled in his mind of late.

"Not now," replied Phoebe. "He is marvellous cheerful since the week-end he spent in the Poultry Compter, of which, by the way, he cannot be persuaded to speak, however much my stepmother plagues him for it. My dear," she added, gulping down a glass of wine and making a face over it, "you might as lief waste your money on treating swine to dinner at an expensive ordinary, as in buying me this Rhenish, for you know very well my gullet relishes better the taste of twopenny ale than the finest wines in the King's cellar."

Derrick smiled absently, his thoughts elsewhere.

"Mrs Jolly," said he, "hath told me that your father's misfortune came of tippling at an unlawful hour, for which he was clapped up by some officious constable. I would not seem to doubt her word, yet it sticks in my mind that Mr Jolly is not the sort of man to neglect his business and tipple in the City."

"I know not what to make of it," said Phoebe thoughtfully. "Certain it is he stank of stale spirits when he came home upon the Monday morning, yet I suspect, though have no proof of it, that his arrest had somewhat to do with our late lodger. He set out in his company that Friday morning, out of charity for the creature's sick condition, but what fell out afterwards I do not know, and my father is obstinate in staying mum upon the matter. He was an ill man, that Mr Baillie; my dogs hated him as much as a tobyman hates Holborn Hill, and you may trust them to smell out wickedness. They hated his visitors likewise, being as eager to fly at their throats as a bulldog at a baited bull at the let-go."

"Do you know who these visitors were?" asked Derrick.

"Not I," replied the girl. "But there was one in particular, a fellow with a wooden leg, who smelled as rank as a he-goat to my dogs. Thank the Lord they are gone, the pack of them, for all the time Master Baillie lived with us there was no peace from them, but such strange rappings on the door by men who looked for all the world like plot-evidences, and such a trotting backwards and forwards to the Bowling Green with letters, that I vow we might have lodged Dr Titus Oates during the height of his fame with less trouble."

Derrick said no more just then, for, having pledged his word to Mr Jolly not to speak of the cipher letter, he could not mention it to his mistress, and feared a hint of it might slip out if he continued to discuss her father and his late troubles with her. All the long ride back to London, personal memories of his evening with his love obsessed him as usual to the exclusion of all else, and as was his habit, he hoarded each word, each look, each touch, that they might sustain him during the period which must elapse ere next he saw her. But when he was in bed at last, and, over-stimulated by emotion, found sleep elude him, his mind returned to the mystery of Daniel Jolly, and in the dark watches of the night, when fears tend to become exaggerated, he discovered something sinister in the chandler's possession of that letter, his secrecy over his manner of obtaining it, and his obstinate refusal to explain the reason why he, a sober, respectable shopkeeper, had spent a weekend in jail.

So disturbed did Derrick grow by these cogitations, which suggested to a well-informed mind some conspiracy in which an innocent man had become involved despite himself, that before he slept he vowed that somehow or other he would probe the matter, discover the real identity of this Mr Baillie and his odd visitors, and assure himself that on the one hand Phoebe's father was not in any danger, and that on the other there was not stirring underground another of those plots against the Government, which, hatched by malcontents left over from the Commonwealth, had disturbed so much of the present reign.

Chapter Two

On awakening next morning, Derrick Calder found his resolution to have hardened, and as he went about his duties at Whitehall his mind toiled over the problem the night had presented to him, seeking a method of solving it.

The more he thought, the more it seemed to him that a clue was to be found in Mr Jolly's mysterious arrest and confinement in the Poultry Compter. Searching his memory, he discovered that this had taken place just after the middle of November; he recollected that he himself had returned in the Duke of York's entourage from Newmarket, where the King and his brother had been attending the autumn race meeting, on the 19th of that month, which was a Sunday, and that next evening, calling for Phoebe at her father's house, he had found the family suffering from the aftermath of some crisis. Mr Jolly, looking very wan and exhausted but oddly cheerful too, had made no reference to this crisis; but his wife, ensconced in an elbow-chair by the fire, her head swathed in a linen cloth which smelt strongly of incense and beeswax, and with hartshorn and spice-ball prominently displayed on her lap, had lost no time in making known to the visitor that he saw in her a victim of man's cruelty and thoughtlessness.

Her dear, weak, foolish and erring old Daniel, she had explained, had behaved on the previous Friday in a manner more fit for a young gallant of the town than for a sober, elderly shopkeeper, neglecting his counter, gadding into London, and there, having got into a tippling company in some tavern, had been arrested by a constable for baiting the bombard at an unlawful hour, for which sin he had been flung into the Poultry Compter and there confined until that very morning. He had bought himself out, she added, with money he ought to have employed in feeding his helpless family. To this story Daniel himself had offered no contradiction, but had sat there silent, smiling to himself, in a secret sort of way which was quite unlike him. Mrs Jolly, obviously furious that her gibes had so little effect, had gone on to treat Derrick to a long description of her own anguished state during the week-end, with many references to genteel ancestors turning in their graves, and a laborious explanation as to why it was correct for gentlemen to tipple and entirely wrong for country shopkeepers to do the like, ending with a solemn statement of her conviction that if her husband indulged in any more such debauches, he would find himself kidnapped and bound as a slave for the Plantations.

At the time, Derrick had satisfied himself with the suspicion that Mrs Jolly's story was only a part of that romancing in which she delighted, and had thought it probable that poor Daniel had been treated by a London acquaintance with some spirits to which he was unaccustomed and, like many another man of his sort, had fallen the victim to the desire of some busybody of a constable to make an easy arrest. But now, reviewing the matter, he was struck by the memory of Mr Jolly's odd manner on that evening, a manner which had remained with him on the occasions when Derrick had seen him since, and which resembled that of a man who had a secret, half disturbing, half pleasant. Further than that, now that he was giving the matter his serious attention, it did seem most unlikely that a man like Daniel Jolly, who hated London and was conscientious in his business duties, should have stayed in the one long enough to get drunk at an unlawful hour (which was after eleven at night), and neglected the other for the same period. And again, Phoebe had told him that her father had gone into London that day to escort their lodger who was very sick; Phoebe strongly disliked the lodger and his visitors, and she was not a girl to take unreasonable dislikes; and now he remembered that this Mr Baillie had left the Jolly residence for good that very Friday. Could there be some connection between this abrupt departure and Daniel's confinement in the Compter? Or, for the matter of that, between either event and the mysterious cipher letter which Mr Jolly had shown Derrick last night?

Having got so far in his meditations, Derrick allowed his imagination some play. Suppose Mr Baillie and his visitors were involved in a conspiracy against the Government, and Daniel somehow had stumbled on the fact? What simpler to such persons than to have the simple shopkeeper clapped up in jail lest he lay an information? Yet if that were the case, there remained the mystery of his swift release. Arrested on a charge of tippling at an unlawful hour, he would be brought before a magistrate on Monday morning, a fine would be exacted, and he would be set free. And this, surely, must have happened; whereas, if these men were afraid of his tongue, they would have seen to it that some crime was laid at his door which would have kept him in jail at least until the Sessions. As it was, he had been arrested on Friday, November 17th, and released again on Monday, the 20th. The question remained, therefore (supposing Derrick's hypothesis to be correct), what had happened between those two dates to make him harmless?

It was during the Duke of York's morning levee, when Derrick was on duty in the ante-room to the Presence Chamber, that a remark made by a fellow Usher, as, during a lull in the arrivals of lords and gentlemen who had business with his Royal Highness, the pair waited idle by the door, gave Derrick the answer to his question, though at the time it seemed too fantastic to be entertained as such.

"I hear," said the other usher, "that my Lord Shaftesbury is made a burgher of Amsterdam, which will save him from the treaty of extradition made betwixt us and the Dutch. I wonder how he passes his time, our Little Sincerity, among the butter-boxes."

Derrick shrugged his shoulders.

"I never could understand," went on the other, who was a young man who liked the sound of his own voice, "why he slipped out of England so suddenly last month, for he were safe enough, you'd think, among his friends the rabble or Wapping. You remember how it was the talk of the town directly we returned from Newmarket on the 19th. Why Bob the Plotter fled is plain, for he was wanted for another seditious paper, but there must have been somewhat out of the ordinary to scare my lord into taking to his heels, he being so sick at the time."

The arrival of some new visitor, and the necessity to greet him and carry his name to the Gentleman-in-Waiting, made further conversation between the Ushers impossible just then, nor did Derrick seek to resume it later. He had heard enough to give him an idea, seemingly fantastic, yet one upon which he could not resist expending some further meditation. If there was a plot against the Government, the two men most likely to be the ringleaders of it were the Opposition leader, the disgraced Earl of Shaftesbury, and his principal henchman, Bob Ferguson the Plotter. And throughout the remainder of his period of duty that morning, Derrick rehearsed to himself all that he knew of both of them.

Living as he had, for over ten years now, in the world of the Court, Derrick knew a great deal about Anthony Ashley Cooper, Earl of Shaftesbury. Since 1673, when my lord had trimmed for the last time in his career of turncoat, he had become the acknowledged leader of all those who opposed King Charles, and had made no secret of the fact that his chief aim was to prevent the Duke of York from ever ascending the throne. With this end in view, he had made the very most of the weapon which the Duke himself had placed in his hands, namely his turning Catholic, had encouraged and fostered the lies of Titus Oates and the rest of that band of disreputable informers, had badgered Charles for a declaration that he had married Monmouth's mother and that therefore Monmouth, that heaven-sent candidate for the role of puppet monarch, was the legitimate Heir, had used every trick he knew to force through Parliament a Bill to exclude York, and having failed in this, had threatened the country with civil war. Defeated by Charles' superior statesmanship, and by the new wave of loyalty which had swept the kingdom at the dissolution of the Oxford Parliament in 1681, Shaftesbury had withdrawn, first to his house in Aldersgate Street and later to some obscure lodging in Wapping, and the Government spies had reported him as being in constant communication with Monmouth and the leading lights of the Opposition, as well as with more disreputable Whigs like Titus Oates and Bob Ferguson. In the previous November, a packed London jury had thrown out a bill of indictment against him, thus saving his head from the block; since then, King Charles had been busy cleaning up the disaffected City, and in September of this year, when Tory Sheriffs and a Tory Lord Mayor were elected, any further bids for revolution on Shaftesbury's part seemed doomed to failure, yet, Derrick was well aware, my lord was not the man to give up hope of doing mischief, and he had an exaggerated faith in those whom he called his Brisk Boys, the rabble of London. Yet suddenly, last month, there had come the news that, for no apparent reason, Shaftesbury had fled to Holland.

So much for the Opposition leader. Turning his attention to that more mysterious and far less important public figure, Bob Ferguson the Plotter, Derrick found that his own knowledge of him was correspondingly vague. If all reports were true, he had been deep in every conspiracy since the beginning of the reign, yet showed extraordinary talent for saving his own skin, while never, so it was said, betraying an associate. Mr Dryden had thought him notorious enough to deserve mention in his *Absalom and Achitophel*; and Monmouth, for his libels concerning the Black Box, had rewarded him by a yearly pension of fifty pounds. His pen had been busy all through the Exclusion rage, and it was known that he directed that secret Whig press from which issued the more violent tracts and broadsheets; as soon as word reached him that a Bill was to be brought in against his leader, Shaftesbury, Ferguson had devoted his lively and vicious quill to vindicating the darling of the Opposition, and in endeavouring to persuade the nation that revolution and plots on the part of the Whigs were mere Papist rumours. Robert Ferguson the Plotter did, in a word, stand for all that was worst in the 'Faction', a strange, half legendary figure, who from an early age had displayed a passion for running counter to the established order, and possessed of a genius for converting others to this point of view, appealing to avarice, patriotism, or fanaticism as he saw fit.

And now he, too, had gone off, suddenly and secretly, to Holland, along with his master, that lord of tiny stature and great brain whom the witty King had nicknamed Little

Sincerity. It was true that, unlike Shaftesbury, Ferguson had an obvious reason for this flight, since he was wanted for yet another seditious paper; yet, like Shaftesbury, he was not the man to flee without there was dire necessity for it, and had lived in England for years under the threat of arrest. The pair of them had fled upon November 19th; and the very next day, a harmless, humble, unknown shopkeeper of Hampstead had been freed from a week-end's mysterious incarceration in the Poultry Compter. Was it altogether fantastic to imagine that there might be a connection between the two events? Suppose it not to be, thought Derrick; then here was the answer to his first problem. Daniel had stumbled unawares upon some information concerning a conspiracy led by Shaftesbury and Ferguson and numbering among those implicated Mr Baillie and his odd friends. It had been necessary at all costs to prevent Daniel from laying an information, and so his arrest had been engineered. But the plot, for some reason, had proved abortive; Shaftesbury and Ferguson had fled; and Daniel Jolly, no longer dangerous, had been restored to the bosom of his family.

So far, so good. But Derrick was not be any means content to let the matter rest here. Apart from his inbred desire to grasp in all its details any matter which interested him, he was not satisfied of Daniel Jolly's safety. To withdraw a charge which they could not substantiate against him may well have seemed, in the circumstances, the safest and simplest course to those he had made his enemies; yet they would continue to watch him at the very least, lest he talked of what he knew and thus brought trouble to the lesser conspirators in the abortive plot. Undoubtedly they hoped that the fright they had given him might keep his mouth shut, and, judging from Daniel's obstinate silence on the subject of his week-end in the jail, their hope was being justified; nevertheless, he might, in all innocence, let fall some word which would embarrass them if spoken in the wrong company, and if he did, Derrick was convinced that they would make no scruple in silencing him. The young man did not know who 'they' were, except that, apparently, this Mr Baillie was of their number; Mr Baillie, so he understood, was a Scotsman, a fact which might not be without significance in view of the recent insurrection in that country and the escape from Edinburgh Castle of its ringleader, Argyll, who was reported to be skulking in London, and undoubtedly had been in communication with Shaftesbury.

After dinner, with a free afternoon before him, Derrick changed out of this uniform, put on a plain dark suit, and hailing a hackney from the stand at Charing Cross, directed the driver to take him to the Standard in Cheapside. Alighting here, he paid off the Coachman, and proceeded on foot until he came to the Poultry Compter. For he had made up his mind that his search for information must begin at the jail.

The wicket in the grate was opened in response to the knock he gave with his sword-hilt, buy a fellow whom he guessed to be the porter, and who looked him up and down with an appraising eye. On the one hand, said this scrutiny, the visitor had no marks of civic authority upon him and was not, therefore, to be treated with any marked deference, but on the other he was plainly a gentleman and might be persuaded to part with a tip. So the porter made a vague gesture towards the verminous fur cap he wore, and civilly enquired the gentleman's business. He was rewarded by Derrick's hand suggestively jingling some coins in this pocket as he said:

"I seek some information concerning a former prisoner of the Compter, and would take it as a favour if we might have a word or two in private."

The porter, eagerly signifying his willingness to be of assistance, ushered Derrick into the lodge, where, having bid a couple of lounging turnkeys go about their business, he ostentatiously brushed the dust from a bench and begged his visitor to be seated.

"Your unwilling guests are many," said Derrick smiling, "and you must be hard put to it to remember them all, yet this man I have in mind may chance to have stuck in your memory, since he is not of the sort who ordinarily enjoys the hospitality of the Compter. His name is Daniel Jolly, and he is a stoutish, elderly man, very decent in appearance, dressed somewhat in the country fashion, with brown eyes and an exceeding kindness about his look. Do you recollect the man?"

"Ne'er stir, I recollect him," answered the porter with unexpected promptness. "For he was the luckiest canary-bird ever passed through my hands. I deemed him started on that journey which ends at the Deadly Nevergreen for sure, and how he escaped Jack Ketch I know not now."

"The Deadly Nevergreen," echoed Derrick, who knew that this was one of the cant names for the gallows. "But was he not jailed only for tippling at an unlawful hour?"

"Lor' bless you no, sir," answered the porter, astonished in his turn. "He was arrested at the suit of a Scottish gentleman, a Master Baillie, for the theft of ten guineas, and was to have appeared before the magistrate on the Monday, had not this Master Baillie sent word that he withdrew the charge."

Derrick stared at the man in silence, horrified by what he had just heard. The theft of ten guineas! If it was difficult to imagine Daniel Jolly neglecting his counter to tipple in London, it was quite impossible to think of his being accused of theft. No matter that the charge had been withdrawn, it could never have been made in seriousness and good faith. And it now seemed likely, horribly likely, that Derrick's theory concerning this mysterious arrest was correct. This Mr Baillie and his friends had intended to keep Daniel out of harm's way for a considerable period, and only the failure of the conspiracy in which they were engaged had made it safe for them to release him. The gravity of the charge which they had made against Daniel argued, surely, that the information upon which he had stumbled must have been something very vital to the plotters, for, as the porter had indicated, such a charge, unless withdrawn, might have cost the poor shopkeeper his life.

"This Mr Baillie," said Derrick slowly at last; "is he known to you?"

The man shook his head.

"I have few acquaintances save the knucks in quod, master," said he, "for I have not to shepherd 'em before the beaks – your pardon, the justices – and scarce ever set foot ouside the Compter. Likely one of the turnkeys may know him; I cannot tell."

Diving into his pocket, Derrick brought out a handful of silver, and offered the man half of it if he would get him the desired information. The porter, his greedy eyes glinting at the coins, rose in haste and left the lodge, returning a few minutes later with a turnkey who informed Derrick that though he had never seen Mr Baillie, he knew him to be a client of Mr Aaron Smith, the lawyer who had acquired so much notoriety during the hey-day of Titus Oates, and who lodged at a tavern called the Horse Shoe, in Queen Street, near at hand. This information, though suggestive, was not very helpful; and after putting a tip into the ready palms of both men, Derrick left the jail.

Outside in Scalding Alley there was the usual crowd of street vendors selling oranges stuck with cloves, supposed to be a precaution against jail-fever. By an association of ideas, their bawling voices recalled to Derrick the cipher letter in Mr Jolly's possession, which, he had told Derrick, he had obtained from a ballad-monger. The rendezvous mentioned in that letter had been the Young Devil, the Fortune, and the Horse Shoe, and though there were several taverns in London which bore the third sign, it was not stretching the imagination too far to infer that this particular Horse Shoe was the one in Queen Street where lodged the notorious Aaron Smith. If there was any sort of plot being hatched, Smith was almost certain to be in it; and by this time Derrick was absolutely convinced that such a plot had been hatched and for some reason had proved abortive. Well, thought he, as he walked slowly up Cheapside again, it proved abortive, Mr Jolly is at liberty, and the wisest thing for me to do is to let sleeping dogs lie. He was not altogether satisfied that Phoebe's father was out of danger, yet if he himself probed further into the affair he might only add to that danger. There was nothing more he could do except hope that at some future date Daniel Jolly might take him into his confidence and tell him the whole story.

But only a few days after his visit to the Compter, an incident happened which made Derrick change his mind.

There was a new comedy of Tom Otway's being performed by the King's Players at the Theatre Royal, and Mrs Calder, having invited a party of friends to accompany her, insisted on her husband's going too, that he might assist her in entertaining the company. These all consisted of Ella's fashionable acquaintances, except for one friend of Derrick's, a Private Gentleman of the Life Guards, Jack Younghusband, invited by Mrs Calder because the party was short of a man. As usual, she insisted on getting to the playhouse by three o' clock, though the performance did not begin until half-past, for there were few pleasures she relished more than that of showing off a new gown in public, admiring or criticising those of her acquaintances among the audience, and spying out the latest amorous affaire by what she perceived of the byplay in the boxes. Therefore, when Jack Younghusband had not arrived at her house by the time she was ready to set out, she made no scruple of going without him, saying she supposed he had sense enough to join them at the theatre.

The party having pushed their way through the usual crowd of idlers who milled around the door, and collected the metal discs which served for tickets, were ushered into their box on the first tier as the clock chimed three, and found the house already half full. Derrick, idly wondering what was keeping his friend, watched with amusement the young beaux in the pit, as they pulled out their combs and made a great play of tidying the curls of their great wigs, sometimes standing up on the benches to ogle fine ladies in the boxes, then, having bought some fruit from the orange-women at an exorbitant rate, presenting it to their choice among the vizard-masks, the prostitutes who infested the playhouse. The sound of gossiping voices and affected laughter rose from all sides, mingling with the impatient bawls of "Show! Show!" from the Upper Gallery where sat the footmen and other servants. Presently the musicians, in their loft above the proscenium arch, struck up the First Music of the Overture, to which nobody paid the slightest attention, but continued to greet acquaintances and crane round to watch fresh arrivals. The Second and the Third Music had been played, and the actor who spoke the Prologue had come between the curtains on to the huge apron which jutted out into the pit; and still there was no sign of Jack Younghusband.

Ella, observing her husband's perplexity, tapped him with her fan and whispered:

"I'll vow he's one of these mean gentlemen, who take advantage of the custom of being admitted free on the excuse of speaking with some friend, provided they don't stay more than one act."

"You forget he is our guest," said Derrick shortly.

"Ours?" echoed Ella with spiteful emphasis. "Nay, methought this famous poverty of yours prevented you from treating any man."

He bit his lip and said nothing. The play began, and it was not until the curtains were drawn again at the end of the First Act that Jack Younghusband slipped unobtrusively into the box. He made his apologies to his hostess with an abstracted air, then turned to Derrick with so worried an expression that his friend enquired in a whisper what was the matter. Mr Younghusband, drawing a side-piece of his wig forward to muffle his voice from the rest of the company, replied hurriedly:

"Something very ill fell out yesterday, and 'tis that which made me so late today. I must speak with you privily, Derrick, and get your advice. Upon my salvation, I believe there's a plot hatching."

Derrick's head jerked up at the last sentence and he stared at his friend for a moment in silence. Then, murmuring to his wife that they were going out for a whet, caught Younghusband's sleeve and hustled him out of the box and into the wining-room at the back. It was not very full, and when they had bought their whets they had no difficulty in finding a secluded corner. There, directly they had sat down, Mr Younghusband began in a low, agitated voice:

"I was on duty at the gate of the Savoy last night (you know I am quartered there), and about ten of the clock a coach drives up, and who should step out but the Duke of Monmouth and my Lord Grey; with them was a third man, so muffled in his cloak I could not tell who he was at first, but only that he had a wooden leg."

"A wooden leg?" repeated Derrick sharply.

"Yes," replied the other. "Do you know him, then?" And as Derrick shook his head: "But I do. His name is Francis Charleton, and is a cousin of Bob Ferguson the Plotter."

"So that's who he is," murmured Derrick, half to himself.

"I thought the party sought to enter," continued Jack, "and challenged 'em, but it was not so. They came up to me and began to engage me in talk; you know such a thing is quite improper for a Life Guard on duty, but what could I do? He is still the Duke of Monmouth, however much in disgrace. After some idle passing of the time with me, he and the rest began to question me in a manner which I thought, and still think, to have been highly suspicious, enquiring what was the present strength of the Life Guards in London, how many sentries were on duty at the Savoy, when was the Guard changed, and so forth. To all of which I gave a sharpish answer, and presently the party got into the coach and drove away. Talking with others of my troop in the Guard Room later, I discovered that several had the same experience at their several posts, and one of them confessed to me that my Lord Grey had gone so far as to offer him a bribe if he would give the information my lord required."

"Was it a drunken frolic, think you?" asked Derrick slowly.

"It was no such thing. Indeed, I protest 'tis the first time for months that I have seen Monmouth stone cold sober."

"Did you report the matter?"

"I was coming to that. This morning I sought audience with my Captain, but it was not to be had until after dinner. When at length I was able to come at him, and had laid before him the whole matter, instead of being concerned at it, he gave me very hard words, rating me for my presumption (as he was pleased to call it) in suspecting his Grace of Monmouth of anything improper, and forbidding me, upon pain of his displeasure, to speak of the matter to any man."

"Who is your Captain, Jack?"

"Why, my Lord Brandon, son to the Earl of Macclesfield, a zealous Exclusionist, as you very well know, and a friend of Monmouth's to boot. Derrick," went on the young man, agitatedly playing with one of the black buttons on his undress grey coat, "I am sure there is some trouble stirring, some plot abroad; why else would Monmouth seek to discover the strength of the Life Guards in London and where the sentries are placed? You do not need to have me tell you that since the Restoration, when we took the place of the Pensioners, we have been the King's chief bodyguard, and likewise have the safety of London in our charge."

Derrick stared down into his wine, and his heart beat sickeningly. The music between the Acts had cased, and a partial quietening of the audience informed the two men that the curtains were withdrawn again. But neither stirred. At last Derrick laid a hand on the embroidered cuff of his companion, and said quietly:

"Jack, I fear you are in the right of if, and that there is a plot abroad. Ere you told me what you have this evening, I was convinced that one had been conceived and laid by; now I very much fear that it breeds again. But don't mention the matter to any other person until you have heard from me, else are you like to be in trouble with your Captain, and to no purpose. We must have proof before we can act. Tomorrow night I shall hope to send word to you at your lodgings, and if matters stand as I fear they do, we will consult together and see what is best to be done."

"You are mighty mysterious," observed Jack, staring at him.

"I have passed my word to a friend to stay mum," replied Derrick, "and must endeavour to persuade him to release me from it."

He sighed heavily, his thoughts on simple Daniel Jolly the village chandler, entangled, perhaps, in some plot which, seemingly dead, had been but sleeping.

Chapter Three

As soon as he was off duty next morning, Derrick took horse and rode to Hampstead, sure of finding Mr Jolly at his shop. But when he arrived there, he found only silly Ned, from whom he succeeded in extracting the information that his master was out at a neighbouring farm, whither he had gone to buy some cheeses. Though he longed to enquire for Phoebe and get at least a glimpse of his love, Derrick decided against it, since he desired to say nothing which might alarm her until he had seen her father, and he knew that his appearance in Hampstead at so unusual an hour would arouse her suspicious that something strange was afoot. Leaving word, therefore, with Ned, that he would be at the Upper Bowling Green, and earnestly desired Mr Jolly's presence there on urgent business as soon as he returned home, Derrick rode up to the tavern, stabled his horse, and desired from the landlord a private chamber and some wine.

 He had to wait an hour before Mr Jolly joined him, and when at length the door opened to admit the chandler, it was plain that he was here sorely against his will. He was in his apron and thrum-cap, and his manner, as he stood upon the threshold and glanced about the room, was oddly nervous.

 "This is an unlooked-for honour, sir," said he. "You must excuse my delay in waiting upon you, but my business – "

" 'Tis I who must make apologies," said Derrick, as the chandler's voice trailed off. "I would not for the world have brought you from your counter, Mr Jolly, but that I had the most urgent matter to discuss with you, which brooked no delay. Pray come to the fire and take a whet; I will endeavour to be as brief as possible."

"Could we not go into the common-room?" asked Daniel, reluctantly advancing a few steps. "I like not this chamber – I mean, I would prefer – your pardon, sir, but the truth of it is this apartment recalls to me something unpleasant; 'ounds, I like it not."

"We must be private," said Derrick, watching him closely, "and it seems this is the only chamber the landlord can put at our disposal. I assure you we shall stay no longer than is necessary, and that meanwhile there is nothing to fear."

Daniel muttered to himself, sat down, then immediately jumped up and going to a small window which looked upon the yard, pulled the red curtains tight across it.

"We could be pried upon through that window," he explained somewhat shame-facedly, as he returned to his chair. "As I should know. Pray, sir, let me hear what you have to say, that I may return to my counter; my 'prentice is but a silly parish-boy, and trade is bad."

Derrick poured the wine, placed a glass beside the chandler, filled another for himself, and sat down opposite, all without a word. He was thinking of the best way of broaching the topic he had to discuss, and at last began:

"Mr Jolly, some few days since I visited the Poultry Compter upon a matter concerning yourself. You will say I tool an unwarrantable liberty in prying into your affairs, but I assure you I did it only for your sake. I was sure there was somewhat more than ordinary in your being arrested last month, and felt bound to satisfy myself that you were no longer in danger. What I learned there was that you had been charged by you former lodger, Mr Baillie, with the theft of ten guineas, but that ere you could come before a justice, the charge was withdrawn. This confirmed my own suspicions that by some means unknown to me you had aroused the malice of certain persons who had a secret to hide; to speak plain, I deemed it likely you had chanced upon some talk of a conspiracy against the Government, and must be silenced by the conspirators. From the fact that you were so swiftly released, I deduced that the plot had been stillborn, and therefore I resolved to pursue my enquiries no further."

"You were right, Mr Calder, you were right," cried Daniel, whose honest face had gone pale during this speech. "It failed, and there is an end of it. Let it rest, sir, for God's sake; you saw what they did to me only for seeing something not intended for my eyes. They are rogues, howsoever highly born, but God in His great mercy hath defeated their wicked plans, and they are scattered."

"Some of them are scattered, Mr Jolly, but alas not all," said Derrick quietly. "There is cause to believe that those who remain are planning fresh wickedness." Then, as the chandler made to rise from his chair in panic, he went on, with a certain authoritative note in his quiet tones: "Sir, you love your King and country and would not see harm come to them. When you showed me a certain letter at your house one evening not long since, a letter writ in cipher, I gave you my word that I would not mention the matter to any man outside that room. I have kept my word. But since it sticks in my mind that this letter had bearing on what I am discussing with you, I ask you to release me from my promise, if the need arise. And I beg further that you will tell me now all you know concerning the plot that failed, for I suspect that the rogues who hatched it are behind this new conspiracy. Come, behave like the honest Englishman that you are, and let me hear what you can tell me."

But a certain obstinate expression had settled on the chandler's face.

"Sir," he said, "you must excuse me. It is as I say; the plot of which I chanced to – to hear some talk was stillborn, God be praised, and those I believe to have been the authors of it are fled overseas. I may tell you now that from what I heard 'twas my Lord Shaftesbury and Bob Ferguson, he whom they call the Plotter, that rogue who was the means of introducing Master Baillie into my house. Well, the great rogues are fled, and I am sure we have little to fear from their under-spur-leathers."

"Whether you are right in calling the Duke of Monmouth an under-spur-leather I know not," said Derrick sharply, "but this I do assure you, that two nights since he, with my Lord Grey, and a man named Francis Charleton who has a wooden leg, were driving all over London, seeking to discover the strength of the King's Life Guards throughout the City of Westminster."

"Monmouth!" exclaimed the chandler, staring at him. "That rogue – nay, I cry you mercy, but from what I have seen of him I look upon him as no other. And the man with the wooden leg – Charleton you say his name is?"

"Francis Charleton, a cousin of Robert Ferguson the Plotter. Nay, Mr Jolly, once again I implore you to be plain with me. If you are not I much fear that one day you will discover the ruin of your country lying heavy on your conscience."

There was a long silence. Derrick watched in sympathy as the old man, rising in extreme agitation, began to pace the room, rubbing his workworn hands together, pushing his thrum-cap on to the back of his head, muttering to himself, and plainly torn between patriotism and self-preservation. At last it seemed that patriotism, and perhaps a human desire to get even with those who had so greatly injured him, triumphed; he returned to his seat, snatched up his wine glass, tossed off the contents, and said hoarsely, but with a show of resolution:

"Mr Calder, I will tell you all, yet I beg that if it be possible my name be kept dark in your investigations, for I am a man with a family, and poor besides. Likewise do I beg of you that you will keep secret the name of the friend (for so he was, and though is not so now, I would not injure him for the world) who, led astray by this Ferguson, was the means of Master Baillie coming into my house. He is one Josiah Keeling, an oil-merchant of the City; and 'twas here in this very room that I spied him in talk with the Plotter near upon two months since."

To these requests Derrick readily agreed, and, prompting and encouraging, at last drew from the chandler the whole story of the coming of Mr Baillie, the strange visitors, the conversation overheard between some of these and the old Scotsman (or as much of it as Daniel remembered), Mr Jolly's folly in obtaining the cipher letter from the ballad-monger, his agitating visit to Mr Keeling at the Amsterdam, his relief at learning that all this secret talk concerned only an innocent project of founding a Scots colony in Carolina, his being sent to Southampton House by Mr Baillie, his encounter with the Duke of Monmouth and Lord Essex, his adventure with the tobyman in the Conduit Fields, and his own reading of the letter already broken open by Captain Cruckshank.

" 'Twas then, sir," cried Daniel piteously, "that I knew into what kind of a company I was fallen, and what rogues I had entertained in my house. Mr Calder, I know my place, and 'tis not for me to judge the ways of great lords and gentlemen, but that letter, albeit 'twas writ by an earl, I mean my Lord of Essex, stank as strong of treason as a close-stool doth of sir-reverence. This General Point, which my poor misguided Josiah had told me was the cant name for the Carolina project, was in truth plain nasty insurrection; they were to attack the Tower and other strong points about London, and slaughter the Lord Dartmouth who commands it, and proclaim Monmouth King – for albeit I am a simple man, I could not doubt that the M in the letter was meant for his Grace – ay, and some declaration of Ferguson's, whom they called Mr Roberts, was to be read publicly to divert the mobile. Happening upon such beastly plots, I straightway ordered Master Baillie to leave my house, and having in my indignation let fall some talk concerning treason (or some such, I remember not precisely what I said), I suppose this Master Baillie thought me altogether too knowing, and so by a trick had me clapped up in the manner with which you are acquainted. And now, you say, there is some fresh conspiracy; bless me, sir, I assure you I know nothing of this."

"I am sure you do not," answered Derrick soothingly. "Yet what you know of the other may prove helpful. I beseech you, Mr Jolly, search your memory again and try to recall any terms you heard used, any names, any rendezvous, anything at all. For I believe there are not two plots but one which, for some reason we do not know at present, was laid-by in November, when Shaftesbury and Ferguson fled overseas, and now is taken up again. Therefore, information which may seem trivial to you, may happen to be vital to my future enquiries."

The old man did his best, though it was plain he hated the subject even more strongly than before, and with the continual encouragement and persistence of Derrick, succeeded in recalling a few scattered details. He was not able to describe, except very vaguely, any of Mr Baillie's visitors except the man with the wooden leg, nor, except on that one occasion when he had listened at the lodger's door, had he heard any talk between them. Of the talk he had overheard between Baillie, Charleton, and the burly man, he remembered something about a map of the City, the original of which hung in the chamber of someone called West, the mention of Goodenough, a former Under Sheriff of London, and that the subject of recruitment had been discussed. Then, at the Amsterdam, he had heard a great many cant terms being used, but could remember only 'the General Point', 'the Lopping Point', 'the Blackbird and the Goldfinch', and 'Prince Perkin'. 'From what had transpired later, he was sure they by 'the General Point' they meant insurrection, but except that 'Prince Perkin' was, he understood, a nickname of the Duke of Monmouth, could not guess at the meaning of the rest.

At Southampton House he had encountered the Duke of Monmouth, Lord Russell, the Earl of Essex, and someone addressed as 'Howard', had been invited by the drunken Monmouth to drink "to the man who first draws his sword against Popery and Slavery", and had heard some indiscreet babblings of the drunken Duke which had informed him that his Grace was confident of gaining the throne. But when it came to his encounter with the tobyman, Daniel's memory failed him altogether, for he had been so terrified, and Captain Cruckshank had used such beastly thieves' cant, that the whole incident had blurred into a kind of nightmare. Patiently taking him through the whole period of his adventures yet once more, Derrick added to his information a few more details which might come in useful later. The password used by the plotters, high and low alike, had been the question "Is all in harmony?" the correct reply to which seemed to have been that given to the fox-coloured gentleman, Aaron Smith, by the ballad-monger: "In harmony and liberty"; the sign by which they were used to make themselves known to one another was the unfastening and refastening of the two top buttons of their coats; and before entering a room occupied by their friends they had rapped upon the door in a peculiar manner, two soft raps, then three loud ones, then two soft again.

Satisfied at last that the chandler had told him all he could remember, Derrick set himself to calm the old man's fears as best he could, promising that he would do his utmost to ensure that no further trouble came upon him as a result of his disclosures, bidding him keep the strictest guard upon his tongue with others, and begging him, if later he remembered some other detail which might be useful, or heard or saw anything suspicious, that he would communicate with Derrick without delay. They parted at the door of the Upper Bowling Green, and Derrick rode thoughtfully back to London.

As he turned over in his mind all that he had heard that morning, he was aware of a deep disquiet which had in it some element of superstition. He was a man who, living so much within himself, was an easy prey to presentiments and premonitions, and he discovered that this morning one of these was lodged securely in his breast. His whole being shrank from a further investigation of this conspiracy (if conspiracy it were); an urgent voice within him cried out that it was none of his affair, that to begin probing might well bring danger to those he loved, that plots were the business of the authorities, that the incident of Monmouth's seeking to discover the strength of the Life Guards already had been made known in the proper quarter and there had met with no credit at all. And all the while as, had he but known it, his reason put before him almost the same arguments which his simple friend, Daniel Jolly, had used before him, he was aware that what he really dreaded was a possible estrangement from Phoebe as a result of his future investigations into this affair. Another voice than that of reason warned him that such investigation might well make him so preoccupied in mind that she would find his company tedious; that even if he could speak to her of what he was about she would not wish to hear; and that if he met with the probable fate of those who meddle in such dangerous matters, a violent and mysterious death, he and his love might part in this world so estranged from one another that his spirit could find no peace in the next.

He tried his best to put such fancies from him, chiding himself for his superstition, holding doggedly to the knowledge of his duty, ruefully admitting that his hopes of any future life beyond the grave and a meeting there with Phoebe were so tentative and lacking in solid foundation that it would be childish folly to guide his present actions by them. Yet, when he reached home and went up to the chamber where he was wont to write and read while his wife was out at her parties, he employed the time before Jack Younghusband should visit him this evening in response to the billet he had sent that young man, in endeavouring to set down on paper something of what he was incapable of expressing in speech to Phoebe, which she would not wish to hear now, but which one day, perhaps, if he had to pay the price of his meddling with dangerous plotters, might convince her of his undying love. He told himself that it was weak and self-indulgent, yet he felt the better for it, unsatisfactory though the written words appeared to him, when he had done his best to express the inexpressible, and sealing the paper, had laid it away in a safe place.

Jack Younghusband was punctual in calling that evening, and the two men sat talking over their wine far into the night in Derrick's chamber. Or rather it was Jack who talked, trying persistently yet vainly to persuade his friend to keep his promise of the previous evening and consult with him frankly concerning all he knew about a plot. But Derrick was obdurate. He knew enough, he said, to make three things clear to him; first, that a plot had been hatching for some while, had been laid-by in November, but was now taken up again; secondly that whoever endeavoured to probe it stood in great personal danger, since the conspirators were desperate men who would stick at nothing; and thirdly that until such probing had borne fruit in the way of solid proof, it would be useless to lay the matter before the authorities. Therefore he, Derrick, was resolved to pursue a solitary investigation, and all he asked of his friend was that he keep his eyes and ears open and report to him if he chanced upon anything which seemed to have a bearing on the matter in hand.

"You have a wife and children, Jack," said Derrick smiling, "and for their sake must not risk having your corpse found with its throat cut in some City alley-way."

Jack glanced at him and away again. He had been about to remind Derrick that he was a married man himself, but having formed the opinion that Ella was a vixen and that her husband, though he would never hear a word against her, was well aware of it, thought it better to keep his mouth shut.

"There is, however," continued Derrick after a while, "a favour I would ask of you, the which lies very near my heart. You and I are good friends, Jack, and I can trust you to ask me no questions if you will undertake it. 'Tis only this: If my meddling with this plot should result in the conspirators putting me out of the way, I beg that, so soon as you hear word of it, you will deliver a letter which I shall give you to the lady for whom I have writ it. I will not tell you her name now, if you please, but you will find it, and directions how to reach her, in a note I have writ to yourself and wherein I have enclosed the other. Will you undertake this for friendship's sake?"

Jack readily undertook the mission, and when he had tucked the package Derrick handed to him in the breast of his uniform, clapped his friend on the shoulder and bade him not to entertain any such morbid fears as those he had expressed.

"I warrant you," he said sturdily, "that when you have nosed out this nasty plot (though I must repeat that I deem you mad to attempt it alone), you'll get a knighthood at least, and that if there are any mangled corpses 'twill be those of headless traitors lying upon Tower Hill."

"We'll drink to that," replied Derrick, laughing and refilling the two glasses. "Here's to King Charles and his rightful Heir, and confusion to all traitors!"

"And here's to the fool who noses out plots single-handed," cried Jack, with an affectionate grimace, "and may he die in his bed!"

Chapter Four

Having become by now quite obsessed with the task he had set himself, Derrick spent many hours in cogitating upon how he cold get upon the track of the conspirators; and the best, indeed the only, idea which presented itself to him was to see if he could happen upon the notice of a meeting advertised by the same method as that of the cryptic letter shown him by Mr Jolly. He reasoned that, no notice or detail of the former plot having come to the ears of the authorities, it was likely that the conspirators would not deem it necessary to lay-by so neat and safe a method of notifying their followers of the time and place of a discussion; even to those who had the key to the cipher such a message as had been contained in the 'letter of condolence' disclosed nothing improper, except that word 'arms', which, thought Derrick, had been unwise.

Having decided upon this preliminary step, he employed all his off-duty time in strolling about the City and scrutinising every ballad-monger, book-woman, and vendor of broadsheets he met. For a week the sole result of such diligence was the collecting of an enormous number of ballads, sentimental, jolly, and obscene, and an equal quantity of assorted pamphlets. Before he bought any of these, he took care to catch the seller's eye and to go through the pantomime of unfastening and refastening the two top buttons of his coat. The street-sellers' reaction to this varied with their character, some advising him on the best way of ridding himself of lice, certain females directing him to the nearest bawdy-house, others taking no notice at all. Blessed with a keen sense of humour, Derrick was fortunate in being able to see the ridiculous side of the business; but by the end of a week the joke had worn thin, his meagre purse was greatly depleted, and he was beginning to fear that he was on the wrong track.

But the very next day the fate which had set his feet upon this perilous path rewarded his efforts. He was walking through St Paul's Churchyard, picking his way round the enormous heaps of stones and the busy crowds of sawyers and masons employed on the rebuilding of the cathedral, when, amid the idlers lounging round a music-shop, watching two dancing-masters' 'prentices practising a new step to the tune of a fiddle, he spied a fellow distributing handbills. More because he was determined not to let slip the slightest chance of attaining his ends than because he retained any real hope of success, he approached the man and was about to make the secret sign when he perceived that the fellow was stone blind. For some reason quite unknown to him, this discovery made Derrick more obstinate in his purpose even than before, and getting as near as he could to his quarry in the throng, he asked in low but distinct accents:

"Is all in harmony?"

The instant response made Derrick's heart beat fast. The answer came pat: "In harmony and liberty," and drawing a paper from the bottom of his pile of bills, the fellow fumbled it into the other's outstretched hand, and, guided by his stick, hastened away before Derrick could detain him.

It was all the young man could do not to turn into some tavern and examine the paper there and then; but, determined to use every possible precaution against discovery before the time was ripe, he carried it home in his pocket, and there, locking himself into his chamber, smoothed out the crumpled sheet. A first glance brought his hopes tumbling, for there seemed to be nothing cryptic about it. It was one of those advertisements drawn up by the quack doctors who infested London at the time; there were the usual extravagant boasts, lying promises and half-intelligible jargon. This particular quack, Dr Amos Bendigo, who was to be found "from three o' clock in the Afternoon 'till nine at Night at this Lodging in St Martin's Lane in the Fields, at the Sign of the Green Posts over against the Head-dressers", professed like all his colleagues to cure by the use of simple pills the most dangerous diseases such as leprosy and cancer; he had his own infallible remedy for the pox; he was expert in astrological predictions, divination by dreams, and palmistry; and he did not consider it beneath him to prescribe beauty treatment for ladies, asserting that he could cure the worst of breaths, make those plump who were too thin and vice versa, and had invented a paste so efficacious for withered complexions that matrons of forty could be mistaken for maidens of fifteen. The bill was decorated with the usual astrological signs and added in large type the customary promise to the unwary, "No Cure, no Money."

A first reading of this long rigmarole had informed the experienced Derrick that if this were indeed a cryptogram it was not enciphered by the method used in the 'letter of condolence' which Mr Jolly had obtained in the like circumstances, for though in some places the phrasing seemed peculiar, the punctuation was normal. Yet from the fact that the fellow had given him this paper in response to his use of the password, and had made the correct reply, he was convinced that it was a cryptogram, and he was determined to break the cipher though it took him all night. Getting out pen, ink, and paper, therefore he set to work.

His knowledge of the art of cryptography was considerable, and therefore he knew at once that, as the writing made sense and the letters were not jumbled together, it was not a key-word cipher, nor a simple-substitution, a double-substitution, a two-step, a transition, or a combination. He frowned, for at the moment he could not recall a system by which the cryptogram made sense to the uninitiated, except the one by which Mr Jolly's 'letter of condolence' had been enciphered. He took down from his shelves the *Steganographia of* Trithemius, Selenius' *Cryptographia,* and Bacon's *De Augmentis Scientiarum,* and wasted several hours poring over these and other ancient works. It was midnight, and his wife was still out at some fashionable assembly, when at last Derrick's persistence was rewarded by a sudden idea. All the while he had been working the conviction had nagged at him that since the conspirators must include among their dupes and minions many illiterate or semi-illiterate men, any method of enciphering they employed for use among these must necessarily be simple. And now, suddenly, he had remembered from his boyhood days a very simple but effective method called the grill. He spent the next half-hour with penknife, a measure, and a blank sheet of paper, and presently laid the latter, now pierced with holes at regular intervals, over the quack's bill. After a few moments' study he cried aloud with triumph; for he saw that at last he had broken the cipher.

There it was, the message or clear, one letter after another appearing though the holes in the blank sheet. When this was removed, it was seen that the spaces between the holes had been filled up in such a manner as to give the appearance of an innocent handbill. His enthusiasm for cryptography overcoming for the moment his desire to search out treason, Derrick was lost for a space in admiration of the ingenuity of those who had penned this paper. There was no awkwardness, or at least very little, in the wording of the advertisement, there was an excellent imitation of the usual jargon, and, once the method of deciphering were known, the simplest man could read the clear. Derrick read it now with a growing excitement:

"Friends in Harmony are invited to attend, according to the Directions given at the foot of this Bill, at the hour of half-past Nine in the Evening, upon the twenty-first instant. They are further invited to bring with them any Honest Man who is a Friend to Liberty and is desirous of hearing Good Tidings."

Reading the message again and again, Derrick could hardly believe in his good fortune. For from the last part of it, it was plain that a stranger would be welcome at this meeting, so he could vouch for his introduction, or, in Derrick's case, invent some plausible excuse for his coming. Almost certainly it was to be a gathering of new recruits, and although at such a meeting it was unlikely that open treason would be talked, nevertheless it was a beginning, it was a getting upon the fringe of the conspiracy, and at this stage of his investigation Derrick could not hope for more. He went to bed at last, worn out with fatigue and excitement, and determined to fill the intervening days before December 21st with a thorough preparation for his appearance at the Green Posts.

The evening of that day, on which, most providentially, he was off-duty at Whitehall at eight o' clock, was bitter cold; a cruel wind sent the dust and refuse of the streets whirling round the legs of pedestrians, buffeted their cloaks about them, rattled such of the signboards as still hung in irons, and hurled itself viciously round corners. Derrick's imagination, the weakest part of him, tempted him with the fancy that the wind itself was a conspirator, striving with might and main to prevent him from taking this first plunge into his dangerous investigation. He had to fight his way against the gale, as, an inconspicuous figure anonymous in the gloom save for that walking-sword by his side which proclaimed the gentleman, he turned into St Martin's Lane and began his search for the Green Posts.

It was not difficult to find, for a newly painted signboard, set flat against the wall in accordance with the new regulations, proclaimed it. It was a tenement, with a fashionable head-dresser's occupying the ground floor, a coffee-house the second, and presumably lodgings above. There was nothing to indicate the whereabouts of the quack doctor, until Derrick spied a narrow alley-way running down the side of the building, and entering the mouth of this, he saw that above an outside staircase, so steep that a rope handrail had been put up, there swung under a lanthorn a board which had the Signs of the Zodiac painted crudely upon it. Here, evidently, was his destination, and squaring his shoulders he climbed the stair and knocked briskly upon a door at the top. After a moment shuffling footsteps sounded from within, the door was opened a crack, and the head and shoulders of a seedy-looking individual, wearing one of those tall hats affected by astrologers, and with a candle in his hand, appeared in the opening, and a voice, accompanied by a stink of brandy so strong that Derrick involuntarily withdrew a step, demanded his business.

"Is all in harmony?" asked Derrick in a stage whisper; and began to undo the two top buttons of his coat.

The man mumbled something, withdrew a chain from the door, and opening it wider, beckoned Derrick within. Here, it seemed, was Dr Amos Bendigo in person, a bizarre figure in a gown embroidered all over in gold with astrological signs, a long chain round his neck from which depended a bunch of tarnished charms, and a pair of steel spectacles balanced upon his nose. Holding up the skirts of his gown to reveal a pair of spindly legs and down-at-heel pattens, he shuffled ahead of his visitor down a dark and evil-smelling passage, and ushered him into a chamber already occupied by some dozen or so men. Then, without a word, he abruptly withdrew.

Left stranded, Derrick propped himself against the wall, the few chairs begin requisitioned, and viewed the company, all of whom had ceased their talk at his entrance but now resumed it. They were a curiously assorted bunch; one or two looked like respectable shopkeepers or small craftsmen, others were plainly apprentices, the rest might have been anything from a disguised lord to a chimney-sweep. Some talked in groups, but here and there a solitary figure sat or stood apart, and these all had the same air of nervousness, keeping their eyes down or glancing furtively at their companions, the while they seemed intent on making themselves as inconspicuous as possible. Here, thought Derrick, were new recruits, the 'Honest Men' who had come to hear 'Good Tidings'. Edging his way towards one of these solitary figures, he smiled, and said in an undertone:

"Methinks you are as strange here as I am, friend. I know no one in this room, nor what is expected of me."

The man's eyes shot up at him, then immediately dropped.

"I'm told there's the rhino in it," he mumbled, "and being out of a post at present, I'm willing to give anything a trial. I – "

He broke off abruptly, as an inner door opened, a man's figure was outlined for a moment against the light from within (this outer chamber was almost in darkness), one of the company who stood nearest slipped through into the other apartment, and the door closed again.

"It seems we are to go in singly to hear these good tidings," said Derrick to the man with whom he had been talking.

The other merely nodded, seeming disinclined for further conversation, so Derrick said no more but set himself to rehearse what he should say when it came to his turn to be beckoned into that inner chamber. He had to wait some time, and meanwhile other figures, some singly, some in pairs, were ushered into the waiting-room by the astrologer. Not one was known to Derrick by sight, and all had the appearance of being new to the business. It was more and more evident that this was some kind of a sorting-house for new recruits, where their credentials were examined, their opinions gauged, and their suitability or otherwise decided upon. Whoever was at the bottom of this conspiracy, he seemed to be a thorough, methodical man.

At last it was Derrick who was standing nearest to that inner door, and who, in response to a signal from the half-seen person within, walked round it and heard it shut behind him. He found himself in a small and extremely stuffy bedchamber, evidently the quack doctor's, for an astrological calendar hung upon the wall and a bunch of horoscopes was kept in place by the frame of a portrait of Galen. The tent-bed took up most of the space, leaving room only for a small table and two rickety chairs. The table was covered with papers, except for one clear space in which reposed conspicuously a pile of silver coins. All these things did Derrick take in at a glance, then turned his attention to the only other person in the room, who now, motioning the visitor to sit in one of the chairs, sat himself down on the other before the table.

He was an old man, well over sixty, a little stooped, but with something soldier-like in his bearing, and with the brightest black eyes Derrick had ever seen. A scar, having the appearance of a sword-cut, slightly lifted one lip and ran up under his unfashionable moustachios almost to his brow; these moustachios were snow-white, and so was his short wiry hair (for he had taken off his peruke and flung it on the bed). His movements were jerky and restless, and from this, as also from the disorder of the papers on the table, Derrick guessed that he was a man of action rather than one accustomed to clerical work. In this first scrutiny of him, his visitor found him oddly familiar, though convinced that they had never met before. He had seen that face somewhere, those fanatical eyes, that disfiguring scar, those heavy military moustachios; but there was no time to ponder on the familiarity just now, for the man was beginning his questioning and Derrick needed all his wits about him. The man's voice was harsh, his tones abrupt and cold, in striking contrast with his burning eyes, which, while he spoke, bored through Derrick like gimlets.

"Who sent you here, friend?"

It was the question which, of course, Derrick had anticipated. He answered glibly:

"Sir, there you have me at a disadvantage. For the friend, or rather acquaintance, who made known to me this meeting, by showing me the handbill you wot of and explaining to me how it was enciphered, did so in his cups, and therefore, by your leave, I must suppress his name, since otherwise he might incur your displeasure. Yet I am sure he blabbed only because he knew me by my talk to be of his way of thinking, and would be close with other men. 'Twas his disclosure to me of the secret method of advertisement that was at fault, said he, and he would not let me go until I had given my word not to disclose his name to you."

It was a somewhat weak explanation, but the best that Derrick had been able to invent. The man continued to stare at him, and snapped:

"And what is your way of thinking?"

"Why," answered Derrick blandly, "I am a great lover of liberty and the Protestant faith, both of which I perceive to be in some peril at this time."

The other nodded briefly, drew towards him a sheet of paper, which seemed to contain a kind of list, and said:

"Let me hear your name and occupation."

"My name, sir," said Derrick, "is Hill, Simon Hill, at your service. I am a gentleman of good estate in the county of Sussex, but at present am on a visit to London. You must know, sir, that we in the country parts hear nothing but stale news and rumours, and being dissatisfied with these, which have informed me only that the principles I serve seem to be altogether decayed, I resolved to come hither to town and discover for myself how went the great world. What I have discovered so far hath made my heart heavier than before, since it would seem that Popery and tyranny are the two gods served at Whitehall, and that even in the City, ever the stronghold of the Good Old Cause, honest men's hearts have failed them, and the chief citizens are become the creatures of the Court."

The man nodded again, this time with a slight air of approval.

"Where do you lodge, Mr Hill?" he asked abruptly.

"There again," answered Derrick with a rueful smile, "I am at a disadvantage to give you an answer. For you must know that my sole remaining kinsman is a rich uncle, and when I come to town I needs must stay at his house, for if I did otherwise it would mad him, and you can scarce blame me for humouring one from whom I have great expectations. This uncle of mine is deep in love with the Divine Right of Kings and other such outmoded tyrannies, and if he knew I had come hither tonight would certainly cut me out of his will. Therefore, under your favour, I think it necessary to keep his name secret."

"Yet if you join with us," objected the other, "you needs must have some place where we can communicate with you." He considered for a moment. "Ere you take your leave tonight, if our talk hath proved fruitful I will give you the name of a tavern where you must call daily for letters and messages which may be sent you as need arises."

Derrick acquiesced readily in this arrangement, and, the preliminary examination of the recruit having passed off satisfactorily, the man set himself to explain the reason for the gathering tonight.

The first part of his harangue was tedious and disappointing in its vagueness; Derrick had heard the same thing a hundred times before, or read it in the Whig tracts. It was the old, old story of a tyrannous king, a Papist heir, free men repressed, parliamentary privileges ignored, proud prelates trampling upon liberty of conscience, patriots persecuted or neglected, the kingdom groaning under manifold abuses, the Court given over to lechery and idleness, and so on and so forth, all stale and trite enough, and saved from intolerable dullness only by the fire in the speaker's eyes which gave to his abrupt tones a kind of icy brilliance. Derrick for his part nodded gravely at intervals, but otherwise sat meek and quiet, apparently digesting the lecture and hanging upon every word. And then, suddenly, he no longer needed to feign interest, for, breaking off his harangue in the middle of a sentence, the stranger crashed his fist upon the table, and cried with a ferocity that was obviously genuine:

"It is intolerable, and is no longer to be borne!"

"Ah!" breathed Derrick, leaning forward eagerly. "That, sir, is what I came to hear."

"We have tried," continued the other, speaking in a quieter but no less intense tone, "every lawful means for overthrowing the designs of Charles Stuart and his brother against our religion and our liberty. We have opened their eyes to Papist plots, and have shown them, through the evidence of Dr Oates, how the Jesuits would stick at nothing in their designs to bring England into slavery. We have endeavoured through Parliament to warn them that the fate of their father will be theirs if they persist in trampling upon the freedom of Englishmen; and, failing in all these measures, we would have appealed to the sword at the time of the Oxford Parliament, had it not been that the nation was become indolent and besotted and would not rise. Therefore one course only remains to us, and that is to band together all true friends of liberty and the Protestant faith, and, when the time is ripe, to make a bid for the Good Old Cause by armed revolt both in London and the country."

"And you think we may succeed, sir?" asked Derrick anxiously.

For the first time the other permitted himself a slight, sardonic smile.

"Mr Hill," said he, tilting back his chair and folding his arms across his breast, "I am an old man and have seen much of the history of the last forty years, ay, and have been concerned in it. I saw the Good Old Cause triumphant in '49, when the head of a tyrant king rolled upon the scaffold at Whitehall yonder, I saw godliness and liberty established, the nation cleansed from the abominations of Popery and Prelacy, the New Jerusalem descending, fair and chaste as a bride. And had it not been for the ambitions of Protector Cromwell, I should see it still. We have no Cromwells now, sir, or if we have they shall meet with scant ceremony once we are established again as a free commonwealth. We are a band of brothers, Mr Hill, owning no man our master upon earth, but resolved to make this kingdom into a republic again, ay, and keep it so, without government by a single person, House of Lords, bishops, or any other tyrant, believing all men to be equal before God, and needing no magistrates or priests. This we are upon is a crusade, sir, no less; the might of Jehovah is with us, and we cannot fail."

Derrick said nothing for a moment, absorbed in a new discovery. For what he had just heard had given him a clue to the stranger's identity; that hot republicanism, that levelling talk, that hatred of Cromwell, that boast of being so much concerned in the history of the last forty years, all combined to inform him where he had seen that scarred face and fanatical eyes before. They had stared at him from many a tract and broadsheet during his youth, and they belonged to Major Wildman, Wildman the Leveller, a soldier in Fairfax's Life Guards, major in Reynold's Horse, arrested for plotting against Cromwell, arrested again soon after the Restoration for republican plots, imprisoned in the Scilly Isles and later for seven years in Pendennis Castle, and at last released on his giving security never more to conspire against the Government. It was said that he had gone abroad; but here he was home again, and plotting harder than ever. Curious that such a man should be a leading figure of a conspiracy which, if Derrick's suspicions were correct, was an attempt to place the Duke of Monmouth on the throne.

"Sir," said he, realising that his cogitations had made him silent, and that Wildman was looking sharply at him, "all that you have told me hath filled my drooping heart with a new hope. I protest, that if there is aught I can do to further your righteous aims, you have but to command me. My fortune, alas, consists chiefly in land, my father when he died leaving me great debts which ate up all the money in his coffers, the which I cannot replenish until the expectations I have from my uncle are realised. Yet if there is any other way in which I can be of service, I beg that you will let me hear it, and assure you I shall not be backward in assisting you to the limit of my powers."

Wildman's face had fallen a little during this speech, and now he said gruffly:

"I had hoped you might be able to aid us with money, Mr Hill, for this is a commodity in which we are somewhat lacking at present. We ask recruits to subscribe according to their means, but many come to us who have to be supported in return for other services. Nevertheless, we make no doubt of getting all we require from the goldsmiths' coffers once we have drawn the sword. For yourself, I must bethink me how 'twill be best to employ you. You have, I observe, a smooth tongue in your head, and it may be we can use that to win over others. For the present, hold yourself in readiness to attend upon any command we may think fit to bestow, and call daily, if you please, at the Young Devil tavern by Temple Bar. When we wish to communicate with you, the message will be enciphered by the same method as that of the hand bill giving notice of this meeting. You are sure you understand how to read such a cipher? 'Tis very simple."

Derrick, smiling inwardly, assured him that he did, and promised to be exact in executing all commands laid upon him by this means. Giving him a nod of definite approval, Wildman rose.

"I have many yet to interview," said he, jerking his head towards the waiting-room, "and our talk hath been longer than ordinary. You will leave, sir, through yonder door which brings you into the house by another way. Pray, one last word, Mr Hill; you will, if you are wise, keep a close tongue in your head concerning all you have heard and seen this night, and likewise all that you may hear and see in the future. If you do not, you will regret it. We are engaged upon the Lord's work, sir, and will stomach neither traitors nor those who cannot keep a close tongue."

Having uttered this threat, Wildman made a curt gesture of dismissal, and making his exit by the door indicated, Derrick found himself in the passage again. There was no sign of Dr Amos Bendigo, so he made his own way out of the house. It was nearly eleven o' clock, he discovered as he emerged into St Martin's Lane; sleepy householders were extinguishing the lanthorns above their doors, prostitutes were scurrying homeward lest they be caught by the Watch, and from the taverns debouched all those cautious citizens who shunned the thief-infested streets after this hour.

But Derrick had no thought of lurking cut-purses as he walked homewards towards his wife's fine house in its fashionable square, being quite absorbed in all that had passed this evening. He had got upon the trail of a plot, and from the use of an identical password it was obviously that same conspiracy in which poor Mr Jolly had become entangled. From Wildman's obvious approval of him, he must have played his part well, and might expect to hear more from the conspirators. He would be watched closely, of course, held at arm's length, perhaps, for a time, and until he had committed himself by actually partaking in treason, would scarcely be trusted with the inner counsels of the gang. There was always the risk that they might happen upon his real identity before he could go to the authorities with proof of the reality of the plot. There was also the counter risk that if the Government chanced upon the scent of the conspiracy before he had informed them of it, he might find himself implicated; either way he stood an excellent chance of losing his life.

But his mood was exultant; he was hot upon the trail of treason; he had made a promising start; and while he risked only his own neck in his investigations, he was resolved to pursue them to the end.

Chapter Five

Derrick had to wait nearly a week before he had any word from the conspirators. Going daily to the Young Devil tavern and finding nothing he had begun to fear that Wildman had decided after all not to employ him. But on Christmas Eve, on approaching the landlord and asking as usual if there was anything for Mr Hill, his hopes leapt again when the man, fishing beneath the counter, drew forth a thick packet which he placed in Derrick's hand.

"If you wish to examine it at once, neighbour," said the landlord, "you may be private in the chamber yonder, and I will see that you are not intruded upon."

Derrick, making a mental note to the effect that the landlord himself most probably was in the conspiracy, thanked him, and entered the parlour indicated. Finding laid ready on the table an ink-horn, a bunch of quills, and some blank sheets of paper (which seemed to confirm his suspicions that mine host was one of the 'Friends in Harmony'), he broke the wafer which sealed the packet and prepared to decipher his instructions. Enclosed within the letter to himself there was another, likewise sealed only by a wafer; it bore no inscription, and for the moment he put it aside. His own seemed to be a letter of business from one merchant to another, but when he had fashioned another 'grill' he discovered that in contained the following instructions:

"You are to deliver the Enclosed, without loss of time, to my Lord Grey at his house of Up Park near Chichester. You being a Sussex man doubtless will know it. You will stay for an Answer, and returning post haste, will put it into the hands of Mr Shephard, a wine merchant, at the Sign of the Bunch of Grapes in Abchurch Lane leading out of Lombard Street."

Having deciphered his own instructions, Derrick's attention turned to the letter he was to deliver to Lord Grey. It would be the easiest thing in the world to break the wafer and seal it up again, since the paste bore no impression of a signet, and he wondered that his new employers should be so trusting of an unknown recruit. But since he was convinced that the landlord of the Young Devil was in the plot, he hesitated to deal with the second letter here, lest he be spied upon or interrupted and his treachery reported to the mangers of the conspiracy. So, curbing his impatience as best he could, he put the letter in his pocket, nodded to the landlord as he passed through the common-room, and hurried home. There, locked in his own chamber, he broke the wafer and spread open the paper on the table before him; then he smiled ruefully, for now he perceived why it had been give into his hands so trustingly. It was a meaningless jumble of letters, enciphered by some method impossible to understand save by the expert in cryptography. His smile broadened into one of triumph, and he blessed the boyhood whim which had made this art his earliest hobby.

There was no time just then for beginning his task, for he had to go on duty, and it being the festive season, when the Court was keeping holiday, he was detained at Whitehall until late at night. While he was there, he sought and obtained audience with the Lord Chamberlain of the Household on a personal matter, and telling my lord that his father the parson was sick and earnestly desired his presence at home, begged leave of absence as soon as was convenient. The Chamberlain proffered a sympathy which made Derrick ashamed of his necessary lie, and told him he might have forty-eight hours' leave of absence on the day after Christmas.

When at last he was able to lock himself into his own room again that night, Derrick lost no time in attempting his deciphering. Once more did he fetch down Trithemius and Bacon from his shelf, and this time studied also his frequency tables, having taken careful note of the number of times each letter of the alphabet appeared in the paper under his hand. He tried the simplest methods first, but after two hours' work had discovered that they would not fit. He began to fear that he had to do with a key-word cipher, and rising once more took down the little book in which he had listed, over a period of many years, the favourite key-words of several centuries. Each in turn he tried, and all in vain. Could it be, he wondered wearily, that most rare of ciphers, the syllable cipher, in which substitution or transposition was made on the basis of syllables instead of single letters? He set to work once more, but again he found he was on the wrong track. There was one last hope: a key-phrase, which, he knew, must be some phrase or sentence containing the exact number of letters, in the alphabet, but, unlike the key-word, could have recurring letters, a fact which made the method only the more difficult to decipher because not only letters but figures were used in it. Looking at the paper again, he saw that certainly figures were mixed up with the letters here, yet this did not necessarily mean that this was a key-phrase cipher. However, he had tried every other method known to him, and it was vital for him to get at the clear.

It was getting daylight, and Derrick's head swam with weariness, but he drew a fresh sheet of paper towards him and began his task afresh. The use of a difficult cipher argued that the clear was of great importance and secrecy, and here was the most difficult of all, for it might be impossible even for the most experienced cryptographer to hit upon the key-phrase employed. Recalling all that ever he had heard of such things, he remembered that what chiefly was used was some text, line of a song, slogan, or common expression favoured by the society or organisation which found a cipher necessary. He tried the most popular slogans of the Opposition, the catch-phrases invented during the Exclusion rage and the Titus Oates plot, but either these had not the necessary number of letters or else they would not break the cipher. Then he racked his brains for some phrase used by the present conspirators, but found he knew scarcely any; there were the few cant terms he had got from Mr Jolly, 'the Blackbird and the Goldfinch', 'the General Point and the Lopping Point', but they would not fit. Neither would the password and counter-sign, 'Is all in harmony?' 'In harmony and liberty' – but stay! What was it they called themselves? – 'Friends in Harmony.' Sixteen letters. Something told him he was on the right track at last. But three must be ten letters more. He tried various words which seemed suitable, but was growing so exhausted that his brain almost refused to function.

Obstinately resolved upon one last attempt before he gave up for the moment, he fetched the quack's handbill from where he had hidden it, and, searching desperately for inspiration, studied it anew. It began "Friends in Harmony"; was there any other possible clue further on? Yes, by God there was! " …any Honest Man who is a Friend to Liberty." 'Friends in Harmony and Liberty' – twenty-six letters. At least it was worth a trial. With a hand which shook more from excitement that weariness now, Derrick wrote down the phrase, and beneath it the letters of the alphabet:

FR I ENDS IN HARMONY AND LI BE RTY
ABCDE FG HI J KLMNOP QRS TUVWXYZ

Then he noted the frequencies; the letter E in the alphabet, the most frequent letter in English text, was represented, if he had indeed hit upon the key-phrase, by the letter D in the message, but it occurred again later in the word 'Liberty'. And there it was 'D2'. He had got it! There remained only the task of the actual deciphering.

The street cries were beginning their raucous chorus, and his wife's maids were bustling about the house, when Derrick, grey and haggard with exhaustion, read the message to Lord Grey:

"All here are agreed that Ferguson must be recall'd, and this without loss of time. Unity is not to be had without him, and delay becomes more dangerous as our Forces grow. If those in the Country be not yet ready, we cannot stay for them as we did in November, but make sure of London first. It must be done when the Blackbird and the Goldfinch are next at Newmarket, which will be in March, for then will the most of the Guards be with them. Argyll has won over Melville and some other great ones, but still insists that the English rise first and likewise that they pay for the Scots rising; he demands 30,000, and the loan of 1,000 horse. In London we have sufficiency of arms, but let us know without fail what strength of them there is in Sussex; we are seeking the same information from Rowles, Drake, Young, and

Courtney in the several parts for which they are answerable.

"Some arms are promis'd from Holland, but Shaftesbury is very sick and his condition is such that we fear to rely upon him. Russell is sure of the Western Counties, and we make no doubt of having Cheshire. The Duke would be advis'd to return without delay to Town and the Council of Six to be set up again, that the Managers here may confer with him and them as the time draws near. We would have you note that 'tis the Opinion of all in London that the General Point cannot succeed unless the Lopping Point be undertaken first, for we remember '41, and are resolv'd that this time the Churchwarden of Whitehall shall not be able to set up his Standard. Yet many here will have assurance first that the Duke cannot turn round on us when 'tis done, and we look to you to bind him to it."

Derrick went about his duties at Whitehall that day with the feeling that he had on his shoulders a burden almost too heavy to be borne. The extent of the conspiracy, as gathered from this letter, terrified him; Scotland and the country parts were to rise simultaneously with the disaffected in London; arms were promised from Holland (he saw in this the connivance of the King's nephew and the Duke of York's son-in-law, the Prince of Orange, whom many thought to be aiming at the throne); old republicans like Wildman had allied themselves with respectable Whigs such as Russell; the vain and ambitious Monmouth was hand-in-glove with those who conspired an armed rebellion; the thing was to be done when the 'Blackbird and the Goldfinch' (obviously King Charles and his brother) were at the Newmarket races and London left unprotected by the Life Guards who accompanied them;

and worst of all, there was that sinister term, the 'Lopping Point', which must be undertaken ere the 'Churchwarden of Whitehall' (the King) could set up his Standard, as his father had done in 1641.

It was not difficult to guess now, thought Derrick with a shudder, at the meaning of the 'Lopping Point'. Yet was it possible that even Monmouth would stoop so low as to connive at a plot to assassinate his father? For the matter of that, it was hard to imagine honest Whigs like Essex and Russell consenting to it. Yet perhaps, he reflected, there were really two plots, one for insurrection, another for assassination; the letter seemed to indicate that this was so. If it were, it would be essential to the second bunch of conspirators to ensure that Monmouth was in some way implicated in their vile scheme, for otherwise, when his friends had foisted him on to the throne of England, he must, for his reputation's sake, bring to justice those who had slain his father. Nor would it be difficult to implicate him; he was stupid, entirely under the influence of those who flattered him, lacking in any discretion, and ridden by his ambition to be king. In all probability it was to unite the two sets of conspirators and fuse the two plots into one, that Ferguson, that prince of plotters, was to be recalled. The only comfort Derrick could find from his reading of this letter was that he himself had some little time in which to seek for solid proof of the conspiracy, since the month mentioned for striking was March, and it was now only the end of December.

It was the heaviest Christmas he had ever known. Bitter indeed was it for him to watch the King and his courtiers enjoying the festive season, carefree and gay, while all the time a mine was preparing beneath their feet and they in utter ignorance of it. Old in his experience of the Court, Derrick was aware that for him to lay an information at this juncture would be useless and perhaps disastrous.

Throughout the reign there had been nothing but real plots and sham plots; the King was heartily sick of them, and although he was aware of the desperateness of a certain faction among those who opposed him, he was confident in the good sense of the nation as a whole and secure in his huge popularity. He would not listen, Derrick was convinced, to any talk of a fresh conspiracy unless the most convincing proof, with chapter and verse, were produced. Especially if such a conspiracy seemed to implicate his beloved Monmouth. And even if he did, if an investigation by the authorities were undertaken straightaway, only the small fry among the conspirators would be caught; the great ones, the managers, would contrive to wriggle out. If, for instance, Derrick produced the letter to Lord Grey as proof, Wildman might hang for it, but Grey himself and his noble friends simply would disown any knowledge of it. No, the lone investigator must travel yet further on his perilous path before he could share the intolerable burden of his knowledge with those whose duty it was to expose and punish treason.

On the day after Christmas, telling his indifferent wife that he was making a visit to his father in Sussex (she held that decayed parsonage in the utmost horror and never went there herself), Derrick mounted his horse early in the morning, lay that night at an inn on the borders of his native county, and next day, with the letter which he had resealed tucked in his breast, continued his journey towards Chichester.

He arrived at Up Park, Lord Grey's country seat, just as the early dark was falling, tired after a thirty-mile ride over roads which were deep in mud and in parts flooded. The great house blazed with light, and from the sounds which issued from it, it was clear that the Christmas festivities were still in full swing. As Derrick dismounted and approached the main doors, out came a party of mummers, the Doctor, St George, the Fool with his bladder, and all the rest of the merry gang, who, by their gait and laughter, seemed to have enjoyed lavish hospitality from my lord. Tying his horse to a post in the courtyard, Derrick went to the doors and peered within. The hall was in disorder, candles unsnuffed and spilling grease on to the rugs, the Yule-log on the hearth half slipped from its dogs, a chair overturned, tables a-swim with wine, and a couple of hounds fighting over what looked like the half-eaten carcase of a goose. There was no one in sight, but from a chamber on the right came an uproar of drunken voices, the smashing of a glass, inane laughter, and other sounds which told plainly of a carouse. As he stood wondering what to do, the door of this room was flung open, a personage in black, with a chain of office round his neck, who was obviously a major-domo or steward and who was as drunk as his masters, came rolling out, speeded on his way by a barrage of apples and oranges which were pelted after him by unseen hands from within.

"I have business with my Lord Grey," said Derrick loudly from the door. "Be so good as to summon a servant to take care of my horse, and notify my lord that a gentleman from London brings an important billet which must be delivered into his hands."

The steward paused, and, swaying gently, rolled a bleared eye in Derrick's direction.

"His lor'ship's engaged," he drawled, with a ludicrous attempt at dignity which was spoilt by a violent hiccough. "Festive sheason – no bhusiness – tomorrow – "

"On second thoughts, I shall attend to my horse myself," snapped Derrick, who feared that the grooms might be in the same condition as the steward. "While I am about it, do you go to my lord and tell him what I have told you. I must have speech with him instanter, festive season or no."

He found the stables without much difficulty; there was not a servant to be seen, but from a building beside it, plainly the mews, issued the sounds of country voices, the squawking of falcons, and a jingle of bells, indicating that my lord and his friends had spent the day a-hawking. Derrick rubbed down his tired horse, found water, oats, and clean straw, and in due course returned to the house, where he found a swarthy-faced man, with heavy-lidded, slightly protuberant eyes and a sensual mouth, pacing up and down the hall in an irritable manner. This was Forde, Lord Grey, who Derrick had seen sometimes at Court, but not lately, for my lord had been prosecuted last month for abducting his wife's sister, being already in disgrace for his part in the assault upon the Lord Mayor of London in the summer. It was said that he had bought his way out of his new trouble, and would never come up for judgement. His condition at the moment, though suggestive of heavy drinking, was controlled, and the eyes that scrutinised Derrick were alert.

"You are the gentleman from London, I suppose," said my lord curtly. "Where a-devil have you been all this time?"

"Attending to my horse, my lord," replied Derrick in the same tone. "I would not trust him to your grooms in their condition. I was bidden carry this letter to you, and to await an answer."

"You know me, it seems," said Grey softly, "and for the matter of that I have seen you somewhere before. I cannot call to mind the occasion, yet am I sure your face is familiar."

" 'Twas with hawk and hound very likely," said Derrick, outwardly smiling, inwardly uneasy. "I am a Sussex man, my lord, from another part of the county, and employ much of my time in field-sports."

"But are at present residing in London, I take it?" queried Grey suavely. "Seeing the sights of the town?"

"Rather endeavouring, my lord," retorted Derrick primly, "to serve certain principles dearer to me than all the falcons and horseflesh in England. For you must know that I am one of the Friends in Harmony. Will your lordship please to take the letter?"

Grey stretched out his hand for it in silence. It was a broad, blunt hand, more honest than the face above it, the hand of a country gentleman. There was one unpleasant moment when Grey turned the letter over and over in this broad hand of his, as though looking to see if it had been tampered with. But he only said to Derrick, with his enigmatic smile:

"I foresee that the reading of this may occupy some time. I have guests, as you may have gathered from the sounds yonder, but will not trouble you with their company, for truth to tell they are somewhat foxed. If you will bide here, sir," he added, opening a door next to that from behind which came the sounds of revelry, "I will have refreshment brought you, and you may take some ease after your long ride. I think you did not tell me your name?"

"Simon Hill, at your lordship's service," replied Derrick with a bow.

"Hill," repeated my lord, ushering Derrick into a pleasant chamber in which a fire of beech-logs was burning on the hearth. "H'm, it doth not recall to me where we met before. But 'tis of no consequence. You will excuse me now, Mr Hill; I shall not detain you longer than is necessary."

He went out and closed the door, and Derrick, listening intently, heard him enter the adjoining room. But when that door closed also, there was silence; not even a murmur of voices came to him, for the mansion was old, well-built, with thick walls. He waited, thinking hard. Presently the drunken steward staggered in with a tray of cold goose and buttered-ale; directly the man had gone, Derrick turned to an examination of the window. It was essential to make every effort at overhearing the conversation which must be going on in the adjoining chamber; he dared not go out and listen at the door for fear of being caught; his only chance, therefore, was to get out of the window of his own room and creep round to that of the other. It was a risky business, and might prove fruitless, but he was resolved to attempt it.

As quietly as possible he opened one of the casements, climbed out, and found himself upon a terrace, bounded on the one side by a balustrade with statues which gleamed palely in the gloom. Keeping himself flat against the house-wall, he crept along until he was come to the window of the adjoining room; it was tight closed, and heavy curtains were drawn over it, but by pressing his ear close to the glass, he found that, when the voices within were raised, he could make out what was said. This was something at least, and as it was impossible to find means of overhearing the whole conversation, he set himself to concentrate on straining his ears to catch a sentence here and there. There was one voice which was raised in a high, petulant tone whenever it spoke; this he had no difficulty in recognising as the Duke of Monmouth's; another with a slight stutter he identified as belonging to Baron Howard of Escrick, once an officer in Cromwell's Life Guards, and lately conspicuous as voting for the death of his poor old kinsman, Lord Stafford, accused by Titus Oates. Neither of these two was speaking at the moment, so that for some time all that Derrick could hear was a confused murmur, until suddenly Momouth cried:

"Wildman only repeats Shaftesbury's lies when he brags of London being ready. We heard enough of the ten thousand Brisk Boys and the invisible army when 'Shiftesbury' was at Thanet House."

It seemed as though someone tried to soothe him, for next moment he retorted:

"Don't fox me with that stuff. Ferguson is 'Shiftesbury's' spaniel, as I very well know, and for the matter of that, there's scarce a man in the business who is not my unfriend. Wildman, Walcot, Holms, what were they but Cromwell's officers, no friends to a king but hot republicans. And you likewise, Will Howard, protest how you will!"

"James," snapped Grey's voice, suddenly raised, "don't talk like a fool. When the blow is struck, you must needs be the rallying-point and refuge for us all, for... "

He lowered his voice again, and Derrick could not hear the rest. Then:

"Not the Lopping Point, Forde," cried Monmouth unsteadily.

"Speak not of that to me, for you know I cannot bear it and must hear nought of it – "

Howard's stutter interrupted him, but it was not distinct enough for the eavesdropper to catch more than a few scattered words – "b-blame on the P-papists," "Oates h-has his lesson p-pat." But Monmouth, it seemed, was not to be soothed.

"Oates is utterly discredited," he cried peevishly, "and must not be trusted with our plans. Nay, if the Lopping Point must be undertaken, let it be the Goldfinch only that is snared. I can manage the Blackbird and he the kingdom, and when he dies I shall get the throne without any more blood."

"Lower your voice for God's sake," snapped Grey harshly. "Not all my servants are to be trusted, and such shouting out of treason may hang us all."

So again there were only stray words and phrases for the eavesdropper at the window. From these he gathered that the discussion had turned upon the amount of arms needed by or in the possession of the conspirators; he caught the words 'public magazine', 'Artillery Ground', 'demi-cannon', and once Grey's voice saying something about "eighty good muskets hid in my" (the next word was inaudible) "since the proposed rising last month." Derrick must have stood there a full half-hour, shivering with cold and nervous tension, before, hearing some sounds which seemed to indicate that the party was breaking up, he slipped quickly back into the adjoining chamber, fastened the window, and, for appearance's sake, ate and drank from the tray. While he was at it, he heard someone leave the chamber next door; from the comparative steadiness of the footsteps it sounded like Lord Grey, but he could not be sure. Whoever it was went upstairs and was absent there some while; when at last he returned, he came straight to the door of Derrick's room, opened it, and entered. It was indeed Lord Grey, and he held a letter in his hand.

"You being such a lover of our principles, Mr Hill," said he (and surely there was a trace of irony in his tone?), "will be eager to return to London with all speed, so I will not seek to detain you further. Here is your letter; pray guard it well, for if it miscarried I fear the consequences for you would not be pleasant."

Derrick, ignoring this politely expressed threat, made a great show of tucking the letter into the toe of his boot, and bidding my lord a hasty farewell, went round to fetch his horse. He rode hard for some fifteen miles, thus putting a comparatively safe distance between him and any of Grey's tenants who might report his movements to their lord, then he knocked up a hedge-inn, obtained a bed of straw in the loft, and by the aid of one guttering candle set to work to examine Grey's letter. He found that it was enciphered by the same system as the one he had carried from London, and so, with the key-phrase in his possession, he had no difficulty in breaking the cipher. But his satisfaction at this soon turned to chagrin when he found how disappointingly short, curt, and uninformative was my Lord Grey's reply to Wildman.

"It is agreed that Ferguson should be recalled, and this may be done though Shephard, who knows his whereabouts in Holland, in a letter under some canting guise. I cannot answer yet for Sussex, and as for Essex, there are not ten men there I can trust. Arms are not lacking, but most men are lukewarm. The Duke will return to Town. Let me alone to manage him, and do you proceed with preparations for the Lopping Point, for until that's done, we waste our time with the other."

Derrick swore. There was nothing which could not be made to have an innocent explanation if the letter were laid before the authorities and enquiries set on foot; even the recalling of Ferguson, a man wanted by the Law, could be passed over, for it was a very common name. Here again the word 'arms' was risky, but it was not nearly enough for his purposes. But wait, there was a postscript; he began to read it without much hope, but had not gone far before he felt his skin prick with apprehension.

"It is advis'd that you make further enquiries concerning the messenger you sent to me with yours. I believe I have met him, but cannot recall the occasion. It was not, I am assured, in Sussex, as he suggests; I know no Simon Hills in these parts. Trust him no further until you have pried closely into his affairs."

Derrick leaned back in his chair and stared frowning at that postscript. So he had not just imagined that Grey had regarded him with suspicion; my lord must have seen him at Court, and by some cursed accident had remembered the face of a humble Gentleman Usher. But he did not yet remember where he had seen him; that was one comfort. Getting out his pen-knife, Derrick very carefully cut off the postscript from the rest of the letter and burnt it at the candle flame. The remaining half-sheet looked odd, and might arouse suspicion, but he would have to risk that. He copied down what was written on it in case this might come in useful, and tucked the original into his boot again. Then he lay down to rest.

But he could not sleep. He was so near getting proof, he thought, tossing from side to side on the lousy straw, and yet so far. He had heard so much, but hearsay was useless. His eavesdropping this evening had rewarded him only with a justification of his previous suspicion that by the 'Lopping Point' was meant assassination, and that Monmouth, though averse to it, would be bullied or tricked into it by his friends. But suspicion was not evidence, and his own word, unsupported by a second witness, would find no credence with Privy Councillors and judges who were in the first throes of their shame at accepting so gullibly the lies of 'Dr' Titus Oates.

Proof he must gain, proof or a second witness; and quickly too, before Grey remembered where he had seen him before and had him silenced. When he slept at last, he still tossed restlessly, like a man in a fever, and as soon as it was light he was spurring on towards London again, galloping break-neck as though he hoped such speed could bring him nearer to his elusive goal.

Chapter Six

Throughout the entire month of January, Derrick's painstaking and solitary investigations went unrewarded. His sole cause for congratulation consisted in the assurance that so far he was not suspected by the London managers of the Plot. He saw nothing of Lord Grey, so supposed he was still in Sussex; but he learned at Court that Monmouth had returned to his house of Moor Park in Hertfordshire, where he appeared to be passing his time in wenching, drinking, and hunting. Meanwhile, Wildman and the others believing Derrick to be a gentleman of leisure, employed him in carrying messages backwards and forwards to their friends in different parts of the town.

From these activities he learned little more than the extent of the conspiracy, which alarmed and depressed him; it was like a pestilence affecting high and low alike. There was a large number of Scotsmen concerned in it, some resident in London, some making journeys to and from their native land, and these, it seemed, were in constant communication with Argyll and other Scots noblemen. The Whig pamphleteers, headed by the fanatical Henry Care, Lord Russell's chaplain, were in it as a matter of course, as also were a group of Cromwell's old officers, Major Holms, Lieutenant Colonel Walcot, Wildman, and others; and there was a sprinkling of lawyers, West, a barrister of the Temple, John Ayloffe, who had distinguished himself by putting a wooden shoe, the symbol of slavery, into the Speaker's Chair in the House of Commons, Aaron Smith, Norton, Wade, and Tyley. Several substantial citizens were involved: Josiah Keeling, Mr Jolly's friend, Zachary Bourn, a rich brewer, and Thomas Shephard of the Bunch of Grapes, a wine merchant. Then there was a host of poor men, some fanatical, some merely greedy for gain: Lea, a dyer, Forbes, a Scots pedlar, Hone, a joiner, and the like. There was another Derrick often heard referred to, but never to his knowledge saw; it was the custom at some meetings to drink to 'Hannibal and his Boys', but who 'Hannibal' was he could not discover.

Of the great ones in it, Monmouth and his friends, Essex, Grey, Russell, Howard, and Algernon Sidney, formed what was known as 'The Council of Six', and so far as Derrick could gather, these had the ordering of the insurrection plan. From the fact that several of them were avowed republicans, it was obvious that they supported Monmouth and his ambitions only because they would need him as a shield against the public indignation when and if their plans succeeded. How far any one of them was committed to the assassination scheme, Derrick could not tell, except in the case of Grey. It was this scheme, referred to always as the 'Lopping Point', that worried him more than all, not only because of its horror, but because he could never discover the slightest detail concerning it. Indeed it was still only a guess on his part that the cant term meant the slaughter of the King. References to it in the messages he carried were few and evasive, and he was never admitted into those private conclaves during which, he supposed, it was discussed.

After so many weeks of investigation which had borne so little fruit yet had told him so much, Derrick Calder was become changed. The awful knowledge which he could not share, the threat hanging over his King and country, the general atmosphere of treachery and hidden violence in which he lived, and the nagging fear lest at any moment this mine should explode before he could prevent it, so preyed upon him that he grew abstracted, irritable, moody; and it was not long before he discovered that the superstitious fear which had made him shrink from beginning on his investigations was being justified, and that he was become estranged from the being he loved best upon earth, his rustic mistress, Phoebe. For, try as he would at their meetings, he could not conceal from her his preoccupation and anxiety. His nerves were perpetually on edge and he could not enter into her gaiety; he became a poor lover; often he drank too much in a desperate effort to lighten his spirits and be good company, and the only effect of this was to precipitate quarrels. Phoebe blamed him for these, roundly accusing him of being touchy and melancholy; but when he sought to unburden himself to her of what was making him so, she would have none of it.

"A fart for politics!" cried she. "They are no business of a rustic wench. Pray keep your plots and plotters to yourself, my friend, and if you are so in love with them that you cannot, prithee stay at Whitehall in their company, while I for my part will seek my pleasures on the Heath."

Painfully just, he accepted her point of view, begged only that she would not cast him off utterly, and tried continually and doggedly to lay-by his cares when he rode to Hampstead and to forget everything save the little heaven he had discovered there. But because of his employment under the conspirators, his visits were necessarily less frequent, and this was an added cause for Phoebe's discontent with him. To all his other fears was added the brooding apprehension of one day hearing her say to him that she did not wish to see him any more.

Then, at the end of January, Derrick's patient efforts to search out treason suddenly promised him success. It began with an occasion when he was sent by Wildman with a letter which he was to deliver with all speed and secrecy to Colonel Rumsey at his house in Soho. Derrick knew Rumsey only by hearsay; he was a soldier of fortune who had distinguished himself in Portugal, had married an heiress, and in the old days was said to have been Shaftesbury's spy on the rest of his associates. As Derrick made his way on foot to Soho, he reflected that Shaftesbury had just died in Holland, and he wondered idly whether this letter contained last messages for my lord's old tool. It was, however, sealed with a wax impression, so that he dared not see for himself.

It was night, a cold, raw, stormy night, with frequent squalls, when he came to Soho Square and knocked upon Rumsey's door. A man whom he took to be the Colonel in person opened to him, and receiving the password, beckoned him inside. The inclemency of the weather, and his own nervous state, made Derrick shiver as he stood in the hall, and noticing this, Rumsey (for it was he) kindly invited him into his parlour where there was a fire, while he himself read the letter. Standing by the hearth and pretending to warm his hands, Derrick surreptitiously watched as the Colonel broke the seal, laid aside an enclosure, and read the letter; while he was about this, there was the sound from above stairs of a curious shuffling footstep, and presently that of a cane being rapped on the floor immediately above: two soft raps, then three loud ones, then two soft again. Derrick stiffened. There was a fellow conspirator hidden up there, he thought, and glanced at Rumsey. The Colonel, with something of an agitated air, was folding up the letter and placing it with the other in his pocket; then, mumbling an excuse, he left the room. Derrick gave him a moment before he quietly followed; he was in time to see Rumsey mounting the stairs and was about to creep up after him when suddenly a door at the head of the staircase opened, a man's figure was outlined in the light from the room behind, and a voice called out an enquiry. Derrick stepped back into the parlour again, for he had heard and seen enough.

That tall lean figure outlined in the candlelight, that great Roman nose, those slightly stooping shoulders, above all that great periwig worn in a unique fashion, pulled so far down upon the brow that it was like a hood, these together with the strong Scottish accent in which the voice had spoken, all told him plainly that the guest Rumsey had secreted upstairs was none other than Robert Ferguson the Plotter, returned again to England in response to the appeals of his fellow conspirators, and without doubt to the management of that plot of which he had been all along, present or absent, the axle on which it revolved.

A strong excitement hastened Derrick's footsteps as he left Soho Square a little later. For here at last, surely, was something with which he could go to the authorities. Ferguson the Plotter was back in England; he was wanted for the writing of a seditious paper before he had fled in November; one at least of his hiding-places (for doubtless so old a plotter would have many) was known to Derrick; he could be apprehended before he became aware that his presence in London was suspected, lodged safely in jail, and in due course brought to trial. Once he, the heart and soul of this conspiracy, was removed, the plot itself might fall to pieces. Yet on sooner had Derrick come to this conclusion than counter-arguments threw his mind into confusion again. Might not the apprehension of their leader drive on the other conspirators to some desperate move in order to prevent themselves from sharing his fate? Their plans were well advanced, and it had been plain to Derrick for some time that the more fanatical among them,

Wildman and his friends, were already fretting under the delay caused by the vacillation of Monmouth and certain of the gentry who were responsible for raising the country parts. The arrest of Ferguson might well prove the spark which set alight the prepared bonfire.

Wrestling with these new problems, Derrick somehow got through his duties at Whitehall, and went home to another sleepless night. When morning dawned he was no nearer a decision, and was so hopeless of reaching one which he could be sure was right that he resolved to let fate guide him. He would go to the Young Devil tavern as usual and see if there was anything for him there; if there was nothing, he would take it as a sign that he should go to the authorities and notify them of the return of Ferguson; he had done all a man could do to uncover this plot, and now it was time for the fate which had sent him on so perilous an investigation to take a hand.

And at the Young Devil there was something. As soon as he saw Derrick enter, the landlord fished beneath the counter and brought out a billet; when he had gone into the inner room and opened it, Derrick found that it contained only some very simple instructions to himself. They were in the handwriting of Wildman, writ in the usual cipher, and they were these:

"Immediately upon receiving this, you are to go to the Sweating House called the Hummums in Covent Garden, and enquire there for the Assistant Rubber. When you come at him, tell him this: That his presence is expected at the Meeting he wots of upon Friday, the day after tomorrow, wherein he is not to fail at his peril."

Well, thought Derrick with a wry smile, if this is the sign I sought from fate, it is a somewhat unpromising one, yet

I will follow it. So he put the billet in his coat and set off for Covent Garden.

He found the Hummums easily enough; though he himself had never been here before, he knew it for a fashionable haunt, where the most expensive whores in town and the high-born rakes and beaux came to sweat away excesses before indulging in others. Here those sensualists of either sex who were too knowing to accept the lying promises of quacks, migrated regularly to supple up their limbs, steep their bodies in essences and sweet herbs, and, under the excuse of some trifling ache, have themselves massaged and rubbed and steeped and cupped and all the rest of it. It was a jest in polite society, but a jest in which all shared; one went to the Hummums as one visited the spas of Tunbridge Wells and Bath, because it was *à la mode*. Already, though it was not yet mid-morning, a long line of chairs waited outside in the Piazza, some with a crest painted on their doors, and as Derrick approached the place a handsome coach drove up, and liveried footmen handed out an extravagantly dressed and painted roué, who from his looks had come straight hither from a debauch.

The door from the street opened into a gallery, and even here there was a suggestion of steam, hot air, and a reek of unguents. A handbell stood upon a table, apparently for the summoning of an attendant, but as Derrick was about to ring it, the roué and his footmen made a noisy entrance behind him, the servants bawling out for someone named Crawley, and at once there came running from the direction of the hot-rooms two attendants, one of whom, who seemed to be the keeper of the place, ushered the roué within with many cries of "At your service, my lord," "Your lordship's bath is a-drawing," accompanied by bowings and congies. When the party had disappeared within, Derrick addressed himself to the other attendant who had lingered behind to enquire what he desired. The man was clad only in a calico gown and hood, his bare feet thrust into wooden sabots, with a rope girdle round his waist from which depended a sort of glove made of horsehair.

"I desire to speak with the assistant rubber," Derrick told him.

"I am he," replied the man, in a voice hoarse from the atmosphere in which he worked. He came a step nearer to Derrick, and added in an undertone: "You need not be at pains to tell me why you are come, neighbour, for I know you, at least by sight. We met, d'you see, at the quack doctor's in St Martin's Lane."

Derrick looked at him more closely, and then smiled.

"I do remember you now. We were both upon probation, and I sought to share my strangeness with you, but you seemed disinclined for conversation. You told me then that you were out of a post; I see you have one now, and offer you my congratulations."

The man sighed heavily.

" 'Tis a good one, if I can keep it. Come, what's your message? Let me have it quick, for bless me I fear it and would know the worst."

"It is," said Derrick, eyeing him curiously, "that your presence is expected at the meeting you wot of upon Friday, which is the day after tomorrow, wherein you are not to fail at your peril."

The rubber put up a hand and wiped his sweaty face, and Derrick noticed that the hand was not quite steady. Indeed, ever since they had begun to talk, he had sensed some barely concealed terror in the man, who now, seeming to forget the presence of another, muttered to himself in extreme agitation:

"I durst not fail in going, yet if I go they will plague me with the old business, and as I am a sinner before God, I will not undertake it."

The significance of these muttered words, coupled with the man's air of terror, was not lost upon Derrick. He shot out a hand and gripped the calico sleeve.

"Harkee, friend," he whispered earnestly, "you and I must have some privy talk, for I believe we are of the same mind in certain particulars. I promise you that you will not regret it if you are plain with me; I will give you proof of my good faith if you will conduct me somewhere where we may be private."

The man stared at him, him lips moving. Then, all of a sudden, it seemed that despair made up his mind for him, and jerking his head towards the hot-rooms he began to walk in that direction, muttering over his shoulder:

"There is but one way we may be private, and that is for you to sweat, after which I will tell the head rubber that you would be cupped for a pain in your shoulder which you got from a fall from your horse. He detests this service, so will leave it to me, and this is done in a private chamber."

Before Derrick could make any comments upon this proposed arrangement, he found himself hustled into the changing-room, where he found the old roué from the coach still undergoing the long process of being undressed by his footmen. They had removed his cravat, coat, waistcoat, and wig, and had got as far as his stays, gradually transforming the aged beau into a sprawling heap of unhealthy fat, slack muscles, and bare bandy legs. There was nothing else for it but for Derrick to strip in his turn; the assistant rubber was waiting impatiently with a pair of sabots which he must put on to save his feet from the burning floor of the hot-rooms. Having donned these, and girded his middle with a linen cloth, he was escorted by his guide into the first of the rooms, where the rubber left him, presumably to arrange with his superior about the cupping.

In any other circumstances, Derrick would have found plenty of entertainment in the hot-rooms, where the beaux, stripped of their fashionable garments, and with profuse perspiration making a woeful mess of their carefully painted complexions, still indulged in that affected drawl and modish gossip which now so comically contrasted with their appearance. But Derrick was too engrossed in this new situation to notice them. He had sought a sign this morning, guidance from fate, and though at first the one he had received had seemed unpromising, he wondered now if it were not the very thing he had lacked all along. This assistant rubber of a sweating-house was a lowly conspirator in the plot; he was being threatened by the managers of it; he was in some deadly fear, and from the few words he had let fall in the gallery just now, that fear had to do with the part allotted to him in the carrying out of the conspiracy. Was it not possible that, if Derrick played his cards correctly in the coming private talk, he might find in this fellow the second witness without whom he had not dared to approach the authorities?

Having stayed his allotted ten minutes in the hottest and last of the rooms, Derrick saw to his relief that his friend the rubber was beckoning to him from the door; the man led him into a private apartment, laid him down upon a slab, and set to work with his hair-gauntlet, grooming him all over as though he were a horse.

"Prithee, friend," gasped Derrick, "use some moderation, for remember I am not here for my health."

"You must seem to be," replied the rubber obstinately, "lest my chief comes in and spies us. Harkee, you told me you and I were of the same mind in certain particulars; what meant you by that?"

It seemed that the man had recovered some caution during the interval while Derrick had been in the hot-rooms, and would need considerable persuasion before he would talk.

"Why," said Derrick, feeling his way, "the company we got into at the quack doctor's have gone too far for my liking, neighbour, and if I could I would withdraw from the business. There you have it, fair and honest."

"Too far in very truth," muttered the other, vigorously pummelling his client's back. "For now they speak nought but of the Lopping Point, and would have me in it up to my neck."

"They approached me likewise on the same matter," lied Derrick, "but I would not be drawn. For the General Point, I am hot for it, and I confess I was won on that."

"So was I also," said the other eagerly. "They promised me pickings d'you see, if the General Point were carried, and being almost reduced to cutting a purse, I was tempted by the notion of loot and plunder, the Tory goldsmiths' coffers broke open after they were slaughtered and a fine livelihood assured me once the kingdom was won. But then they drew me in deeper, d'you see, and there was nought but this Lopping Point spoke of, and I must act a principal part in it, else would they rub me to the Whitt. I'd been upon the budge, d'you see, a little matter of a cotton counterpane which I prigged at a trugging-place and got a few pence for it from a rumbo-ken. But the Common Side of the Whitt is one thing, neighbour, and Ketch's quartering-knife quite another, d'you see, and 'tis that I fear if I do as they bid me in the matter of this Lopping Point."

"You are in the right of it there," said Derrick warmly, "and speak like a wise man indeed. There are rogues among 'em who care not what comes to such as you and me once we have done their dirty work for them."

"Yet they would pay me well, say they," sighed the rubber, going to a cupboard to fetch his glasses for the operation known as cupping. "Forty guineas, no less, if I'd be one of those chosen for the Lopping Point. But then I do remember that them Geometers were promised fifteen thousand guineas if they'd take off the King as he walked in the Park (so said Dr Oates), and 'twas not long after that I saw 'em hanged, drawn and quartered at Tyburn."

Derrick sat up so suddenly that he sent the glasses, which the man had been about to clap upon his shoulder, crashing to the floor. Swinging his legs over the slab, he seized the rubber in a tight grip and stared into his face a moment without speaking. Then, in a tone of deadly urgency, he said:

"Now listen, man. Hitherto I have not been entirely frank with you, but now I will be, and thereby put my life into your hands. I am a gentleman of the Court, attached to the Household of the Duke of York – nay, you must, you shall, hear me out. I have feigned to be one of these rogues only that I might smell out their beastly plots, and even as I came hither today was meditating an immediate approach to the authorities. Yet I lacked a second witness to back up my information, and this I must have to be believed. I have found him now; he is yourself. I am sure now, what I have all along suspected, that by this 'Lopping Point' they intend the assassination of the King and the Duke of York."

"I did not say so – 'tis a woundy lie!" yelped the man, struggling to free himself from Derrick's grip. "God damn and rot you, I have a mind to fetch my bleeding instruments and sham an accident here, for if you leave this place alive and blab of what you bubbled me into saying, there are some will cut my throat for sure."

"They will have no chance to do so," retorted Derrick, still holding him strongly, "if you will do what I bid you now. Come with me to Whitehall immediately and tell all you know to one of the Secretaries of State, and thus not only save the life of your Sovereign Lord and his rightful Heir, but earn yourself the royal protection and a rich reward into the bargain."

"So thought Master Prance during the Popish Plot," snarled the other obstinately, "and what he got instead was a taste of the rack, if all the tales be true. Nay, I know you not, nor what faith is to be put in your promises – "

"Listen, you plaguey fool," cried Derrick, shaking him in his exasperation, "I have told you who I am, and therefore 'tis I who must fear you, not you me, for if you blab to our fine friends the conspirators my life would not be worth a leather farthing token. But mark this: whether you go with me or not, I shall lay an information this very day, for I have learned somewhat lately which may get me credit, though I have no man to back up my tale. If I go alone, you may lose your life and a reward into the bargain." Then, as the rubber still glared at him sulkily, he tried another tack. "Come, friend, when I encountered you this morning you were troubled by what was demanded of you by the plotters; I am sure you are not a murderer at heart. If you put your hand to regicide, you will have no peace henceforth all your life long from the remembrance of that vile deed, even though you escape the vengeance of the law. I swear to you that you have everything to gain, nought to lose, if you will come with me now to Whitehall like an honest man and lay bare this foul conspiracy ere it be too late."

Before the rubber could make any reply to this speech, there was a perfunctory tap upon the door, if opened a few inches, and a sweaty face beneath a calico hood was poked in.

"Are you not done yet, Jack?" asked the voice of the head rubber. "There is a Crown Bath Extraordinary to be prepared, Italian paste to be got ready for my Lord Peterborough, and many stay for this room."

"Anon, master, anon!" cried the assistant rubber tremulously. Then, when his superior had withdrawn again, he muttered to Derrick, not looking at him: "I cannot stay for more talk or I shall lose my post. Come, master, put on this robe and I will conduct you to the room where you may rest ere you go home; and hasten, pray."

"I shall not stir a step," answered Derrick definitely, "until I have your answer. Will you come with me to Whitehall, or refuse and take the consequences?"

"Why, I cannot leave here until my work be done for the day," whined the rubber, making a great to-do about gathering up his towels.

"This evening, then," persisted Derrick. "You are acquainted with Holbein's Gate which stands at the Charing Cross end of Whitehall? If you will come thither as soon as your work here is done, I will be awaiting you there and will conduct you past the guards. At what hour are you free?"

"Why, at eight of the clock, master," admitted the rubber reluctantly, "but I cannot appear at Whitehall amid lords and gentlemen – I have no change of linen – I am but a poor man – "

"You have vital information," cut in Derrick impatiently, "which, I promise you, will make you a kindly reception, let your outer man be what it will. I will be at Holbein's at eight of the clock and will stay till you come. Now, let me have your answer."

The man stared at him a minute, then gave a brief nod, and before Derrick had time to detain him had scuttled out of the apartment without another word; his voice could be heard in the passage answering some shout from his superior, and it was plain that nothing was to be gained by endeavouring to have further speech with him.

Keyed up now to the highest pitch of excitement, Derrick, without troubling to go and cool off in the waiting-room, hastened to the chamber where he had left his clothes, flung them upon him, and leaving some money on the table in payment for his involuntary sweating, ran out of the Hummums and hailed a hackney from the stand in the Piazza. Thank God he was off duty today, he thought, as the vehicle jolted him towards his wife's house, for there was a world of things to be done before eight o' clock this evening. Alighting at his home, he went straight up to his own chamber and there collected the copies he had made of all the various written messages and letters he had carried for the conspirators. They were but copies, and hitherto had been useless to him, but now, possessed of the information that Robert Ferguson was in London, and hopeful of a second witness to his story, he would need them as additional evidence when he approached the authorities. Having tucked the papers into his breast, he went directly to Whitehall, for he was aware that the arrangements for a private interview with someone in authority would take some time.

The obvious personage for him to approach was one of the two Secretaries of State, but Derrick being attached to the Court, he had to observe a certain rigid etiquette. All the Court Officers, with the exception of the Gentlemen Pensioners, were under the jurisdiction of the Lord Chamberlain of the Household, and if they had petitions to make, grievances to air, or any business of like nature, it was the rule that they do so either through the Lord Chamberlain's office, or, if the matter were private and personal, to the Chamberlain himself. If Derrick attempted to approach one of the Secretaries of State, he would almost certainly be told that anything he had to say must go through the proper channels first; and therefore, though chafing at the waste of time this would involve, he directed himself towards the Chamberlain's lodging.

This was situated on the west side of the Banqueting House, next door to that of the Lord Keeper, and overlooking the Privy Garden. As Derrick hastened down the street which divided the palace into two, he heard the trumpets sounding for dinner, and swore under his breath, for now some long time must elapse before he could have a chance of seeing the Lord Chamberlain. As he passed the entrance to the Great Court, which lay between Scotland Yard and the Banqueting House, he saw the procession forming which would conduct his Majesty to dinner, the Gentlemen Pensioners resplendent with their gilded pole-axes and their chains-of-office, the picturesque Yeomen of the Guard with their partisans, the trumpeters and pages, and in the midst the Lord Chamberlain himself, fussy as ever, and making great play with his white wand. Derrick passed on, and on reaching the Chamberlain's lodging, told the man on duty there that he designed to catch my lord for a private word as soon as he came from dinner, and begged leave to await him in the ante-room.

He had to curb his impatience for two hours, pacing up and down the chamber, listening to the familiar sounds of the palace, the orderly bustle, the cries from the Cockpit over the street where some courtiers were enjoying the sport, the trumpets sounding at intervals, the clink of steel and hollow clatter of horses' hooves from the Horse Guards Stables, and the drum-beats which announced that the Foot Guards were being changed. When at last footsteps on the stair announced that the owner of the lodging was returning, Derrick in his impatience hurried out of the ante-room and met the Lord Chamberlain in the corridor. Before he could accost him, the Chamberlain, panting from the effort of climbing the stairs (for he was a very fat gentlemen), halted among his attendants and with an exclamation of pleased surprise cried to Derrick:

"Mr Calder! The very man I wished to see. You are off-duty, I am aware, Mr Calder, yet I would ask a favour. One of your fellow Ushers has been taken sick, and therefore another must needs take his place in the ante-chamber of his Royal Highness this evening. Unless you have an urgent engagement which may not to put off, I beg, Mr Calder that you will be so kind as to accept a spell of duty there from six to eight of the clock."

Courteously termed though it was, this was obviously a command rather than a request, and Derrick could not refuse it. But he was not altogether displeased, since it made it easier to ask a favour in his turn.

"I am honoured, my Lord Chamberlain," said he with a bow, "and shall be there without fail." And then as the Chamberlain made to proceed along the corridor: "I took the liberty of waiting upon your lordship here at present that I might beg from you a private audience this evening betwixt eight and nine."

The Chamberlain's gracious smile lost a little of its graciousness. "A private audience?" he repeated. "Why, Mr Calder, I am promised to sup with her Grace of Cleveland. Nevertheless," he added, "you are aware that I look upon the Officers under my jurisdiction as my own sons, and if this matter of yours be a personal one on which you seek my advice, I will indulge you. But pray be punctual to the appointment, sir, for I must not keep her Grace waiting. I shall expect you soon after eight of the clock when you come off duty."

Derrick bowed again and murmured his thanks. As he made his way out of the lodging he was aware of a sudden and enormous fatigue, both of mind and body. Only a few hours now separated him from that moment when he might share at last the dreadful secret which had burdened him for so many weeks. Would he be believed? Would the Lord Chamberlain act, and if so, would it be in time? But the question which racked him worst of all was this: Will Jack the assistant rubber at the Hummums keep faith with me and come to Holbein's Gate this evening?

Chapter Seven

As the innumerable clocks of the Palace struck the hour of eight that evening, Derrick, relieved by the Usher next on duty, fairly ran out of the Duke of York's apartments, along the Stone Gallery, jostling the crowd of petitioners who waited there to see the King or the Duke, down the stair into the Great Court, through Palace Gate, and into the street. Here was the usual throng of chairs and coaches, all in a blaze of light from the lodgings which occupied both sides; he pushed his way through them and the innumerable pedestrians, nodding to acquaintances, making the proper bows and congies to the great ones, and so hastened along towards Holbein's Gate. He had nearly reached it when, his mind entirely occupied with his chances of finding the assistant rubber waiting at the trysting-place, he cannoned into a gentleman who came suddenly out of a gate upon his right. Pausing to lift his hat and make a brief apology, Derrick found himself looking into the swarthy face and protruding eyes of Forde, Lord Grey.

There was an instant's complete silence between the pair as they stared at one another. Then:

"Mr Simon Hill!" exclaimed my lord, gently sardonic. His glance strayed significantly over Derrick's uniform. "Why, this I protest is an unexpected honour. Yet methinks it should not be unexpected, for now at last I recollect where I had seen you before, ere you paid me the honour of a visit to Up Park in December. In the days when I was received at Court, before my sad misfortune, I have spied you often in the train of his Royal Highness, the Duke of York – God bless him!"

"You mistake me, my lord," said Derrick dully, for he had no hope of convincing Grey. "My name is Calder, Derrick Calder, at your lordship's service. I do assure you, I never had the privilege of waiting upon your lordship at your country seat."

"No?" queried Grey, and now he did not trouble to hide his ugly amusement. "You have a twin brother, perchance, who masquerades under a false name. A dangerous thing to do, Mr Hill – a thousand pardons, Mr Calder – you should rebuke him for it, you really should. Otherwise I fear he may find himself inconvenienced by his frolics."

"Your lordship is pleased to jest," observed Derrick curtly, yearning to hit the man on that sensual mouth of his. "I protest, I have no twin brother, and know nothing of what your lordship is speaking. I beg you will excuse me now, for I am in haste."

"An amorous tryst, perchance?" teased my lord softly. "I wish you joy of it. Let all your trysts be amorous ones in future, Mr Calder; believe me, you will find them safer than certain other pranks in which you have indulged in times past."

He bowed ironically low, and turned away. Derrick stood staring after him for a moment, cursing the chance which had brought him to Whitehall this evening. He had hoped to be safe from Grey at least in the palace, for since my lord's abduction of his sister-in-law he was forbid the Court. Glancing at the gate through which Grey had come into the street just now, Derrick remembered that among other noblemen Lord Stamford had lodgings hereabouts. Stamford was a crony of Monmouth's, and had accompanied him on that semi-royal progress last September which had resulted in the Duke's temporary arrest. In all probability, Grey had been visiting Stamford – but what did it matter what he had been doing, reflected Derrick bitterly, as he watched my lord's figure disappearing from view in the crowded street. Grey now knew that 'Simon Hill', one of the 'Friends in Harmony', was really a Gentleman Usher in the Household of the Duke of York, and would lose no time in notifying his fellow conspirators. The cursed encounter had dashed any lingering hopes Derrick had entertained of being able to unearth further information supposing his story were not credited tonight. The only comfort was to be found in the fact that it had happened now and not earlier in his investigations.

With this reflection he hastened on towards Holbein's Gate, and as he reached it, heard the clocks chime a quarter past the hour. The assistant rubber should be here by now, but there was no sign of him. The great gates stood open, admitting coaches and chairs after their occupants had been scrutinised by the Life Guards on duty, and a stream of pedestrians entered and left by the wicket. Among the Life Guards, Derrick spied Jack Youndhusband, and although it was altogether improper for him to speak with a guardsman on duty, he seized a moment when the commanding officer was bending down to greet some lord in his coach, to ask Jack in an undertone whether any man had been enquiring for himself. Jack shook his head, and on Derrick's hastily describing the assistant rubber, told him that no man of that sort had been at Holbein's this evening, but that if he arrived after Derrick had gone and Jack was still on duty, he would direct him to the Ushers' Parlour.

"Nay, to the lodging of the Lord Chamberlain," said Derrick. "I – " he broke off as Jack's officer looked in their direction.

Derrick waited at Holbein's Gate for a full half-hour, scrutinising every pedestrian who approached, expectant of seeing the man on whom his hopes were pinned. His spirits sank lower and lower as no rubber appeared, and now he cursed himself that he had not at least asked the man where he lodged. Also, he reflected agitatedly, he ought to have got more details from him concerning the 'Lopping Point', the method to be used, the time and place. When the clocks chimed a quarter to nine, a new fear struck him; the Lord Chamberlain was not a person to be kept waiting, and unless Derrick hastened to him now he might find that my lord had gone off in a huff to keep his appointment with the Duchess of Cleveland. So as he had hastened to Holbein's Gate three-quarters of an hour earlier, so now he raced along in the opposite direction, and arriving breathless at the Chamberlain's lodging, was told with a wink by the man on duty at the door that my lord's patience seemed nearly exhausted and that he was only just in time to catch him.

The Lord Chamberlain of the Household was a man whose character appeared to go in layers; the surface one was an exaggerated kindliness and condescension, an avuncular patronage. It was one of his favourite boasts that the lowlier the Officer in Ordinary, the more accessible did my lord become to him, as a father should to the weaker among his sons, and young gentlemen at their first coming to Court were almost overwhelmed by the unctuous welcome they received from the Lord Chamberlain. But it was never long before these unwary youths were dismayed by reaching the second layer of his lordship's character, which was composed of a childish vanity and touchiness, which, appearing suddenly through the veneer above, was apt to be exceedingly disconcerting to the uninitiated. In the bottom layer of all, the kindliness reappeared again and this time was entirely genuine; if it could be reached, all was well, but unfortunately it took a great deal of tact and effort to reach it.

Apart from these peculiarities of character, the Chamberlain possessed certain idiosyncrasies which made him the butt of the Court wits. He was fanatical in his dislike of the fashion of wearing false hair, which, he averred, not only carried infection but bred lice, and whenever it was possible it was his habit to remove his peruke and incase his head in a silk turban, Turk-wise, an ornament not very well according with his fat and cherubic countenance. He lived in constant terror of catching some disease or ailment, and had been known, in the very Presence Chamber, in a loud whisper to order some page to close a window because he suspected a draught. The malicious asserted that at the time of the Great Plague he had been the very first of all the Court to leave London; and even now, when the pestilence had not been seen in the metropolis for nearly twenty years, he never stirred abroad without continuously sniffing at his silver spice-ball, never entered any public vehicle, and regularly, once a week, had a sulphur candle burnt in every apartment of his lodging.

On being admitted to the presence of this personage tonight, Derrick found him pacing up and down with his watch in his hand, his turban pushed slightly on one side of his head, and the innumerable cloaks and wrapping with which he enshrouded himself whenever he must venture into the night air, laid ready near him on a couch. The room stank strong of garlic and incense (because of the belief in the efficacy of the latter to ward off disease, the poor man had very nearly found himself suspected during the height of the Popish Plot), and prominently displayed under a glass case above the fire was his bezoar stone, supposed to be an antidote to all sorts of poisons. Scarcely had Derrick made his bow than the Chamberlain snapped at him:

"Now, Mr Calder, I must be sharp with you, I really must. This is most unfitting, most unmannerly. You craved the favour of a private audience with me betwixt eight and nine of the clock; it is now precisely seven minutes to nine, as you may see by my watch, and you should be aware that I am not accustomed to being kept waiting by my Officers in Ordinary. I should not have to remind you, Mr Calder, that it is a mighty condescension on my part to grant you this audience; you have been long enough at Court to know that any petitions you have to make should be made through my Office."

"I beg your lordship to excuse this seeming discourtesy," said Derrick. "I stayed for a man whom I hoped to present to your lordship, but he came not. I must even endeavour, therefore, to convince you of the truth of what I have to say without him, and I most earnestly beg, that despite the inconvenience I have caused you, your lordship will hear me out."

"Well then, be brief, if you please," sighed the Chamberlain, seating himself in a winged chair close to the fire. "Now what is this matter which is so urgent that none but myself can advise you upon it? Nay, I remember now that your father was sick at Christmas-time, and you had leave of absence to attend upon him. It will be somewhat connected with this, I suppose. I trust you have not bad news – it was not, Mr Calder," added the Chamberlain, in sudden alarm and snatching up his spice-ball, "some infectious sickness, was it?"

"No, indeed, my lord, it was an ague, but this is not – "

"Ah, an ague," interrupted the Chamberlain, before Derrick could go on. "Country air, damp mansions – yes,

yes, quite understandable, poor gentleman. I never stir into the country myself. You look somewhat pale, Mr Calder; you are not ailing, I trust?"

"It is no personal matter which brings me here," said Derrick, so desperate to come to the point that he ventured to ignore this query. " 'Tis a public one, and lies very heavy upon me." He took a deep breath to steady himself. "My Lord Chamberlain, I have to tell you that there is a plot abroad the which must be investigated without delay."

"A plot?" repeated the Chamberlain vaguely, blinking a little as he spoke. "Bless me, what's this? Mr Calder, I do hope that you are not wasting my time with coffee-house talk; the town is ever full of rumours, and young gentlemen like yourself are apt to set too much store by 'em – 'ounds, sir, I am sure there is a draught in this chamber. Can you not feel it? Pray draw the curtains a little farther over the door – so. Now, what was I saying? Ah yes, concerning this plot. I protest, I have heard no talk of such a thing."

"That was as I feared, my lord," said Derrick shortly, "and it is for this very reason that I have approached you. So far, it seems, the conspirators have kept their plans very quiet and are the more to be feared for that. Have I your lordship's leave to tell you all I know concerning the matter?"

"Why yes, I suppose so," said his lordship reluctantly, drawing a fur rug over his knees and still appearing much more concerned with a possible draught than in what his visitor was saying. "But pray be brief, Mr Calder, for I must remind you that I am engaged for supper with her Grace and am already late. I am sure we can clear up this little matter which is troubling you, if you will but be brief."

So Derrick, trying desperately not to be discouraged by the obvious hint that the whole thing was but a figment of his own imagination, marshalled his facts and told his story. He kept out of it the names of Josiah Keeling and Daniel Jolly, and explained that he had first got upon the scent of a plot by the accidental obtaining of a paper, not meant for his eyes, which advertised a meeting; and at appropriate intervals he laid before the Chamberlain the copies of the letters and messages he had deciphered in the course of his investigations. My lord fingered these as gingerly as Daniel Jolly had done with the paper he had got from the ballad-monger, eyeing them with undisguised distaste; several times he made to interrupt, and at last, when Derrick came to relate his visit to Up Park and mentioned the Duke of Monmouth, my lord fairly leapt from his chair in his extreme agitation, gave his turban such a push that it rocked upon his shaven head, and bleated shrilly:

"Now, sir, I must really chide you. What you have said is most improper, and if spoken outside this room might bring you to the Provost Marshal for daring to accuse so great a personage. 'Ounds, Mr Calder, would you have me believe that his Grace would so lay aside his duty as to connive at a rebellion against the King, to whom, sir, let me remind you, he is bound by – ahem! – more tender ties than those of a subject to his Sovereign."

"It is well known that Monmouth –" began Derrick, but again was interrupted. The Chamberlain's face was red with fury.

"Monmouth, sir, Monmouth, quotha! Odsblood, how dare you speak so of a duke! His Grace, the Duke of Monmouth, if you please, sir; upon my salvation, Mr Calder, you forget yourself. I never thought to hear the like impertinence from one of my Officers in Ordinary."

"It is well known that his Grace the Duke of Monmouth," continued Derrick, metaphorically grinding his teeth, "is mighty discontented at being turned out of his posts, that he so far aspires to the crown that he has taken the bend sinister out of his coat-of-arms, has gone upon progresses in a manner fit only for royalty, has even presumed to touch for the Evil when he was at Hinton Park, and that when in private he encourages his friends to address him as 'Your Royal Highness'. Likewise, that he hath been used by the opponents of the King in all their machinations, was the close friend of Shaftesbury, and has made no secret of the fact that he will prevent, if he can, the accession of the rightful Heir when the King shall die. Under your favour, therefore, my lord, I see not why you should be so incredulous when I inform you that his Grace hath been so far seduced from his duty as to implicate himself in this plot."

"Mr Calder," said the Chamberlain, in a voice which trembled with indignation, "you, are a Gentleman Usher, not some great lord whose privilege it is to speak freely of personages like his Grace, nor are you, sir, one of His Majesty's Life Guards, whose duty it is to smell out and report disaffection. You have presumed, sir, upon both counts, and I must let you know that thereby you have merited my extreme displeasure – my extreme displeasure, Mr Calder, I can call it no less."

Derrick bit his lips to keep back the rage and frustration which longed to find vent in an oath.

"My lord," he said abruptly, "I am a loyal subject of his Majesty, howsoever lowly my birth and post at Court, and I believe your lordship will hardy deny that as a loyal subject it is my duty to report disaffection, much more plain treason, if such comes to my knowledge. If your lordship will only hear me out, I hope to convince you that here is not only rebellion being plotted, but the assassination of the King and the Duke of York."

"Proceed and have done, sir," cried the Chamberlain, who nevertheless gave the impression that he longed to stop his ears. "I will strive to have patience, and God is my witness I was never more in need of it."

Made dogged now by this hostile reception of his story, Derrick related the rest of it in short, sharp sentences, keeping control of his voice, yet allowing the strength of his feeling through sufficiently as to make his abrupt tones the more impressive, so that, as he proceeded, he saw that the Chamberlain was listening with more attention, was forgetting to push his turban about or peer around for imaginary draughts, and was even turning a little pale. But when at last Derrick came to the events of that morning, of how he had hoped to bring this fellow, the assistant rubber, forward, who so amply could confirm the worst part of his story, and of the man's failure to keep faith with him, the Chamberlain pounced on him like lightning.

"Ah, sir," cried he, with something resembling triumph in his tone, "there you have it. You have no second witness, no exact proof either that this nasty conspiracy exists save in your own noddle, and therefore is there only your word that it exists at all. As for these papers you have shown me, they are but copies, sir, you have confessed it, and so are worthless and must not be admitted as evidence. Mr Calder," continued my lord, holding up an admonitory hand as Derrick would have protested, "what you have told me, if it had foundation, would be horrid, very horrid indeed, sir, I grant you that; but has it foundation? I think it hath not." The Chamberlain, in his relief at this conviction, became a little playful, and wriggled in his chair like a fat kitten. "All this talk of passwords and countersigns and secret writings and – dear me, what was it now? – fastenings and unfastenings of coat buttons – I protest, Mr Calder, this is child's talk, not fit to be taken seriously. I fear you have let your imagination (which I perceive to be very strong) override your better judgement, sir; noblemen and high-born gentlemen do not indulge in such fiddle-faddles, you must believe me they do not. Yet you are not to take me wrong, Mr Calder; no doubt there is some trifling disaffection abroad; there be always some who are discontented even under the best of monarchs; yet if such disaffection had reached the dreadful proportions you would have me believe, be assured your superiors would have word of it. You must not imagine that the King's Ministers are so blind to their duty as to let treason run rife without smelling it out. Bless me, Mr Calder," continued the Chamberlain, somewhat breathless from this long speech, "you are old enough to know better than to make me late for supper with her Grace all for such nonsense as this."

"And suppose it is not nonsense," snarled Derrick, shivering with the rage which threatened to overwhelm him. "Suppose that, my lord; what then? 'Tis true what you say that I have no exact proof to offer you, yet neither hath your lordship proof that this which you are pleased to dismiss as nonsense is not in fact treason."

"Pray use not that tone with me, sir," began the Chamberlain; but Derrick swept on.

"For two months now," he cried passionately, "I have risked my life daily in searching out, single-handed, the bottoms of this plot. I have feigned to be one of them, thus endangering myself, not only by courting their malice if they discovered my true character, but likewise by putting myself in peril of being implicated in their treason if it should be discovered ere I could lay an information. All this I have done because 'twas my plain duty, the duty of any man, be he lord or mechanic, who is a loyal subject of King Charles. My lord, I have been at Court now many years, and let your lordship's opinion of me be what it will, you cannot, I believe, deny that I have ever shown myself loyal and honest. You tell me in one breath that young gentlemen like myself are too apt to listen to rumours and coffee-house talk, and in the next that I am old enough not to fox your lordship with such nonsense. Under your favour, I take leave to tell you that I am thirty-four years of age, have been at Court since I was twenty, and am indeed old enough to recognise plain treason when I see it, and to be aware that conspirators in all ages have made use of passwords and secret signs and all else your lordship is pleased to term fiddle-faddle."

The passionate sincerity with which Derrick had spoken had penetrated, it seemed, to that bottom layer of the Chamberlain's character which was composed of a genuine kindliness. He said mildly:

"I perceive that you have acted according to your lights, Mr Calder, and have shown some courage and much care for the safety of your King and country. Therefore I am pleased to pass over your improper method of addressing me and shall not remember it against you. But as for this plot, methinks your zeal hath a little blinded your common sense, yet if you will set down upon paper, calmly and without heat, all that you think you have discovered concerning it, and will submit it to me, together with these – these copies of letters and other such things, I will do you the favour of examining into the matter with due care, and will let you know my considered judgement."

Derrick lost his temper altogether.

"And meantime," he shouted furiously, "the King and the Duke may be murdered and the kingdom plunged into civil war."

The Chamberlain rose.

"One word more like that in my presence, Mr Calder," he shrilled, "and I shall summon the serjeants-at-arms and have you warded in your lodging. Never in my long experience hath one of my Officers in Ordinary so far forgot himself."

Derrick threw out his hands in a gesture of despair.

"Do what you will with me, my lord," he cried hoarsely, "only for the love of God take measures to prevent these rogues from putting into action their hellish plans."

The Chamberlain softened again.

"I will tell you what I will do, Mr Calder," said he, with the air of one indulging a fond but foolish child. "I will advise the Majesty's Secretaries of State that Robert Ferguson, called the Plotter, hath returned to this kingdom, and since a true bill was found against him by the Grand Jury last December for writing and publishing a seditious libel, doubtless they will issue out a warrant for his apprehension. For the rest of those you have named, we have nothing against them, though 'tis true that several among them are of the fanatics and have behaved themselves in past times not at all as they ought, yet the Law of England, sir, will persecute no man unless sure proof is offered against him." He pulled a tasselled bell-rope at his side. "And now, Mr Calder, you have my leave to go, and pray, sir, be guided by the advice of one who is old enough to be your father, and hath your welfare as much at heart as though you were in truth the fruit of his loins. In future, Mr Calder, attend more to your duties, which are most honourable ones and should content you, and gad less about the coffee-houses and taverns of the town where many a young gentleman before you hath been affrighted by the wild talk and rumours of the disaffected."

Derrick stared at him. There was no possible reply to this pompous speech; there was nothing more he could say; he was defeated. With a formal bow he turned to leave the room, and at the door nearly cannoned into my lord's valet, who was hastening in with his master's peruke on its stand.

As Derrick stumbled down the stairs, his head whirling with the anguish of frustration, desperate resolves raced through his mind. He would go to the Duke of York, to the Secretaries, to the King himself; he would make them listen, force them to act. But he knew in his heart that it was useless; from the criminal credulity with which they had drunk in the lies of Titus Oates, the Privy Council had gone to the other extreme and now laughed at plots in general; the Duke, indeed, would listen with his customary seriousness and justice, but the Duke could do nothing by himself. If he brought the matter before the Privy Council, his enemies therein would not hesitate to say that he sought to discredit the fanatics in revenge for the late persecution of his co-religionists. The King would not listen to talk of any conspiracy in which his beloved Monmouth was involved; the Secretaries would ask Derrick why he had not taken the matter to the Lord Chamberlain. He was entangled in a web of etiquette, officialdom, and incredulity; and all this while the conspirators were going forward with their hellish plans.

The guard was being changed again when Derrick came to Holbein's, but he had time for a word with his friend, Jack Younghusband, who told him that no one resembling the assistant rubber had sought admittance or enquired for him this evening. Jack was inclined to be curious, and invited his friend to come home with him and explain the matter over a whet, but Derrick, utterly depressed and despairing, excused himself. When he reached home, he found that his wife was entertaining, and before he could escape to his own chamber, he was obliged to be polite to her guests. When at length he could escape, he flung himself, fully dressed, on to his bed, and endeavoured to examine the situation without emotion.

First, his own usefulness was finished. Grey would lose no time in making known to his fellow conspirators the real identity of 'Simon Hill', and besides this it was not at all unlikely that the assistant rubber, seeking to curry favour with those of whom he was obviously afraid, would report the disclosure made to him by Derrick at the sweating-house. One thing was almost certain: that if by any means they could compass it without risk to themselves, the plotters would silence Derrick as soon as possible, either by bringing a false charge against him, as they had done in the case of his humble friend, the chandler, or else by the more certain way of murder. Against neither threat could he guard himself; and indeed he scarcely cared.

As for the rest, he had done all he could. If Ferguson was arrested, some good might result, for undoubtedly he was the heart and soul of the conspiracy; but he was known to be a most slippery customer, had a dozen different aliases and retreats, and unless the Lord Chamberlain acted at once (which was most unlikely, thought Derrick with a bitter smile), the Plotter might very well escape. So far as Derrick himself was concerned, there was only one chance, a mighty slender one, of producing that proof the lack of which had defeated him tonight. He would go tomorrow morning to the sweating-house and endeavour to speak again with the assistant rubber and persuade him to come forwards as a second witness; it was the only hope.

Lying there exhausted on his bed, Derrick had to bite his lips to prevent himself from crying aloud with rage, horror, and frustration. He could hear the Privy Councillors echoing the Chamberlain's words, and adding some of their own for good measure: Here we have the Oates game played again; great talk of letters but only copies produced; many accusations but no second witness; sensational stories but not a shred of evidence. Where is your proof, Mr Calder? Bring us proof and we will believe you. All night long these mocking voices pursued him in nightmare, and each time he woke the sweat was pouring down his face.

Chapter Eight

He was awakened finally by his own voice crying "Treason! Treason!" and sitting up on the bed saw that it was dawn. There must be, he thought, some little fever on him, for even now, with his eyes wide open and the grey light of morning seeping through the window, he saw a procession of faces leering at him, seeming to pass at the foot of the bed, Wildman's with its military moustachios and livid scar, Grey's, swarthy, sensual, with heavy-lidded eyes, the assistant rubber's, sweaty beneath a calico hood, the Lord Chamberlain's, peevish and flushed beneath the absurd silk turban. He rose with a groan and began to change and shave. His mind, he found, was drained of emotion; he felt dull and calm with despair.

Before it was time for him to go on duty a Whitehall, he made his way to the Hummums and enquired for the assistant rubber. It was no surprise to him when he was told by the indignant keeper of the sweating-house that the fellow had not turned up this morning, and that the keeper had no idea where he lodged. Derrick thanked him and turned away. As he walked back to Whitehall, he had the sudden feeling that he was being followed. Though he had expected this, he had so far forgotten his personal peril that the notion came as a shock to him; he whipped round on the foot-path and scrutinised his fellow pedestrians sharply, but could see no one who seemed to be dogging him. Through the dullness of his mind there shot a little thrill of fear; horrible to be flung suddenly under the wheels of a hackney without a chance to fight for his life. Then he shrugged and walked on, deliberately refraining from glancing over his shoulder. He had always believed that no man could escape his fate, that death came only when the right hour struck. He was not going to demean his manhood by getting obsessed by assassins who might or might not exist.

But as he went about his duties at Whitehall that day, observing the correct expression and posture of an Officer in Ordinary, making the right congies and greetings, the cold despair which filled him began to give place to a burning desire. If these plotters designed his destruction (as indeed they must do now), they would waste no time in attempting it, and before they struck he must taste again, perhaps for the last time on earth, the companionship of his love. More important than this, he must recapture for both of them that old precious harmony which his late preoccupation and disturbance of mind had threatened to destroy. As a subject he had done all he could and had failed; he was free to be the lover again, and to endeavour, if by any means he could, to make success of the only human relationship which mattered to him.

Then he remembered that today was Tuesday; on Tuesday evenings he was off duty after five o'clock, and it had been a standing arrangement with Phoebe that she should go to Jack Straw's and stay in the common-room between five and six. Lately it had not always been possible for him to join her; his activities among the plotters had kept him much in town; and although so far as he knew Phoebe had been faithful at the trysting-place, he had become very fearful lest his frequent failures to join her might so offend her that she would cease from going there on Tuesday evenings. However that might be, he would ride to Hampstead as soon as he was off duty today, and pray God that he would find her waiting at Jack Straw's.

It was a dark, wet, raw evening, more like November than February, when he trotted his horse along that familiar road. The sky lowered and seemed to press the cold into the earth, making a mockery of the approach of spring, and when he had left the town behind him, the tree trunks stood out like corded black velvet against the grey fields. From the moment he had left Whitehall, after changing out of his uniform, he had experienced the sensation of being followed, and despite his resolve to ignore such a possibility, had turned his head several times to see. Each time he saw, at some little distance behind him, a fellow on horseback leading a pack-horse; he was hunched forward in the saddle, chewing a straw, and seemed quite uninterested in Derrick. Probably he was a perfectly innocent countryman, bound for some farm; on the other hand, he might be an assassin. To hell with him, thought Derrick. He will hardly dare to shoot me in the back in daylight, even in this lonely place; let me but get to Hampstead and Phoebe in safety, and afterwards, on the dark ride home, he may do what he will.

He felt a lump rise in his throat as he came to the familiar village. There was the Black Boy and Still, there the forge, and now he was passing Mr Jolly's shop; the air was sharp and cold and clean after the smoke-laden atmosphere of London; pigs were straying about the street as usual, and an indignant housewife was shooing one from her clean doorstep. He felt as though he had been absent many years in some distant country, and was returned after much peril to the only home he knew. His spirits soared so dizzily from the depths to the heights when, having stabled his horse, he hastened into the common-room and saw Phoebe sitting in her accustomed place, that he could not speak for a moment, but stood silent, drinking in every detail of that beloved face and figure, warming his cold heart at her smile.

She sat on a stool at the counter as usual, leaning her elbows among the mugs and tankards, her feet crossed and her skirts tucked up to expose several inches of shapely leg. She was in her red-hooded cloak, which she had thrown back in the warmth of the room, and her bright brown hair was tumbled about her shoulders. She had kicked off her pattens and her stockinged feet swung gently a few inches above the floor, the toes wriggling sensuously in comfort and freedom. Through the hatch above the counter showed the head and shoulders of the Pirate, his bearded face grinning with surprise and pleasure as he saw who had come in. There were no other customers, for it was too early for the shopkeepers and labourers, and Derrick, savouring each detail of this evening, glanced affectionately about the empty room, noticing anew its sanded floor, its shovel-board table, its clinging aroma of ale and tobacco, its framed advertisements for horse-medicine and cures for the diseases of sheep and cattle, and its tattered copy of an Act of Parliament, written over by rude rustics, nailed above the hearth.

"I had begun to think I had grown stale to you," said Phoebe, looking at him mischievously over the rim of her ale-can, "for you have deserted me for three weeks, you rogue. Come, give account of yourself, pray; you will not bubble me with tales of accompanying your royal master out of town, for though I am a rustic wench I hear the news and know very well that the Court hath not stirred from Whitehall since Christmas."

"You'll be away to Newmarket next month, Master Calder," interposed the Pirate eagerly, before Derrick could reply. "Come, what will win the Town Plate this spring? There was a party of horse-coursers from Smithfield a-drinking in my house yesterday, and they spoke of nought but this grey gelding called Dragon belonging to my Lord Lovelace, which they swore was the best running-horse ever ran a heat."

"Bless me!" cried Phoebe, "but I would like well to go to Newmarket and see the sport. How goes the song now? –

'To horse, brave boys of Newmarket, to horse!
   You'll lose the match by longer delaying;
The gelding just now was led over the course,
   I think the devil's in you for staying.' "

The pirate, keeping time with his tankard, joined in the chorus:

" 'For I'll have the brown bay if the blue bonnet ride,
   And hold a thousand pound of his side, sir;
Greybird would scour it, but Greybird grows old,
   He cannot endure it, he cannot, he will not now run it.' "

Listening to the pair of them, merry and carefree, Derrick felt a lightening of his own spirits, and presently was deep in a discussion as to the chance of the King himself riding the winner of the Twelve Stone Plate which his Majesty had instituted soon after the Restoration. It was good to distract oneself with such talk, and he determined to maintain this light note during the evening, and to give no hint to Phoebe of the troubles which had come upon him since last they had met. He knew her well enough by this time to be aware that one of her rules of life was that troubles should be kept to oneself; she never told him hers, and did not expect to be burdened with his; she accepted the fact that life had its dark side, but saw no good in dwelling upon it, and despised as a weakness any reference to it. For herself, she could always find pleasure in little things, and she expected her fellow mortals to do the same; if they could not, she shunned their company.

There came at last the longed-for moment when Phoebe, having sufficiently regaled herself with ale and jests in the Pirate's company, made that motion with her head, half tender, half saucy, which told her lover that she would be private with him, and collecting the usual quart of wine from the landlord, he followed her to their little retreat abovestairs. It was strange, he thought, seeing her turn to him with that old eagerness and ardour as soon as the door was shut, how neither of them ever tired of this invariable manner of spending their evenings together. When he was absent from her, the cold thought sometimes nagged at him that Phoebe felt nothing but a sexual passion for him; yet each time he was with her he knew that there was affection as well, though whether she was aware of it or not he still did not know. Nor could he guess from what source this affection sprang; they had nothing in common, they were of different worlds; yet they had forged that strange link which transformed passion into a genuine love on his side, something at least resembling it on hers. Sometimes when the reality of her affection for him seemed suddenly to strike her, she would stare at him, and frown, and exclaim in surprise and almost with irritation, as she did this evening:

"Pox on't, what have you done to me to make me love you so? I have had a-plenty satisfaction in my life, but never any happiness until I met you."

In the early days of their association, he had been jealous enough to try and draw her into an enlargement of this statement, desiring assurance of her future fidelity, hoping one day he would hear her swear that their mutual love was enough for her and that she could never now indulge in those casual affairs for which she was notorious. But those days were past. He had come to accept her grudging confessions of affection as the best he could ever hope for from her, and took care not to mar the compliment by crying for that which could not be.

Presently they drank their wine together, and Phoebe, still in a particularly lively mood, told him little anecdotes of her doings during the past three weeks. It was sweet to him now, where sometimes it had been bitter, to hear how happily occupied she had been without him, how full was her life, how satisfying she found her days; she had been out with poachers in Cane Wood, and had narrowly escaped being caught by the keepers of the lord of the manor there; her dogs had dug a badger on the Heath; she had persuaded Mr Dubs the farmer to let her doctor a sick sheep, and had been so successful that he had presented her with a dozen of eggs and a pound of fresh butter. She related these small triumphs with zest and liveliness, taking Derrick's interest for granted; and then, drinking the heady wine she never touched save in his company, grew first a little bawdy, then frankly amorous again, employing by instinct all those arts of love which ladies of fashion and high-born courtesans spent years in learning for the capture of husbands or wealthy lovers.

And so the time fled by. Often before when he was with Phoebe, Derrick had noticed the curious behaviour of time; an hour seemed a minute; the evening was scare begun ere it was time for him to escort his mistress home. As she dressed herself tonight, Phoebe surprised him by asking suddenly:

"When shall I see you again?"

It was a question she had never asked before, for ordinarily she was content to know that he would come to her whenever he could, and that if he did not come it was because of circumstances over which he had no control. Before he could answer her, Phoebe went on:

"You are sick in mind and body, Derrick. Oh, you have been mighty gay this evening, but your flesh is dry and burning as though you had a fever, and your eyes when they look at me see always something else. Come, what ails you? You may as well be plain with me."

He was straightening the curls of his peruke before putting it on, and despite himself he found that his fingers were unsteady. A desperate urge to unburden himself to her of all his troubles fought with a conviction that it would endanger their harmony, mar the perfection of what very well might be their last evening together. His troubles were his own, and he must keep them so. It was comfort enough to know that Phoebe most uncharacteristically had asked to share them. But as, readily accepting his silence, she turned smiling at the door to see if he were ready, his conviction that his parting with her tonight would be a final one so racked him that he caught her in his arms, pressed her closely to him, and spoke deep and quiet into the bright hair which nestled against his cheek.

"My dear and only love, you know that while I am in this world I shall never cease to come to you, or, if circumstances prevent me, to send word to you why I cannot come. But alack, we have no legal claim on one another, and so it might chance that, if some accident befell me, you would not hear of it, for there is no one who would think of letting you know. For this reason I have writ you a letter, which I have given into the hands of a trusted friend of mine, with instructions to him that – that if aught befell me of a fatal nature, he is to place it in your hands. Read this letter with charity and understanding; what I have writ in it comes from the depths of my heart."

He stopped, half regretting having spoken, wondering how she would take it, for he knew she did not like this sort of intense talk. Then he heard her laugh a little, whether from embarrassment or to cover some emotion he durst not decide.

"Bless me," murmured Phoebe, patting his cheek, "what is all this talk of fatal happenings? Are you to fight a duel? Nay, I know very well what 'tis," she went on, laughing now in a natural manner, and seeming quite to have forgotten her late anxiety for him, "this wine we have been guzzling hath given you the melancholy; pox take it, the grape's a spiteful thing, as often I have told you. Come your ways and let's wash it out with ale, for you are in the country now, and will find its potations more comfortable than your town-bred clarets."

He was grateful instead of hurt that she had resumed this light note, and was ashamed of the self-pity which had driven him into forsaking it just now. They went downstairs and into the common-room, crowded now, and spent an hour in light talk and jest. Phoebe, always a little tipsy by this time, became rustically lewd in her conversation, exchanging broad jests with the Pirate and the other customers; Derrick noted, as so often before, the curious innocence which made her bawdiness so different from that of the fashionable world in which he lived.

When at last he must go to the stable to fetch his horse, he noticed without interest that there were two other animals there, the sorry nag and the pack-horse which he had observed coming along behind him as he had ridden up to Hampstead. Leading his own horse by the bridle, he went round to the front of the tavern and found Phoebe awaiting him at the door, her hood drawn over her head to shield her from the rain which was now falling in a light drizzle; she was exchanging last jests with the Pirate, who stood in the entrance, but on seeing Derrick went up to him and tucked her hand under his arm in an affectionate gesture. They walked slowly down the hill, not speaking; she hummed under her breath the racing song she and the

Pirate had sung together in the common-room earlier, cheerfully cursed the pot-holes into which she stumbled now and then, and appeared altogether carefree and contented. When they came level with her father's door, he caught her in his arms in the kind darkness, and kissed her lingeringly, unable to trust his voice to speak; so he watched her go, with a last gay wave of her hand; the door opened and shut, and he was alone in the night.

Mounting his horse and walking it slowly down the long slope which led to London, he set himself deliberately to relive each moment of this evening in his mind, almost childishly striving to take it all in order, pausing to search for some sentence of Phoebe's which eluded him, trying to picture her exact look and tone and gesture as she had said this, done that. Such was his invariable custom, making a store of sweet memories until they met again, but tonight he was particularly industrious in his collecting of tiny details, for the fear lay strong upon him that he had seen her for the last time on earth.

Once, as he came to the loneliest part of the Conduit Fields, he reined-in suddenly and sat listening. He had been sure, somehow, that his enemies would choose just such a situation as this for putting him out of the way; it was night and very dark; when his body was discovered it would be taken for granted that he had been waylaid by tobymen, like many another solitary traveller foolish enough to brave the perils of the night abroad, and the usual hue and cry would go on with the usual vain result. He had almost hoped that they would strike tonight, while the scent of Phoebe's hair was still in his nostrils, the sound of her voice still lingering in his ears, the happiness of their time together still warming his heart. But he heard nothing save the melancholy drip of the rain, the hooting of a distant owl, and the creek of leather as his horse moved restlessly. He touched the animal with his heel and rode on, suddenly anxious for bed, for he knew that tonight at least he would sleep sound without nightmares.

The next day was uneventful, and the next likewise until evening. Then, arriving at Whitehall to go on duty, a servant met him at the door of the Ushers' Parlour, where he must change into his uniform, and told him that a fellow had been enquiring for him, and was still waiting within. Derrick's heart missed a beat; he thought instantly, it is the assistant rubber; he has changed his mind and will come in as a second witness after all. He pushed past the servant, flung open the door; and found himself face to face with Daniel Jolly.

Derrick exhaled a sharp breath. He was shocked, not only by the unexpectedness of finding Mr Jolly here, but by the old man's appearance. His kindly face was unshaven, grey and drawn; he had an old cloak flung over his working clothes and apron, with its hood still pulled over his head; and his face was working with some violent emotion the nature of which Derrick could not make out. Becoming aware of the presence of two fellow Ushers, who were lounging here in the Parlour before going on duty, and were staring with frank curiosity at the incongruous figure of the visitor, Derrick stepped quickly up to them and took an arm of each.

"Tom, Ned, do me a favour. Let me have the Parlour to myself for a space. I must have privy talk with this man, and there is nowhere else I can take him."

They agreed good-naturedly, and after reminding Derrick that he had not much time before he must go on duty himself, left the room.

Derrick closed the door after them, faced round and leant against it, and opened his mouth to speak. But before he could get out a word, a voice he scarcely recognised snarled from before the hearth:

"Villain! Where's my wench?"

"Your wench," repeated Derrick stupidly. "Phoebe?" And then, sharply and on a note of gathering anguish: "Phoebe? What mean you, sir? Is she at home? Hath something happened? Tell me instantly."

He strode over to the chandler as he spoke, and as he came near he smelled a strong odour of spirits from the man. This added to his mounting terror, for he knew that Mr Jolly seldom indulged in anything but ale. The chandler stared at him, his former rage dying, and a look of piteous weariness taking its place.

"Your pardon, sir," he mumbled. "I knew you could not have done her any ill. But I am distracted and scarce know what I say. I have not slept – you must excuse me."

"Mr Jolly," cried Derrick, seizing him by the shoulders, "for God's sake tell me what is this to-do. I take it that Phoebe is missing; when did she vanish, and what do you suspect to be the cause?"

"Last evening," began the chandler, making a great effort to control his shaking voice, "I went to the Black Boy for a whet, as is my custom when the shutters are up and my 'prentice gone. Phoebe was within doors then, but my wife was out a-visiting a neighbour. When I returned, I found my wife but not my daughter. I thought it did not signify, since the wench is prone to gadding, and when she had not returned at ten o'clock, I locked the door and left the key under a flower-pot on the window-sill. She knew where to find it, for often she – she – "

The old man hesitated, glancing at Derrick in an embarrassed way.

"She is often late in returning home," the young man prompted him impatiently.

"Ay, that's it, that's it," agreed Mr Jolly. "I went to bed and to sleep. During the night I was disturbed by the noise of Phoebe's dogs, which came a-scrabbling at the outer door and making such a touse I feared they would arouse the neighbours. Methought she would be with them, but when they still continued I went down and let them in and there was not a sight of her. Well, thought I, they have missed her on the Heath very like, so I shut them into her chamber, but bless me, how they whined and scratched at the door. This morning I arose ere my family was astir, as is my wont, but when I had lit the fire and performed other little tasks and Phoebe came not to bring me my 'morning' of bread and small-beer, I began to wonder, and when 'twas time to take down the shutters and I heard the dogs making as great a touse as ever from her chamber, I went thither and made so bold as to enter. She was not there and her bed had not been slept in."

He paused, sighed shudderingly, and passed a hand over his face.

"Then I went in to my wife, and she being newly awake, enquired of her whether Phoebe had said aught concerning where she had gone last night. My wife said no, the wench had not been in the house when she returned from her visit. I began to have some disquiet, yet Phoebe being a wench well able to take care of herself, and known to all the people round, I kept a rein on my anxiety, being besides very occupied with my business, until mid-day. She being yet not come home, and her dogs near beside themselves with howling and whining, I put on my cap and went to make enquiries with the neighbours, and so I learned that one of them had spied my daughter, somewhere around nine of the clock last night, hastening towards the Upper Bowling Green in company with a stranger, and at this time, said they, she had her dogs at her heels. Thither I went with all speed and addressed myself to the landlord."

Again he paused. He was sitting huddled in a chair now, with Derrick, cold and silent with apprehension, leaning against the chimney-breast near him.

"Charlie Weems, the landlord of the Bowling Green, sir," went on Mr Jolly, "is a man I never could abide, though I confess I have no near acquaintance with him. If all the tales be true, he is hand-in-glove with the tobymen, and I suspect likewise that he was deep in the confidence of my former lodger, Master Baillie – but let that pass. When I asked him if he had seen my daughter last night, he said Yes, he had seen her in his house; she had come thither, said he, in company with a gentleman, they had drunk together in the common-room, seeming very fond of each other's company, and some time later he had seen them drive away towards London in the coach which had brought the gentleman to Hampstead. I begged of Mr Weems to describe this gentleman, and from what he said, sir, I thought it to be you."

Daniel broke off again, and glanced up at the other in wistful appeal.

"It was not I," said Derrick shortly. "I have not seen your daughter, or been to Hampstead, since Tuesday night."

There was a short pause.

"I went home and told my wife what I had heard. She – she was pleased to insist," said Mr Jolly, with an evident embarrassment, "that you had – you had kidnapped my girl, and told me I ought to go to a justice and lay an information of it, adding that thereby you – your pardon, Mr Calder, I do but repeat what she said – might be constrained to have your wife divorce you and so marry my daughter. I would not hearken to such foolish talk, but being by this time in great anxiety of mind, persuaded some of my neighbours to assist me in making a search of the Heath. I feared, d'you see, that some mischief had befallen the foolish wench; she is headstrong, sir, and sometimes conducts herself in so free a manner that I have feared for her safety before this. We could not find a trace of her, but a swine-tender we met with informed us that last evening, being upon the Heath (and a-poaching, if I know aught of him), he had seen a coach which was not a hackney driving with great speed in the direction of Hendon. He could not see who was within, but this he swore, that for some distance it was followed by two dogs, the which he knew to be those belonging to my daughter, and that these beasts kept up with it, barking loudly, till they were whipped off by the coachman."

"Go on, man, go on for God's sake!" cried Derrick, as the old man paused again for breath.

"So I being altogether desperate," pursued Mr Jolly, his words now coming in a rush, "resolved upon seeking you out, sir, ay, I resolved to penetrate even into the King's palace to get news of my child if in any way I could. I did not intend, Mr Calder, to address you as I did when you entered here; I knew you would never harm my Phoebe; but I was distracted, sir, altogether distracted, and I came to you for assistance, you being a gentleman and knowledgeable of what I ought to do in these straits, and having so great a tenderness for my foolish little wench – "

And with that he broke down and wept openly, his head bowed in his hands and sobs shaking his old shoulders.

In the silence of the room, broken only by this piteous sound, a clock chimed musically, and Derrick realised without interest that the hour when he should have been on duty in the Duke's ante-chamber had just struck. The knowledge faded from his mind almost before it had come there; he began to pace the room, twisting his hands together, fighting for control.

"Mr Jolly," he said at last abruptly, as he halted by the old man's chair, "you and I will find your daughter, but only if you will trust me and give me all the assistance in your power."

"D'you know where she is, then?" asked the chandler, lifting his head to stare at Derrick with a new suspicion.

"I know, I fear, who hath abducted her, and why. Do you remember your late lodger, do you remember the man with the wooden leg, the tobyman in the Conduit Fields, the paper you got from the ballad-monger – "

"No more of that, for the love of God," interrupted Mr Jolly, rising in great agitation. "Why fox me with such things now, sir, when all I desire is the return of my daughter – "

"These things and the disappearance of your daughter are parts of one foul plot," Derrick interrupted in his turn. "Harkee, sir, you must not ask me now for explanations; all I beg of you is that you search your memory, even as I have been doing while you spoke, and let me know if there was any place you heard mentioned which was used by these conspirators and the which you did not remember when we talked together at the Bowling Green that morning. Mr Jolly," he added authoritatively, as the other made to speak, "positively you must do as I say and ask no further questions. Your daughter's safety may depend upon this memory."

He walked away to the window and stood staring out. They would not hide her in London, he reflected, striving desperately to be calm; it was too dangerous. Where else? There was Lord Grey's country seat, Up Park, in Sussex. It might serve, for it was secluded; but no, my lord having been so recently in serious trouble for the abduction of one woman, would scarce risk his head by another kidnapping. Had they carried her to Scotland, or into one of the disaffected country parts? Even as he fought against the despair this idea engendered, he heard old Jolly's voice, tentative, hesitating, speak from his chair by the hearth.

"There was one place mentioned," said he slowly, "but I knew not what it meant and so forgot to speak of it to you when we met at the Bowling Green that day. I think, I am almost sure, 'twas Captain Cruckshank, as he calls himself, that rogue of a tobyman, who mentioned it; he spoke of someone with a name which sounded mighty strange and foreign to me – Handibel or some such – "

"Hannibal, was it?" interrupted Derrick sharply.

"Ay, that was it," replied Mr Jolly, brightening. "Hannibal, a most heathenish sort of a name, fitter a Turk than a – "

"I have heard it myself," snapped Derrick. "But I know not whose it is. Did you hear him described? Was he, perchance, a one-eyed man?"

"Nay, why should he be that?" asked Mr Jolly wonderingly.

Derrick made a gesture of impatience.

"It doth not signify. Go on, man, what else? What of this Hannibal?"

"There was somewhat about Hannibal and his boys, and then a place mentioned – somewhat to do with – nay, it hath escaped me. Stay! Somewhat to do with – corn, was it? Nay, not corn – wheat? no – I have it! Rye! Hannibal and his boys at Rye."

"There is only one Rye that I know of," said Derrick, frowning, having hung in anguish upon this slow search after what might be a most vital clue, "and that is in Sussex. But then, this coach, it did not turn south as it ought to have done. A fig for that, we progress; a one-eyed man (for I'm sure that will be the reason for the by-name) at Rye in Sussex. I shall ride thither tonight."

"But your duties at Court, sir," exclaimed Mr Jolly astonished.

"Are ended, Mr Jolly," answered Derrick, smiling without mirth. "I am already somewhat under a cloud with my Lord Chamberlain, and since I have missed his Royal Highness' evening levee, where I should be on duty, undoubtedly I shall be dismissed. Have no thought of me; only be assured that come what may I shall find your daughter. Go home now, sir; speak of this to no man; only if you have further news, come to me with it yourself, or, if I am absent from London, enquire for Private Gentleman Younghusband, of the Third Troop of Life Guards. He is quartered at the Savoy; you must seek him there, and when you come at him, give him a message for me, or beg his own assistance. He will not deny you, for he is my very good friend."

Before the chandler could indulge in any further talk, Derrick bustled him out of the room, down the stair, and along the street, parting from him finally at Holbein's Gate. Then he called a hackney and bade the man drive him home; he must collect a few necessaries before starting forth on his difficult quest. Jolted along in the stuffy darkness, he beat his forehead with his clenched fist in wild self-accusation; fool that he had been, fool, fool to imagine that he alone was in danger. Here was the answer to the puzzle as to why they had not struck him down as soon as Grey told his fellow conspirators who 'Simon Hill' really was. They had dogged him, they had followed him to Hampstead, they had seen him with Phoebe, they had marked, without the shadow of a doubt, the fondness of his manner towards her. And just in case he might contemplate a further meddling in their affairs, they had issued a warning: Mind your own business or you will never see your mistress again.

Well, he would do so; he had laid his information before the authorities; his duty was done. His life was narrowed now into one single purpose: to find Phoebe and restore her to her home.

Part Three

Chapter One

As soon as her father had gone off to the Black Boy for his evening ale, Phoebe took the opportunity of having the house to herself to prepare a more than ordinarily offensive medicament, invented by herself, for the doctoring of animals. One of her dogs had a tooth which needed extracting; she had discovered that this could be done without the pain of dentistry by mixing raven's dung, cow dung, and the soles of old shoes, all burnt together into a powder which, mingled with honey and May-butter, she put into the hollow tooth; after five days the tooth fell out of its own accord. Or at least it should do.

It was Wednesday evening, the day after she had been with Derrick Calder to Jack Straw's. She talked cheerfully to her dogs as she filled the kitchen with the fearsome odour of her firing, annoyed with herself because she was worried, but determined not to admit it. She was a very simple girl, was Phoebe, and somewhat selfish besides, yet it had been plain enough to her the previous evening that her lover was sick in mind and body, so seriously sick that it had aroused the womanly compassion in which she was not lacking but which ordinarily she despised. So today her heart was reproaching her for the way she had snubbed Derrick when sometimes of late he had attempted to unburden himself to her of what was troubling him; she had gathered that it was something of a public nature and therefore no concern of hers, nor, she comforted herself, could she have been able to advise him upon it.

Nevertheless, thought she to herself, next time we meet I'll make him purge himself of this pother and plague my ears with conspiracies and other tiresome matters. God damn him, why am I so fond? she wondered irritably, pulling her cooking-pot from the fire by its long handle and investigating its loathsome contents to see if they were ready for the next stage of mixing; I'll vow he'll turn me into a love-sick wench despite myself, and then farewell peace of mind. Shift your silly arse, Tangle, or you'll have it burnt; if I were sensible, I'd hie me up to Jack Straw's and have a bout with the Pirate, for there's no better remedy for such a humour as has gotten into me.

Scarcely had she thus addressed herself, when Phoebe was interrupted in her labours by a knock upon the outer door. She did not hurry to answer it, supposing it to be some crony of Mrs Jolly's come hither for a gossip. When at length she did, she was surprised and pleased to see a man's figure standing in the doorway; then immediately intrigued when a strange and deferential voice enquired if she were Mistress Phoebe Jolly.

"Herself in person, sir," answered the girl saucily. "What would you with her? If it be something which must take me abroad, you must even stay a while, for I am about an important task and cannot gad out till it be done."

"Mistress," said the stranger, with a courteous bow, " 'tis a very urgent and privy matter on which I seek you. I carry a message from a gentleman who has the honour to be a friend of yours, one Mr Calder. This message cannot be given you in a few words, being weighty, and since I would not intrude into your father's house for reasons of delicacy – you understand me? – I beg that you will accompany me to the Upper Bowling Green, where, if you will oblige me by partaking of a whet, I will endeavour to make all plain."

Adad, thought Phoebe, here's gentlemanly talk. But underneath her flippancy she was experiencing an intensification of the worry which had lain on her ever since last night. There had been that strange talk of Derrick's about fatal accidents and his care in making arrangements for her being told if anything untoward befell him.

"Stay a moment while I fetch my cloak," said Phoebe abruptly to the stranger. "I will come at once." She ran upstairs, and returning after a moment dressed for out-of-doors, called to her dogs to accompany her.

"Must these brutes come with us?" enquired the stranger, eyeing the mongrel curs with distaste.

"I stir not abroad without my dogs," replied Phoebe firmly. "You need not be afeared, sir, they have companioned me in many situations wherein ordinarily a wench would be private, and I assure you tell no tales."

As they walked up Heath Street together, Phoebe cast surreptitious glances at her companion, in an endeavour to make out what sort of a man he was. But it was a dark night, and only when they passed the lighted window of some cottage could she make out more than a mere outline; he was, she thought, a man in early middle age, tall and spare, walked with his head downbent and his hat pulled low over his brows, and seemed to her to have a faint air of uneasiness. For a while she attempted to make conversation, but her companion answering only in monosyllables, and her own anxiety for Derrick growing, she soon fell silent, and thus they came to the tavern.

The happenings of the next few minutes were so swift and so unexpected, that afterwards Phoebe could scarce place them in their proper order. To reach the common-room, she and the stranger had to cross the yard, and in the centre of this there stood a coach, a four-horsed vehicle, with the leather curtains close drawn at the windows. Weems, the landlord, was standing beside it, talking to the coachman on his box, and as Phoebe and her companion made to pass, Mr Weems stepped forward as though to greet her. Phoebe was surprised, for he was no friend of hers, and being a haughty sort of man, he tended to ignore his humbler customers. She paused to hear what he would say, and as she did so the stranger who had brought her here stepped quickly up behind her and threw an arm round her head, pressing hard against her mouth. In the shock of the moment she stood flaccid in the stranger's grip, and before she could regain her wits Weems had flung open the coach door, the man behind her propelled her forwards, and as she was half lifted in this fashion, another man, who had been secreted in the coach, dragged her roughly into the interior. A wild barking of dogs followed, and then a yelp as someone kicked at them; the first stranger leapt in beside her, the door was slammed, the curtains pulled over the windows again, the coachman shouted to his team to "Git up there!" and the vehicle rattled over the cobble-stones and into the road.

Phoebe was not the sort of girl to respond to this rough treatment by swooning away. As soon as she had recovered from her first shock, she began a robust struggle for freedom, using teeth, feet and nails without ceremony and to such purpose that she soon drew a yell of pain from one of her captors. The coach progressed to the sounds of wild confusion, Phoebe's two dogs careering along behind it, barking furiously, the interior of the vehicle a-whirl with flailing arms and kicking legs, accompanied by the sounds of harsh breathing and muttered oaths. Clutching one of her captors firmly by his short curly hair, Phoebe, kicking backward at the other, made a dart at the handle of the door and was in the very act of turning it when a terrific jolting of the coach over a particularly deep pot-hole in the road, tumbled all three of its occupants into a heap on the floor.

"Nay, let me knock the trull senseless with my pistol-butt," panted one of the men as he picked himself up. "She was near leaping out just then, and if she be not silenced we'll never get her to the Rye."

"Put up your pistol, Zachary," commanded the other, he who had accompanied Phoebe to the Bowling Green. "We want no violence on the road, our orders being to bring her safe to my brother. Mistress," he said gruffly, holding the girl down upon the seat in a strong embrace, "do you forbear this touse; we mean you no harm if you stay quiet, but if you do not will be constrained to use force."

At these words Phoebe, reluctantly releasing the new hold she had got upon the other man's ear, ceased her struggles which she saw were quite in vain, and tossing back her disordered hair, thus addressed her captors:

"Force, quotha! And what a-devil have you been using during the past ten minutes? Now I long for the day when I shall see you both hanging in chains upon the Gibbet Trees yonder, you shitten rogues, which will come soon, I promise you, for I am not to be used in this fashion. If you think to abduct me and go unhung, you are much beside the cushion. Tangle! Mumper!" she bellowed at her dogs which were still racing and barking behind the coach, "go home, mine honest curs, for here is no company for you, and I would not have it said that dogs of mine consorted with such whoreson villains. As for you, my hempen-looked friends, let me tell you that besides there will be a hue and cry made for me so soon as my absence is known, I have powerful friends who will stick as close as a crab-louse to you till they have brought you to the Sessions for your insolence. So if you are wise, you will order the coachman to turn rightabout and head back for

Hampstead before my father comes home and finds me to be missing."

"If by your powerful friends you intend Mr Derrick Calder," replied Phoebe's late caller drily, "allow me to inform you that he is the very reason why you have been constrained to come with us, since he has presumed to stick his foolish nose into what doth not at all concern him, and in order to teach him to forbear it in future, we are removing his fair bedfellow as a warning."

"So that's the tune of it," said Phoebe thoughtfully. "By this I perceive ye are not only kidnappers of innocent wenches, but nasty plotters likewise, and therefore I shall have the pleasure of seeing ye quartered as well as hanged at Tyburn. And now I do bethink me, I have seen you before," she added, addressing the man whom his companion had called Zachary, "which was when you called upon that decayed old Scotsman, Baillie, who at his age should rather have been meditating upon what account he could give of himself to his God, than occupying his time in beastly plottings. Bless me, there'll be a goodly company of ye a-mangled by Jack Ketch when the time comes, and I assure you I shall be there to see it done. Meantime, is a poor jilt permitted to ask whither she is bound in your custody?"

"You are bound for a most genteel mansion," replied the other stranger, "called the Rye House in the country of Hertfordshire. There you will be entertained with all conveniences, and if you are wise, and make no pother, you will have security and fair treatment, and may divert yourself very pleasantly until such time as we see fit to give you your liberty again. Only for your sake I trust Mr Calder will take heed of the warning we are bestowing upon him, and will lay-by his inquistiveness into our affairs, for if he doth not, I fear we may be constrained to arrange it so that some accident befalls you, which extreme measure we hope to avoid."

"You have a sweet pretty tongue in your head," snapped Phoebe tartly. "Pray save it for your last dying speech and confession, for I assure you that such coffee-house answers are quite wasted upon me."

After this interchange there was silence save for the rumble of the wheels and the drumming of the hoof-beats; Phoebe's dogs, it seemed, had given up their vain chase and were gone home. Now that she had given an account of herself with her tongue, the girl was almost enjoying herself. It was an adventure, and she had a great relish for anything novel or exciting, especially when it gave her the opportunity of using her wits. She had a great respect for her own wits, had Phoebe, and not without reason, for they were sharp. Moreover, despite her recent words, she was a trifle fascinated by the smooth speech of the man who had conducted her to the Bowling Green, and curious to see what sort of a person he was. New acquaintances of the male sex were always welcome to Phoebe, and she never lost a chance of trying out her arts of fascination upon them. Thus she comforted herself and drove down her anxiety for her father. He would be distracted when he found her missing; so, of course, would Derrick, but in a manner of speaking it was Derrick's own fault, and moreover he was a man of the world, and in touch with powerful personages; she did not doubt that he would find a way of rescuing her, whereas her poor old father would merely anguish in distraction, and fritter away his time in futile enquiries among his neighbours.

After what seemed a long while, Phoebe perceived by the increased jolting of the coach that they were come upon some little-used country lane, and shortly after this she heard the coachman cry to his team to "Wh-oa there!" and with a great scraping of hooves the coach pulled up. One of her captors immediately leapt out, and Phoebe, peering after him, saw that it was moonlight, and that she was able to get a glimpse of the place to which she had been brought. Directly in front of her she saw a wooden bridge which led over a moat to two stout oaken doors set in a tower which looked as high as a church's. This tower, she could see, was battlemented at the top and had small windows pierced at intervals into its red brick; from the look of this brick, the tower could not have been built many years. Above the doors was a bell, attached to a stout rope which hung down on one side; the more genteel of her captors, who was the one who had leapt out, crossed the wooden bridge, and catching hold of the rope gave it a sharp jerk. The bell spoke janglingly, and almost at once there was the sound of bolts being withdrawn; one of the doors was opened from the inside, and the figure of a man holding a lanthorn appeared and exchanged a few words with the other.

"Come," said Zachary, catching Phoebe's arm in a firm grip. "Get you out, wench, and hasten, for we are arrived at the Rye."

Keeping hold of her arm, he marshalled her across the bridge and past the open door. When she and her two captors were through, the man with the lanthorn closed and bolted the doors again, turned the great key in the lock, and raising his light, surveyed the prisoner, while she in her turn eyed him with equal curiosity. She saw a short, but powerfully built man in his sixties, with arms so long in proportion to his body that he somewhat resembled an ape. He wore buff boots pulled up to his thighs, boots which were curiously in contrast with his grey country coat and oaken staff. His head was shaved as though ordinarily he wore a wig like a townsman, and he had about him an air of extraordinary surliness and even savagery, an impression heightened by the disfigurement of this face;

for he had only one eye. Where the other had been was a hideous complicated map of wrinkles, drawing up his cheek as though he were perpetually winking; the lids were puffed and of a dull purple colour, showing between them a small blood-shot aperture.

"There's a bear-garden countenance!" exclaimed Phoebe, to conceal the horror she felt of this man. "I'll warrant you there's many a matron hath miscarried at the sight of those hanging looks, and if they wish to affright children in your country, they have no need to tell them of Raw Head and Bloody Bones."

"Keep a civil tongue, you," growled the man. "My name is Richard Rumbold; I own this house; and if you look to enjoy your security while you are in it, you had best take a care to treat me with respect and carry out my orders. Will, take her within. You are confident you were not followed from Hampstead?"

"Not we," replied the man addressed as Will, and who was the genteel one of Phoebe's captors. "All fell out as we designed, and Weems knows what to say when the hunt begins."

He touched Phoebe's arm, and motioned her to follow him. They were in a small courtyard around which the house was built. In the moonlight she could see that it was partly a large farmhouse, partly a semi-fortified mansion; the only access to it appeared to be by way of the bridge over which she had just come. It was strongly built, of bright red brick, dominated by the tower which stood northwards of it; here and there a light showed in windows, but most of the place was in darkness; there was a damp smell as of a river close at hand, and the whole building had an air of melancholy and brooding evil which, despite herself, fell upon the tired Phoebe like a weight.

"I like your Rye House no better than its master," said she, as her conductor led her through a doorway into the mansion. "Pray, what manner of man is he, if one may ask?"

"He is my elder brother," replied the other shortly, "and an ill man to cross, I do assure you, so you had best use him civilly. He entered the army of the Parliament when he was but a lad, and had risen to the rank of lieutenant in Packer's Regiment of Horse ere all was done."

"Then he should have his bellyful of rebellion by this time," said Phoebe tartly, following Will Rumbold up a stair. "Adad, why cannot you be quiet, you outmoded Roundheads, and leave honest men in peace?"

"I'll tell you this, mistress," said the other, pausing suddenly and lowering his voice. "My brother Richard was one of the guards who stood about the scaffold when the late King lost his head, ay, and dabbled his handkercher in the tyrant's blood with the rest. Such men think little of taking life, I do assure you, and if you will not behave yourself while you are here, he will not scruple to knock you on the head and fling your corpse into the Ware River. So be advised."

Even the spirited Phoebe was somewhat shaken by this threat, and she was silent as her conductor led her up the stair and into a chamber where two women, one old, the other in her late thirties, sat spinning flax.

"Here's the wench," said Will Rumbold shortly. "Give her some meat and show her where she is to lie."

And with that he went out and closed the door.

Both women had risen on Phoebe's entrance, and the elder now came forward to greet her, the other remaining at her wheel.

"Do 'ee come in to the vire, me dearie," said the former, in a broad country voice. "Ee'll be cold and tired after thy long ride. I be Mistress Rumbold, and this be my daughter Miriam."

"Gossip," replied Phoebe, seating herself before the hearth, "by your looks you are an honest matron, howsoever you have the ill luck to be married to a rogue, and therefore you would be advised to lend me every assistance in returning from whence I came, for there is a law against abducting of innocent wenches, and though 'twould be no loss to you if you were made an hempen widow, you will scarce escape punishment yourself if you connive at my kidnapping."

Before Mrs Rumbold could make any answer to this, her daughter gave a short, hard laugh.

"Spare us your threats, wench," said she contemptuously. "My father is master here and brooks no interference with his plans. There will be no leaving the Rye House for you until he gives the word, and if you seek to persuade my mother to assist you, I shall report it to him and he will whip you soundly."

"Why as to that," retorted Phoebe with spirit," 'twill be he who will be whipped at the cart's tail anon, and so I promise you, and make no doubt, likewise, of seeing your madamship belaboured at Bridewell and set up to the hemp and hammer. Damme, this mutton is roast as 'twere prescribed for the pox, of peases-fed sheep as rank as he-goats; I would not give such stuff to my dogs. Would they were with me, those two honest curs, and I'd show you how prettily I have taught 'em to lift their leg at a rogue."

Beguiling herself with such verbal attacks and insults, Phoebe meanwhile observed the mother and daughter, estimating her chances of interesting them in her escape. It did not take her long to decide that her efforts to coax or frighten Miriam would be in vain; Richard Rumbold's daughter was a sullen, embittered spinster, small, dark, thin, with very pronounced eyebrows which met over her nose. It was plain that she hated her life here, but found some compensation in making everyone in her vicinity as unhappy as herself. Mrs Rumbold was more promising; she was timid, cowed, obviously in mortal fear of her husband, fundamentally kind and gentle, with a great deal of thwarted maternal instinct. Phoebe took care, during the remainder of the time before she retired to the bedchamber she was to share with Miriam, to behave towards the elder woman in a manner calculated to arouse her liking, though she feared the poor soul was so browbeaten that even if she wished to help Phoebe she would never dare to do so.

The girl found next day that she was to be allowed the liberty of walking whither she pleased about the house, the inner courtyard, and the garden. Her spirits rose at this, for a close confinement was a fate she dreaded more than all. But when she had made a tour of her prison, any hopes that escape from it would be easy quickly died.

The Rye House and its garden lay enclosed within a very strong high wall, looped for muskets, and this in its turn was surrounded by a moat of considerable width. The only access to the outer world was through the gateway in the tower; the doors of this were kept permanently locked, only Richard Rumbold having the key. Beyond them, and across the wooden bridge, was a large outer courtyard, around which were built stables, corn-chambers, and a malting-house, for Rumbold was a maltster by trade. His numerous apprentices and labourers, who worked in the out-buildings, were never permitted to cross the wooden bridge, nor were the inhabitants of the Rye, other than himself, allowed to do so in the opposite direction, so that the Rye House seemed to be in a state almost of siege. On peering through the loops in one stretch of the surrounding wall, Phoebe could see a country lane, which, she learned, was a by-road running between Hoddesdon and Bishop's Stortford; this road, after crossing the River Lea (known locally as the Ware River), which it did by a narrow bridge, ran parallel with the garden wall, then, turning sharply, passed over a causeway through a meadow close beside the outer courtyard of the Rye.

All this Phoebe either observed for herself or learned from Mrs Rumbold during her first day of captivity, and having thus satisfied herself that escape from the Rye House would be next to impossible unless she could win over one or other of its inhabitants into being an accomplice, turned her attention to accomplishing this feat. The persons among whom she was come did not seem promising, but Phoebe was a girl not easily daunted, and one very confident of her powers of persuasion so far as the male sex was concerned. In what precise was Derrick had so far offended the owner of the Rye House as to drive him to the abduction of an innocent girl she did not know; it had something to do with a plot which Derrick, it seemed, was intent on investigating. Well, plots were none of her business; all she desired was to get home to her father; if, she thought, she could convince one or other of the inhabitants of the Rye of this, she might succeed in gaining the assistance she needed for making her escape. It would be in vain, she was aware, to try and coax or frighten Richard Rumbold himself or to waste her efforts on the female part of the household; there remained four persons from among whom to seek an accomplice, the maltster's younger brother William, the burly fellow named Zachary, and two other men who seemed to be part friends, part henchmen, of the owner of the Rye.

The sole duty of these four appeared to be taking turns in mounting guard in the turret of the tower; from sunrise to sunset, Phoebe observed, this turret was never without its sentinel, though for what they were watching she could not at first make out. Zachary and one of his companions were of the most bitter type of fanatic, larding all their talk with texts, raving against the sins of the Court and the nation generally, exchanging reminiscences of the days of the Commonwealth (both, she learned, had served in the Roundhead army), and talking mysteriously of the time when the Good Old Cause should be triumphant once more. For all she caught them casting sly glances at her figure, she knew it would be a waste of time to try and win them over; and therefore concentrated all her efforts upon the only two persons at the Rye who just possibly might be willing to fill the role of accomplice, William Rumbold and a man named John Rouse.

Chapter Two

Phoebe had not been in captivity a week before John Rouse was whispering an invitation to come and take a whet with him in his chamber.

He was a man contemporary in age with the elder Rumbold, and had been a surgeon in the regiment in which Richard had served as lieutenant during the Civil War. Like all the other inhabitants of the Rye, he was plainly in fear of the one-eyed malster, and from hints he let fall, Phoebe suspected that the latter had some particular hold over him, going back to their soldiering days. Rouse was an educated man and frankly despised the brutish company at the Rye House; for the greater part of the day he was sullen and sarcastic, but there were intervals when, emerging from a period spent in his bedchamber, he would be filled with self-pity, wistfully seeking someone in whom to confide his wrongs and troubles, desperate for congenial companionship. At these times he smelt strong of spirits, and from this, as also from the way in which his hands shook in the mornings, it was obvious that he had some secret store of liquor in his room. From his first sight of Phoebe he had ogled her, and when she accepted his invitation to take a whet in his room, immediately began to take some senile liberties. Well able to manage men of his age, Phoebe played up to him, and by permitting him to stroke her calf and steal a kiss or two, soon had him so far infatuated that he began to talk.

On her first visit to his chamber, Rouse talked solely of himself and of this past, cataloguing a long list of his misfortunes and wrongs, raving against the ingratitude of friends, inveighing against the adverse fate which never had rewarded his talents and qualities. But the second time she accepted an invitation to drink with him, Rouse was more interesting, for he began upon his present situation, whining for her sympathy in that he, a man who loved good talk and genteel company, must stay locked up with oafish countrymen and mad fanatics.

"If I could but get me to Bishop's Stortford for a few hours," he grumbled, "I am sure I could find some company more human that these animals with whom I must stay cooped up. And I would take you with me, my pretty dear, and you and I would try what we could discover in the way of a good Rhenish or Canary in the principal tavern there."

This was distinctly encouraging, and Phoebe, seating herself upon his knee, whispered that they ought to attempt it, for it would please her mightily.

"There is not space for a dog or a cat to creep through into the outer world from this place," answered Rouse gloomily, "and Hannibal alone hath the key to the gates. He is obstinate in keeping us close prisoners till all is done, lest one of us should blab in our cups; I suppose he is in the right of it, yet 'tis an ill situation for one who loves good company."

"Hannibal?" repeated Phoebe. "Do you speak of Master Rumbold?"

" 'Tis the cant name for him among our friends," replied Rouse, "because he lacks an eye – nay, I perceive you are not read in the ancients, and why should you plague that lovely head of yours with reading of dull books? Hannibal, my sweet, was a soldier of Carthage and led his people against the might of Rome, during which operations he had the misfortune to lose an eye, but in the end of all took poison rather than fall into the hands of his foe."

"Methinks your modern Hannibal will be fortunate if he cheats the gallows by the same trick," said Phoebe tartly.

"Nay, he'll wear an earl's coronet, my pretty, when all is done," Rouse assured her, laughing. " 'Tis a neat plan and cannot fail, and by and by, my charmer, you and I will drink together in a king's palace, and pledge the fate which brought us together in a common captivity here."

"Since I know not what this plan is of which you speak," said Phoebe, yawning, "I will not presume to contradict you."

She got off his knee and walked to the window, turning her back on him. She was cross, because it appeared to her that she was wasting her time with Rouse after all; besides, he was growing very drunk, and when he was thus he dribbled at the nose and his speech was a trifle incoherent. Not easily disgusted, her present captivity and the diminishing hopes of escaping from it, were making her so irritable that she felt nauseated by the man, and feared to let him see how his tipsy maulings disgusted her. Mistaking the reason for her releasing herself from his embrace, Rouse lurched up behind her, and ducking his head down began to whisper in her ear.

" 'Tis a shame to keep so pretty a bird in a cage and let her know no reason for it. List you, sweet dove, since you are a prisoner and cannot blab, there can be no harm in letting you into our secrets. You must know, then (but let not Hannibal know that I have told you, or he will do both of us some mischief) that the King and his brother, when they return from the races at Newmarket, are accustomed to leave the main road at Bishop's Stortford and take the by-way to Hoddesdon, forsaking the other because it winds much about on the right hand from Stanstead. They are settled to go to Newmarket upon March 12th and return upon the 26th, but they will never reach London alive."

She stiffened in the arms which he had placed about her body; keeping her face averted, she strained to hear every word of his half coherent speech.

" 'Tis known that they travel with very few Life Guards, and that by the King's order his coachman drives at such a rate that often he quite outdistances those there are. When the royal coach is to pass the Rye and is upon the causeway yonder, there will be a farm cart overturned which will cause it to halt, and immediately upon this, those within it will be surprised by an ambuscade, who will open fire upon them at point-blank range. Ay, 'tis a neat plan, and cannot fail, I promise you. Come, my sweet rustic, let's drink to it, and to the fine times which are coming for those who 'complish it."

"There'll be fine times at Tyburn," said Phoebe, with pretended scorn, "and this I promise you. Are you so mad that you think to murder the King and escape the vengeance of the Law?"

"You understand not, you understand not, my little simpleton," chuckled Rouse, hugging her close. "Here is a deep-laid scheme which goes back a long while and hath many concerned in it, among whom are several noblemen. When we have done our part at the Rye, immediately there will be a seizing of the public places in London, risings in the country parts, the proclaiming of the Duke of Monmouth King, and the murder of Charles Stuart and his brother laid upon the Papists. Had it not been that several in the country were not ready and failed us at the eleventh hour, we would have struck in November last; the disgust he took at this postponement caused the Earl of Shaftesbury to flee overseas. But on this occasion there will be no hitch, and then! what feastings and bonfires and rewards handed out to us who have risked so much, and you shall share in these junketings, my rustical Venus, and have silk gowns and pearl necklaces and ride in your own coach."

He applied himself to the bottle once more, and Phoebe, pressing him to drink yet deeper, soon brought him to the state when he scarcely noticed that she escaped from his chamber. She fled to her own room; and there astonished herself by bursting into tears.

For the horrible secrets she had heard from Rouse had pierced the shell of her shallowness and selfish indifference to public matters. Vague talk of a plot was one thing; the details of a plan to murder, in cold blood, the King and his Heir, were quite another. Her captors were not only ruffians and abductors of innocent wenches; they were butchers, king-killers, the worst sort of traitors; and she was altogether in their power. But she must escape now, she must; somehow or other she must get out of the Rye and inform the authorities of this plot before it was too late. Failing this, she must find a way of conveying a message through the country folk around. The more she learned of the Rye House and its peculiar situation, the less could she delude herself with the hope that the assassination plan would fail. Though it stood but eighteen miles from London, the surrounding country was as lonely as could be found; there was no village near, not even a solitary farmhouse or hedge-inn; and from the tall tower the sentinels had an excellent view for many miles, so that the conspirators would have ample warning of the approach of the royal coach. Immediately they had accomplished their bloody work, the assassins would be able to barricade themselves into this stronghold of a house, while one of them galloped breakneck to London to bear the tidings to their friends.

Phoebe's horror at what she had just heard soon was overwhelmed by a sturdy determination to thwart the plans of the conspirators. It was now plain to her that in any scheme she might form for escape, Rouse would be as useless as the others; sullen when sober, maudlin when drunk, he lacked the strength of character to carry out a daring plan even if she could persuade him to enter into it in return for her favours. Yet an accomplice she must have if she were to get out of the Rye House; there was no possible chance of slipping out by the gateway at some unguarded moment, for the gates were locked by day and bolted by night; however often Richard Rumbold must go in and out about his business, he never did so without turning the key in the lock. At night this key reposed beneath his pillow, and he was not the sort of man to sleep so sound that one might risk stealing it at dead of night. Therefore, shunning Rouse's company, Phoebe turned to a bettering of her acquaintance with the only other possible candidate for the role of accomplice, the maltster's younger brother, William.

William Rumbold was indifferent to female charms; his one fleshly vice was gluttony, and when Phoebe, discerning this, took care to tempt him with little tit-bits whenever he passed the kitchen, he began to take an interest in her company, and presently to talk. From her first sight of him she had sensed that he had some trouble of mind, and now she learned that while his comrades looked forward to the deed of murder with lively anticipation, William had some qualms concerning it. For the greater part of his life, he told her, he had served as a mercenary in foreign service; she gathered that the profession of arms was dear to him for its own sake, and that he was proud of a reputation for courage in the field and for discipline in the camp. He had his code, therefore, and though it was but the code of a mercenary, he prided himself that he had lived up to it. This, he confided to her, was the reason why the thought of murder in cold blood was distasteful to him; an armed rebellion, yes, assassination, no; and it was only his fear of his brother which had persuaded him to become one of the actors in the latter. From the way he talked of Richard, Phoebe learned also that he had some jealousy of his brother, who, though he lacked his wide experience of military matters, and had been a stay-at-home, ordered him about like a lackey. It was this knowledge of William Rumbold's character which Phoebe tried to use for her own ends.

"Where lost your brother his eye, master?" she would ask, as greedily he devoured a pie she had smuggled him. "Nay, fox me not with tales of old battles, wherein he knew more than ever his General did, for I warrant you he lost it in some drunken brawl. He's a terrible figure in a country town, i' faith, and must make the old wives watch their poultry more than a gang of gipsies. I'll swear that when he went a-soldiering with Ruby-nose, he was beloved by but two sorts of companions, whores and lice, who were ever great admirers of a scarlet coat. Why d'you let him order you so? Have you faced the enemy so often in the field to be in dread of this malt-worm?"

Then sometimes she would try to appeal to the man's better nature.

"Come, friend, you are no murderer; you have heard prayers read, though 'twas only when you were obliged to hear 'em upon a drum-head, and must know the fate which is promised against the spiller of innocent blood. Will you obey your brother as Indians do the Devil, not through love but fear? What commander would employ you after you have stained your hands with this foul deed? Take shame to yourself to consort with such a company as we have here, who, for all they boast that they are soldiers, love fighting no more, I'll swear, than a chicken, and though a dozen of drink and an affront will make 'em draw their swords, a pint and a trifle of lip-lechery will serve to put 'em up again."

As the days went by, Phoebe noticed with secret glee that her taunts, flattery, and appeals were having some effect upon William Rumbold. He sought her company now not only for the delicacies of the table, and his grudge against his brother became more open in his talk. He confided to her his deepest wish, that he should meet his death upon the field of battle, as a solider should, his sword unstained by any offence against the military code, his face to the foe. Phoebe seized upon this to give him a detailed description of the punishment for high treason, which she herself had seen meted out to the Five Jesuits in the time of Titus Oates, dwelling with grisly relish upon the choking figures swiftly cut down from the gallows, stripped, and laid on the straw-strewn scaffold, upon Jack Ketch's notorious unhandiness with the disembowelling knife, upon the entrails dragged out smoking from the bloody bodies, the stink of the cauldron, the hideous dismembering. The man roughly bade her hold her tongue, but she saw that her description lingered in his memory and added to his uneasiness of mind. In a few days now, she thought exultantly, I'll have him in the mood to listen to me when I suggest that he engineers our escape from the Rye and the laying of an information which will save his own neck. He has a sort of courage, and is not without resourcefulness; and he grows so hot against his brother that he may not scruple to betray him.

But it was at this very moment that the maltster chose to send William away from the Rye on some mission. What that mission was, Phoebe did not know at the time, nor could she be sure whether it was not just an excuse to remove William from her growing influence over him. All she knew was that, when she came to serve breakfast one morning, William Rumbold was absent, and she was told by Rouse that he was gone. Whatever the reason for this abrupt departure, it was a stunning blow to Phoebe, and for a while seemed to make impossible all chances of her own escape. But she was not a girl to despair, and quickly recovering from this disappointment, became absorbed in a new idea: to seek an accomplice from outside the Rye.

She wrote, very laboriously, for she was unhandy with her pen, a brief and simple appeal for aid, stating that she was an innocent and helpless girl who had been kidnapped and was kept a close prisoner in the Rye House; the paper containing this appeal she thrust into an empty bottle, which she stole from Rouse's chamber, and armed with this she took to haunting that part of the garden which was separated by the high wall and the moat from the country lane. For surely, she reasoned, it should be possible to catch the attention of some passer-by, who, being made cognisant of her plight, would rouse the local people to her aid. Rumbold had committed a criminal offence in abducting her, and it was the kind of offence which ought to make honest countryfolk so indignant that they would attack the Rye in force.

With the bottle secreted in her petticoats, she would go into the garden on the excuse of plucking herbs for culinary purposes, and as she stooped as though seeking them among the weeds of the overgrown beds, she kept a sharp look-out through one or other of the loops in the wall for countryfolk passing in the lane beyond the moat. It was not long before, at considerable risk (for she could be seen from the windows of the house behind her and suspected that Miriam Rumbold was for ever spying upon her movements), she attracted the attention of a country fellow who was driving by with a load of vegetables. At the sight of a female arm frantically signalling to him through a loophole, he reined-in his horse and sat stupidly staring in her direction; the moat was too wide for Phoebe to address him save in a shout, so, thrusting her arm through the loop as far as it would go, she flung her bottle into the water, then urgently beckoned him to draw it to his side with his whip.

The result was so disappointing that Phoebe could have wept. The fellow, instead of dismounting from his cart, whipped up his horse and drove furiously away down the lane, glancing over his shoulder with an expression of terror as he went. And there was Phoebe's message bobbing gently up and down in the moat; she could not recover it now, and if it chanced to be picked up later by Rumbold or one of his labourers, she would be confined to her chamber at the least. The only hope left was that some other passer-by would see it and have the curiosity to fish it out, but after some days of waiting in vain for this, and in continuing to scrutinise all who went along the lane, Phoebe realised that the local people lived in mortal fear of the one-eyed malster, and that when they had to pass his house did so in nervous haste and with averted heads.

Her message was still floating in the moat when Phoebe received an order from Rumbold to keep within the house until he gave her permission to walk in the garden again. At first she thought this must be because he knew of her perambulations in the vicinity of the wall and guessed their purpose, but then she found that the order extended also to Mrs Rumbold and her daughter. Neither knew the reason for it, or at least would not tell her, but as she was preparing dinner in the kitchen that morning she heard certain sounds from without which made it easy for her to guess what was happening today. There was first a clatter of hooves in the lane, accompanied by a ring and clink of steel, and then the thunder of coach wheels, accompanied by more hoof-beats, all at a canter; there was an order shouted, and though she could not hear what it was, it was plainly military; and so without pause the little cavalcade came rapidly round the far side of the outbuildings, over the causeway, and away along the road to Bishop's Stortford. The King and his brother, thought Phoebe, her hands clenched in the dough she was kneading, driving to Newmarket with their pitiful few guards. No other coaches passed and it would seem that the noblemen and courtiers took the main road when they went to enjoy their sport.

Two evenings after this, Phoebe was crossing the courtyard having gone to draw water at the well. It was almost dark, but she could just make out a figure lurking near the gateway in the tower. Those long dangling arms could belong to no other but Richard Rumbold, and there was something so vigilant and attentive about his attitude that the girl dodged back into the shadows and watched him, curious to know what he was doing there. She had not waited long before she heard the rumble of wheels coming into the outer court beyond the tower; they halted, and she waited to hear the jangle of the bell, but instead there came the thud of a whip-handle against the gates, a peculiar thud like a signal, two soft raps, three loud ones, then two soft again. The figure of Rumbold, hitherto statue-like, leapt to life as he thrust the great key into the lock, and dragged the heavy gates wide. A covered cart came through, drawn by two stout horses, and from it leapt down some three or four men; they talked in low voices as they began to uncover the cart, and were presently joined by Rumbold who had been busy refastening the gates. One of the men had a lanthorn, and though she was too far off to see clearly what the cart contained, Phoebe caught glints of steel in the wavering light and could just make out that the objects the men were unloading were of the sinister shape of muskets and carbines.

After this there was scarce a day passed without there were visitors to the Rye House. All were men; some rode in singly, others came in carts or leading pack-horses, yet others staggered in bowed down by the weight of chests which they carried on their backs. The men were lodged in the house, dossing down at night anywhere on the floor; the goods they brought were taken into a store-chamber to which only Rumbold had the key. This sinister activity made Phoebe so apprehensive and curious that she sought out her old friend Rouse and asked him frankly what it meant. Since she had begun to shun his company, he had taken a dislike to her and scarce ever spoke to her without a taunt, so he answered her question only because he hoped it would frighten her:

"These brave lads are Hannibal's Boys, my punk, who very soon now will be at the work you wot of. And the stuff they bring with them are the tools of their trade, muskets and pistols, sent down from London secreted under coals in the carts, or loaded into boats beneath oyster barrels and conveyed up the Ware River. You have the honour now to live in an armed fortress, and soon those pretty ears of yours will hear the music of flintlocks which will play a tyrant to his death."

She said nothing, but turned away and left the man chuckling to himself. She was desperate now; she could expect help from no one, certainly not from these forty armed ruffians who overcrowded the Rye. All along at the back of her mind had lingered the hope that Derrick somehow would find and rescue her, but her common sense told her plainly that it was a hundred chances to one against his even discovering her whereabouts. She had only herself on whom to rely, and the time was getting short. There was one plan of escape which had occurred to her, but it was so full of risk, so unlikely of success, that she shrank from putting it into action while there was any hope of a substitute for it. Now she must chance it; it was the only way.

Ever since she had been at the Rye, Phoebe had continued to cultivate the friendship of Mrs Rumbold on the off-chance of the old woman's proving useful to her in some way. Poor Mrs Rumbold, browbeaten by her lord and despised by her daughter, was only too eager to respond to the girl's advances, and was accustomed to confide to her long tales of her bodily ailments which comprised her only real interest in life. She had pains in her back; her ankles swelled sometimes of an evening; she could not take her meat with any relish, and often she could not go to stool for days at a time. Hitherto, Phoebe had merely listened sympathetically and murmured condolences; but now, seizing an opportunity when she and the old woman were alone in the kitchen, she told her that these symptoms closely resembled those of her own mother which had appeared shortly before that lady's premature decease.

"I would I had learned more of the apothecary's art at that time, neighbour," sighed the girl, "for then I might not have been motherless all these years. But having had the sole care of my widowed father for so long, and living, you must know, in the country, I have made myself very skilled in the preparation of herbals, and there is one I know of would do you more good than any physician's pills."

Mrs Rumbold exclaimed in surprise and astonishment at this, and begged her kind Phoebe to try if she could find the herbs for this sovereign remedy in the garden, only stipulating that she say nothing to Miriam concerning it, because her daughter was so unkind as to scoff at her ailments and tell her she imagined them. She would see to it, she said, that Miriam was elsewhere when Phoebe went upon her charitable errand; and thus, having found so willing an ally in the first part of her scheme, Phoebe made another excursion into the garden, this time genuinely seeking herbs.

Her luck was in, for she found all she sought, and presently returned to the house with her apron full of ground-ivy, nightshade, lettuce, and poppy-roots. Her unwitting accomplice, Mrs Rumbold, was waiting in the kitchen, and kept watch at the door while Phoebe pounded her herbs in a mortar, and, a little ashamed of herself because of poor Mrs Rumbold's innocent enthusiasm, prepared the strongest sleeping draught she knew.

Chapter Three

The one-eyed maltster, Rumbold, was a man of habit. Even now, upon the brink of executing a most desperate crime, he kept strictly to an orderly routine, rising and retiring at a set hour, requiring his meals to be punctual, attending to his malting with as much care as that he bestowed upon the business of assassination. One of his habits was to take a draught of strong ale just before retiring for the night. This draught was brought him by his wife, and was never imbibed until all his duties were done, he had gone the round of the house like a jailer to see that all the inhabitants of the Rye were in their beds, and had satisfied himself that the gates in the tower were fast closed and bolted. Then, entering his bedchamber, he would place the great key beneath his pillow, undress, drink his nightly potion, and retire to rest. All this Phoebe had learned from Mrs Rumbold during the time the girl had been a prisoner at the Rye.

On the evening of the day when she had prepared a pretended herbal for Mrs Rumbold's ailments, it was simple for Phoebe, as she went backwards and forwards between the kitchen and the dining-chamber at supper-time, to slip three-quarters of her potion into the maltster's strong-ale, which, as usual, was placed ready at this hour in a special tankard in the pantry. The little that remained of the stuff she reserved for the maltster's wife, to whom she had asserted that the herbal was most efficacious if drunk immediately before retiring. Two questions worried her; first, would Richard Rumbold detect the presence of the drug? Secondly, was the old herbalist from whom she had got the recipe right when he asserted that it was so strong that it would make a man sleep like the dead? Sniffing hard at the contents of the tankard, and even sipping at it, she felt pretty confident that neither taste nor smell were marked enough to arouse the suspicions of a weary man, for the strong-ale was very strong indeed, and so sweet that it masked the slight bitterness of the herbs. She must await the answer to her second question with what fortitude she could muster; hitherto she had used the drug only upon animals as a simple anaesthetic; she had only the old herbalist's word for it that it would work upon a man.

The household of the Rye retired at its usual hour, and presently the stumping tread of its master announced that he had completed his nightly round and was retiring. Lying tense in the darkness of the bed-chamber she shared with Miriam, Phoebe gave him half an hour to undress, drink his strong-ale, and succumb to what was mixed with it. Then she began ostentatiously to toss and turn, and presently to groan a little; sitting up in bed, Miriam Rumbold swore at her, and asked crossly why she could not be quiet.

"I have such pains in my belly I would swear I were in labour if I was not an honest maid," replied Phoebe, groaning again. "That pesty chuck-beef we ate for supper must have poisoned my guts, and if I cannot void it I am sure I shall die."

"More like it is this fancy method of cooking you have," snapped Miriam, "forever mixing herbs with honest food. Get you out of here, you nasty jilt, if you must vomit, for I'll not have my bedchamber nastied, I promise you."

Inwardly gleeful, outwardly in the extremity of physical discomfort, Phoebe slipped out of bed, lifted her hooded cloak from behind the door, and made something of a noise in going downstairs as though towards the privy. At the bottom, she turned and stole softly up again, having slipped off her shoes and laid them at the stair-foot; and now she was ready to start upon the most perilous part of her plan.

Before she had gone to bed that night, she had taken care not to undress, but to slip a nightgown over her clothes, so that it was not cold which made her shiver as she padded down the innumerable passages of the old house. Well-endowed with courage and spirit though she was, it needed all her will-power to beat down the terror which threatened to overwhelm her as she tiptoed past doors from behind which came the snores and heavy breathing of Hannibal's 'Boys', and flattened herself against the wall, scarce daring to breathe, as some branch, tapping at a window, alarmed her with the idea that she was being followed. Arrived at last outside the maltster's door, she drew a deep breath, lifted the heavy wooden latch with the utmost caution, stifled a gasp when it creaked a little, then pushing open the door, slipped inside.

The great bed, its curtains closely drawn about it, occupied the middle of the apartment, and from behind the hangings she could hear strange animal noises, grunts and growling snores, which assured her that her drug had worked. Heartened by this, she made her way cautiously in the direction of these sounds, and since the night was clear and starlit, and the curtains at the window undrawn, she was able to do so without bumping into furniture. The familiar lidded tankard, with an ale-mug beside it, stood on a small table at the side of the bed on which the maltster lay; she listened intently a moment till she could hear the even breathing of his wife upon the other side, then, inwardly cursing her hands which shook despite every effort she made to steady them, she lifted one corner of the bed-curtain and peered within.

The maltster lay on his back with his mouth wide open, and it was plainly no ordinary sleep which had overcome him. Now he groaned a little, now breathed stertorously, now grunted and muttered, his head turning restlessly, his squat body heaving as if with fever. It was not light enough for Phoebe to see with any clearness that hideous, one-eyed countenance, but her imagination painted it all too vividly, and a dreadful fancy caught her that the one good eye was open, staring at her, fixing her like a snake before it strikes. Beating down her panic, she held the curtain apart with one hand, and with the one groped gently beneath the pillow until her fingers closed upon something metallic. Inch by inch she drew it towards her, her gaze fastened all the while upon that drugged figure, expecting at any moment to see it spring up and seize her; until at last the great key lay in her hand, warm from its resting-place, and a thrill of triumph dispelled something of her horror.

Speed was now the one thought in her mind. Dropping the corner of the curtain back into place, she ran on tiptoe from the room, not troubling to close the door behind her; it was all she could do not to race along the passages and down the twisting stairs, but she had not braved the supreme moment of danger to be caught on the verge of success. She went at a hurried walk, her bare feet soundless on the boards, looking neither to left nor right, but keeping her gaze fixed straight ahead, as she tried to ignore those many doors which might open and confront her with one of the ruffians. She was nearly at the stair head, and was passing the door of her own bedchamber, when she froze in terror at the voice of Miriam calling sharply from within:

"Who's that?"

Opening the door, and at the same time giving vent to a soft groan, Phoebe faltered:

" 'Tis I, neighbour. I was returning to bed, but am seized with another vomiting. Your pardon, I hope it is the last, but I cannot stay to parley further."

She closed the door again, and listened fearfully. Suppose the woman was moved with an unusual compassion and came to see if there was aught she could do? But no: there was an angry mutter, and then silence in the room; Miriam was not going to leave her warm bed to aid a wench she had always detested. Blessing her lack of charity, Phoebe hasted down the stairs, slipped on her shoes, drew back the bolts of the door which gave on to the inner courtyard, and stepped out into the cold air of night.

There was a last ordeal to be faced: the opening of the gates in the tower. She had made herself acquainted with the position of their bolts, and of the way in which the stout wooden bar was worked, but she knew that to deal with them entailed a certain amount of noise, and as ill luck would have it, the night was still.

The house seemed full of watching eyes as she ran across the courtyard; an uneven flagstone all but tripped her; every deep shadow seemed like a lurking figure. But she came to the gates without accident, and addressed herself to her difficult task. First she fitted the great key in the lock, fumbling a little to find its keyhole; then she turned her attention to the bolts. They were strong and heavy, and when at last she shot them back, tearing the skin of her fingers, the rasping noise they made sounded in her affrighted ears as loud as musket-shot. There remained the wooden bar; she placed both hands beneath it, as she had seen Rumbold do when he went out to his malting house in the mornings; but when she attempted to lift it from its hooks, it would not budge an inch. The sweat started out all over her body as she heaved and strained; she was sure she had heard a casement opened in the house behind her and someone call out. The breath rasped in her throat and her muscles ached; the bar was like an enemy resisting her; it was the inanimate keeper of the Rye, determined to thwart her in the very moment when, having braved so many dangers, she was on the brink of escape. She cursed the wooden thing with all the oaths in her rustic vocabulary, fighting with it as with a human foe, sobbing with mingled terror and fury, and expecting at any moment to hear the heavy feet of men pounding across the courtyard in her rear.

And then, just as she despaired, the bar shot up from its hooks with such force that she was almost flung over backwards. Staggering and swaying, she yet managed to keep upon her feet and hang on to it until she could lower it to the ground. Careless now of caution, oblivious of the noise she made, she turned the great key in the lock, dragged open one of the gates sufficiently to admit of her passing, slammed it behind her, relocked it, and, with a wild whoop of triumph, flung the huge iron key into the moat.

As she raced across the wooden bridge, over the outer courtyard, past the silent malting-house, and into the lane, she no longer imagined that she heard sounds of pursuit. But now she exulted in them because it was Richard Rumbold's turn to find himself a prisoner; he had seen to it that his gates, the only egress from the Rye House, were stout, and, locked from the outside, they would need a battering-ram to make them yield to his efforts to get out of his own stronghold.

"A fart for you, you murdering ruffian!" cried Phoebe to the night. "You will get out of the Condemned Hold at Newgate with more ease than from your marvellous Rye House at this time. Stay there, my hanging-looked canary-bird, till the constables come to drag you hence to the Deadly Nevergreen and Jack Ketch's knife."

Indulging in such verbal insults, she stumbled along the country lane, hearing from behind her a confused uproar, of men's voices shouting and the dull thunder of wood upon wood; they were trying to batter down the gates from the inside, and though it must take them some time to do so, Phoebe quickened her hurried walk into a run. The night was no longer starlit and clear, but cloudy with now and then a spitting of cold rain; unable to pick her way, she fell into pot-holes, sank ankle-deep in mud, and tripped over large stones, shivering all the while with cold and nervous excitement, and trying to decide on what was best to do next. There was no other dwelling in the vicinity of the Rye House, and even had there been she would not have dared seek shelter there lest its owner be some creature of Rumbold's; her only course was to make her way to Bishop's Stortford, some five miles distant, and there, when morning came, seek out a justice of the peace to whom to tell her story.

It was a long, anxious, and fatiguing walk; all the while she was straining her ears to catch the sounds of pursuit and getting ready to crouch down in some ditch; parts of the lane were under water from the winter storms and through this she must wade up to her knees; and though she was not imaginative, she could not help feeling a little uncomfortable when she reflected that she was walking solitary through a lonely countryside at night when witches and bogies might be expected to be abroad. As for the human denizens of the dark, she had no fear of them, for she had not so much as a penny-piece in her pocket and therefore could be of no interest to foot-pads. Besides, after her notable triumph over the one-eyed maltster, she felt herself capable of dealing with any rogue who attempted to interfere with her.

It was beginning to get light as she approached the little town of Bishop's Stortford. Cocks crew in the neighbouring farms, a boy herded cattle to be milked, and thin skeins of smoke became visible above the trees. Phoebe's spirits rose; and she fell to picturing the further triumphs and excitements which awaited her here. She would seek out the Watch House and demand of a constable there that she be taken before a justice of the peace without a moment's delay; she could imagine some sleepy and pompous local gentleman being roused from his bed, his disgruntlement changing to consternation, and then to awe, as he listened to her story and learned that she, a mere wench, had outwitted a whole horde of desperate ruffians, and, more marvellous still, was to be the instrument in preventing the King and his brother from falling victim to the assassins' musket-fire; she imagined the wild confusion of orders, the frantic saddling of horses, men spurring towards Newmarket to notify the King, and perhaps she herself driving thither beside the justice in his fine coach.

Regaling herself with such pleasant fancies, and at the same time growing more and more conscious that she was enormously hungry as well as dead tired, Phoebe entered Bishop's Stortford. There were few people about at this early hour, but as she entered the High Street she spied a housewife come out of her house upon some errand; the women came a few paces in Phoebe's direction, stared hard at her, turned abruptly, and opening her door again, shouted to someone within:

"Betty lass, do 'ee lock the door behind me and look well to the chickens and the pig. Here's a gipsy trull come a-begging, and as nasty-looking a creature as ever I see."

Phoebe, glancing all around her, could see no one answering this description, and was about to accost the woman with the intention of asking the way to the Watch

House, when the housewife, seeing her approach, crossed hurriedly to the other side of the street and hastened away, glancing covertly in the girl's direction with such an expression of distaste and loathing that it was borne in upon Phoebe that she was the 'gipsy trull' in question. Such an insult was not to be endured in silence, and Phoebe was about to run after the woman and give her a piece of her mind when round the corner came a milk-walker, loaded with his pails on their wooden yoke. Deciding that the obtaining of information was more important at this moment than the dealing with rude housewives, Phoebe stepped up to the man and asked to be directed to the town Watch House. The milk-walker paused in his chalking of a score upon a customer's doorpost, stared at his questioner a moment in silence, then displayed toothless gums in a grin.

"Zure, there's a foolish question to asken," said he. "If 'ee be wise, my wench, 'ee'll shun all zuch places like the plague."

"Now do I begin to think I am come into a town of Bedlamites," exclaimed Phoebe crossly. "Is this your way of greeting strangers who ask you a fair question? Prithee, gape not at me like some booby at the Tower lions, but answer me short and plain: where is the Watch House? For I must tell you that I have exceeding weighty business there."

"Zure, I'll tell 'ee where 'tis, wench," replied the man, still grinning broadly, "but don't 'ee rail at me arterwards if when 'ee have come to it 'ee find it hard to leave it again."

He gave the necessary directions, and Phoebe, thanking him shortly, started off to find it. As she went, she noticed that the few people she met stared at her as curiously as the housewife had done, and that a couple of boys, playing in an alley-way, shouted rude things after her. It began to dawn on her, therefore, that her appearance was in some way unusual, and stopping abruptly in front of a shop window, from which an apprentice had just removed the shutters, she peered at what she could see of her own reflection therein. She saw a figure with wildly tangled hair, shoes and skirts caked with drying mud, and a cloak torn in several places from the trifling accidents she had met with on her walk; grimacing at her own image, she understood why she had been mistaken for a beggar-maid, and began to fear that the milk-walker's warning was like to be justified. Heartening herself, however, with the importance of the information she had to give, she continued steadily towards the Watch House, and arrived just as the Watch, which consisted of one decrepit old man huddled in a woollen gown, and with his dog on a string and his lanthorn slung at his belt, was going off duty.

The Watchman was tired with his night's perambulations; he was likewise very deaf; when at last Phoebe had succeeded in making him understand that she had urgent business with the town Constable, to whom she must be taken immediately, the Watchman, yawning between every few words, informed her that the hour had now struck which changed him from a keeper of the peace of Bishop's Stortford into an ordinary citizen again, that he was about to go home and get his breakfast, and that he would be obliged if she would take herself off. On receiving a sharp answer from the increasingly exasperated Phoebe, he became the Watchman again, and threatened her that if she did not stop plaguing him with silly questions and get out of his sight this moment, he would have her whipped out of the town as a vagrant, adding that the local justice of the peace was a gentleman very hot against beggars of either sex and would not stomach them in any place under his jurisdiction.

Torn between fury and despair, and cursing the entire population of Bishop's Stortford for their stupidity and narrowness, Phoebe left the Watch House and began to wander aimlessly about the streets. I must get to Newmarket, she thought; no good is to be had by lingering in this pesty little town. She did not know how far it was, but plainly she must have some sort of conveyance; and as she thought this, she noticed just across the street an inn which, from its size, seemed to be the principal one of the town. Its sign proclaimed it to be the Lamb, and through the wide passage which ran down on one side of it, she could see a man bustling about with buckets in a courtyard. There will be stables there, she thought, and where there are stables there will be horses, and since Bishop's Stortford will not treat me honest, I shall do my endeavours to get away from it by stealing one of its cattle. With this desperate intention, she marched boldly across the street, darted a glance to right and left to make sure that she was not observed, then slipped unobtrusively into the yard. Keeping close to the wall, she made an observation of the stables and coachhouse; the ostler had disappeared and there was no one in sight, but standing ready saddled and bridled at the mounting-block was a big bay gelding with a white blaze.

It was an opportunity too good to be missed. Shedding her cloak and tucking up her petticoats, Phoebe ran softly into the courtyard, unhitched the reins, and was about to leap into the saddle, when the ostler reappeared in the doorway of the stable. He took in the situation sufficiently as to give a shout, which was so loud and sudden that the bay gelding shied; Phoebe, not yet securely seated, lost her balance and was fain to fling her arms round the gelding's neck to save being thrown to the ground; and at the same time a second man, pushing past the ostler, ran to catch the reins and secure the female horse-thief. Hoisting herself back into the saddle, prepared, if need be, to make a fight for her freedom, Phoebe glared down at the man at the horse's head; and then, for the first time in her healthy life she nearly swooned.

For the man was Derrick Calder.

Chapter Four

The next ten minutes were dream-like and unreal, and when she was recovered enough to take stock of her surroundings, Phoebe found herself seated in the common-room of the inn, on a settle by a new-lit fire, with her lover beside her, his arm close round her waist. As she could not yet trust herself to speak, she stared at him in silence for some moments, and so noticed a great change which had come upon him since last they had met. Never foppish, he had been always neat and trim in dress and general appearance; but now his clothes were put on anyhow, his linen was crumpled and dirty, his peruke uncurled, and he had not shaved for several days. But the change went deeper than this. His face had thinned, and upon its greyish pallor were unfamiliar lines; his kindly mouth had a new set to it, almost bitter, and his eyes, deeply shadowed, looked enormous and feverishly bright. His free hand touched her gown, lightly caressed her cheek, half raised itself to her hair, as though he could not convince himself that she was flesh and blood and not some ghost. At last, kneeling down, he began to unfasten her mud-caked shoes, and as he did so he said, in a strained hoarse voice, not attempting to conceal his emotion:

"My love, I have been seeking you for a month, ever since your father came to me at Whitehall with the news that you were missing. I knew instantly who had abducted you, and why; and howsoever long I live I never shall forgive myself that I was the cause of this crime against you." He paused a moment, then went on more steadily: "I did not know whither they had taken you, and have wasted precious time in searching for you in Sussex and in London; not until yesterday did my search lead me into these parts. It seems that I was right at last, and I will hazard a guess that all this while you have been imprisoned in a place they call the Rye House."

"My curse upon it!" exclaimed Phoebe heartily. She sipped a measure of brandy which Derrick had put into her hand and felt better every minute. "A nest of as nasty a parcel of rogues ever you heard of, as I will inform you shortly. But first let me hear from you how you lit upon my whereabouts, and what kind of providence brought you into the yard yonder just as I was about to turn horse-thief."

So Derrick told her of all his activities during the past month. For his failure to appear on duty on the night when Mr Jolly had visited him at Whitehall, he had been deprived of his post at Court, and this had left him free to devote all his time to searching for Phoebe. He had started off with the assumption that the conspirators would not think it necessary to hide her at any very great distance from London, and three possible places had occurred to him: London itself; my Lord Grey's country seat, Up Park; and Rye, in the same county. The third had been suggested to him, he said, by Mr Jolly who, most unfortunately, had forgotten that when he had heard the place mentioned it had been referred to, not as Rye, but as 'the Rye'. Starting in London, he had applied himself to several magistrates in a vain attempt to interest them in the girl's abduction; taking Mr Jolly with him, he had so far prevailed with one of these gentlemen as to persuade him to send out a hue and cry; also he had put an 'advice' in one of the news-sheets for the missing girl, offering a reward for information concerning her, and though at imminent peril of his life, had haunted the London resorts of the conspirators in the hope of obtaining some clue to her whereabouts.

All these efforts proving in vain, Derrick had ridden down to Sussex, and had wasted further time, first in cautious questioning of the local people in the neighbourhood of Up Park as to whether my lord had some lady concealed there, and afterwards in searching the town of Rye for a one-eyed man of questionable character. Despairing of obtaining the information he sought in Sussex, he had returned to London, with the intention of making enquiries in Hampstead, and there, perhaps, of lighting upon some detail regarding the actual abducting which had not been given to Mr Jolly at the time.

"I arrived in town the evening before last," continued Derrick, "and as I was riding through the Strand whom should I meet but a good friend of mine, Jack Younghusband, whose name I have mentioned to you before. Jack was not on duty, and so it was not improper for him to be seen speaking with one who was dismissed in disgrace from Court. He asked me where a-devil I had been all this while, and told me I had best not go home because my wife had given out that I had deserted her, which had put her into a high good humour – nay, I'll not plague your ears with those sordid matters, my love. Then he began to say that the town was woundy dull now, because the King and the Duke were at Newmarket, and he lamented that it was not the turn of his troop to accompany them thither. When he said that, I remembered of a sudden that in a letter, writ in secret writing, which I had carried upon one occasion from the plotters in London to my Lord Grey, there was mention of something being done when next the King should be at Newmarket, and since that time I had discovered that in the plot I was investigating was included a scheme to slay his Majesty and his brother, only that I knew not the details of it. But now it struck me, perchance the deed is to be done while the King and the Duke are at their sport, and from the plotters speaking of this 'Hannibal' always by his nickname, I suspected that he was the man chosen to strike the blow. 'Twas a long chance, but I was desperate, and so I persuaded Jack to enter a tavern with me, and, engaging a private room, began to question him as to whether he knew, either a one-eyed man living in Newmarket, or some village in its neighbourhood which was called Rye."

Derrick rose to kick a smouldering log on the hearth into flame, and leaning his arm on the chimney-breast, smiled down at his mistress.

"At first Jack gaped at me," he went on, "and desired to know what a-devil I was talking about. I know no one-eyed men, saith he, save a valiant old dragooner who taught me how to handle a firearm when I was a lad, and as for villages in the neighbourhood of Newmarket, I protest that when I have the luck to go thither, I am too much occupied with sport of all sorts to waste my time learning how these are called. But wait, saith he, there is a place called the Rye, but 'tis near forty miles from Newmarket, and is not a village but a house, a mighty strange and solitary house, but who lives there I cannot tell. Whoever he is, he likes his own company, for 'tis liker a fortress than a mansion, having strong walls and a moat."

"Had you not marked it for yourself," asked Phoebe, "when you have gone in the Duke's train to the races?"

"No," answered Derrick, "for none but his Majesty and the Duke, with their escort of Life Guards, take the by-road by which it stands; the Officers in Ordinary go with the rest by the main road through Stanstead. But when Jack told me of this secluded place, I was sure that at last I was come upon your whereabouts, therefore I posted down here yesterday, and when you encountered me in the yard yonder, was about to mount the gelding I had hired and ride to the Rye and force an entrance."

"You were like to have failed in that," answered Phoebe, speaking rather shortly to cover the emotion aroused by this account of her lover's desperate and persistent efforts to find and rescue her. "For I vow a mouse could not creep out or in without that wicked one-eyed rogue of a maltster knowing it. But I have crept out, and if you will have patience, I will tell you how I did it."

So, warmed with brandy, and cheered by the presence of her lover (a presence which, being so long denied, was more agreeable to her than she would have thought possible), Phoebe told her story, with spirit and verve, somewhat exaggerating her own cleverness as women will, and being not entirely fair to the chance or Providence without which she could not have succeeded in her daring escape. She concluded with an account of her adventures in Bishop's Stortford earlier that morning, vowing they must be the stupidest people in England who dwelt there, and that she verily believed a stranger must have his throat cut in the street before they would afford him the courtesy of interesting themselves in him.

"Nay," said Derrick smiling, "simple folk, in particular those who live in remote parts, are ever distrustful of strangers, and as for your Watchman, like all his kind he is earnest in seeking to avoid trouble which he deems none of his business."

"Then you and I," said Phoebe briskly, "had best start upon our way for Newmarket, where we shall find gentlemen who will deign to give us a fair hearing when we make known to them this beastly plot."

Derrick's smile died.

"For the matter of that," said he, "my experience makes me fear that the gentlemen of whom you speak will become as deaf as your Watchman when we tell our story. It will be a great labour to come at them in the first place, for I am in disgrace at Court and assuredly will be refused audience by anyone in authority who knew me there. Yet by some means we must get our information laid, for there are but four days ere the Court returns to London, and I am sure those rogues at the Rye will not lay-by their wicked scheme because you are flown. They know what time and labour 'twill cost you to come at the proper authorities and compel them to take action, and will hope, no doubt, that their plan will have succeeded ere you can do so. As soon as you are rested, therefore, we will hire a coach and drive post to Newmarket, and being come there will make shift to convey a warning to the King."

"As for rest," replied Phoebe sturdily, "I have had it already, and am as impatient to be on our way as a broken merchant to escape the duns. So do you go hire this coach, if there be such in so wretched a little town, and in the meantime I'll get water and clean myself, for I cannot come near majesty looking like a wallowed bacon-hog."

Scarcely had Phoebe completed a hasty toilette when her lover returned to say that he had found a horse-dealer who had a coach and four stout Flemish mares for hire, and that, it being but mid-morning, they might make the journey before nightfall if they set out at once. Phoebe exclaimed with delight at riding in such state, as she termed it, and speculated as to how much money it must cost.

"Fie, you rogue!" cried she, squeezing her lover's arm as they were jolted over the country roads, "I swear you must be as rich as some fat Alderman, and yet not let me know it all this while. I protest, you should not have used me so."

He did not tell her that he had sold every valuable he possessed, save his sword, to maintain him during his search for her, or that when the coach-hire was paid for he would have but a few guineas left in the world, but instead, entered into her bantering mood, and passed the journey, now in light-hearted chatter, now in more tender talk.

It was still light when they came to the outskirts of Newmarket, and Phoebe, craning from the window, was beside herself with excitement at the evidence she saw of the Court's being here. A party of finely dressed ladies and gentlemen rode by with hawks on their fists; a cart, on which reposed an elegant bath, evidently sent for in haste by some fair dame who had forgot to bring it with her, overtook them; and as they came into the one long street of the town, she could see that it was lined with private coaches and sedans. Forgetting for the moment the urgent mission which had brought her here, Phoebe feasted her eyes upon coronets and coats-of-arms painted on coach-doors, on liveried servants bustling hither and thither, and with the greatest pleasure of all upon a string of beautiful 'running-horses' which were being ridden to their stables by their boy-riders.

Alighting at one of the many inns of the town, Derrick paid off the coachman while his mistress went within to find accommodation for the night. It was not to be had here, and after trying every other inn in Newmarket they discovered that the little town was so overcrowded with the Court that there was not a bed to be had.

"Sleep I must," announced Phoebe at last, "though it be in some running-horse's manger. 'Adsblood, and now I do bethink me; the coach in which we travelled hither stays till the morning to rest the horses. A quart of strong-ale from you, and a trifle of pretty glances from me, will persuade the coachman to let us sleep in that snug vehicle,

I'll warrant you that, which I shall like better than some lousy bed in an inn."

Phoebe had a way of getting what she wanted, and presently was snuggling down in clean straw in the coach which stood in one of the inn-yards. Laying her head against Derrick's shoulder, she drowsily reminded him of how, on that last evening they had met at Jack Straw's, she had cried that she would love to go to Newmarket and see the sport, and behold, here she was, though, she added with a sigh, with little likelihood of viewing the races. When she awoke next morning, Derrick was nowhere to be seen, but soon appeared to say that he had arranged for breakfast in the inn; and while she was attacking this with a healthy appetite, he said to her:

"You shall view the races after all, my love, or some part of them at least. For during the night I have bethought me, and am resolved that instead of wasting our time in endeavouring to come at some of the Privy Council, we would do best to approach his Majesty himself. When he is here at his diversions, he is wont to lay aside all state, wears a plain dress, loves to go about almost unattended, and, so they remember their manners, will allow all sorts to approach him without ceremony. Therefore, you and I will go up to the course with the spectators, and watch for some opportunity for approaching his Majesty and making known to him this plot."

This was cheering news to Phoebe, and she was in high spirits as she and Derrick mingled with the crowds of country folk who trudged up to the race-course. The day was bright and cold, with a rough wind and a powder of snow lying on the roofs, not a good racing day, for the going would be hard, but this did not damp the enthusiasm of the multitude jostling in the direction of the large level meadow in which the heats were run. There was a holiday atmosphere abroad; everyone was gay and excited, and plots and plotters seemed to belong to another world. Men decked out in gay uniforms rode by with drums and trumpets strapped to their saddles; ladies, dressed for all the world like cavaliers, in plumed hats and tight-buttoned jackets, trotted in company with their male escorts; gentlemen wagered vast sums on what would win the several heats; and itinerant musicians, tumblers, jugglers, and vendors of gingerbread and oranges made the place like a fair.

It was some while yet before the first race, and Phoebe had an opportunity of strolling about the course, which was marked out by tall wooden posts, painted white and placed at regular intervals, the last having a flag mounted upon it to designate the winning-point. At the other end were the stables wherein the horses awaited the heats for which they were entered, and here also was a weighing-room for the boy-riders or jockeys; mingling with these were many gentleman riders, certain races being exclusive to them, all decked out in bright taffety jackets and long spurs and tight-fitting drawers, those who had to carry weight having it quilted into their waistcoats. The metal on the horses' bridles twinkled like silver in the sun, their coats gleamed, satin-smooth, their hooves were as highly polished as a fine gentleman's shoes, and some of their long tails were plaited most cunningly. Phoebe had not been on the scene ten minutes before she had persuaded one of the horse-keepers to permit her go to into the stables and feast her eyes upon the precious beasts, and what with her wonder at seeing the way they were treated, more like princes than animals, their oats washed with white of egg, their bits with muscadine, and their mouths with ale, and her eager drinking up of the stories told her by one of the boy-riders, she had almost forgotten the mission which had brought her to Newmarket, when a noise from outside reminded her of it.

Penetrating the din of the crowd came the high, thrilling notes of a trumpet, and answering it went up a great roar of acclamation. Running out of the stable, Phoebe observed that every man in the neighbourhood had uncovered, and looking in the direction in which all eyes were turned, she saw a small cavalcade of horsemen approaching from the town. One of them rode ahead of the rest, a tall figure, his horsemanship superb, controlling without effort the liver-chestnut stone-horse which displayed its spirit in many bucks and curvettings. The rider wore a plain suit of country grey, unadorned save for a broad blue ribbon from which hung a medallion, winking in the sunshine; his long legs were encased in thigh-boots, and beneath his fashionably cocked hat he wore a small plain wig, which flopped upon his neck with the dancing of his steed. It did not need the frantic acclaims of the crowd to inform Phoebe that here was King Charles the Second.

It was the first time Phoebe had seen the King, and as she watched that tall figure approaching, so unexpectedly simple in dress, so absorbed in the joy of his own horsemanship, so at one with his people in this friendly atmosphere of sport, she felt a sudden sharp stab of feeling go through her, to which she could not give a name. It was this popular, accessible gentleman for whom a bunch of conspirators even now lay in wait, with loaded muskets, behind the walls of the Rye House, prepared to shoot him down in cold blood as he drove back from a well-earned holiday to the cares of his kingdom. Had her first sight of King Charles been of him in crown and robes, surrounded by obsequious courtiers, hedged in from the common herd by Ministers and noblemen and Life Guards and Pensioners, Phoebe would not, perhaps, have experienced so sharp a feeling of outrage; it was his defencelessness, and the trust from which it sprang, that worked in her so hot an indignation against his would-be murderers that she felt shaken with rage.

It was but for a few moments that she had this sight of the King. Then the crowds blocked her view, and she saw only now and again his head and shoulders as he walked his horse to a spot whence he would gallop alongside the running-horses and so see the whole race.

"Why, any man in England may come at him here," she observed to Derrick excitedly. "Observe these crowds, how they flock about him and are not driven off. I warrant he is pestered by petitioners of all sorts, being so accessible."

"It is known that he will have no petitions presented to him while he is at his diversions," answered Derrick, "and no talk of public matters either. That is why I fear our task will prove difficult, for though his Majesty is the kindliest of men, my dear, he is apt to be sharp if his commands are not observed. We must await our chance and be patient. Hark, there are the drums beating for the riders to mount; the first heat will soon be commencing, and his Majesty will be off along the course."

The excitement had grown intense; wagers were shouted thicker than ever, and men and women jostled one another to get a good view. But Phoebe had lost all interest in the sport. Unimaginative though she was, that first sight of the King had filled her mind with horrid pictures; instead of the riders in their bright colours she saw the one-eyed maltster, Rumbold, directing his ruffians to their posts; instead of the running-horses, so sleek and slender, dancing with impatience to be off, she saw the powerful Barbaries in the stables at the Rye House, kept ready saddled, that the conspirators might spur to London as soon as their beastly deed was done; instead of the cheerful chatter of the crowd, the heart-stirring notes of drum and trumpet, the clink and ring of bit and stirrup-iron, she heard a volley of musketry fired at point-blank range from behind a high wall. And there was the unconscious victim, his gloved hands firm yet light upon the reins, his swarthy face flushed with the sharp air and the anticipation of his favourite sport, the cares of a stormy reign laid aside for this brief interval as he waited to gallop off as the signal was given.

Three heats and a course were run, the winner acclaimed, and wagers collected. Derrick and Phoebe anxiously watched every movement of the King, hoping for a favourable moment to get near him. But his very accessibility was a handicap to their purpose, for though he was free of the presence of his ordinary attendants, he was dogged everywhere he went by the country folk, who pressed near in case they might catch some specimens of his famous wit, or to give themselves the pleasure of being able to boast afterwards that they had actually touched him.

And then, as Phoebe began to fume with impatience, suddenly her lover caught her arm.

"His Majesty is going to dine," said he, "which he doth *al fresco* on the course. See, they are spreading a cloth for him yonder among the trees; he permits the crowds to see him eat, and we will make one with them. What chiefly troubles me is this," he added, as they walked in the direction he had just indicated, "that among his attendants here there may be some who know me and that I was sent from Whitehall in disgrace; if such there be, and they chance to observe my approaching his Majesty, I shall be stopped ere I can make known to him what I have to tell."

"There is no one who knows me," answered Phoebe briskly, "and for this reason you had best leave me to tell our tale. Besides, I'm told Kind Charles hath a kindness for my sex which might persuade him to hearken to a comely wench, and you must not think that I shall be tongue-tied from awe of him, for having seen him here, so free and open, I shall make no more of accosting him than if he were a neighbour."

"Well, then," said Derrick, smiling, "you shall be our spokeswoman, yet this is a great matter, Phoebe, and you needs must have a second witness to what you have to say. Therefore shall I stick close to you, and be at hand to come in to your support."

Pushing their way through the straggling crowds that were following the royal horseman, they were soon in the front ranks. Some little way before he reached the group of trees beneath which his collation was spread, a groom came running to hold his horse while he dismounted, and approaching at a distance behind the groom walked several Court officials, hat in hand. It was at this moment that the liver-chestnut stallion chose to give the spectators an exhibition of his own high spirits and his master's horsemanship. Refusing to stand still, he began to buck, and then to rear, his ears laid flat, his nostrils dilated, foam flying from his lips, and his powerful body quivering with excitement and mischief. The crowds drew back out of respect for those wicked heels, and even the groom kept at a wary distance, so that for a brief interval the King was quite alone. It was Phoebe's chance and she seized it. Snatching her arm from Derrick's, she ran to within a couple of yards of the prancing stallion, bobbed a small curtsey, and cried:

"Sir, I perceive that there is no horse ever foaled that could put you down, but there are rogues can do so, and I beg that you will listen to me while I tell you of them and of how they plot against your Majesty's life."

The King, who had now succeeded in quieting his mount, stared down at her for an instant in silence, as with one hand he patted the sweating chestnut neck of the stallion. He saw an obvious country wench, her face flushed and eager, her hair dishevelled and her clothes travel-stained and dirty, with bits of straw adhering to them from her night spent in a coach. One of the royal eyebrows shot up, the deeply curved mouth twisted into its famous smile, and the heavy-lidded, melancholy eyes quizzed her with dry humour.

" 'Odsfish!" exclaimed King Charles. "Here must be Mistress Titus Oates."

"I have to tell you," pursued Phoebe doggedly, irritated but not abashed by this reception of her news, "of a plot against your Majesty's life, to which I and this gentleman here can bear witness. They are lying in wait even now to shoot you – "

"In the Park," interrupted the King, leaping suddenly from the saddle and throwing his rein to the groom, "with screwed bullets. There are others who will poison my wine, yet others who have sanctified knives with which to stab me, for they are very thorough gentlemen, these plotters of yours. You see, my wench, I have heard it all so many times before. Who may it be on this occasion, prithee? The Papists, the French, the Fifth Monarchy-men, or is by chance the Quakers for a change?" He laughed outright, then added kindly: "Lord! So pretty a mouth should not let fall such nonsense. Enjoy the sport, my wench, as I am resolved to do, and harkee, if you would make a shilling to buy a new ribbon, lay a wager on the bay mare which runs in the next heat; she belonged to my Lord Rochester and hath never been beaten yet."

During this speech, Phoebe's flush had deepened into one of anger; all the pent-up anxiety and nervous strain of the last few weeks boiled up in her so furiously that, forgetting in whose presence she was, she was about to relieve her feelings in a spate of rustic invective, when Derrick, stepping to her side and putting a tight grip upon her arm, said quickly to the King:

"Sir, I implore you that your Majesty will grant to this lady and myself some privy talk at your convenience, for I swear to you that 'tis true what she says and that there is a plot abroad – "

"What's this? What's this?" interposed a new voice in great agitation, and Phoebe, whipping round, saw that the group of Court officials had now arrived, and that the voice was that of a short, fat gentleman, dressed very unsuitably for a race-course and carrying a white wand. "Your Majesty is being pestered; I know it is always so when your Majesty condescends to let the mobile come at you. Away, wench, away instanter! I'll give you over to the constables and have you whipped for your insolence. And you, sir – wounds! who's here? Now marry come up, you knave, how dare you show your face in the King's presence? Sir, I must inform your Majesty that this fellow was one of my Officers in Ordinary, an Usher to his Royal Highness, but lately sent away from Whitehall in disgrace."

The King glanced at Derrick, and his face clouded. Now that the smile was gone, Phoebe noticed how aged was that face, how seamed with lines of weariness and anxiety.

"You do ill, sir," said Charles shortly to Derrick, "if you think to regain your post by these means, and worse to enlist the aid of this simple wench."

"I beg that your Majesty will permit me to have the fellow warded," chimed in the fat gentleman officiously. "I suspect that if enquiry be made 'twill be found that he is a dangerous person, for whiles we were yet in London I heard talk that he was got into the company of rogues, and moreover from my own knowledge I know him to be insolent and mischievous."

"My Lord Chamberlain," said the King, with bored patience, "be so good as to remember that I am come hither to divert myself with sport, and will not – I say, I will not – be foxed with talk of dangerous persons or the misdeeds of Officers in Ordinary, even from your lordship. Let the fellow be gone about his business; a few days' sport will cure his folly, and from the look of him I think he is too honest to bear a grudge. As for this pretty maid," he added, smiling suddenly at Phoebe, and giving her a wink as he patted her beneath the chin, "I will not have her tormented in any way whatsoever, but will leave her free to follow some advice I have given her which is a secret between her and me. And here, my sweet rustic," said he, fishing in his pocket and putting a shilling into Phoebe's flaccid hand, "is that which will enable you to do so; couple it with the bay mare and let it breed."

And with that he turned and strode away ahead of his attendants, leaving only the fat gentleman whom he had addressed as 'my Lord Chamberlain', and who, ignoring Phoebe, was puffing out his cheeks at Derrick like an angry cherub.

"You may thank his Majesty's famous clemency that you are not under arrest, Mr Calder," he cried. "But this I promise you, that if you seek to intrude yourself into his Majesty's presence a second time, or show your face as much as in the neighbourhood of the Court, you will not escape so lightly."

Having uttered this threat, he waddled away in the wake of King Charles, leaving Derrick and his mistress staring after him, speechless with despair.

Chapter Five

"I tell you," said Phoebe, for the twentieth time, "that he may be shot or stabbed or poisoned for aught I care, and I will concern myself no more at the news of it than if he were an occupant of Jack Ketch's cart. For all the pains I have endured in my care for his life, I have received a chuck under the chin and advice upon a wager (which was ill advice, and there was not a hackney coach horse in London which could not have beaten that pesty bay mare), and therefore am resolved not to plague myself further with his safety."

She and her lover were sitting in the most secluded corner they could find in one of the Newmarket taverns. It was evening; all the rest of the day since their encounter with the King on the race-course and its unlucky termination, they had wandered in the meadows surrounding the town, Derrick silent and thoughtful, Phoebe raging against the King and the Lord Chamberlain; they had not discussed their own personal predicament, which was daunting enough since the coach which had brought them from Bishop's Stortford had returned thither, and they had not even that refuge for the night. Now, laying his hand over hers as they sat close together in the tavern, Derrick said, with that curious calmness which had come upon him since the morning:

"My dear, your indignation against his Majesty is understandable because you do not know, as intimately as I do, the events of his reign and their effect upon him and his Ministers. From the very beginning of the Oates plot, King Charles deemed it a sham, but durst not say so because the public madness ran so high that there would have been revolution had it attempted to curb it. So was he obliged to let it run its course and permit men whom he knew to be innocent to be persecuted, imprisoned, and butchered. The Privy Council, credulous at first, feigned later to believe Oates' lies because the Opposition was using that knave as a weapon against the Duke of York, and was out for any man's blood who ventured to discredit the informer. Therefore, since the defeat of the Faction, the very word plot is anathema, both to the King and to his loyal Ministers, and would be more so to his Majesty did he know that the Duke of Monmouth was implicated in this conspiracy."

"A pox on politics!" said Phoebe brusquely. "I know nought of what you say, and care less. What mads me is that I have been kidnapped and confined and shoved about like an owl fallen into the company of rooks and jackdaws, and can have neither revenge upon that whoreson one-eyed knave of a maltster nor the satisfaction of having the King do me the courtesy of harkening when I tell him of this plot. 'Tis a sweet state of affairs to which I am come when, for all my pains, I can but sit on my arse and wait to hear the news that King Charles and his brother are shot dead."

"Phoebe," said her lover earnestly, taking her chin and forcing her to look at him, "there is one thing you can do to better purpose, and that is to go home to your father. I have a little money left, sufficient to convey you to Hampstead. Consider that all this while your father will have been in an agony for your safety; for his sake, prithee go home, my love."

She stared at him a minute in silence; then asked shortly:

"And what will you do?"

"I shall stay here," replied Derrick quietly, "and wait upon the fate which all along, I believe, hath guided me in this investigation, to show me some way, even at the eleventh hour, of defeating these conspirators."

"So that's the tune of it?" observed Phoebe. She turned from him and took a deep draught from her ale-mug. "Now I tell you what I think," she continued in a level tone and rather carefully not looking at him, "I think you talk like a heathen when you chatter about this fate of yours, and I think further that you are an obstinate, pigheaded fool, and since such a madman is not fit to be at liberty without a keeper, I am resolved to stick close to you, and shall not budge from your side till you have got yourself either slain by the conspirators of flung into prison by your Lord Chamberlain, so do not you think to be rid of me."

"Phoebe," he said; and his voice broke on the name.

"Prithee do not fox yourself with arguments," continued the girl severely, "for I have made up my mind. I shall endeavour to regard you as my cross, as good Master Mole, our parson, would say. And until I am rid of you by the means I have mentioned, pray let's boose; 'twill make us more cheerful while you stay for this fate of yours, and by and by I shall escort you to a horse-keeper whose acquaintance I chanced to make upon the race-course yonder, and persuade him to let us share a bed with his charges. Come, a yard of ale will – "

She broke off so suddenly that Derrick glanced quickly at her. She was frowning as she stared intently at the back of a man who at that moment was walking quickly out of the room in which they sat.

"Adad," muttered Phoebe in a different tone, and clutching Derrick's hand, "I will swear I have seen that back somewhere before, ay, and very lately. A moment, pray."

She rose, and, signalling to Derrick to remain where he was, slipped out of the common-room in the wake of the stranger. Only a few minutes elapsed before she returned, looking puzzled and disquieted.

"He had too good a start on me," she sad, reseating herself by her lover's side, "and 'tis pesty dark without. Damme, I vow I know him, and it sticks in my mind that 'twas at the Rye we met. Yet I cannot be sure, and durst not roam the town lest I get myself abducted a second time. Upon my salvation, Derrick, this fate in which you believe seems altogether out of love with us, and like a jack-o'-lanthorn entices us forward with a glimmer only to disappear when it hath led us into a bog."

"You mock at my superstitions," said Derrick, smiling and taking her hand again, "and I cannot blame you, yet they are all I have to guide me through life. I have no sure belief in an omnipotent God, I would I had, yet struggle to believe that our lives are woven upon some pattern which cannot be seen by us till all is done; for my reason revolts against the notion of blind chance."

"You are, I perceive, in a fine preaching vein," teased Phoebe. "Pray continue, sir, for I stand in need of a sermon to divert my mind from other things."

He seemed not to hear her, but, fondling her hand which lay in his, continued:

"I cannot believe 'twas chance which led me to Hampstead on that day when first I had the happiness of meeting you; chance which set my feet upon the trail of these conspirators through my acquaintanceship with your father; chance which brought me into the stable-yard at Bishop's Stortford at the very moment when you most had need of me. Fate is a term I like not, yet can hit upon no other to designate the Power which I believe orders our lives from the beginning."

"Howsoever you call it," observed Phoebe with a sniff, "it appears to have forsaken the pair of us so far as this plot is concerned. Pox take it, say I."

"Reserve your judgment, pray," answered Derrick quietly. "It calls upon a man to do all that in him lies, and then, and not till then, it declares itself plainly. 'Tis on its mettle now, and perchance will oblige us with some miracle." He glanced at her, squeezed her hand, and added in a different tone: "But for the present, no more of it; let's drink, as you say, and pretend we are at Jack Straw's Castle."

Phoebe entered readily into such congenial pretending, and for the remainder of the evening neither spoke of the troublesome matters which had brought them to Newmarket; they recaptured without effort that private world they had shared at Hampstead, discovering indeed an even deeper harmony than any they had known before, exchanging old familiar jests, absorbed in one another. When the last customers had gone, the landlord, who at intervals throughout the evening had overheard some specimens of Phoebe's rustic wit and had taken a fancy to her, invited them into his private parlour to sample a wine of which he was inordinately proud, and at last, becoming very drunk, and understanding that the pair of them had nowhere to sleep that night, insisted on accommodating them in his own bedchamber while he slept in a chair by the common-room fire.

The first grey light was beginning to creep in through the window when Phoebe awoke and could not sleep again. After an interval of tossing and turning, she experienced the annoyance of all healthy persons in this predicament and searched about for some reason for it. The bed was not large enough for two? Damme, she had spent the previous night cooped up in a coach and had slept like the dead. She had drunk too much ale, or maybe that plaguey wine of the landlord's had undone her? Pish, she had consumed far greater quantities of the first and had been forced, out of politeness to her lover, to imbibe more potent varieties of the second, many a time at Hampstead and never had been troubled. Perhaps it was the weather; certainly the rough wind of yesterday had risen to gale force, and was rattling the casement and creaking the inn sign in its irons outside. Then, to complete her annoyance, she remembered that she had awakened from an evil dream, an affliction to which she was quite unused. It had seemed to her that the man whose back she had seen going out of the common-room last night, and whom she had thought to be someone from the Rye, had come creeping into the bedchamber and, seizing her in his arms, had carried her off. She had tried to scream for help to Derrick, but as is the way in nightmares her throat would not emit a sound, and her lover had gone on sleeping calmly while she was borne inexorably back to the Rye House.

" 'Twas all that heathenish talk of fate," said Phoebe aloud, severely. "Such meddling in high matters begets a melancholy and should be shunned."

She got out of bed and pattered bare-foot to the window; she needed a breath of good country air, she thought, to restore her to herself. Opening the casement, she leaned out; it was not yet light enough to see the sleeping town, and the wind was so strong that it made her gasp; in a moment it had banged the casement shut again. Exerting her strength upon it, she forced it open and so held it, her nostrils dilating a little and a frown appearing on her smooth young brow. Surely there was a strange smell abroad, blown to her on the gusts of wind which buffeted the casement? She sniffed harder; the smell was acrid and unpleasant, and – did she imagine it, or was the greyness of dawn darkened here and there with drifting skeins of something which might be mist, or smoke?

"What is it, my love?" asked Derrick's voice from behind her, and turning she saw that he was sitting up in bed.

"There is an evil stink abroad which likes me not," replied Phoebe shortly, and turned again to the window.

He came at once and stood beside her; and after an instant gripped her arm. It was taut and rigid, for now she too had identified that odour; it was the reek of burning.

Each at the same instant sprang into feverish activity and began to drag on their clothes.

"I fear it comes from the stables of the running-horses," muttered Phoebe, as she dragged her gown over her head. "God damn those tobacco-loving grooms!"

"With this gale, the whole of Newmarket will be a-fire within an hour," observed Derrick, shrugging himself into his coat as he ran from the room.

"Let it burn!" cried Phoebe heartlessly, as she followed him, "so we can save those poor beasts."

They pelted down the stairs, wrenched open the outer door, and debouched into the street. Newmarket still slept peacefully, unaware of the peril which had invaded it during the night, and the presence of which grew more ominously observable to the girl and her lover as they raced along in the direction of the royal stables which stood at one end of the town. The skeins of smoke were thickening into a cloud, the reek of burning stung their eyes and throats, and intermingling with the dull roar of the wind they could hear a crackling, confused shouting, and the terrified neigh of a horse. As they ran they banged upon the house doors, shouting "Fire! Fire!", so that by the time they reached the stables, casements were flung open, alarmed voices demanded to know what was to do, and here and there figures appeared, in shifts and nighgowns, with cloaks hastily flung over their shoulders, beginning to form a small, panic-stricken crowd. And all the while the sinister crackling grew in volume, and a wicked tongue of flame spurted up and died, like a danger-signal in the grey light.

The horse-keepers and grooms who lived over or in the vicinity of the stables were already up and doing when Phoebe and Derrick reached the scene of disaster. In the growing light of day, which was being swiftly transformed into a more evil illumination by the flames which now flickered and flared from several points at once, men and boys worked like demons to coax the demented horses out of the stables, yelling directions of questions, the sweat pouring down their blackened faces, while others, forming a chain of buckets, strove desperately to quell the growing fire. Phoebe, without a word to any man, plucked off her cloak, and plunging it, with her kerchief, into the nearest bucket, draped the first over her head and mouth and with the second in her hand ran boldly into the stables. Careless of the danger from the fire or the wildly kicking hooves, she approached the first horse she saw, deftly twisted her sopping kerchief over its eyes, and running a soothing hand down its neck, set herself to persuade it to come forth.

Looking back afterwards upon this terrible period, it seemed curious even to the unimaginative Phoebe that these few hours, so tragic in themselves and immediately preceding both public and personal danger, should have been the happiest of her life. Yet so it was. From the moment when she felt that first horse respond to her, that beautiful, high-bred creature which with its fellows she had so much admired upon the race-course yesterday, and which was now but a quivering, terrified, defenceless dumb beast, she was filled with a kind of ecstasy, never before experienced; she was suddenly and completely at home, with danger and animals as her companions, and even Derrick clean forgotten. A feeling of power thrilled through her, of benevolent power such as she had experienced less intensely when she had doctored successfully some sick animal at Hampstead; coaxing horse after horse out of the inferno, completely comprehending their panic, instinctively knowledgeable in the method of overcoming it, she was herself, exaltant with the fulfilment of her own personality, inspired. And when at last, as she stood in the meadow to which the rescued horses had been brought, one of a group of bedraggled and exhausted figures, Derrick Calder found her again, he knew that here was a glimpse of the real Phoebe whom he had not dared to hope he would find in this world.

"Not a single beast hath perished," cried she, in a voice almost unrecognisable from her labours, but vibrant with victory. "Observe them, pray, these lordly thoroughbreds, as poor-looking now as any scrubbed tit you may see at Smithfield Rounds."

He took off his coat and laid it round her shoulders.

"My love," he said very quietly, "I raved last night about a miracle. It hath come, in the tragic guise of this fire. His majesty and the Duke are taking coach immediately, to return to London."

She stared at him; and something like anger moved in her at this reminder of a world she had so happily forgotten.

"Good luck to them," she said indifferently.

"I wondered at first," continued Derrick, taking her arm and drawing her in the direction of the burning town, "whether the plotters had sought this way after all to kill the King and his brother, but it seems 'twas an accident caused by a careless knave of a groom a-smoking of his pipe in a hay-loft. Half the town is burnt, and though the King's palace is untouched as yet, it stands in peril since the wind is carrying the fire in that direction, and his Majesty hath been persuaded by those about him to be gone without delay. Even I myself had begun to lose faith in this fate of which I spoke so much, but never again will I doubt its existence. They cannot have news of this disaster at the Rye, since 'tis near upon forty miles away, and news travels slowly in the country parts. Therefore will the King's coming take them unprepared, and I believe, nay, I know, that he will drive by in safety."

She said nothing; the reaction from her recent ecstasy had made her sullen, and for the moment at least she had lost all interest in the safety of the King and the Rye House plotters. And then, when Derrick halted her at a spot whence they could see, without danger, the one long street of stricken Newmarket, she forgot everything in the scenes of horror which met her gaze on every hand.

The fire had by this time demolished all the wooden houses on the south side of the street, and the wind, carrying sparks and burning brands across to the other side, threatened that likewise. The roar of the flames, the crashing of timbers, the screams of terror, the confused shouting of orders, the rumble of cart wheels as the inhabitants drove their families and what goods they could succeed in rescuing to the safety of the surrounding country, all merged into one dreadful cacophony. Here and there, men under the leadership of a constable worked frantically but vainly to stem the fury of the flames with the half-gallon syringes dignified by the name of 'fire-engines' then in use in the country parts. Others, in the pathetic manner of pigmies hurling pebbles at a giant, flung buckets of water into the inferno, and both parties were hampered by the panic-stricken, half insane persons who milled around, searching for missing relatives or fighting to penetrate into the burning houses to snatch some treasured possession. The street was almost blocked by carts and piled furniture, and on all sides some isolated tragedy met the eye, here a women running shrieking with hair and clothes alight, there a trapped child screaming at a window; a local justice of the peace and his servants were wrestling with some of the riff-raff of the town who, even at such a moment, were engaged in looting the shops; and everywhere men coughed and retched and choked from the suffocating smoke and the inflamed air.

And all of a sudden, as she gaped at this hideous confusion, Phoebe ceased to see it. It was eclipsed by one solitary figure, the sight of which sent her reeling dizzily back into a world she had almost forgotten, the foreign nightmare world of treason and plot.

"That man!" she shouted to Derrick, clutching his arm with one hand and pointing with the other. " 'Twas he whose back seemed familiar to me last night, and now I know him, for all his face is blackened with the smoke. He is William Rumbold, the maltster's brother, and now I know why he was sent away from the Rye. 'Twas to skulk here and spy upon the King. See, he has gotten him a horse; death and hell! He's away to warn them to be ready at the Rye House when the King drives by this day."

The arm she had gripped shook itself free as she spoke, and she saw her lover thrusting and jostling his way across the street in the direction in which she had pointed. For the first time in all her life, she experienced panic; for the first time she knew that she needed Derrick, and that he was going away from her. With a sobbing cry she rushed after him, towards the figure of William Rumbold who, wigless, hatless, but fully dressed and armed, was engaged in trying to drag a terrified horse out of an inn yard into the cluttered street. Before her went Derrick, inexorably pushing his way through the seething crowds, and drawing his sword as he went; and in another moment she saw it, that thin line of steel glinting in the light of burning Newmarket.

He was but a few paces from Rumbold when the latter, with a quick, skilful movement, suddenly swung himself upon the maddened horse's back and hit it with the flat of his sword. It bounded forward, then it reared; for Derrick, careless of the prancing forelegs, had leapt at it, had caught it by its long mane, and hanging on with all his strength, prevented its further progress. With a volley of curses, Rumbold bent down to beat him off, but as he did so the horse reared again, he was thrown over its side, and he and his assailant lay in a heap upon the ground.

They were up on the instant, and their swords rang together. Phoebe, hovering fearfully behind her lover, heard nothing but that ring of steel, saw nothing but those two gracefully dancing figures, who thrust and parried as absorbedly as if they had been in the fencing-school. The frantic crowds milled round them, ignoring the strange duel, only side-stepping as the steel twinkled and rang in their immediate neighbourhood, too engrossed in securing their own safety from the fire to concern themselves with the odd spectacle of men fighting a duel in the open street. The general uproar drowned the sound of this private battle; the light of the flames glinted red upon the snickering steel, and the smoke curled about the two bodies which lunged, vaulted, bounded, and turned round each other.

Both men were excellent fencers, and though Phoebe knew nothing of the art of swordsmanship, she could see that the combatants were well matched. Every thrust met its parry, every pass was delivered on some set plan, the attention of neither was distracted by the showers of sparks which fell around and over them, the noise and movement of the crowds, the heat or the smoke. Rumbold had the advantage of height, but Derrick was younger and would tire less easily; moreover, he seemed the more expert in those feigned passes and tricks of swordsmanship which every gentleman learned in the fencing-school.

Desperate for the outcome, Phoebe looked around for some weapon with which she could come in to her lover's aid; she had just spied an iron bolt from a door, and had snatched it up though it was so hot that it shrivelled the skin on her fingers, when a sudden succession of new sounds approaching down the street made her pause and stare.

They came from the direction in which was the King's little palace. Men's voices shouted urgently and persistently "Make way! Make way in the King's name!" and mingling with these shouts came the whinnying of horses, the hollow clatter of many hooves, the rumble of wheels, and the jingle of steel. Even the demented crowds took notice of these sounds, and made haste to clear the middle of the street; it was both gallant and pathetic to see how the men among them, even at such a moment, remembered to remove their hats. Momentairly forgetful of that duel to the death which continued uninterrupted near her, Phoebe pushed her way to the front rank of the crowd in her immediate neighbourhood, and so saw, looming out of the smoke, the figures of men on horseback, whose scarlet cassocks, stiff black jack-boots, plumed helmets, and steel cuirasses proclaimed them to be Life Guards. Disciplined and smart as became this famous regiment, they looked startlingly incongruous in the tattered, dishevelled, panic-stricken mob; even the horses, though they snorted and sweated with terror at the reek of burning and the flickering flames, behaved themselves bravely, answering to every order of heel and voice. At the head of the little troop rode an officer, with his fringed silk sash, embroidered holster-cap, and ribbon epaulette, his sword drawn and held in one buff-gauntleted hand;

behind him rode his trumpet-major and his ensign with the colours of double damask unfurled, the rest of the troop riding alongside the royal coach.

And at the sight of that coach, with its six grey horses, the Arms of England painted on the doors, the coachman and postilions with the crown and royal cipher blazoned on their sleeves, the trumpeters shrilling their heart-stirring music beside it, and the Gentlemen Pensioners with their gilded pole-axes and white taffeta sashes riding close behind, Newmarket forgot its tragedy, and in a voice which overtopped the roaring of the flames yelled spontaneously:

"God save the King!"

In response to the acclamation, a figure in the coach leaned forward, a gloved hand was raised in salutation, and a lined and swarthy face smiled through the new-fashioned glass; it was the same face which Phoebe had last seen scowling a little on the race-course yesterday at mention of a plot. Then the officer of the Life Guards barked an order, his men put spur to their horses, the coachman whipped up his greys, and the tiny cavalcade broke into a canter and so passed in a cloud of smoke and dust along the road to London.

As the noise of it died away, Phoebe remembered the fateful duel. She swung round sharply; and saw that it was ended. One of the figures who had been lunging and thrusting so absorbedly just now had vanished; the other, that of William Rumbold, stood panting and sweating and wiping his sword blade on the skirt of his coat. With a yell of fury and despair, Phoebe fought the crowd to get at him; he turned and saw her, and now she perceived that his had been no easy victory. Blood mingled with the sweat which streamed down his face, and there was a dark and growing patch upon one sleeve. He scowled and muttered curses, for he was aware that his victory had come too late; the

King and the Duke were on their way to London two days ahead of their appointed time, and he himself had been prevented from riding on ahead of them to warn his comrades at the Rye. As Phoebe, hitting out at those who separated her from him, came face to face with the maltster's brother, he spat viciously upon a prone figure which lay bleeding at his feet. She raised the iron bolt she still carried, and with all her force struck him across the face.

She did not see him clap his hands to his mangled features and stagger backwards; she did not hear the bellow of anguish which was torn from him. She saw and heard nothing but the faintly stirring and muttering figure of her lover on the littered ground. Flinging herself down beside him, she lifted him a little in her arms; from a jagged hole in the breast of his coat blood was oozing thickly, and as he opened his lips to speak to her, two red trickles flowed from either side of his mouth. His face was ashen, and the sweat of death glistened on his forehead, but his eyes held recognition in them, and a last fear.

"Ne'er stir, I've knocked the rogue on the head as neat as a butcher does an ox," Phoebe assured him, in answer to that unspoken torment of mind. "There will be no warning given them at the Rye".

It was plain that he heard and understood, for the fear drained away from his eyes and a sigh of contentment shuddered through his limp body. Frantically striving to staunch the wound in his chest with her petticoat, Phoebe implored aid from the scurrying, preoccupied figures around her, but no man paused to notice. Her lover was trying to speak, and laying her cheek close to his, she made out the muttered words:

"Money in my pocket...home to Hampstead...your father...promise me."

"I swore I would not budge from your side till – till all was done," said Phoebe, squeezing her eyelids together to keep back her tears.

The bleeding mouth mumbled urgently:

"Must to home...lay an information...plotters may strike yet...Jack Younghusband...I entreat you... "

"It shall be done," promised Phoebe tremulously. "Don't fox yourself, they shall pay for their treason, and we'll be at Tyburn to see it." And then, all the a sudden, she could not keep back any longer the unfamiliar anguish which racked her. "Derrick, oh Derrick," she sobbed, burrowing her face against his coat, "don't die, pray don't leave me."

She felt his face turn to her, and into her ear his voice spoke with sudden clarity and enormous tenderness:

"I shall never leave you now, my dearest life, for there is no separation save estrangement. My faith was weak; forgive me. I shall wait in peace until you come to me."

Then he died, very quietly, in her arms.

Chapter six

The landlord of Jack Straw's Castle at Hampstead, taking a Sunday afternoon siesta in his elbow-chair, awoke with a start at the sound of the outer door of the tavern being opened, and footsteps coming down the passage. They passed the kitchen wherein he sat, and went on into the common-room. The pirate, who had imbibed freely during the morning, had eaten a huge dinner, and had awakened with a bad taste in his mouth, grumbled to himself about the ill habits of customers requiring a drink on a hot Sunday afternoon in July. Nevertheless, he heaved himself out of his chair and padded across in stockinged feet to the hatch which opened on to the common-room counter. Unlatching it, and peering in, his scowl gave place to an astonished smile; for seated in her old place at one end of the counter, with her dogs at her feet, was none other than Miss Phoebe Jolly.

"Now marry come up, sweet heart!" exclaimed the Pirate, "here is a welcome sight. Yet I must chide you, I really must, for your base desertion of me and my house. You have not put a foot across my threshold for near upon five months, I swear, which I have taken most unkindly of you."

"Well I am here now," replied Phoebe shortly, "and desire a quart of good red, of which you shall partake with me for old times' sake."

The Pirate was about to suggest that a quart of red wine was scarcely a suitable drink for a hot afternoon, when something in the girl's manner made him hold his tongue. As he went to draw the wine, he surreptitiously observed her, and noted that the change which rumour said had come upon her of late was plainly evident. She looked as pretty as ever in her Sunday gown of muslin and the ribbon confining her bright hair, but there was a kind of new reserve in her eyes and something almost subdued in her manner.

"Adad," said the Pirate, placing the wine flask on the counter together with two of his best glasses, "you are become the most talked of wench in Hampstead these last months, my dear, and I have longed extremely to hear of all your adventures from your own fair lips. Kidnapped, they tell me, by a pack of nasty conspirators, and then away with your father to lay informations at Whitehall, and – "

"My friend," interrupted Phoebe sharply, "all this is stale news, and must be as familiar to you by this time as the neck-verse to the Ordinary of Newgate. Pray don't plague me to rehearse it yet again, for I did not come hither for that."

It was on the tip of the Pirate's tongue to ask her why she had come here, but again something in her manner restrained him. After a pause during which Phoebe sipped her wine, she said abruptly:

"As for the late plot, we shall hear the end of it this week, methinks, when my Lord Russell goes to the block, and Rumbold and two others to Tyburn. You'll have heard that my Lord Essex cut his throat in the Tower yesterday, which will save Ketch a labour, and that the Lords Grey and Howard are turned evidence for the Crown. They say that Monmouth will back 'em up, if he can find courage sufficient to dare the vengeance of his fellow plotters, and that Algernon Sidney likewise will lose his head. Ferguson's escaped, as it seems he always doth, and the rest are either fled or are hasting to turn evidence."

"They tell me 'twas your father's friend, Mr Keeling the oil-merchant, who laid the first information last month, but was not credited," the Pirate prompted her eagerly, "and that he was moved to confess by remorse that he had countenanced so bloody a design."

"His remorse was as difficult to arouse as a malt-worm who hath guzzled all night," retorted Phoebe scornfully, "seeing that my father applied himself to him directly I returned from Newmarket in March, and he did not stir until June. And when he did, 'twas only for fear some of the others in the plot would be beforehand in laying an information, for there were rumours of the conspiracy going round the coffee-houses. Yet he has his reward, and good luck to him, and so have I, for telling my tale so neat and pretty to Mr Secretary. Fifty golden guineas, my friend, which will serve me as a portion when I am married next month."

The Pirate's mouth fell a-gape at this statement.

"Married!" he exclaimed. "Why, bless me, here is news. Nay, Phoebe, will you break all the hearts in Hampstead?"

"Pray don't fox me with that sort of talk," snapped Phoebe. "Did you think I'd dance the shaking of the sheets for ever without getting myself set up in life? You will please to drink to my future husband, who, I may tell you, is Alfred Dubs, the farmer."

The Pirate sniggered.

"Oho!" said he, nudging her arm and winking, "so you are marrying wealth, my dear, and though you must have a most tedious dull husband to go with it, I warrant you 'twill not be long ere you ornament that wooden head of his with a pair of horns."

He had scarcely completed the sentence when Phoebe, leaning over the counter, bestowed upon his bearded cheek an extremely smart slap with the flat of her hand.

"Take that, sauce-box!" cried she. "And you may inform any of your gossips who entertain the same bawdy notions that I shall be pleased to pay them the like compliment if they durst void 'em in my presence." Then, all of a sudden, she smiled. "Nay, you big booby, here's a kiss to take away the sting of the other. Go back to your sleep, my friend, and leave me in peace. I am come here today upon a fool's errand, which I must accomplish privily; harkee, I will tell you honest, 'tis to lay a ghost. You stare at me, and no wonder, but this I promise you, that the next time we meet I shall not appear so like a Tom o' Bedlam, but shall be myself again. So! Close the hatch and sleep off your morning's tippling. Leave me the remains of the wine, and lock the outer door. You do not expect customers for an hour or two, I warrant, and I for my part desire my own company for that space".

As she was speaking, it came to him like a flash why she had come here this afternoon, the reason for her strange manner, and even for her choice of drink. For he had seen her glance at the empty stool opposite, and had remembered the tragic end of Derrick Calder. He gave her a big sheepish grin, which was all he could manage by way of sympathy, and almost with reverence closed the hatch and went to lock the outer door.

Alone in the common-room, Phoebe permitted herself to give rein to an uneasiness which she had concealed from the Pirate by a display of irritability. She talked to her dogs, got up and wandered restlessly about the familiar room, feigned to study the Act of Parliament nailed above the hearth, snatched off her hair-ribbon and tossed her curls into disorder. Then, with an oath, she marched deliberately back to her stool at the counter, reached into the bodice of her gown, and drew forth a letter, unfolded it, and began to spell her way through it. It had been in her possession for nearly five months, yet never until now had she so much as broken the seal of it. She would read it now; out of compliment to the writer she would read it where assuredly his ghost must linger; and when she had read it she would tear it up. For she was a young woman, and a realist, and she had sense enough to know that she could not live with ghosts.

"My dear and only Love," she read,

"It hath become my duty as a subject to enter upon a certain Investigation the which may well cost me my life. I care not for that, save that it will part us in the body; what plagues me is that what I have to do must so occupy my time and thoughts that you will be offended at me, and that perchance we may part estranged. I will not weary you by describing the nature of this Duty of mine, for you never relished talk of public matters; suffice it to say that Honour will not permit me to refuse it.

If this Letter comes to your hand, methinks you will be a little sad, because it will mean that I am dead. My most Loved One, all my life I never could prevent myself from speculating and meditating upon Eternal Things, God, Fate, the Immortality of the Soul, and so forth, and all my life I have groped vainly in the dark. Yet there is a Notion which often returns to me, and though I can offer no proof of its Reality, I will venture to describe it to you here, knowing that you will be indulgent to my Folly, if Folly it is, and hoping even that it may afford you some comfort, as it doth to me.

This Notion, my beloved Phoebe, is that we come to this World not once but many times, because the

Lessons we are requir'd to learn therein are passing difficult and cannot be learned in one lifetime. The Mistakes we make, the Crimes we commit, the Errors we fall into, these, I think, are such as occur in our childhood, before we have learned better. Here alone, to me, is Justice. If we refuse a Lesson, we must come back until we have mastered it, and each time we refuse it, it becomes more difficult. You and I in this Life could have but the most incomplete Relationship; if I do my best with this, if I give you all I have to give, and fret not to bestow that which it is not my privilege to bestow, I endeavour to hope that I shall earn the reward of returning with you and having you for my wife. Nay, I find I cannot express myself without the risk of being tedious, so will say no more concerning these old Notions of mine, which must appear to you plain heathen. This only I know: That You, and this World, of earth and sky and sea, of trees and flowers and creatures, are all I am capable of desiring, now or hereafter.

So I will come to that which, more than all, impels me to write you this Letter. It is to thank you, and to let you know how greatly I am in your Debt. I thank you, first of all, for being yourself, for all that the name PHOEBE means to me, the strengths and weaknesses, the faults and virtues, the looks and gestures, the tone and the footstep, the laugh and the frown, which all together comprise the Woman whom I love. I thank you for the Happiness you have brought me, and equally for the Pain. And lastly, I thank you for the little things, which, while we are in this School-house of a world, signify so much to us. For the common-room at Jack Straw's and the first sight of you awaiting me there; for the Quart of good Red, which you have ever despised; for foolish Jests most private to ourselves; for the climb abovestairs to that narrow Chamber which to me is the most beloved space on earth; for the Paradise of your embrace; for the Heath, and your Dogs, and the Pirate, and all the persons and the things sanctified to me because I have shared their acquaintance with you. For all this, my Love, and for so much more that I cannot find it in me to express. They have made up the pattern of my life; they are the Pledges of my soul's survival.

Wherever I am, when you come to read this Letter, whatever I am doing, be assured that I love you, and you alone, and that if anything of me exists, it will exist only to serve you."

She laid the letter down, and stared at the empty stool opposite. She had scarcely understood a word of what she had read, yet the impression it had conveyed to her of the dead man was so strong that almost she expected to see his form take shape on that stool, to see his hazel eyes adoring her, his mouth curve into its well-remembered smile. She poured the last of the wine into her glass, and lifting it towards that empty stool, said aloud, without shame:

"Here's to you, and our next meeting, my love, since that's the way you'd have it. Here's to you in your own tipple, which I shall never drink again, but stick to honest English ale."

Then, very deliberately, she tore Derrick Calder's letter across and across until the bits of paper were as small as dice, and dropped them into the dregs of the wine; since ghosts, she had heard, are less likely to rise if they are drowned. So at last, calling briskly to her dogs, she walked out of the common-room without a backward glance and shut the door, with a sort of finality, behind her.

It was not yet five o'clock when she came out into the sunshine, and the Heath was still thronged with people taking their Sunday promenade. Merry family parties clustered about the Hampstead Elm, young people, arms entwined, sought the kindly privacy of the sand-pits and the gorse-bushes; a party on horseback trotted up 'Du Vall's Lane', a portion of the village especially shunned after dark because it was said to be haunted by the ghost of that notorious highwayman; and a stream of folk flowed in the direction of Mother Huff's and her famous cheese-cakes. Phoebe stood undecided for a moment, then, crossing the road which led to Highgate, she descended the steep slope of the Heath and strolled along the less frequented paths; for she was not yet in the mood for company.

Incapable of analysing her own emotions, which in any case she would have deemed a thoroughly unhealthy occupation, still Phoebe was aware that she had changed since the cataclysm of those days in Newmarket. She felt infinitely older and mature, and was conscious, not without regret, that certain pleasures in which she had been used to indulge so freely no longer appealed to her. She was too much of a realist, and too lacking in sentimentality, to mope after Derrick; she was annoyed with herself that, all unawares, she had allowed her emotions as well as her senses to be stirred by him, and thus had threatened her peace of mind. His love for her, a love of which she herself was quite incapable, and the strength of which she had never guessed while they were together, had sobered herself despite herself, and though she had no intention of allowing the memory of it to spoil her life, it was, unknown to her, the reason why she was now determined to settle down and become respectable. Her marrying Alfred Dubs, that middle-aged and somewhat stolid farmer, was her tribute to the memory of Derrick Calder, though she would have been hard put to it to explain why. It was not in the nature of a penance, for what she was really marrying was Alfred Dubs' farm. For the rest of her life she would be surrounded with animals of all sorts, and since that half-dreadful, half-ecstatic morning when she had assisted in rescuing the running-horses from their burning stables, she knew that to be surrounded with animals was happiness enough for her.

As she strolled about the Heath this afternoon, with Tangle and Mumper at her heels, she took pains to avoid her promenading neighbours, for by this time she was weary of being 'the most talked-of wench in Hampstead', as the Pirate had described her. Her public importance had meant little to her, and she had been merely bored by her interviews with the great and mighty. It had been satisfaction to her to know that her evidence had gone far in convicting 'Hannibal and his Boys', and she had every intention of witnessing the one-eyed maltster's death at Tyburn; but since her encounter with the Lord Chamberlain at Newmarket she had conceived a contempt for all Court officials, and her interviews with a Secretary of State who had grown increasingly polite and cordial had left her unmoved. The Rye House Plot had failed, thanks largely to a lone investigator who had been rebuffed in life and was forgotten by the world in death, and to a most tragic but opportune fire; and there, so far as Phoebe was concerned, was an end of the matter.

Keeping to the trees, she was about to cross a little path upon the Heath when she paused abruptly with an impatient exclamation. For there, approaching her arm-in-arm, were none other than her father and stepmother, returning from their Sunday walk. It was too late to avoid them, for her dogs were already barking them a greeting.

"Why, there you are, my love," said Mr Jolly cheerfully. "Bless me, we knew not where you had got to."

"Nay, husband," chided Mrs Jolly, panting a little because her stays were laced too tight, "I told you the sweet child would be desirous of her own company at this time, being quite wrapped up, I'll warrant you, in the blissful thoughts of a maid who is to be wed next month. Fie, for shame, Phoebe, your hair is all in a tangle and there is a rent in that pretty gown of yours. You must come home, my little bride, and make your toilette, since your dear betrothed is to sup with us tonight."

"My dogs need exercise," said Phoebe shortly, "and so do I likewise, and since 'tis near upon three hours till supper-time, I beg you will excuse me."

"Such a wild thing still!" sighed Mrs Jolly, "but marriage will tame you, ne'er stir. Bless you, child, go your ways, and I will hasten home to make our preparations. I am accustomed by this time to having it all upon my hands, and I promise you, you shall not blush for the entertainment this evening. Your father, my dear good Daniel here, hath sworn to me that he will take pains to appear very genteel in the presence of Master Dubs, and I am sure his example to you – why, good day to ye, neighbours," she broke off to exclaim, bowing graciously to a family party which was overtaking the Jollys. "What a sweet fine afternoon! I was just a-going home, and will walk with you, if you please, for I must tell you that my son-in-law to be, Master Alfred Dubs, is invited to my house for supper, and I have a stubble-goose to cook, the which he is pleased to tell me I prepare more sweetly than anything he hath tasted at his own board, substantial farmer though he is. But Lord! I think I should be a fair housewife, seeing that my dear father (God rest him) was Warden of his Livery Company, and when there were feasts in his Hall, my honoured mother would oft let me accompany her to the kitchens to oversee the cooks aroasting of swan-standard, sea-hog, and leche-lombard, which latter I must tell you is prepared... "

Her voice prattled away into the distance, as, surrounded by an admiring throng of neighbours, she picked her way homewards on unsuitable high heels.

Phoebe, turning to continue her walk in the opposite direction, was surprised and not too well pleased when her father, putting a hand through her arm, intimated his intention of accompanying her.

" 'Tis too fine a day to go home yet," said he. He glanced back over his shoulder, ascertained that his wife was out of sight, and, with a sigh of relief, lifted his hat, pulled off the peruke which Mrs Jolly now compelled him to wear on Sundays and holidays, and stuffed the uncomfortable thing into his pocket.

"And since I am soon to lose you, my wench, pray let me have your company while I can."

Phoebe said nothing, but pressed his arm. The old affection between father and daughter was as strong as ever, though during the last month even Phoebe had found him a little trying at times. The truth of it was, Daniel's new role as a witness against the plotters had gone to his head, and he had become tedious and boastful. From being for so many years a struggling and obscure tradesman, he had become, overnight, a minor public figure, his name even appearing in the news-sheets, his shop always full of folk who came from far and near to buy from the famous Daniel Jolly and hear details of his adventures from his own lips. Bullied and bamboozled by great lords and low intriguers, suddenly he had found himself cossetted and deferred to by Secretaries of State and Privy Councillors, while his former tormenters were being tried for their lives; he rode backwards and forwards to the Secretary's lodging at Whitehall at his Majesty's expense; he was paid handsome compensation for the time he must spend away from his counter; Josiah Keeling, once so high above him in business status and so patronising in manner, now almost fawned upon him; and even Elizabeth, though she playfully nagged at him in private, in public paid him a new respect.

It was only natural, therefore, that this simple good man should inflate himself a little. He could scarce open his mouth nowadays without dragging in some reference to his altered circumstances: "As Mr Secretary Jenkins observed to me but yesterday," he would begin, or "My Lords of the Council were good enough to inform me, neighbour, that the news-sheet you mention was in error when it stated that… " He was talking of engaging a second apprentice; he loved to call at the Upper Bowling Green and enjoy the new deference with which Charlie Weems treated him (for that landlord, though he had known too much about the plotters for innocence, had escaped implication in the conspiracy), and whenever he drove to Whitehall to make his depositions, he took care to have the coach glasses down so that he might bow graciously to admiring neighbours.

Yet beneath all this surface change in him, Daniel Jolly remained the same doting father. He had shown an unexpected delicacy in never referring to Derrick Calder when he and Phoebe were alone together, and quite sharply had rebuked his wife for pressing the girl for details of the young man's death. Once or twice he had questioned his daughter, very gently, as to whether she was sure she wished to marry Alfred Dubs, observing that money was not everything, and that for his part he would welcome her presence at home unless her affections were engaged; and sometimes, when he had bidden her good night, she had felt his work-worn hand linger for a moment on her curls with an increased tenderness.

They walked in silence this afternoon through the trees of the Heath, instinctively avoiding the groups strolling in their neighbourhood. Presently they came to the high brick wall which enclosed the estate of Cane Wood, where lived the widow of John Hill, son of the Royal Printer, who had built this wall around twenty-five acres of parkland. Walking slowly along beside it, neither speaking, Mr Jolly and his daughter came anon to the spot where there was a door, fast closed, and overgrown with ivy. Phoebe felt her father hesitate, and glancing at him, saw that he was staring at the door with rather an odd expression on his face.

"I never pass this wall nowadays," murmured the old chandler, speaking in a reverent undertone as though he were in church, "without I think of a dear friend of ours, and of what he said to me on the evening when first I had the honour of entertaining him in my house."

Phoebe stiffened a little, but made no reply.

"It was deep talk," continued Mr Jolly, sighing and shaking his head, "and I understood but little of it. Only I remember that he said to me something after this sort: That when he was a boy he used to wander by a high brick wall, which separated him from his former playmates with whom his father had forbidden him to have any further intercourse. And that since that time he had come to fancy that our mortal life is somewhat akin to a high wall, we being in exile upon one side of it, while on the other lies our home. And further, that for each of us there is a private door in this wall, the which hath our name upon it, and the door is death."

He paused, seeming to have forgotten the presence of his daughter, as he cogitated upon something only half-understood yet profoundly moving. Then he added:

"Our friend hath found his private door and hath passed through it out of our sight. God rest him; I like to believe he hath found upon the other side of it all that he sought and loved so much."

And then, simply and without embarrassment, Daniel Jolly made a motion of salute with his hat.

EXPLANATION OF THE THIEVES' SLANG, IN THE ORDER IN WHICH IT APPEARS IN THE TEXT.

Part I   Chapter 6

1. *Pickers and stealers:* Hands.
2. *High-lawier:* A highwayman.
3. *Buzzard:* A simpleton.
4. *Boarded:* Addressed or accosted.
5. *Geck enough to scamper:* Fool enough to run away.
6. *Oakes:* A highwayman's accomplices.
7. *Frisk:* Search.
8. *Coney-catch:* Cheat.
9. *Rhinocerical:* Full of money.
10. *Duds of a swad:* Clothes of a country clown.
11. *The generous way of padding:* Highway robbery.
12. *Meg, smelt, scout, famble, sice:* Guinea, half-guinea, watch, ring, sixpence.
13. *Pluck out porker:* Draw my sword.
14. *Caravaned:* Cheated.
15. *Martin:* A highwayman's victim.
16. *A cully for hookers and anglers:* A prey for petty thieves.
17. *I say by the Solomon:* I swear by the Mass.
18. *Hay in my horn:* Ill-tempered.
19. *Play crimp:* Another term for cheating.
20. *Snck up:* Go hang.
21. *Clack-dishing:* Careless talk, from a beggar's wooden dish clapped smartly to attract alms.

Explanation's

22. *Red-lattice:* Most taverns had red lattices before their windows.
23. *Three Legged Mare:* The gallows.
24. *A nip draws you:* A cur-purse robs you.
25. *Silly cheat:* Petty theft.
26. *Bum-bailly:* Sheriff's officer.
27. *The Whitt:* Newgate, so called because built by Whittington.
28. *High-law:* One of the many terms for highway robbery.
29. *Clem:* Starve.
30. *Stale:* A cut-purse's accomplice.
31. *Bolter of Whitefriars:* A debtor in the ancient sanctuary of Whitefriars or Alsatia.
32. *Bluebottle and his nut-hooks:* A beadle and his constables.

Part I   Chapter 7

1. ***Sucked the rhino from a shot-shark but had got so clear upon it that I was putt enough to lose it to a tat-monger:*** He had obtained money from a tavern-waiter, but had got so very drunk upon it that he was silly enough to lose it to a man who played with false dice.

Part II   Chapter 6

1. *Prigged at a trugging-place:* Stole at a bawdy-house.
2. *Rumbo-ken:* Pawnbroker.
3. *Geometer:* Jesuits.

JANE LANE

A CALL OF TRUMPETS

Civil war rages in England, rendering it a minefield of corruption and conflict. Town and country are besieged. Through the complex interlocking of England's turmoil with that of a king, Jane Lane brings to life some amazing characters in the court of Charles I. This is the story both of Charles' adored wife whose indiscretions prove disastrous, and of the King's nephew, Rupert, a rash, arrogant soldier whose actions lead to tragedy and his uncle's final downfall.

CONIES IN THE HAY

1586 was the year of an unbearably hot summer when treachery came to the fore. In this scintillating drama of betrayals, Jane Lane sketches the master of espionage, Francis Walsingham, in the bright, lurid colours of the deceit for which he was renowned. Anthony Babington and his fellow conspirators are also brought to life in this vivid, tense novel, which tells of how they were duped by Walsingham into betraying the ill-fated Mary, Queen of Scots, only to be hounded to their own awful destruction.

Jane Lane

His Fight Is Ours

His Fight Is Ours follows the traumatic trials of MacIain, a Highland Chieftain of the clan Donald, as he leads his people in the second Jacobite rising on behalf of James Stuart, the Old Pretender. The battle to restore the king to his rightful throne is portrayed here in this absorbing historical escapade, which highlights all the beauty and romance of Highland life. Jane Lane presents a dazzling, picaresque story of the problems facing MacIain as leader of a proud, ancient race, and his struggles against injustice and the violent infamy of oppression.

A Summer Storm

Conflict and destiny abound as King Richard II, a chivalrous, romantic and idealist monarch, courts his beloved Anne of Bohemia. In the background, the swirling rage of the Peasants' Revolt of 1381 threatens to topple London as the tides of farmers, labourers and charismatic rebel hearts flood the city. This tense, powerful historical romance leads the reader from bubbling discord to doomed love all at the turn of a page.

Jane Lane

Thunder on St Paul's Day

London is gripped by mass hysteria as Titus Oates uncovers the Popish Plot, and a gentle English family gets caught up in the terrors of trial and accusation when Oates points the finger of blame. The villainous Oates adds fuel to the fire of an angry mob with his sham plot, leaving innocence to face a bullying judge and an intimidated jury. Only one small boy may save the family in this moving tale of courage pitted against treachery.

A Wind Through the Heather

A Wind Through the Heather is a poignant, tragic story based on the Highland Clearances where thousands of farmers were driven from their homes by tyrannical and greedy landowners. Introducing the Macleods, Jane Lane recreates the shameful past suffered by an innocent family who lived to cross the Atlantic and find a new home. This wistful, historical novel focuses on the atrocities so many bravely faced and reveals how adversities were overcome.

OTHER TITLES BY JANE LANE AVAILABLE DIRECT
FROM HOUSE OF STRATUS

Quantity		£	$(US)	$(CAN)	€
☐	Bridge of Sighs	6.99	12.95	16.95	11.50
☐	A Call of Trumpets	6.99	12.95	16.95	11.50
☐	Cat Among the Pigeons	6.99	12.95	16.95	11.50
☐	Command Performance	6.99	12.95	16.95	11.50
☐	Conies in the Hay	6.99	12.95	16.95	11.50
☐	Countess at War	6.99	12.95	16.95	11.50
☐	The Crown for a Lie	6.99	12.95	16.95	11.50
☐	Ember in the Ashes	6.99	12.95	16.95	11.50
☐	Farewell to the White Cockade	6.99	12.95	16.95	11.50
☐	Fortress in the Forth	6.99	12.95	16.95	11.50
☐	Heirs of Squire Harry	6.99	12.95	16.95	11.50
☐	His Fight Is Ours	6.99	12.95	16.95	11.50

ALL HOUSE OF STRATUS BOOKS ARE AVAILABLE FROM GOOD BOOKSHOPS
OR DIRECT FROM THE PUBLISHER:

Internet: www.houseofstratus.com including author interviews, reviews, features.

Email: sales@houseofstratus.com please quote author, title and credit card details.

OTHER TITLES BY JANE LANE AVAILABLE DIRECT
FROM HOUSE OF STRATUS

Quantity		£	$(US)	$(CAN)	€
	THE PHOENIX AND THE LAUREL	6.99	12.95	16.95	11.50
	PRELUDE TO KINGSHIP	6.99	12.95	16.95	11.50
	QUEEN OF THE CASTLE	6.99	12.95	16.95	11.50
	THE SEALED KNOT	6.99	12.95	16.95	11.50
	A SECRET CHRONICLE	6.99	12.95	16.95	11.50
	THE SEVERED CROWN	6.99	12.95	16.95	11.50
	SIR DEVIL-MAY-CARE	6.99	12.95	16.95	11.50
	SOW THE TEMPEST	6.99	12.95	16.95	11.50
	A STATE OF MIND	6.99	12.95	16.95	11.50
	A SUMMER STORM	6.99	12.95	16.95	11.50
	THUNDER ON ST PAUL'S DAY	6.99	12.95	16.95	11.50
	A WIND THROUGH THE HEATHER	6.99	12.95	16.95	11.50
	THE YOUNG AND LONELY KING	6.99	12.95	16.95	11.50

ALL HOUSE OF STRATUS BOOKS ARE AVAILABLE FROM GOOD BOOKSHOPS
OR DIRECT FROM THE PUBLISHER:

Internet: www.houseofstratus.com including synopses and features.

Email: sales@houseofstratus.com please quote author, title and credit card details.

Order Line:
UK: 0800 169 1780,
USA: 1 800 509 9942
INTERNATIONAL: +44 (0) 20 7494 6400 (UK)
or
+01 212 218 7649
(please quote author, title, and credit card details.)

Send to:
House of Stratus Sales Department
24c Old Burlington Street
London
W1X 1RL
UK

House of Stratus Inc.
Suite 210
1270 Avenue of the Americas
New York • NY 10020
USA

PAYMENT

Please tick currency you wish to use:

☐ £ (Sterling)   ☐ $ (US)   ☐ $ (CAN)   ☐ € (Euros)

Allow for shipping costs charged per order plus an amount per book as set out in the tables below:

CURRENCY/DESTINATION

	£(Sterling)	$(US)	$(CAN)	€(Euros)
Cost per order				
UK	1.50	2.25	3.50	2.50
Europe	3.00	4.50	6.75	5.00
North America	3.00	3.50	5.25	5.00
Rest of World	3.00	4.50	6.75	5.00
Additional cost per book				
UK	0.50	0.75	1.15	0.85
Europe	1.00	1.50	2.25	1.70
North America	1.00	1.00	1.50	1.70
Rest of World	1.50	2.25	3.50	3.00

PLEASE SEND CHEQUE OR INTERNATIONAL MONEY ORDER.
payable to: STRATUS HOLDINGS plc or HOUSE OF STRATUS INC. or card payment as indicated

STERLING EXAMPLE

Cost of book(s):..................... Example: 3 x books at £6.99 each: £20.97
Cost of order: .... Example: £1.50 (Delivery to UK address)
Additional cost per book:.............. Example: 3 x £0.50: £1.50
Order total including shipping:.......... Example: £23.97

VISA, MASTERCARD, SWITCH, AMEX:

☐☐☐☐☐☐☐☐☐☐☐☐☐☐☐☐☐☐☐

Issue number (Switch only):

☐☐☐

Start Date: **Expiry Date:**

☐☐/☐☐   ☐☐/☐☐

Signature: _____

NAME: _____

ADDRESS: _____

COUNTRY: _____

ZIP/POSTCODE: _____

Please allow 28 days for delivery. Despatch normally within 48 hours.

Prices subject to change without notice.
Please tick box if you do not wish to receive any additional information. ☐

House of Stratus publishes many other titles in this genre; please check our website (**www.houseofstratus.com**) for more details.